VOIDVERSE

ALSO BY DAMIEN OBER

Doctor Benjamin Franklin's Dream America

VOIDVERSE

DAMIEN OBER

LONDON · **NEW YORK** · TORONTO
AMSTERDAM/ANTWERP · NEW DELHI · SYDNEY/MELBOURNE

AN IMPRINT OF SIMON & SCHUSTER, LLC

1230 AVENUE OF THE AMERICAS, NEW YORK, NEW YORK 10020

For more than 100 years, Simon & Schuster has championed authors and the stories they create. By respecting the copyright of an author's intellectual property, you enable Simon & Schuster and the author to continue publishing exceptional books for years to come. We thank you for supporting the author's copyright by purchasing an authorized edition of this book.

No amount of this book may be reproduced or stored in any format, nor may it be uploaded to any website, database, language-learning model, or other repository, retrieval, or artificial intelligence system without express permission. All rights reserved. Inquiries may be directed to Simon & Schuster, 1230 Avenue of the Americas, New York, NY 10020 or permissions@simonandschuster.com.

This book is a work of fiction. Any references to historical events, real people, or real places are used fictitiously. Other names, characters, places, and events are products of the author's imagination, and any resemblance to actual events or places or persons, living or dead, is entirely coincidental.

Copyright © 2026 by Damien Ober

All rights reserved, including the right to reproduce this book or portions thereof in any form whatsoever. For information, address Saga Press Subsidiary Rights Department, 1230 Avenue of the Americas, New York, NY 10020.

First Saga Press hardcover edition March 2026

SAGA PRESS and colophon are registered trademarks of Simon & Schuster, LLC

Simon & Schuster strongly believes in freedom of expression and stands against censorship in all its forms. For more information, visit BooksBelong.com.

For information about special discounts for bulk purchases, please contact Simon & Schuster Special Sales at 1-866-506-1949 or business@simonandschuster.com.

The Simon & Schuster Speakers Bureau can bring authors to your live event. For more information or to book an event, contact the Simon & Schuster Speakers Bureau at 1-866-248-3049 or visit our website at www.simonspeakers.com.

Interior design by Lewelin Polanco

Manufactured in China

1 3 5 7 9 10 8 6 4 2

Library of Congress Cataloging-in-Publication Data is available.

ISBN 978-1-6680-6560-0
ISBN 978-1-6680-6562-4 (ebook)

to my parents, who always encouraged the big dreams

He came from so distant in the void
it may as well have been another void,
a battle so far away
its words meant nothing.

All he carried with him was the anomaly
he had used to win a terrible half victory,
a power only he knew the method to unlock.

After an endless sink, he arrived at a cluster of seven rocks.
There he settled in the familiar embers of a scorched dome.
Through the high glass eye,
he could watch the void above,
should old, distant dangers
form again.

So that all in every breath to follow would know
it was the truth, he used the anomaly again,
to set and hold the seven clustered rocks in a perfect line,
each one equidistant in exact.

He created a Sword to guard the anomaly,
a Sword that would not pass down hand to hand,
but mind to mind, heart to heart, fist to fist,
for the anomaly held the alignment in perfect balance;
if it were ever moved, the formation would come undone.

He lived a life and two and for forever,
for he did not age nor ever would.
Then arrived a rumor of a rumor of a rumor,
of an old enemy loose in the void.
He knew it was the truth because what was said
was impossible otherwise.
And he knew he could not leave his fate
to some other person's fate.

Before his hunt began, he told
them one last thing.
Keep the Sword always sharp.
Some rest, a shifting
in the void will bring a challenger.
Look first in the glass eye of the dome,
to take the anomaly and undo
the alignment,
from the topmost rock
to the very
bottom.

"THE IMMORTAL FIRST SWORD"
—a legend from the Kingdom of the Scorched Dome

VOIDVERSE

I was lost in the void again, the friction whipping angrily, its roar obliterating all sound, even the thumping of my heart, the pulsing of my blood, and I felt that downward pull, the pull from inside, seeming to suck me into the vast depths below, and I looked and spun and looked, but all there was was the total darkness of the void, in every direction, as far as I could see, with no idea which way was back, sink or rise and at what angle, so I rose, for I don't know how long, until I panicked and, full of doubt, tried straight outwide, then thought better and followed that inward pull and sank at absolute, starving and dehydrated and desperate for anything to form from the void, but all there was was more emptiness, more endlessness, more nothing, until the dryness of my mouth crept down my throat and I ground into stillness and was given over to the roiling friction, some dead thing adrift forever in the endless sink . . .

PART 1
EMERY

THE RISERS OF FAIRVIEL

The sink was loud at the edge, the friction roaring endlessly by, battering my clothes and skin, whipping my hair up wild toward the overvoid above. The cow had been milked and fed and put on her tether. She looked back at me from where she floated out there, the friction rippling her hide, jostling her baggy udder. Shifting my weight, I tilted forward, and the uprushing friction pushed back, holding me up, leaned out over the edge. Below, the darkness of the sink was so uniform and complete, I could have closed my eyes and it would look no different. I leaned farther, and the roar roared louder, and there was the first subtle lift, a cupping into the friction's harsh embrace, and I remembered then the breath from my youth when I first realized that in addition to other rocks below and above, there are ones outwide too, rocks in all directions, sinking forever through the void. I felt its pull, the compulsion to let go, to dive into its infinite darkness, its bottomless depths, all of everything there could ever be if you went far enough.

Distantly, through the roar of the edge, I heard the back door bang open. I could feel him there watching me, my husband Tim. When he spoke, he had to shout to be heard above the roar. "You're not still thinking of going to the Deciding?"

I leaned out a breath longer, my hair and skin and clothes rippling so hard it seemed they could all fly apart, everything. Then I let the friction ease me back, my weight shifting onto my feet. The overpowering roar receded. My windblown hair settled.

Tim had come down to the low step. His voice was closer, softer. He didn't have to shout now that I'd moved back from the edge. "Don't you think it will be too upsetting," he said, "seeing all those boys deciding, knowing Del will never have the chance?"

Finally, I turned and looked at him. It was an argument we'd already had, and I was too tired to wade back in. Tim was right in one sense, though; I *was* thinking of our little boy, but also of myself, how neither Del nor I would ever leave Fairviel: born, live, and die all on one rock in the great vastness of the sink. At least that's what I thought then.

"Please, Emery," he said. "Why don't you come on in?"

I walked past him instead and kept on going, to the wide walkway that looped between the edge homes and the crosshatching of farm plots in the center. Other people were trickling out, speckling the path. As I mixed in, I looked back and saw Tim still watching me. Our eyes met briefly before he melted back into the shadows of our house. The others who lived on the edge had their cows out too, dangling on their tethers. It was to save space for the gardens the families toward the center of the rock all kept. Fairviel was small, so I was told, and we used every bit of surface.

As with all Decidings, most of the rock had gathered to watch. There were five new boys of age, lined up on the edge platform. Always the boys looked on display, things people had tidied and set up. The rise instructor beamed, his pocked, beefy face and beard all gone gray. He nodded encouragingly to the boys, and the friction rippled them as they stepped to the edge. Their faces looked like apples, shined up with fear. I could see each boy's breath, the heaving of their lungs, ribs expanding wide and contracting in. I felt the full extension of my own—full inhale, full exhale—and I thought again of Del's round little face. I don't always remember all of this exactly right, and some of what is to come was told to me or learned much later, but I do remember my son's face. I remember it clearly, in all the forms I saw it over the short rests we were together.

A cry burst from the platform. One of the boys had turned back to the crowd, face skin twisted around wild eyes, red cheeks about to rip apart from the rictus. He broke and ran into his mother's arms, and they became a tangle of gripping the other tighter. They sobbed and scuttled away, and the only sound again was the roaring friction past the edge.

The other boys were pulling down their pack straps, clipping them tight. They moved fast, their hands trembling. None wanted to be the next to lose his nerve. With no further hesitation, they began leaping out into the void, one after the other, all four spreading their arms and legs in Kolatchi position as they'd been taught. They hovered a breath in stasis—as if the sink itself was now deciding—and then the friction took them and they began to rise, slowly, then picking up speed. Their faces lost distinction, their bodies smaller and smaller and then only specks in the overvoid.

It was hard to see at first, but a fifth speck had appeared, this one getting larger. "A sinker!" someone shouted.

The crowd mumbled and shifted as the sinker came slicing downward at impossible speed, arms and legs pinned tight, chin tucked under a matte-black helmet. A clear circle spread in the crowd, and the sinker swooped and landed smoothly. His helmet was not matte black, after all, but scratched up and dulled by dings and scuffings. Only the snapped-down visor was polished, reflecting us back as he scanned the crowd. He was thin, lean and sleek, in a suit of tight-fit leather with lots of straps and buttoned-up pockets. The hilt of a sword protruded from his back, snug beside a pack as tight as an angry fist. Then the visor flipped up, and I could see this sinker was a woman, had been since she first appeared way above.

Everyone was silent and still as she moved through the crowd, studying faces. Finally, she settled and fixed on me, and in the wide black centers of her eyes was the empty darkness of the void. From the tight overlappings of her suit, she took a folded sheet of paper and held it up for all to see. "I call upon the code of this rock," the Sinker said. "I have a letter."

THE OLDEST DREAM

The dream was the same, always the same, lost in the total darkness of the void, the friction ripping at every surface of my body, the roar overpowering, the downward pull from deep inside, no idea which way back or how far, and so I rose, for rests and rests and rests, then outwide as far or farther, then even farther midoutwide, then, finally following the inward pull, straight down at absolute, but as always there was only more endless nothing and hunger and thirst, and again I felt my body tighten and shiver and then go still and become light as I faded into the endless darkness . . . but this dream was different, this stillness was not death, not an end, only a new endlessness I was trapped inside forever, a new darker darkness, somehow even more cold and empty than the void, and the only sound was a cracking echo reverberating through the fabric of it all, and then again and again, and the sound cleared and sharpened and became the crisp snap of a knife on the chopping block. I opened my eyes, and the floor of the living room took shape from the darkness, the lumped blankets of our makeshift bed. I could hear more clearly now the sound of my mother in the kitchen. She'd finished chopping. Pans were clinking. Water was spitting its way toward boil. I closed my eyes again and pressed them tight and caught the last echo of the dream, darkness and panic and rippling friction and the stillness of death.

Tim was asleep on the floor beside me. Before every exhale, a wet click came from inside his nostrils. I lay there listening to a few mucousy snaps. Suddenly, with a hard snort, he sat up. "My fucking back," he said. He stood and hinged at the hip, letting his arms hang. "Oh my fucking back." He straightened again and said, "I'll go check on him," and then he was gone down the hall, toward Del's room.

I'd had one other lover before Tim, a boy named Bristle who'd grown up with me on Fairviel. My clearest memory of him was the off angle of his face, how it slanted more and more left the longer you looked. He was always so careful when we made love, careful to stop and leave before it was over. To Bristle, a child was the end of any chance he'd ever have. When his Deciding came, he rose off with the others and, like all the boys who left, was never heard from again.

I got up and stretched and went to stand in the doorway to the bedroom. The Sinker was still asleep, laid out straight on our bed, her body like an insect's, condensed and hollow-seeming. On the floor sat her sword and tightly wrapped pack and on top, her helmet. I picked up the helmet, feeling its compact lightness.

"Please put that down."

The Sinker's eyes were two gleaming dots in the dark room. I did as asked, placing the helmet softly on her pack.

She sat up in the bed, looking at me. "There is a child who lives here," she said. "I've not seen them."

"We have a son," I said. "Del is his name."

I led her down the hall to Del's room. Tim was in there, neatening the blankets. When he saw us, he stepped aside, then farther, until he was still and inanimate beside the door.

The Sinker moved into the emptied space and I beside her. There Del was in the bed, shivering and sweating and barely conscious. He'd grown past the little-boy stage, and now his face held the ironed-out, puffy features of my father's old face, with tufts of wild hair so thick it seemed fake. The Sinker reached out to touch him, but I grabbed her wrist and held it. I could feel her forearm muscle as tight as an iron rod, but alive too and simmering with tension. "It could spread," I told her.

She nodded. "It's okay." I let her go, and, with the tips of her fingers, she moved Del's hair so it was all on one side of his face. His lips made damp poppings with hardly a noise. Lazily his eyes moved about, dimly focused on things not there.

The Sinker looked to me once more, then a short glance at Tim. I caught his look back, a subtle downcast of his eyes that made me think of a cow caught chewing its tether. The Sinker moved to the end of the bed. She took the blanket's low hem and lifted it carefully back. The pus smell rushed us warm and sour. Leg flesh had gone black around the seeping bandage, bruising in purple and yellow contrasts to his ribs.

"He was cut by the meat knife," I said. "It's got his leg. It will be his hip next, then his heart."

▼

My mother was washing dishes as she talked about the boy who ran off from the Deciding. She didn't leave the house much anymore, but the gossip had reached her fine. "At least he didn't decide to sink, that boy. Because staying right where you are, well, at least that's better than sinking."

I'd seen it happen before. Those poor young boys out there looking into all that vastness, and it's just too much. Some of them would leave the next Deciding, but mostly once they'd missed their first chance, they could never summon the courage. None of them ever decided to sink, though, not as long as anyone could remember. Really, the boys weren't deciding to rise or sink, they were deciding to rise or stay. We were a rock of risers, founded by risers, trained in rising. I wondered if my mother really cared at all about that boy from the Deciding. Maybe it was just easier than talking about my own boy, her grandson, who was down the hall in his bed and would never get the chance to decide anything at all.

Tim was sitting opposite me at the table. He looked asleep except for his eyes. He rolled his neck. Popping came from it like stepping on gravel. "My fucking back," he said. I was sore from sleeping on the floor as well, but it didn't do any good to complain. It was the code of our rock: bring a letter, get two meals and a rest.

"A letter from my brother," my mother said. Her hands moved mysteriously in the dark of the basin. Clean dishes appeared, set off dripping. "I wonder how far he's risen. A few hundred rests? A thousand?" Her eyes went soupy and distant. "He always said he'd go a thousand, but he can't have gone that far. But maybe." She turned to look at me over her shoulder. "Your father was a riser too. From that shithole rock where he started. He came pretty far to get here." Turning back, she took to the dishes with vigor.

"My rock sure was a piece of shit," Tim said. "Couldn't get out of there fast enough." He laid his hand on mine. "And I'm so glad I did." It was the same way all risers who settled there talked. They said Fairviel was smaller than other rocks but had more food, more milk, good water collection, that life there was easier than the rest of the sink. Tim never talked of his life before Fairviel, not in any detail. When I asked about his home rock, he'd tell me it was pretty much the same but not as nice, not as easy, not as much food. It was the exact answer my father used to give. He'd died when I was a girl, my father, and was more a memory of a memory than a real memory. I wondered now and then if I really recognized his face in the face of my son, or if Del's face had simply become the memory of my father. I did remember his droll, impatient way of talking about the wider sink, as if all that was out there were just more tiny rocks like ours. But how could that be true, in all the endlessness?

Bristle had not been like that. He was full of wonder, dreamy about what was out there; he couldn't wait until his Deciding. Something must happen to them once they're out in the void to turn them quiet and boring and dead inside. All these men were like the sink, only darkness past the edge.

"Thank you for the rest." The Sinker was standing in the doorway.

She had entered without disturbing even the stillness of the air. This is how she moved, like not moving at all, but already where she intended to be. She was in the doorway, then seated at the table as if nothing had occurred between.

"How did you come about the letter?" Tim asked.

The Sinker peered at his face. For her, all of this was temporary and soon would be gone. "I had a long stretch out in the sink," she said. "Landed on a rock, got some well-needed rest, food, kind treatment. A man there wanted to get a letter to his sister. He knew which way I was headed, told me the code here." She pressed a smile for my mother. "He looks a lot like you, like both of you." And she nodded to me.

My mother said nothing. She put on one of the big leather gloves and went to the oven.

"Have you traveled far?" I asked the Sinker.

"Yes."

"How many rocks have you been to?"

"Lots. Hundreds."

"Hundreds?" Tim whistled.

"And what did you do to end up a sinker?" my mother demanded. She was standing with her back to the oven, that big mitt on her hand. "A woman out there alone in the void." And she shook her head.

The Sinker eyed her with an even gaze, her voice flat when she answered. "I'm not really a sinker, though I have been sinking for a stretch now. But I've risen far, gone outwide too."

My mother scrutinized her. "Sinking," she scoffed. "Takes a few rests of it to get the distance you can in one of rising." Turning, she reached into the oven with that big mitt, took out a steaming plate, and set it down in front of the Sinker. Her part of the code complete, my mother straightened, as tall as she could make herself. She looked right at me, but it was clear what she said was for the Sinker. "To really get somewhere, you have to rise, put out some resistance, let the friction take you, let all the rocks sink right past. That's why men rise instead of sink. Through generations of male lineage, the family eventually reaches Center City."

"Have you been there?" I asked the Sinker. "To Center City?"

She looked at me, a long measuring gaze. I could feel Tim watching her, my mother too, waiting for her answer. "I have not," she finally said.

"But it *is* up there, right?"

"Of course Center City is up there!" my mother shot out. "We pay our tribute to risers headed there. We obey the codes passed down. Where does the tribute go, where do the codes come down from, if there is no Center City?"

When my mother was done, I looked at the Sinker, but she refused to react at all. "It's up there," she finally said, "from what I've heard."

"See?" Satisfied, my mother pushed a fist into the lumpy part of her hip and nodded down at the plate she'd set on the table. "Two meals, and a rest." And she held out her hand.

The Sinker's fingers went into the folds of her dark clothes, and the letter emerged. She put it flat on my mother's palm. "Thank you," she said.

My mother stared at the letter for a breath, then, with gentle fingers, unfolded the page and began to read.

"Where has he settled?" Tim asked.

My mother shook her head, reading to the very end. "It doesn't say." She turned to the Sinker. "From how far up did this letter come down with you? A few hundred rests? A thousand?"

The Sinker sighed and looked around, then set her cold gaze back on my mother. "A ten-rest rise from here," she said.

My mother went still, a full puffing and unpuffing of her small body. She turned and looked into the basin. Her hands held the edge. Her voice was so quiet, I couldn't hear it over the distant roar of the sink, whatever it was she said.

▼

I had finished with the cow and was urging her to the edge. Like always, she reached out her hoof, uncertain, pawing the void for some purchase. I gave her an encouraging slap on the rump, and she went for it, stepping off with a frightened moo. I watched her shift and sink, relax, then waver and rise, tether out taut, her supple face settled into the calm embrace of the friction. Her black empty eyes looked back at me, always confused.

From where I was, I could see past the next house over, to the meeting hall, where the boys of the rock were gathered for the once-a-rest lesson with the rise instructor. It was how the boys learned to become the kind of risers our rock was known for. Probably they were listening to some lecture about the future of their lives and the need to prepare now no matter how far away their Deciding seemed. Or maybe using the funnel hole in the center of the floor to hone their rising, working meticulously through all the fine details of Kolatchi position.

Several girls were gathered outside, standing atop an empty barrel to peer through the hall's high back window, exactly as I had done when I was their age. I could still picture that diagram every boy was made to learn and draw from memory—a pyramid pattern of rocks like ours with Center City way up at the top and biggest of all.

One of the older girls was up on the barrel, a younger tapping her calf because it was her turn to climb up and have a look. But the older girl wasn't relenting, and some bickering broke out, until the rise instructor appeared, chasing them off with his fluffy beard, as wild and as windblown as some scavenge hauled in from the sink.

As the girls scattered, screeching and giggling, I noticed the Sinker behind the meetinghouse, way out on the far edge. She was gazing outwide, her helmet up under her arm, her pack and sword strapped tight to her back. Her hair whipped upward, lashing back at all the other lives she'd already passed. And soon, off she'd sink, to wherever it was she was headed, gone again into the void, and I'd be just another tiny life somewhere above.

I'm unsure how long it took me to cross to her. At each breath, she could have slipped on that helmet and leaned forward and been gone, but at each breath, she did not. It was silly to think she didn't know I was approaching, but she never turned or acknowledged me at all until I was by her side. Even then her gaze stayed focused on the far outwide.

"Is there an end to it?" I shouted, loud to be heard over the roar.

A breath passed. I wasn't sure she'd answer, but then she did, her voice low and clear, piercing the friction somehow with its quiet surety. "There doesn't seem to be. Rumors abound. People believe what they believe."

"Is sinking really slower, slower than rising?" I was shouting still. It was the only way I could be sure she'd hear me.

"That's a myth," she said. "If you know how to sink, you can get going just as fast, faster even."

I nodded. "It doesn't seem like he went that far, my uncle. Ten rests from here. After all the training, all the expectations. He could have gone further if he'd sunk instead?"

She shrugged. "It's harder than you think out there, to be in the void, sinking or rising or going outwide. A single rest is more than most people can handle. After two or three, they crack, from the darkness, the solitude, the hunger, the uncertainty. Most people, once they get back in, they never go out again."

"Most people, but not all?"

She smiled. "No, not all."

Some part of me knew it was the wrong thing to say, but I thought then that I would never have another chance. "Did you betray your family?" I asked. "One girl was made to leave here once. It was because she'd betrayed her family. But it was before I was born." In the silence, I felt foolish and naive and wished I could take it back.

"Rocks are all different," she told me. "With different codes and preconceptions about rising and sinking."

"That's why you decided to sink? Because of the code where you grew up?"

"My rock had no code. I wanted to be as far away from it as possible."

The friction warbled as it will, swirling and churning as it roiled by.

"I dream about the void," I told her, nodding into the vastness of the sink. "But I've never been out in it, not really."

"What is the dream like?"

"Longer than when I sleep, because it always feels like I've been out in it forever."

"It seems like you're lost," the Sinker said, "just empty sink, and you can't find anything, up, down, outwide."

I nodded and wiped a tear I hadn't felt forming. "And there's a feeling of something tugging me," I continued.

"The friction feels that way."

I shook my head. "But it's something more than the friction, a separate something. A pull, but from the inside. A pull downward."

The Sinker was looking at me and I back, into her thinning eyes. A long roaring of the sink passed. I thought that would be it. I could feel her about to slip away and be gone. "Your son has an infection," she said, "an organism that got into the wound."

I nodded. "The knife fell off the table and hit his thigh and he cried a bit, but we didn't think a thing of it until a few rests later and it already had him." Talking about it was like pulling my heart back to that moment, the knife there on the floor. The silly boy crying, I'd thought when I saw the tiny nick. "I know it's dumb to think, but if I'd just washed it when it happened, it might have made all the difference."

"It might have," she said. "Probably not, though. It's no use to worry about it, either way, what you could have done. Breath is not like the void. You can't choose which way to go. It only goes forward. From here. Then here. Then here. Forever."

"You're right," I said. "It's best for me to just accept it. Talking about it, thinking about it, it only makes it more upsetting."

"On some rocks people don't die of infection."

"They don't?"

"On some yes, but not all."

I wondered about my uncle, about Bristle, about all the other boys who'd left. If they'd reached such a place, wouldn't one of them have come back and told us? But none of the boys ever sank back down. They vanished into the blackness of the void and never returned. Occasionally a letter, filled with empty mystery.

"I can take you to Roseblood," the Sinker said. "I'm headed that general direction."

"Roseblood?"

"A rock. A few rests' sink from here. We can get medicine there that will save your son."

THE VOID

The Sinker led me out, slowly, into the uprushing friction. "You know how to sink?" she shouted, loud to be heard over the roar. I shook my head. Her face showed through the front of the helmet, the visor snapped up, but her expression was flat and unreadable. She'd had me tie my hair down and given me a tight cap to keep it from whipping around. I could feel the ties shifting and tugging at my scalp as the friction pulled and battered me.

"A lot of surrender," the Sinker shouted, "and a little bit of control." She gestured for me to follow her lead, then angled her shoulders and hips in a way that turned her upside down, helmet pointing into the undervoid. I did the same, and my body flipped and I started to sink. I could feel the friction, harder on my shoulders and head, then lighter as it lapped and curled past my feet. The surface of Fairviel tilted away as we went down below the edge, and then I was looking up at the jagged, craggy underside.

"Let it shape your shape," the Sinker shouted. "Then adjust." She bent at her hips and drifted away, then came easing back. "Use the flow, the coursing of the friction going by. Let it scoop in behind you and push you along." She snapped her visor down and leaned away and picked up some speed.

I mimicked her, legs together, arms tight to my sides, and I felt the friction crackle along me as my speed increased, and I looked back at Fairviel getting smaller and smaller, then smaller than I'd ever thought it could be, then only a speck, then gone, and in all directions there was nothing but the dark endlessness of the void, and the only thing I could see was a subtle gleam off the Sinker's helmet, and I tilted and wobbled and settled in on her flank and we plummeted downward together, the roar overpowering, sinking positions held tight, the void forming more and more darkness below, nothing changing for what seemed like an entire rest or more, until the Sinker began to move and her pose loosened and she went into her pack, and I let my arms and legs loosen too and felt the blood flow easing and then painful and then soothing, and the Sinker pressed a pill into my hand and I put it into my mouth and swallowed and felt it filling my insides, and a drop from a tiny dropper, the liquid iron-tasting on my tongue, then back into position, arms and legs pinned tight, the void smearing into a sameness and then an even deeper and extending sameness, as if all of the sink was only a single dragging breath, and I eased into the cupping fabric of the roar, the soothing cradle of its deafening warble, and *all sounds and sensations were the same and seamless but for a dull, confused tunnel I could not remember passing through, and the Sinker was gone, or perhaps I was the Sinker, and I looked around, but in no direction could I see anything, and I felt again the thinning of all I was, my body becoming lighter and lighter, and when there was only the thinnest sliver left, something did finally form in the distance below, a faint hint of blue, a wavering of light, and the sensation of the sink began to change to more of a floating, and, looking below, I could see the thing I'd been sinking toward was water, a plane of it extending in all directions, as endless as the endless sink, and the roar was gone and the friction too and above me stretched out all I'd fallen through, and the void began to waver and something grabbed hold of my arm and I looked and saw a dark tentacle had attached itself to me and I pulled away and it doubled its strength and yanked* me back into the uprushing of the sink, and where the tentacle had gripped me was the Sinker's hand, shaking me awake.

She tapped the side of her helmet and the visor flipped up. She was yelling again, to be heard over the roar. "Risers!" And then I could see them, two glinting specks way below and coming up fast. "They've tracked us awhile now, adjusting their course."

"Why?" I shouted back.

"To kill us and take whatever we have. Give me some space. Rise a little."

I spread my arms and legs wide and felt the friction crashing harder into me and my descent slowing, and the distance between us grew. The specks had formed into two men, both with dim headlamps, one with a sword and the other with what looked like a spiked net. The Sinker's visor flipped down and her body straightened and she accelerated away like an arrow released. As the three forms converged, there was a flash of thin steel; then the risers were rising limply by. In the headlamp lights I saw their frozen grimaces, pools of blood in shifting oblongs around them. The Sinker spread out her arms and legs and rose back to me. Her visor flipped up. "They find you sleeping and you're dead."

"I'm sorry," I shouted back.

She wiped and sheathed her sword and was cold with indifference again. "Sleeping isn't your fault. When you're alone out here you have to."

I looked into the darkness from which they'd come. It seemed impossible there could ever be anything down there. "How much further?"

The Sinker took out a small device, almost a cube but slightly elongated on one side with a tiny lens, a few knobs and buttons, and a row of input jacks. She settled it into her palm and pressed a button on one end. It crackled with crisp green light, and a complex of clustering dots projected out around us. She must have seen my awe and confusion. "It's a map," she shouted, and I could see it then as I never had, the ghosted layout of the wider sink. Her thumb rolled the top knob, and a section of the projection grew larger, the clusters separating and thinning. She pointed out a tiny red light moving downward. "This is us." Then she pointed to a nearby dot. "And this is your home rock, Fairviel." Scrolling again, she homed in on a dot in the path of our descent. "This is where we're going. Not too far. Under a rest."

I looked longer at the projected motes all around us. "How big is it, the map?" The Sinker smiled into the lashing friction. Her thumb scrolled and flicked, and we were enveloped by a cloud of projected specks, too many to count or even pick out from the near-uniform haze, all of it sinking together endlessly through the void.

And then the map was gone and we tilted and plummeted, and there was another pill and another of the metallic-tasting drops and ever more unfolding darkness spreading out in waves and peeling back to reveal only more layers of the endless void beneath, and then there was another type of light, faint in the distance far below, not one light but hundreds, set atop a high stone wall, a square perimeter around the edge of an equally square rock.

The Sinker's visor snapped up. Inside the helmet was dark, with only peekings of her face as she yelled above the roar.

ROSEBLOOD

As we sunk closer, the true size of Roseblood became clear. Ten of Fairviel would have fit on its surface. More awe-inspiring than its size was its density. Within the enclosing walls, houses were packed in tight rows, rows upon rows, no empty space but for a few wide walkways cutting length- and crosswise. There were more lights, dotted throughout, on the fronts of buildings, hanging above the paths, glowing from inside windows. The high wall surrounded it all but for a thin outcropping on one side where even more lights illuminated a sparse cluster of tents and trading booths. Bulky generators along the edge sucked up friction from the void to spin turbines like we had on Fairviel, but as big as a house. From high atop the walls, three bright plumes ignited and headed toward us.

"Centurions," the Sinker shouted. "Do as they say. And don't talk."

They swooped in and hovered around us, backpacks on that shot fire from the bottoms. All three had cubist-hilt swords in sheaths on their belts. "What is your business at Roseblood?" one shouted.

"Just a stop," the Sinker shouted back.

The centurions bobbed slightly, in tune with the fluctuating exhaust from their packs. Each had a control in their left hand with a wire snaking back. "Stay on the traders' side of the wall," one finally shouted. The Sinker nodded, and the centurions went hurtling back to their posts.

We sank toward the small clearing, and the surface widened and picked up detail. Then it was coming on too fast, and I thought for sure I would break both legs. The Sinker was at my shoulder. She made an upslicing motion with her hand, then dove downward and angled her body that same way, and the friction scooped under her and her coiled legs caught her as perfectly as if she'd stepped off a kitchen stool. I tried to mimic her motion, but the upcurving friction came on too sharp. My feet hit first, but the surface yanked itself out from under me. I threw my hands down to break my fall, but they collapsed. Pain bit through my ribs and chest, then dulled and contracted as if pulling me into it. I could feel the hardness of the surface now, holding me up, and I rolled onto my back, gasping for breath.

The Sinker's face appeared, hovering against the darkness of the void. "You're all right," she declared. She helped me to my feet. I stood and arched my back and had to suck in hard to get any air. "You knocked out your wind," she said. I imagined all the traders and travelers entertained by my sloppy landing, but not a single one had noticed, or if they had, they didn't care. They sat at their fires or in the front flaps of tents, not paying attention to us in the least.

I'd been in the sink before, but only floating out in it, and never beyond sight of Fairviel, never for longer than a few dozen breaths. Now, after two full rests out in it, walking on rock felt incomplete, a half sensation. I was relieved to have something solid pressing back up again, but it was so quiet without the roar. I missed the darkness too. Everything around us was lit bright in the high, searing lamps, looming like big glowing eyes. Against the light, the dark outlines of the centurions could be seen, pacing slowly on the wall above.

At an open tent, the Sinker traded a few glass bearings for a mysterious hunk of meat she called pig. We took it to a fire where others were cooking similar meat and meat in links and iron pots of boiling juices. We settled in with looks and nods from the others, and the Sinker set to cooking. I noticed immediately that some of the people around the fire were women. I knew the Sinker was right when she told me not all rocks were the same, but now I knew she was even more right. Maybe Fairviel was an exception, not a norm.

"You rising or sinking?" an old man asked us.

The Sinker only stared into the fire, offering nothing.

"Sinking," I said. "For now anyway."

A younger man spoke up, a kid really, barely older than the deciding age back on Fairviel. "Better make your mind one way or the other. Lest you don't plan on getting anywheres your whole life. Me, I've been sinking since I first came to. First chance I got."

The old man's eyes thinned on the kid. He caught me watching him and pressed a smile. "Are you sinking too?" I asked him.

The old man nodded, once for me, then at the kid. "Since I was about this one's age."

"All that breath," the kid said, "and we in the same spot now, you and me."

The old man's eyes darkened as he looked into the lapping flames. "It ain't where you are that's important, kid, but how far you've sunk to get there."

The kid thought about it, then laughed.

"Where are you going?" I asked the older man.

More laughter mixed into the crackle of the fire, but the old man's face stayed soft and kind. "Just down," he said. "Been going down a long while."

"Did you come from Center City?"

The question hung. I could see a few of the faces snickering. I looked to the Sinker, but she only stared into the fire, minding the meat she'd bought. The kid was talking again: "Never heard of no Central City. Maybe you mean the Big Gather. Where you from?"

"Fairviel."

The kid's eyes turned inward; he didn't seem to know it.

"Fairviel," another said, a plump woman with a face as rounded and soft as a pillow. "I thought women don't leave that place?"

"They usually don't, I guess."

"How far is this Central City?" the kid asked.

"Center City," I corrected. I could hear the tone of my own voice, like it was something they already knew and I was only reminding them. "Two thousand, three thousand rests? No one's quite sure."

There was more laughter around the fire, and the kid whooped and slapped his leg. "Three thousand rests?" he said between chuckles. Even the Sinker was smiling.

"Center City! Not real. Old scavenger legend." It was a rat-faced man across the fire. He was glancing around nervously under the brim of a furry helmet. "Legend was they would tell families on small rocks, and these people used to give over their food out of fear at just the mention. The mention of Center City. They let you sleep in their daughter's beds too."

A lost-looking man was wagging a finger at us. "I heard of the place where this woman is from, thought about going there myself once or twice maybe, maybe see if I can stop this constant drift and settle down. Rise, sink, outwide, a dozen rests in one direction, then change my mind and drift off in some other. Fairviel . . . They say a riser can settle there and go stationary."

The Sinker, at some point undetermined, had moved her hand to her sword hilt. Now she pulled it, a hard, short yank; a gleaming sliver of her blade hovered over her shoulder. "Any of you go to Fairviel, you'll be dead before your toe hits rock." The threat simmered, the sword reflecting in the eyes of everyone there.

"I hear it's boring anyway," the lost man replied, indifferent.

The rat-faced man hadn't stopped laughing. "Center City? Like some place in charge of the whole thing, ruling the whole of the sink?" He laughed again. "What you really need to worry about is what's at the bottom." He pointed out into the void. "A place where all the rocks land, all piled up, one on top of another, broken to bits. And everything on them."

"The Great Flat," someone whispered.

"The Great Flat?" I asked. "What's that?"

The old man pressed a smile. "Maybe real, maybe not. Maybe just some way to explain the end."

"The end of what?"

"The end won't come from above or below or even outwide!" It was a ragged old woman, made thin-boned and sinewy by a life in the sink. Her face was disproportionally teeth; they snapped, clicking while she talked. "It will come from within." She waited to continue, lapping up the attention. "There's a rock... a rock that consumes other rocks, has iron tentacles to suck them right in, eats them and every thing and every person on them. That is what's coming for us all."

The Sinker's eyes had fixed on her. I was the only one who noticed, the others all focused on the woman's toothy voice, the searching way her eyes probed.

"And not sinking, this rock," she continued, "nor rising even, but making whatever way it wants through the void."

"That's not possible," someone said.

The woman frowned. "Not *possible. Is!*"

"Who told you all that?" the Sinker demanded. All eyes turned to her, then followed her hard gaze back to the woman.

She stared at the Sinker, daring her. "No one told me! I saw it! Pulled the whole rock right in, smashing and chewing it, until all that was left was void where it'd been!"

"Where?" the Sinker asked. "Where did you see this? What rock was it?"

The woman's face fell. Her teeth seemed to float out free of her lips. She remained that way through a full breath. "Chancetville," she said. "Next sector over."

Someone laughed. "You've never traveled a sector in your life!" Others around the fire were chuckling too.

"Yes I have, you tit! I've been further than any of you! I started at Flagtop and went outwide as far as Kel. Down to the Green, then out and up past the Scollord Arc." Her face burst into a mad, toothy grin, hand up, finger pointing into the darkness of the void. Loose flesh flapped the underside of her arm. "It's out there. It is! And you will all find out some rest when you're chewed up slow by it too."

There was no more laughing or taunts.

"After Chancetville," the Sinker said, "you rose to here?"

The woman shook her head, her brow knitting. Her mouth moved silently, trying out the shapes before she'd say the words. "I sliced off midoutwide . . . to Treckell . . . then Flellwool . . . Strattatta . . . then straight rise more or less to here."

"Strattatta," someone hissed. "There is no Strattatta."

The woman was too tired now to argue. Her lips were stretched and bloodless, a fleshy bulge covering her misaligned teeth.

With a sudden burst of coughing fire from the high wall, three centurions launched. Three tubes of dark smoke, milky and opaque against the pure black of the sink. They coagulated in the void to meet a riser coming up, just as they had met us. There was a shout, and all eyes looked up as a bright plume of sparks flowered in the void. One of the centurions had killed the riser, and off he went, rising now in no direction.

The kid leapt to his feet.

"Let it be," the old man said.

The kid smiled. "Must be something on that riser worth checking for." He ran for the edge. A few breaths later, I could see him rising expertly. I'd never seen anyone accelerate upward so fast. As he reached the riser's limp body, a single centurion swooped by, sword out, and sliced the kid in half.

I looked around the fire, but no one seemed to care. They watched him float away a few breaths, then went back to the depths of their own minds. Only the old man seemed affected, a slight misting of memory or regret in his eyes. "Why did they do it?" I asked.

He looked up at the two pieces of the kid's body vanishing into the dark void above. "Code is code. And code here is no scavenging in sight of Roseblood."

▼

We found an empty spot to bunk down, set off from the other tents. The Sinker was encouraging me to get some rest, but I could tell she had no intention of doing so herself. "I have to go inside," she finally said.

"Inside?" Up on the wall, I could see the centurions pacing along. I thought of the Sinker, cut in two like the kid and left to drift off, meaningless forevermore. But it didn't seem possible.

She dug in her bag and came out with a piece of iron pipe about as long as my forearm. It had a second, shorter pipe welded perpendicular. "This is a bolt sling," she said. She held the shorter pipe so the longer rested on the top of her hand and wrist. I could see the main pipe was cut lengthwise in half with a pull and a spring inside it. The Sinker's hand came out of her bag again, now with a small metal bolt in her palm, which she fit into the trough of the longer pipe. "Pull it back like this," she said. She eased the bolt back along the groove until there was a click, then, lifting it, showed me a push trigger on the shorter pipe. "It's only accurate if someone is within a few steps." She carefully released the bolt and handed it all over. "In case anyone messes with you while I'm gone."

I took the bolt sling and the bolt.

"You won't need to use it," she said. "If someone gets close enough, you load it, show them, and they'll leave you alone." She looked me over a breath longer and seemed satisfied. "I'll be back soon." And off she went, weaving between the fires and tents until I could no longer see her.

I tucked the bolt sling inside my coat and the bolt in the easiest pocket to reach, then settled down on the roll the Sinker had put out for me. All the traders and travelers had gone into their tents and bedrolls, only the occasional shifting somewhere in the big pools of light. A centurion arced off and returned. Another swooped low, then was gone with the fading cough of his jetpack. If I was home at Fairviel,

Tim would be settled in beside me. Del would be down the hall, his pending death filling all the space between. But it felt so far away, farther than the couple rests of void we'd traveled, farther than all of the sink.

A man shuffled loudly past and glanced down at me. His face was terribly scarred by burns and seemed frozen in the process of dripping off. He went to a bedroll and lay down, and I watched the soft stillness of his body for I don't know how many breaths and *I was not aware of a darkness slipping over me, but the lights from the high wall were gone as if slowly faded out and in their place the dark emptiness of the overvoid, and forming below me was that same plane of water, churning and roiling and flowing over itself, more water than there ever could be, outwide as far as the outwide went, and when it seemed the water would roll on as endlessly as the sink, a rock appeared in the faraway distance, except this rock wasn't sinking through any void; it was in the water, completely surrounded by it, with only the rock's surface visible, and sinking closer I saw an edge of white sand and clustered trees running off into the distance, and I swooped low, and as the surface rushed to embrace me, I opened my eyes* and could see an odd shape moving in the deadened light of the fire.

It was the Sinker, rolling up her gear, packing it away in her ever-tightening pack. When she saw me awake, she held up two tiny jars. "You put this on your son's wound. And this into his food. One per meal until they're gone. It will be about thirty-five rests or so. Did anyone bother you?"

I roused further, shaking my head. She went back to working her pack. It seemed to get smaller as she added things. "You were in that dream again," she said.

"How could you tell?"

"Your eyes. They were moving wild behind your lids."

I nodded, feeling the lingering downward tug of the sink inside my dream. "But there was something different. There was water."

"Water?"

"A lot of water, more than there could be. More water than is possible."

The Sinker contemplated it as she packed more things, folding up flaps and weaving in ties.

"Will you tell me the truth about Center City?" I asked.

She was still a breath, then sighed as if tired of it. "There is no High Careless, no Center City, no Great Flat. Only endless void and rocks sinking through it."

I nodded. "I sort of knew that." I looked at the jars, one filled with pills, the other a clear goo. "This medicine, all of this, this place. A couple rests from Fairviel and no one even knows about it?"

"The men probably do, the ones who've settled there. They hear a rumor about a place with women waiting to hitch a riser. They learn the code, the things to say. Their real pasts vanish."

My stomach felt suddenly heavier in my gut, like it had shifted down lower than my hips. A heat worked up the back of my neck, and the lapping friction cooled it and chilled me.

"You're going to have to get back on your own," she said. Some part of me already knew this, knew it as soon as I agreed to come. The Sinker had other destinations that didn't involve backtracking. "You'll be all right," she said. "You've been out in it now, and it seems like you can handle it."

She pulled out a small metal cube, dented on one side with a row of cracked lights. She pressed a button, and a crude image flickered to life, not much more than a few dozen blue specks. It was a smaller, dimmer version of the way the Sinker's map projected. "This map is for you," she said. "It's a piece of shit but will get you home. Without one, you're dead out there. Into the void and you never come back."

The Sinker pointed out a brighter, purple dot. "This locator beacon is set to the map itself. So it's you, your location." She indicated one of the blue specks. "This is where you're headed, Fairviel, straight shot at fifty-five from absolute, radial seventeen. You know what absolute is?"

"Straight up," I said. "Or down."

She nodded, then pressed a button on the map, then another. A guideline appeared, straight up and down, bisecting the map perfectly. "And you know how to set the radial?"

I shook my head.

She held the map so I could see the water-filled disk with the pointer floating in it. As she did, the pointer rocked and settled. "This always points outwide true zero," she said. "Line up the two pointers." She moved the map so the floating pointer touched a pointer on the main body. "Then put in the radial from there. Got it?" I nodded. She thumbed and scrolled, and a second line appeared, angled off from the first. "You'll need to tilt your body so you rise at fifty-five from absolute, marked by this line here." She indicated the line between the beacon and Fairviel. She pointed out the same angle in the dark void above us. I hadn't realized until then that we'd not sunk straight. It unsettled me, this difference between what had happened and how I'd perceived it.

"Keep the beacon on the guideline, and Fairviel will be there. It'll come right out of the darkness." She handed me the old, beat-up map. "Put it in your pack until you need it."

"Thank you," I said. "It must have cost you something."

"I let them download a chart from my map, so not really."

"What about this?" I asked, taking the bolt sling out of my coat.

"Keep it," she said. "Remember: let them get close. It's a pain to reload fast, so make each shot count. Bolts are best, but any chunk of metal will work. The closer to the width of the pipe, the more accurate it will be. Hopefully you'll never need to use it."

I thought long about it, the map, the angle, the transit back, the bolt sling, the things that had been said around the fire, that kid the centurions cut in half. "Can I come with you?" I blurted, not thinking what it would mean beyond the frank asking of it.

"Not if you want to save your son."

I nodded.

"You'd slow me down too much," she said finally. "And you don't want to go where I'm going."

"I've slowed you down already. Taken you off course. I'm sorry."

"I had no course," she said, "not until now."

"What are you going to do?"

She pondered it a breath. "Same as always, I suppose, a lot of surrender, a little bit of control."

"What that woman said, about the rock that doesn't sink but makes its own way through the void. That was real? You've heard of it, seen it? That's where you're headed?"

The Sinker looked at me but offered no answer.

"Is it true what she said, that it consumes other rocks? How is that possible?"

"Everything's possible, if you go far enough."

"Will it come this way?"

She stood, finished with her pack. She strapped it on beside her sword and pulled it all down tight. "I don't know," she finally said. "But if you hear that it is, you flee, you take your family or you don't, but you flee."

I nodded. "Thank you," I said. "For saving my son."

"You're the one who has to save him."

"But I couldn't have if you hadn't stopped. If you hadn't listened."

She paused and looked inward, and maybe it meant more to her than another thing passing in the void, or maybe not. "Remember," she said, "straight shot, fifty-five off absolute. Don't second-guess and you'll be fine."

I nodded, willing myself to believe she was right. Easy as that. "Emery is my name," I told her suddenly.

The Sinker only gazed outwide, into the darkness and the darkness beyond the darkness. She gave me a last reassuring look, then slipped on her helmet, walked to the edge, leaned out into the friction, and dropped off into the endless sink.

THE PLACE THAT ONCE WAS HOME

The friction tugged at my skin in a way that was familiar now, even soothing, the roar a calm place my other senses could crawl into for some shelter from the endless darkness, and I had an awareness then that the map was gone or lost or stolen, but I didn't need it because I knew the direction was down, toward something I'd forgotten about until I saw the water forming again, so far off it was only a fluffy haze of blue, and I bore down and tightened my dive, using everything the Sinker taught me, but no matter how I angled my body, how much resistance I stripped away, I couldn't get any closer, and the hazy blue faded and thinned until the depths below me were dark and empty again, and I realized I was not sinking but rising, and was aware then that some other, more crucial part of me had been pulled into the darkness below and I was the leftover pieces, and the rising slowed as the friction eased back and the roar went down to a distant

whisper and I opened my eyes and lay there looking at the ceiling as Tim snored beside me.

I had always wondered if Kolatchi position actually worked or was just men boasting. But I'd used it the whole way back from Roseblood, spine arched, shoulder blades in, almost touching. I'd locked my elbows, my hands wide, knees rolled, and I'd felt that extra lift from the turned-out ankles. The more I held it, the more the friction pushed back. It became work to keep the pose, and then the friction pushed even harder back and felt like a hand thrusting me upward. I knew I was still falling in relation to the void itself, but with Kolatchi it did feel as if I was actually going upward, rising, and not only in relation to the falling of everything else.

It had been more than thirty rests since I returned from Roseblood, and Del was healthy and fine and running around again. I gave him the pills and used the goo as instructed, and when it was all gone, his bruising had receded and the seepage had turned clear. Again Del would have a chance to decide, thanks to the Sinker.

I spent his recovery studying the map, practicing how to set the angle and radial, to lock in a beacon line and use it as a guide. I'd done it once already on my own, straight shot back from Roseblood, just like the Sinker had said. I imagined her somewhere, somehow aware of me, proud of my self-learning. But I knew I was only some face she'd sunk past like all the others. After putting out the cow, I'd stare into the sink for even longer than I'd always done before. Forever its darkness had seemed like a thick wall, but now it was thin and as airy as the whipping friction. I could see Roseblood when I closed my eyes, its lights, its hugeness, the faces of the people around that fire. I knew it was real, that they were real, and not just some things I'd imagined to fill the empty sink inside my mind.

The women of Fairviel could hardly believe Del's recovery. They'd been coming to the house since he got back on his feet, asking where the medicine had come from. There was talk of training sinkers, sending them off for more. The men had become uneasy, but none of them were bold enough to argue. How could they after a child was saved? My mother treated Del's recovery like some dark trick. As she watched him climb out of bed, her face revealed this possibility to me: maybe she would have preferred him to die rather than be saved by something she didn't understand.

Sitting on the front porch, watching Del play with the other kids, I knew the breath had come. I fit out my pack with supplies and prepared my tightest clothes, adding some extra tie-downs and straps. I'd studied the map and plotted out a few stops; I'd go back to Roseblood for a quick resupply, then a three-rest sink to a rock labeled Vallio, then Muckers a few rests outwide from there.

I roused myself very early next rest, even before my mother was awake. I left Tim still snoring in our room and went to see Del. It would be a silent goodbye, a last look before I slipped away mysteriously. But when I was standing there above him, I could not stop myself from reaching out to lay a hand on his soft cheek. When I did, his eyes popped open as if he'd been awake, waiting for me. My tears welled and dappled his blankets.

"What's wrong?"

"I have my own Deciding to make," I told him. "I've been here too long, and it's not the right place for me. If I wait, even a rest more, I'll lose my nerve and my chance will be gone and I'll never leave."

His face spiraled in. "I thought only boys were made to leave."

"Anyone can leave," I told him.

He took it like any other piece of information a parent imparts, a set fact he'd just been made aware of. His thin arms emerged from the blankets and wrapped around me. I could feel all his weight hanging from my neck. "Are you going to rise or sink?" he asked.

Tim was there when I slipped from Del's room. Our eyes met over the clicking of the door. "A few hundred rests until his Deciding. You're sure you won't wait until after he's gone?"

I nodded that I was, as sure as I would ever be.

He sighed and shook his head. "I can't hold it against you, wanting to leave this place." His eyes filled with tears, but he blinked them away and rubbed his sleeve over his face. "I'm sorry," he said, "that I never told you the truth, what it's really like out there." He was digging in his pocket. "You'll need at least a few things to trade, to get yourself started." He took out five silver disks and put them into my hand. There was the face of a woman on them, a star framing her head. He hugged me, and I hugged him back. I hadn't ever loved Tim, but I knew him. What portion could really be a lie? All? How could he not be who he had been to me, even if really he was just some drifter who'd heard a rumor at Roseblood?

At the bottom of the back steps, I turned to see Tim had followed me. He was leaning in the doorway, watching me tighten up. "Are you going to rise or sink?" he asked. But then his eyes lifted and his brow curled in, focused on something past me. There was a sound too, a few layers I could hear faintly under the roaring void: a high ring and a deeper low rumble. I felt something lift from a place in the center of my chest, and suddenly the roar and the sink and the strange layered sounds were gone, and *all there was was the darkness of the void, the nearvoid and farvoid, the overvoid and undervoid, in every direction, as far as I could see, emptiness and darkness and more endless nothing, and the friction rippled and howled and roared, and there was that same pull, pulling me from the inside, downward into the void, and when I* woke, I really was in the darkness of the deep sink. All around me was blackness and nothing. My head pulsed, then pulsed lower as the roar rushed in. Something had hit me. I could feel the bruise on the back of my neck. Right then, I didn't really remember what had happened. It felt as if I'd been asleep in my bed, then woke in the void, but now it wasn't a dream. I had my pack on still, and I remembered then that I'd packed it, and the intention of going to Roseblood, of leaving. My stomach turned, and I realized I was slowly flipping, head over feet. I spread my arms and let the friction stop and settle me, and I floated there in the dark roar of the void.

My neck and shoulders were sore when I moved them, but I could move them. I went into the pack and got out the map. It plumed to life, and I set the beacon and found the radial. If I was reading it all right, I wasn't far from Fairviel. I tilted and sunk the way the map said. Soon I came across a glint in the nearvoid, a small piece of dark metal floating loose. It was so close I could touch it, and when I did, it was warm. There were more metal shards, and other debris as well: wood chunks, tufts of fur, a washbasin floating off on its own. All of it was part of a cloud of loose refuse with what looked like a rock at the center.

As I got closer, I could see the rock was Fairviel. The entire surface had been broken like a huge shattered plate. Everything was torn up: the houses, the fences, the meeting hall, the platforms, and the small turbines. There was nothing left but the rock itself. Lashed to it with thick metal wires were several giant bundles laced in chain netting, big cubes of slaughtered cows twine-wrapped into blocks and somehow frozen solid and several houses ripped up intact and made into storage containers, heaped with collected household goods and timber and clothing.

I remembered right then: Tim's face, the odd expression that had come across it, the sudden panicked widening of his eyes. I'd turned, and something huge and metal was streaking at me. I must have been thrown by the impact, flicked out into the void. How long was I knocked out? A rest, several rests? My hands were shaking hard, but I got out the bolt sling and slid in the bolt until I heard the soft click.

As I sank closer, I could see that one of the houses was filled with dead people, their bodies stuffed in like compacted trash. I was too far to see the details of the faces beyond the dark pits of a few open mouths. It looked like a red-and-pink mush, fuzzy with the shifting debris all around. I sank closer, and the horrible collaging effect shifted back, and individual faces became clear. And there, stuffed atop the pile of dead bodies, as if arranged for me to return and find, Tim and Del.

Right then the sink turned inside out with me at the center, all of its darkness and emptiness pulled through me, then extended back to endless. I wish I could say some future I'd imagined died or was crushed right then. When Del was only a baby, I would picture his then-long-off Deciding, the prideful breath when your son chooses to rise and takes Kolatchi and vanishes into his future in the overvoid.

But those weren't my real dreams. They were the echoes of the things my mother and father and Tim, and all the people of Fairviel said. The truth is I never imagined what the future would be like there, for Del or me or anyone. My life was just happening, the rests sliding by.

 I realized my eyes were closed, though I didn't remember closing them. I knew if I looked, I would see Del, and I didn't want to. I could rise up to the next rock in the map and see if anyone else had escaped and gone that way. I could search the sink for them, rock to rock, ever up into the overvoid, hoping to find someone I knew or knew before, maybe one of the boys who'd left long ago; maybe I could find my uncle, ten rests away. Or I could go down, as my dream seemed to want, and make my own life in the sink somewhere.

I was sinking faster, then faster, then faster than a person had ever sunk in the void, then even faster as everything else began rising, rushing up past me at greater and greater speeds, and there was a subtle rotation to it too, impossible to resist as the sink propelled me downward into darker depths that folded out and spread and unfurled and bloomed into even greater endless darkness, and then the feeling of the sink began to change, to something thicker, my plummet slowed by a more resistant friction, until it was impossible to tell if I was sinking at all or rising or going outwide or asleep in my bed on Fairviel, and there was that familiar pull, pulling downward, the feeling of sinking, not to some place, but into myself, and I could see a distant speck that bloomed and unfurled, and the water was there below me as if it had always been, deep and frothing and roiling, as dark blue as the deepest void was black, and a smell reached me, of brining fluid and decay, and in the sink above a sourceless light was forming, dim but everywhere, brightening the void in ticks, and the dark surface of the water had upfaded to milky blue and the white froth spread apart to show spears of light punching into a wavering void below, and the light became more than a dimness, then was even more, and the overvoid vanished and the water too, and a stabbing pain shot through my face and all of everything was swallowed by a bright colorless nothing that erased everything but itself . . .

PART 2

THE SINKER

FROZEN ROCK

The Sinker angled her hips and shoulders and pointed her helmet and held her arms tight, and her speed increased and the friction rolled past her and pressed her on faster, and Roseblood faded into the overvoid and all there was again was the pure darkness of the void, and she thought about her name, which she hadn't in a thousand rests, three thousand perhaps, and she remembered what her father used to tell her, about the way the water moved, different where he was from than on any other rock, but he was a liar, all of it a lie, at best a fanciful exaggeration to entertain a young girl, and she thought of the toothy woman's story, the different maths of the sink that would need to line up to make it true, the numbers and distances rattling in formation through the Sinker's mind a whole rest straight, without the slightest loosening of her dive, arms pinned tight, legs pressed together, the bulbs of her ankles interlocked, the clicky sound of the woman's voice ghosting thinner and thinner, until it too was gone behind her like Roseblood and Fairviel and all the other rocks, and when she finally did break her pose for pill and drop, the Sinker could feel the settled blood moving cool through her veins, warming as it pumped faster and her fingers and toes tingled and she shook them out and put the pill into her lips and the drop sucked down and a last full-body resettle, then arms and legs tight again, chin tucked, cutting downward through the void, the curling friction propelling her onward as it rushed past, the pressure smearing her farther into the fabric of the void to reappear where she wasn't yet a breath before, and more unfolding void and more endless darkness and more pills and drops and short slivers of shifting and stretching and back into a knifepoint plummet, all the way across the Gratting sector before stopping a single rest to resupply and feel the wobbling of solid ground beneath her feet, then up the Degloss Updraft midoutwide, rising faster than ever in her life, only pills and drops and her long, even breaths and the dull encased drone of the sink in her helmet for ten rests straight, to the little cluster of Brund, where the rumors were more than rumors, firsthand reports of rocks stripped and bundled up square and pulped into fragments, and she plumed her map to trace the recent line of her travel, calculating her shortcut through the thinner sector and up the Degloss had saved a half dozen rests, and if her geometry was correct, she would find what she was looking for about here, her finger circling an isolated cluster of dots.

She slipped the map away and pointed her helmet, and the sink thinned and widened and she arced outward and accelerated and settled again into the droning ever darkness, a long, slicing tangent across the outer rocks of the Freehold, a last stretch of dark void and droning friction and pills and drops, until a coolly glinting speck appeared in the far outwide: Frozen Rock, its icy gleam diffused by a cloud of smoke that trailed up into the overvoid.

There in the darkness above it was the jagged shape of a Far Machine; and if a Far Machine was here, it meant the Construct was not far behind. The Construct, a rock that consumes other rocks. But not a rock, or not only a rock. A machine rock, fueled by the rocks it absorbs. All of it became true for her then: the woman's clicking story, the rumors, and the more than rumors she'd tracked all the way. She could see it now, the converging paths, the symmetry, her past's unlikely reemergence into her life after so many random directions in the sink.

She swooped in closer, and the jagged shape of the Far Machine became more clear, its wide metal fins like giant saw blades, chain cannons limp along both sides, tether wires dangling from its belly, but its engines were off, tri-flaps out to float there in the uprushing, its sleeping mouth a vague darkness of gears and grinders. It was one of the larger ones—bigger itself than all of Frozen Rock—and could reduce it with little effort or resistance. So why was it waiting? the Sinker wondered. The Far Machines usually ranged out ahead in several directions, harvesting resources, or laying out possible paths for the Construct to follow. Speed, haste, and surprise were the Far Machines' most effective weapons, appearing from the dark and reducing a rock before much could be done to resist. But there it was, hovering like some gigantic trade barge.

As the Sinker angled and sank closer, a hatch on the bottom of the Far Machine opened, and a pilot ejected from the under carapace. A small team of droppers fell into flank behind him, all wearing the same drab canvas jumpsuits, all sinking in formation for Frozen Rock below. When they landed on the rear of an ice swell, the Sinker angled out and put down farther off. From a shelf away, she watched them gather, the pilot talking to them and waving his hands directionally. Going into their packs, they took out thicker jackets and put them on over their faded canvas suits. Better dressed for the cold, the pilot led them on foot toward a high wall of white ice. The Sinker followed, unnerved by the coldness of the place. It was a different cold than out in the void, a cold that radiated up through her feet, more inside the body than whipping at it from outside. It was a strange imbalance, she felt, to come in from the sink to a place even more cold.

Soon a town came into view, dark iron buildings cut into the face of the sheer cliffs, stretching vertically above a wide ice floor. Along the base, several furnaces glowed, pipes webbing out to the homes above.

Soot-faced workers milled about, their eyes gleaming. They nodded to the droppers and the pilot but didn't slow their work or watch them at all once they'd passed. The smell of whatever they were burning was awful, chemical. Smoke burping from release valves draped the place in a foul obscuring mist. Several other workers were busy chipping off chunks of ice, piling them in wagons with teeth-tread tires. Everyone else was inside somewhere, the metal homes glowing with warmth high above.

The town had a small center along the ice floor, a dozen crooked buildings clustered tightly around a supply store. All of it looked as frozen as the rest of the rock. What few people were out moved slowly, fighting a soul-deep battle against the cold. The Sinker slid along in the furnace shadows, watching the pilot and his men vanish one by one through the door of a dining hall. She readied her sword and unclasped her boot knife. She had determined not to let them kill if she could. But fight them all? Did they have chain guns on them? Pocket razor retracts? And if they didn't and she did kill them all, then what? Kill the whole crew of the Far Machine? It was futile. This place was already dead, no matter what the Sinker did. But still, she was here; the droppers and the pilot were here; the people of Frozen Rock were here. Little violences she could stop with her own. The larger ones would need to be figured out later.

▼

The Sinker crept down the alley to look in the window. The dining hall was all but still. The pilot and his men were the only customers, seated at a few tables in the back, all quietly looking at a menu painted on a board above the bar. A barman as large as two men was smiling as he stepped over. The pilot smiled back and began talking, but it was only a hushing murmur to the Sinker, out in the cold alley. There was no bullying or wild behavior. They seemed to treat the big barman with the upmost respect.

"Where you coming in from?"

The Sinker looked to see an older woman leaned out on the porch of the supply shop next door, huddled in a puffy fur jacket, smoking a root as thick as her finger.

"Get out of here," the Sinker said.

"What?"

"Take your family, whatever you can carry, and get off this rock."

The root hung limp in the woman's fingers. She remembered it and took a long drag. "Code here is I got to be nice to people when they arrive, but after that I'm allowed to tell them to go fuck themselves." She tossed the root, and it sizzled where it hit the ice floor.

Inside the dining hall, the orders were all in and the drinks arrived. The pilot was up, patting shoulders, waving and joking as he made for the door. When he reemerged out onto the main walkway all alone, the Sinker slipped from the alley and became part of the dark, leaning shadows behind him.

At a distance, she followed the pilot through a fissure in the wall and up a series of catwalks to a small iron house jutting from the high ice cliffs. The Sinker watched as he knocked and waited outside the door, his breath punching out curt tufts of vapor. When the door opened, a woman was there, pulling him into a big hug. Even from a distance, the Sinker could see a change come over the pilot's thinly bearded face, a softening of his eyes, a tight, wavering lip.

When the pilot reemerged a short while later, the Sinker tracked him back down the tilting stairs, then looped wider and dropped to reach the ice floor ahead of him. As he passed, she formed suddenly from the darkness. The pilot's eyes went wide. He stumbled and was yanked upright and pressed back against the ice wall, sword edge to his throat.

"Move and my sword moves," the Sinker told him.

He went still, glaring at her, his outrage failing to hide his fear.

"Why are you here?" the Sinker demanded. "Why is the Construct coming to this sector of the sink?"

He looked at her differently now. "Who are you?"

She pulled him away from the wall and slammed him back, thunking his head off the ice. His eyes rolled as the Sinker pressed her sword in snug under his chin.

"This place is already gone," he spat. "If you really know what the Construct is, you know what I say is true. You know there's nothing you or anyone can do."

"This is your last chance to answer. You won't be able to when your head's not attached to your body." And she pressed the sword edge deeper, drawing a single rivulet of blood that ran down his shivering neck.

"Orders!" he blurted. "They want something! The Garent and the barons. They've altered course to come and get it. The Garent himself ordered it."

The Sinker loosened her grip for the slightest intake of a breath. "What is it they want?"

The pilot shook his head, outraged and amused at once. "They don't tell us! Look at me!" He tugged his canvas suit, filthy and overworn and now stained with fresh blood. "We haven't been to the Construct in a thousand rests. They relay instructions. We obey. All the Far Machines have been reassigned."

"What is its destination? Where is this thing it wants?"

He bit his lip, his face trembling, working to hold her gaze.

"Those people up there," she said. "Your family, or an old lover, someone you care about. You came down to warn them to leave." She let this sit on him a breath. "You know I can't stop it. But I can warn the people there."

The pilot's gaze flicked away, to that wall-clinging house way above. "A place called the Slant," he finally said. "The Kingdom of the Scorched Dome. Three other Far Machines are set to converge there, thirty rests from now. That's all I know."

The Sinker's eyes stepped back, seeing in her mind the map and its projected motes, the layout of the sink around her, the angle and radial that would take her to the Slant. "The Garent," she said, "what does he look like?"

The man was confused for a breath but did not hesitate. "Old," he said, "an old man."

The Sinker caught a shifting of the pilot's eyes, to something in the alley behind her. She turned to see a pasty-faced officer holding a chain gun, his eyes fixed hard on the pilot. "Traitor," he hissed. His young face was filled with confusion and rage, and with no further hesitation he pulled the trigger.

The Sinker spun the pilot into the storm of razor and chain. She heard the crisp, wet tearing of his flesh, then felt a hard bite in her thigh. She screamed, and when she opened her eyes saw the pilot's stunned face, so completely still. The only motion was a worm of red blood escaping his eye. She heard the clacking, then the distant thunk and tumble of the chain gun firing again. A hard jolt shook her hips, and she felt the wood-cracking sensation of her own head knocking off the ice floor. She swam in the hazy layer between sub and conscious. She was crawling, the rock surface cold on her forearms; then she realized she was no longer crawling but lying face down. She heard a high hiss, thin and piercing, and a deep crack under her, then an explosion along the ice wall as the furnaces burst and all turned dark and everything was erased.

BIG IRON

The Sinker woke in an unfamiliar bed. There was a ceiling above her and walls, and through a window she could see the darkness of the void, its hushing roar dulled but not far off. A small rock, then, but she was not on the surface, maybe the second floor of a building. She felt a presence and rolled over and saw a man standing in the doorway.

"I'm Randy," he said. "It's good to meet you finally." When the Sinker didn't respond, he said, "You were out for three whole rests. Three of mine, I guess. For you it was just one long one." He smiled and laughed. "You're aging slower than me." He let his smile spread wider.

The Sinker looked at him from the bed. The last thing she could remember was Frozen Rock: that young officer firing his chain gun, the pilot's face, as surprised as her, and then he was dead and still his eyes were boring into hers. "Where am I?" she asked.

"Big Iron," Randy said. "Well, one of the satellites of Big Iron. Near the Chain."

The Sinker tried to remember the map. Usually she could see it as easily in her mind as when she had it projected, but her head was foggy, an ache pulsing in her brain stem. "Do you know how far to the Slant?" she asked him. "The Kingdom of the Scorched Dome?"

He worked his tongue around inside his mouth. "I guess ten if done real right. I've never been, though."

Her eyes retreated inward, working the math in her head. Ten rests to the Slant, three already spent here, six at most in the void . . . so she could spend five more here, recovering, and still be sure to get to the Slant ahead of them. She relaxed looser in the bed. She looked out the window again: some unplaceable stretch of void. "How did I get here?"

Randy ran fingers through his hair. He put his hand into his pocket. "One breath you weren't and the next you were, there in the corn." He nodded toward the window. "You stood there, a breath or two, covered in blood. You were still holding your sword; it was all bloody too. Your clothes, that leather suit, all covered in it. I thought you were about to come slashing through the corn and kill me." He smiled. "But you fell over unconscious instead and that was three rests ago, but I said that already."

The Sinker scooted herself up a bit. She had a sore rib, but it didn't feel broken. One wrist and one ankle throbbed with sprains. Her thigh was the worst of it; it burned and itched deep inside the muscle. Lifting the covers, she saw, beneath a corn husk bandage, a peeking caterpillar of stitches. "You did this?"

"Not the slash, no, but the stitching." The Sinker swept her gaze across the details of his face. It was soft and made thick-looking by deep pocks and a dusting of faded acne scars. "We don't get many visitors, or any really," he said.

"Thank you," she finally said.

"Well, it was Dot who did the bandage. I just sewed it up like an old shirt."

"Who's Dot?"

"Dot? She's my wife you could call her, if you have the term where you're from. Though I guess officially we were never joined in any formal way. She says they don't do that where she's from and she can't fully right the idea. But we are all the same, Dot and me, man and wife."

The Sinker roused further, taking in the small room, the big bed stuffed thick with something soft, the small chest of drawers. The walls were faded yellow. Randy stepped closer, holding out a shard of mirror. "Looks better than when you first arrived. Looked like ground beef when you did, your face."

The Sinker took the shard. She tilted it to see her mangled features. How many rests had it been since she'd seen her reflection? She couldn't remember. Now it was this bloated, lumpy blue-black thing looking back. Usually when she imagined her face, it was her childhood face she saw. There were plenty of mirrors back then; she could look at herself whenever she wanted. If she flexed her brain, the Sinker could see her face as the face of her mother, but it felt forced and unreal, a strain to hold, a few breaths at most before it softened into a grotesque mush in her mind's eye.

The Sinker held the shard back up for him, and he took it and wiggled it. "Floated up as scavenge from the void, this mirror did. Wasn't on this rock, though. No scavenge reaches any of the satellites really. Everything with any trace of metal that gets close enough gets sucked in by Big Iron."

"My sword, my helmet, my pack?"

"I have them, your sword and pack. You didn't have a helmet."

The Sinker lay back. She supposed if she had to lose something, the helmet was the easiest to replace. She was feeling lucky to have anything left, lucky to be alive.

"Well," Randy said, long and slow, "I got some clothes there for you. A tad big, I figure, but it's all we got. Some of Dot's old things." He hooked a thumb back at the house behind him. "I'll have dinner ready in . . ." He trailed off and shrugged and smiled. "Just come on down when you're ready to eat." Then he turned and slipped out, closing the door behind him. The room was still, the house creaking as he moved off somewhere in it.

The Sinker worked herself out of bed, carefully shifting her weight onto her legs. They wobbled but held. The triple rest had done her good. Checking her pack, she found the map, exactly where it was supposed to be. The one thing she could not lose.

She dressed in the clothes left out for her, loose, dark canvas, with ties to tighten them up. Limping slightly, she went to the window and looked out. The rock was covered by sprawling cornfields, shimmering and shifting and swaying in the upcurling wind. The farmhouse appeared to be the only structure, otherwise the rock was corn from edge to edge. In the distance, the friction whipped harder, stalks lying over and popping up wildly.

The Sinker leaned down on the windowsill, craning her neck to look up. And there it was, Big Iron, dominating the overvoid. It really was as she'd heard, millions of chunks of random metal clumped together, harsh and sharp, rotating with no discernable regularity, some central magnet somewhere in there holding it all together.

▼

The table was set for three. In the center of each plate was what appeared to be a thick cut of cow steak, except the meat was yellow. The gravy was the same color, but a slightly different shade. It was the bread that was most naturally set in its yellowness, spongy and cakelike. Randy was coming in from the kitchen. He held up a decanter filled with brown juice. "Corn can be made into about anything with practice and patience. But spirits is its most natural product."

He poured them each some and sat. The Sinker sipped. She felt the warmth flood down her throat, into her stomach. "Will Dot be joining us?"

"It's up to her, I suppose, but . . . I suppose if she has not yet been enticed by the aroma, she may be already to bed until next rest, when it starts all over again."

The Sinker tasted the corn steak. "It's delicious." She took another bite, chewing slowly. She had not had a real meal since Fairviel, and nothing like this in she couldn't remember how long. She took a few patient forkfuls, feeling each separate smushing in her teeth. She looked at the stark patterns of the wallpaper, overlapping geometrics in thick, offset rows. Wide-framed doorways led to other large rooms. "Did you build this house?" she asked.

He laughed, shaking his head. "Found it as is. I was working out on the Chain back then."

"What kind of work?"

"Spider. Sifted through the nets. The Chain's where I got the mirror glass. Floated right up to my hand and I slipped it into my jacket. Spidering wake-long for some scavenger lord, it felt right to keep a little something for myself now and then." He shrugged. "Some of them on the Chain talked about Big Iron. You've traveled. I imagine there are other anomalies throughout the sink, probably far more impressive ones."

The Sinker nodded. It was true. She'd spent a dozen rests on a rock that was sinking within the emptied core of another, two separate cultures living concentrically. There were legends on the inner rock about a rock even farther in, while on the outer rock, they spoke of a people on some even-more-outer layer within which the entire sink was contained. On a rock called Torsque a crystal fire burned eternally over a full third of its surface. A small community of monks flourished there in perfect economic and spiritual synch with the roiling blue flames, in some places only a dozen steps from their homes. There was Four Rock, four identical fragments, each enormous and exact, in constant regular rotation around one another. "There are some strange things out there," she said. "Far more strange than a giant magnet."

Randy swished something around in his mouth and swallowed. "Well, it's the strangest anomaly in this sector of the sink, or so far as most of the workers on the Chain are concerned, the other net spiders. They would talk about the dangers of long-term exposure to the magnetism, the impossibility of ever building anything so close to Big Iron's pull, about the instability of the satellites that could break their perfect counter valence any breath and be sucked in. For me, back then, Big Iron was just a scary idea. But the longer I spidered those nets, the more I heard about it, the more it sounded like a place that might be right for me. I'd got tired of the Chain. Wasn't any space. The links felt familiar to me in a way that betrayed every excitement about the sink from my youth."

He sipped more corn liquor only to find his glass empty. He refilled it and topped hers off and sat back sipping and tapping his chest. "I packed my pack, took heed to the warnings and folded them away into my mind, and made the long trip out." He used his glass to indicate the closer environs of the house. "The farm was already here. The corn too, planted and thriving. I'd checked out a dozen or so of the satellites. There was debris on a few. Old camps, black dust of long-ago fires. But no people. I told no one, and for a few hundred rests it was a private retreat. I'd work out a contract, then pack off to Big Iron, to this house here. Eventually, Dot came into the picture. We met at a tavern out on the outer link, out past the last knuckle. She didn't believe me at first about this place, beautiful and serene, without the clutter of the Chain. A small house. An awe-inspiring—if a little scary—view of Big Iron. All the corn you can eat. And then one rest she came along."

The Sinker had a long sip, watching him trying to sort out the next detail. "Dot isn't here, is she?" she asked.

A strange confusion settled on Randy. His gaze drifted upward, toward the ceiling, as if better to hear any sign of her, but there was none. "No. I suppose she's not. She was, though, for a while. Used to be she came and went, some breaths here, some breaths not. The trip isn't so bad if you're prepared, a tiny stretch of dark void really. She used to travel it with me when I had the contracts. Made a regular trade run for a while and she tagged along on that too."

"Where did she go?" the Sinker asked.

"Oh . . . maybe to live back with her family, or where she was when we met, or maybe off for some other life altogether. She was a hard woman to keep satisfied, to be honest. After a while, she got tired of it and left me." He forced a smile that made his face look waxy and about to melt. He shook it off with a laugh and took a big sip, and suddenly his glass was empty again. He looked at the decanter but didn't pour himself any more.

"Do you want to know what I think?" he asked her. "About the corn, why it grows so strong, how this house was built despite the magnetism of Big Iron? I think this rock satellite is a sliver that's still preserved. Maybe something inside Big Iron—some effect of the magnetism—has kept it this way, all this breath."

"Preserved?" she asked. "Preserved from what?"

He smiled with his lips gleaming and his eyes offset. "From *before*."

THE CODE ABOVE ALL CODES

The Sinker woke from a sleep as deep as the darkest stretches of the void. Rousing, she sat on the edge of the bed and rubbed her eyes. She ran her fingertips over the lump of her stitched thigh and saw again the young officer's pasty face in the alleyway on Frozen Rock, outraged and betrayed, the jerk of his gun as he fired, the darkness closing around her. More came back as she sat there on the bed, in that farmhouse room, way out on that satellite of Big Iron. She'd been knocked out a while when she came to, face down in that alley, stumbling, then crawling from the town, to the lip of a high icy shelf, the loud grind of the Far Machine powering up, the crunch of its gears when it fired, the rock jolting as the grapples hit, the high hissing of the furnaces before they burst, the sharp crack of Frozen Rock breaking apart, her knees watery as she pressed to her feet, a few desperate, stumbling steps and then headfirst into the void, all of it spinning away, the wreckage of the metal houses turning loose in the void, people sporing out, the broken chunks of Frozen Rock collecting in the Far Machine's chain netting, then the vague darkness of the sink, the endlessness.

How long, how many rests, unconscious in the void? And somehow she had landed here, and on her feet, Randy told her, still holding her sword. The Sinker smiled at the image. It overlaid suddenly with her younger self, out on that first sink, the same sword in hand. Thirteen, fourteen thousand rests ago when she was little more than a child . . . All she had traveled since, the long reaches of her wander, what symmetry was at work to bring it all around again? Now that she was sure it was true, that the Construct was near, the Sinker knew it would go one of two ways. She would plummet away, exactly as she did before, or she would follow the arc, back into the great wheeling of her life in the sink. A lot of surrender, a little bit of control.

▼

Randy may have been drunk when he said it, but the Sinker took up his offer to slash as much corn as she wanted if it helped her recovery. As she thrust and stabbed and parried through the fields, she could see the farmhouse, seemingly afloat atop the swaying stalks. Above, Big Iron, all sharpness and angle, spinning its odd asynchronous rotation, this way, then that, then shifting to turn around some new axis. Every so often a loud clang would pierce the roar, distant and hollowed out, another piece of metal debris added, becoming magnetized itself, increasing Big Iron's pull, pulling more in, from farther off, always growing, always bigger.

Back on the porch after her workout, her sweat cooling in the lapping updrafts, the Sinker looked down on the jagged line through the corn. It was nothing, an insignificant marring of the field, all but unnoticeable.

She kept this pattern up for four rests. When the sweat thickened on her, it felt as if a thin layer of armor was added. Muscles worked past breaking, then built up stronger by the over-input of corn. Her wounds lost their itchy twinge. Her sword became a smooth extension of her arm again. For dinner, she joined Randy and always an empty chair for the ever-absent Dot. Their corn-based meals were varied nicely and stretched by liquor. Drunk, Randy would tell her stories about his home rock, the family he'd left behind, *grapevine farmers*, he kept calling them. "I don't know what became of them," he said. "I've never heard, and even if anyone cared to inform me, who would ever think to find me here, way out on one of the satellites of Big Iron? No one actually lives out here. Except for me and Dot."

"But Dot isn't here," the Sinker reminded him.

Randy nodded, still chewing, as if remembering something he'd forgotten long ago. "Tell me about the rock you grew up on," he said.

The Sinker leaned back, had a long sip of her liquor. Her mind raced through it all in a smear, the rocks, the void, all the faces, all the way back to the very beginning. "I left when I was pretty young," she finally said.

"There must be something you remember."

"Yes," she admitted. "It was warm. Not everywhere. But there were these hot places in the undersurface. I didn't realize it was strange then, but now that I've been out in the sink so long, how cold it is. I remember a few of those warm places, where I'd go as a girl. I can picture them pretty well."

"Doesn't sound so bad," Randy said. "I gotta heat up that old corn-burning furnace if I want to have a bath that's even lukewarm."

The Sinker sipped again. "There was one spot I remember. Because I eventually got too big for it. It was at a joint on the edge where they would hang these tiny bolt turbines to collect the static charge."

"That's an interesting way of doing it."

She nodded. "If you edged out around the turbine hold, you could slip into this underspace where the welding had been done. It wasn't much, but big enough for a small child to lie in. I would get in there and turn face down and watch the undervoid below me. But that's all vague. My clearer memory is from when I was older, looking at the same spot, knowing I no longer fit inside it." She thought. "There was a sound that came out of it, the friction scraping it." She whistled a low note. "Like that."

Randy considered it. He took a sip and pointed the glass at her. "You were a kid then when you left? What have you been doing since?"

"I have a map. I'd pick a sector, poke around. I wanted to see, to extend."

"Extend what?"

"The sink, what it is. What it could be. I collected more mapping data, built mine out pretty well. I'd try to find new sectors, add them in."

"And?"

"There does always seem to be more and more."

He smiled. His eyes moved over her, gathering what clues he could see. "But not now," he said. "Now you're not exploring the sink, charting, data collecting. Now you're chasing whatever it is did that to your leg."

The Sinker was holding up her glass, looking through the liquor at the color it made things behind it. "No, not chasing," she said. "Until recently I was just trying to find out if it was really so close, if it really could be." She glanced at her leg. "But now . . . now it feels more . . . as though I am sinking toward it, when standing still, when sleeping, when rising or sinking or gone outwide, that maybe I always have been."

Randy nodded, looking off distantly. "Like Big Iron," he said. "Some rest it will pull this whole place in; it must, the bigger and bigger it gets. You can't see it happening, but it sure looks different than when I first came. Fills the whole overvoid now! Forks and knives and pieces of wall junk, net buckles, cans and pieces of cans and frayed wire and stray barbs. Some rest there won't be satellites anymore, even if they don't fall in. Big Iron will add and add and build itself out around them. Until it's all a huge magnetized metal clump sinking through the void, if it really is endless. And maybe some rest, some other people will build something new on it, or in it, or out of it." He laughed and shook his head and had another sip. "Damn," he said, and laughed again.

▼

The Sinker was feeling hairy from the corn liquor and so took to the fields early to break her sweat. She had been at her slashes awhile when she split a wall of stalks like any other only to find herself in a tiny clearing. A large stone dominated the center, a thick gouge in the ground where it had been dragged and rolled over. The discoloration of the dirt was not recent but could be seen. A few hundred rests, she guessed. At the base, a small bouquet of picked weed flowers lay dried and bundled. There was a marking too, chiseled into the stone: a single dot.

The Sinker went back to the house. From the porch, she could see Randy, little more than a disturbance in the distant waving stalks. She drifted backward, into the house, and slipped silently up the stairs. There were three rooms besides hers and the bathroom. The doors were unlocked, and she opened them each and peered in. There was a sewing room, a plain unfurnished bedroom, and then a third bedroom, dim, with blue muslin hung over the windows. There was a large bed, immaculately made, a sitting chair, and a dresser beside a thin door. On the dresser was an old gear box, cleaned and repurposed. She flipped up the lid and saw it was filled with sparkling rings, common enough scavenge, but polished with astounding care. By the bed, the Sinker came upon a loose floorboard. Beneath was a hidden compartment. Inside, a piece of lace and a small knife. Looking up, the Sinker noticed, above the bed, tiny holes punctured in the ceiling and several long marks. Scratches, she could tell, scratches made by fingernails.

The Sinker checked the dresser drawers, filled with neatly folded clothes arranged by color. Moving the clothes revealed only more clothes and the bottoms of drawers. She opened the closet and slid aside the hanging dresses, and there, tucked deep into a back shelf, a large iron cuff and a small controller. There were two buttons on the controller. The Sinker pressed one, and the cuff tightened around itself. The other button produced a low hum from the cuff, and it leapt suddenly off the shelf, pinning itself to the ceiling.

▼

The Sinker found Randy in the corn, not far from the edge. He turned at her approach and smiled, but his smile faded when he saw what she held. Her eyes were as cold as the void, her sword in its sheath on her back, her hair held down tight with interlocking ties. In one of her hands was the iron cuff, the controller in the other. "This is a magnetic shackle," she said. "Dot didn't go off to live with her family, did she? She didn't find some new life. She wanted to leave and you kept her here and she died. On purpose or by accident, you killed her."

Randy remained still, but his neck reddened, his cheeks turning ashy.

"Were you planning on trapping me here?"

Finally he moved, shaking his head. "One look at you and I knew I wouldn't be able to."

"You're right."

His fingers rubbed his palm, and he flattened his hands and wiped them down the sides of his pants. "So, what will you do now?"

"Exactly what the code demands: kill you for killing her."

"That's the code where you're from?"

"It's the code everywhere. It's the one code above all."

He nodded, seeming to agree. "I saved you. Isn't there some code for that?"

"Thank you for what you did for me. But it doesn't matter." She tossed the big cuff to his feet. "Put this on."

He watched her calmly for a breath, then complied, looping the cuff around his ankle. The Sinker pressed the first button, and the cuff hissed and tightened snug. Randy looked up at Big Iron, its sharp, jagged angles slowly turning. "I have a last request."

"What is it?"

Smoothly he drew from his jacket a folded piece of paper. "You're off to the Slant. To the Kingdom of the Scorched Dome. It's on the way. Spurl. Almost midpoint between here and there. Would you . . . deliver this, to my parents." He smiled, his lips trembling. "The grapevine farmers."

"What is the code for letters on your parents' rock?"

"A full resupply, camp spot for two rests. You'll need it." He remembered something. "They're suspicious of sinkers there, but you'll be coming in almost outwide, I guess, so . . ."

The Sinker vanished the letter into the folds of her jacket.

Randy smiled. "Thank you." His eyes drifted off, looking into the corn. "I wrote that letter so long ago, I've forgotten what it says. I wrote it back then. Back when Dot really was here and alive and we were happy. When you got here, I put it into my pocket, and I guess now I know why." A tear broke down Randy's cheek. His eyes were sinking into his face, deep caverns, filled with shadows.

"You didn't ask me why," he said. "Why I did it."

The Sinker's sword flashed and then was back in its sheath. Randy's face fell open with sublime surprise as torrents of red blood gushed from his throat. The Sinker pressed the second button, and Randy flipped feet overhead. She watched the tiny lines of his dangling arms as he lifted away, smaller and smaller, until he vanished into the jagged layers of Big Iron, way high above.

Stepping to the edge, the Sinker thumbed the map. It crackled to form around her. She entered in the angle and radial, then tucked it away and pulled everything down tight. Leaning forward, she let her body rest there in balance with the friction pushing back. A breath cycled, and she leaned more and slipped into the uprushing friction and the roar swallowed her, deafening now without the helmet. Four rests, she estimated, to Spurl, to deliver the letter. Six more to the Slant, the Kingdom of the Scorched Dome. If it went smoothly, she would arrive there just before the converging Far Machines. And soon after, the Construct itself. The Sinker could feel it, the endless wideness of her own sink narrowing down.

I could not tell if I was sinking, or rising, or going outwide, or drifting at the whim of the void, but then there was that same downward pull, then a soft acceleration, then a loosening of the friction, then an ease, and then a drawing out and an uncurling, as if I'd passed through an invisible barrier into some other, separate void, and the friction grew warmer, and my speed increased and increased again, and all of it became an indeterminate wave of passing breaths, and I realized it had been dozens or hundreds or a life of rests since I last ate or drank or had a drop or pill, and when finally something did form below me, it was too small to be a rock and not coming up or remaining still or sinking away, but seeming to unform and form again with each closer breath, until I saw it was a person, their back to me, and when they formed again close enough, I reached out and gripped their shoulder and turned them toward me and looked into their face, but there was only emptiness, a darker, deeper void than ever had existed before, and the only thing there with me in the endless nothingness was a sound . . . a voice . . .

PART 3

THE KINGDOM OF THE SCORCHED DOME

THE IMMORTAL FIRST SWORD

Crooked Arm was the name he was given at birth. At this point, he knew he'd never earn another. Chosen names were for the elite fighters who'd won tournaments on their rocks and could compete for First Sword of the Slant. There was a fleeting breath when it could have happened for him, but Crooked Arm was too old now, and too well-born to get another chance. He would never earn a new name, but he would *get* one. When his father died, he would become the Lord of the Scorched Dome. Not a warrior, but a politician, an administrator, the guardian of some old faith.

Dismissing the cynical thought, Crooked Arm released his bad arm from the back of his belt and let it dangle. His shoulder went cool, then warm with blood flow. The arm had been bothering him more lately. It always gave him some discomfort, but discomfort had become pain these last few hundred rests. Something inside the arm was tightening. The flow of blood more labored. As he squeezed the elbow joint and gently massaged the muscles, he scanned the crowd gathered in the palace courtyard.

Another Sharpening was breaths away, a named warrior sent up from Haven. And so the sub-lords and important families from up and down the Slant and their subalterns and their fluttering entourages had gathered with their daughters and sons all dressed up. The soft chattering din spiked with the occasional exclamation or sharp bark of laughter. He looked up at his father's box in the high tiers, still empty. It was not like the lord to be late. Crooked Arm felt this indicated something, but he did not know what.

Turning, he rested his good hand on the low stone railing and gazed up at the Scorched Dome, high on the hill opposite the palace courtyard, its charred arc a curve of flatter dark against the empty void. From a rectangular opening in the center of the dome, the giant glass eye peered out into the darkness of the sink. If a straight line were drawn downward through the optical axis of the lens, it would bisect perfectly all seven rocks of the Slant. This line was the justification of all their codes, the proof of their foundational legend: that long ago an immortal swordsman used an anomaly called the Nest to set the rocks of the Slant in place, and if this anomaly were ever removed, the alignment would come undone.

To protect the Nest and the alignment of the Slant, the Immortal Swordsman appointed the first First Sword, to be kept always sharp should a challenger arrive. And so they trained their warriors in master weapons and held tournaments and named the winners, and each rock in the Slant periodically sent one of these named warriors up to Vertex, a Sharpening in the palace courtyard, with the Scorched Dome on the hill above as a reminder of the one indisputable fact: the rocks of the Slant *are* perfectly aligned—at twenty-three off absolute, radial one ninety-eight—from Vertex to Widescape, then Haven, Greventon, Middrop, Stanley, all the way to Dropoff. Seven rocks in all, plummeting forever together through the void.

Deep Crystal was feeling her way along the railing to Crooked Arm's side. Her gaze moved aimlessly, then shifted and settled on a closer strata. The dark centers of her eyes were only pinpricks, pushed tiny by her thick blue irises. "What do you see, my love?"

Crooked Arm retucked his bad arm into the back of his belt. "My father still has not arrived."

"And that troubles you?"

"A little."

She considered it, her mouth curling with amusement. "Tell me about the crowd."

Turning, Crooked Arm sat on the railing and watched the peeking sideways eyes, the toothy mouths. "A spilling of grubworms over old meat."

Deep Crystal laughed. "And the Sharpening? You think we will have a new First Sword?"

"No."

Deep Crystal pressed a frown. "I don't understand how he's going to beat Fast Daggers with a rope."

There was a bustle in the crowd. Crooked Arm could see the lord had finally come out into his box above the courtyard, working toward his high-backed chair. "My father is here," he told Deep Crystal. He watched him, smiling, bowing, greeting the highest of the high families. Crooked Arm's father was one of the greatest lords to ever rule the Slant. Not only had he earned his name as a fighter, but he was one of a very few lords to have also served as First Sword. His name was Bloody Hatchet then, but it was many rests ago and that man was gone. After ascending to the Lord of the Scorched Dome, he'd widened and turned square and fat. No one had seen the actual hatchet since. Crooked Arm imagined it in a velvet case somewhere.

A bell rang, and the crowd began moving to the risers that rimmed the sunken fight pit. Crooked Arm took Deep Crystal's hand and led her up the tiers. The lord greeted them warmly, a firm handshake for Crooked Arm and a long, embracing hug for Deep Crystal. Separating, the lord smiled at them. Though his thick body still shimmered with hard vigor, his face—sagging in the center—lent an unintentional air of kindliness. It reminded Crooked Arm of the separate man, not the lord or the First Sword, but the father who played Kruntle with him and trained him with that wood sword and tucked him into bed and told him tales of the Slant from rests long ago.

Crooked Arm was the eldest of two young boys then, his father the First Sword, his grandfather the lord, and his mother still alive. Now, some ten thousand rests later, things looked very different. Their mother had hemorrhaged while giving birth to a sister. Neither mother nor child had survived. When Crooked Arm's grandfather died, his father retired as First Sword, undefeated, to become the lord himself. Crooked Arm's brother, Mighty, won the tournament to succeed their father as First Sword. Eventually, Mighty lost a Sharpening, but his life was spared. It was rare for this to happen, but Mighty was the son of the lord. After his loss, Mighty left for self-imposed exile, now of no consequence to the Slant at all. If Crooked Arm outlived his father, he would become the next Lord of the Scorched Dome. And some rest farther off, some ambiguous child of his would be the lord after, and so on and so on and so on.

The lord stepped away from them and turned to face the gathered crowd. All went still and silent with anticipation. Crooked Arm moved to stand behind Deep Crystal, his lips close to the curl of her ear. "They're entering the pit now," he whispered. Below, a thin door opened, and a young man emerged. He'd won a tournament on Haven and earned a name of his own choosing, and he had chosen Lariat.

Deep Crystal leaned her head back to whisper to Crooked Arm. "How does the rope look?"

"Not as bad as it sounds. It's made of razor wire and has some burrs on it."

Her gaze focused on something not there. "Tell me about him."

"Reedy, handsome, uncertain."

On the opposite side of the fight pit, another door opened, and out stepped Fast Daggers, First Sword of the Slant. She was short and wisp thin, her tight-fit jumpsuit sparkling with throwing knives. Crooked Arm had sparred with her and so had some understanding of what

Lariat was about to face, the seldom and fleeting targets, obscured always by the whirling of her arms, daggers flying fast from the glinting hilts. Crooked Arm knew the person as well as the warrior. Outside the fight pit, her cold deadliness thawed; she was full of wry humor, smiling usually at something private in her mind. But Fast Daggers was reckless, and brash and dismissive of her opponents. She treated these Sharpenings as glib rehearsals for some mysterious thing of vast importance in the future. Crooked Arm knew some Sharpening it would be her death. But not this one. Not against a warrior named Lariat.

The lord raised his hand. Hard muscles still hinted under his looser flesh. Perhaps he did have that hatchet ready somewhere, still crusted with the blood of the opponents he never once washed off it. "This rest we gather to sharpen our First Sword," he said, "so that the Nest can be protected, and the arrangement forever preserved." A perfect quiet hung. The lord held his hand high a breath more, then brought it down. All eyes focused on the sunken pit.

"They are ready," Crooked Arm whispered.

The razor rope began to circle Lariat's head, a loosely shifting oblong, his arm looping slow with a fast crack of speed as his elbow straightened to whip it around again. Crooked Arm could see the rhythm forming: there would be a throw and then a yank, and the rope would circle smoothly back into rotation and be ready again. But Lariat never got the chance. With the razor rope still turning anticipatory circles above him, a dagger hilt appeared in his throat, another in the center of his forehead. Lariat fell over dead, the razor rope landing in a limp pile on top.

The tiers of seating and the courtyard and the fight pit fell just as still. Distantly, the soft hush of the sink could be heard, even as far from the edge as they were. Crooked Arm swiveled to see his father's reaction, but the lord was already slipping out. Confused, Crooked Arm looked back to the fight pit; Fast Daggers was gone as well.

▼

Doors flew open, that one good arm out to hold off the protests of the guards. He was the firstborn son of the lord; he would be the lord himself one rest, and no one wanted to be the guard who once tried to stop the lord from seeing his father. After Lariat's body was dragged from the fight pit, Crooked Arm asked some questions around the kitchen and the guardhouse and discovered a few things. A dozen rests before, a riser had come and spoken hushed words to the lord. The visit was expunged from the records; in the end, no one but the lord, Fast Daggers, and the guards on duty knew the riser had been there. A few rests later, a sub-lord personally relayed reports brought to his rock by the survivor of a mysterious calamity. This last bit was more gossip, an aside between the lords, overheard by a rock gardener's apprentice, possibly false. Lastly, a matriarch from Greventon brought more than her family to the Sharpening. Arriving a full rest early, she'd gone not to her suites but into direct conference with the lord. Fast Daggers had been called in, but no one else was told what the meeting was about.

Pushing past the last guard and through the doors into the executive study, Crooked Arm found the lord in a tense discussion with his First Sword. His father simmered, outraged to be intruded upon this way, even by his own son. He looked to Fast Daggers, but she was hiding a smile. The lord huffed, and Fast Daggers disengaged to lean against the wall. The lord circled, calming further. When he spoke, his voice was hard and curt. "What is the meaning of this?" he demanded.

"A meeting?" Crooked Arm almost sang. "And I was not invited?"

"Because it's a meeting between the lord and the First Sword," Fast Daggers informed him flatly.

Crooked Arm glared at her. "Custom is to humor them a little longer, Fast Daggers. Now you've embarrassed Lariat's family, and all of Haven too."

"They try to kill me, I try to kill them; it's how we keep the First Sword sharp. If Haven wants a better showing, they should produce a better warrior."

"It's bad politics," Crooked Arm said. "Let him throw the rope at you at least. Now they'll take that bad blood back down the Slant with them."

Her smirk faded.

"Your cockiness will cost you your life some rest," Crooked Arm told her, rubbing it in.

She considered it. "The rests pass. No blade stays sharp forever. Some rest I *will* lose, and the First Sword will be sharper for it. My position in the end is temporary." She flashed a grin and folded her arms.

"Don't blame her," the lord broke in. "It was my command to end the Sharpening as fast as possible, with as little risk as possible."

"Why?" Crooked Arm demanded. "Tell me what you know! This secret you have been keeping from me. I will be lord of this rock one rest, and the whole Slant too. Why have I not been told?"

His father barked back, "Because you are droll and cynical! You do not want to be lord. You are not interested!"

"I still have to do it!"

Their eyes held longer, until finally the lord turned and sought a new position a step farther away. He crossed his arms, and his frame seemed to thicken. "A shipment arrived at Greventon," he said. "But it was meant to arrive at Frozen Rock."

"Frozen Rock is five rests outwide from Greventon," Crooked Arm said. "How did they miss it?"

"The shippers hadn't run the line before," Fast Daggers said. "It took them longer than expected, but they'd followed the angle and radial and thought they were where they were supposed to be."

Crooked Arm looked to Fast Daggers, then to his father. "There's a chance these shippers got off course and missed Frozen Rock," Crooked Arm speculated loosely. "Right past it somehow and arrived at Greventon."

"A chance, yes," Fast Daggers admitted, "but not a good chance."

The lord sighed. "'. . . *a shifting in the void will bring a challenger*. . . .'"

Crooked Arm's eyes thinned on him. "That is why you had Lariat and his family humiliated? Because of an old poem?"

"You know it's not simply an old poem," the lord said. "It's the history of the Slant. It is all we are and will be. A shifting in the void is the sign of the coming of a challenger. Someone who will seek to take the Nest and undo the alignment of the Slant. If it's true, and a challenger is coming, I can't have my First Sword risk some fluke in the fight pit. Not for politics."

"But why have you kept this information so secret? Even from me?"

"I kept it secret because I want no alarm. Rumors catch echoes in the sink. Echoes bring fear. Fear is—"

Crooked Arm did then the unthinkable, interrupting the lord. "Is that what you take me for, a panicking villager? I am not some gossiping servant or nervous sub-lord or some trainee loitering about the courtyard!"

The lord was enraged but held it in. He glared at Crooked Arm, then looked away, took a few steps, and turned to face him from farther off. "What would you suggest we do?" the lord inquired calmly.

Crooked Arm took only a breath. "Send someone to Frozen Rock."

The lord nodded. "That is already done. We sent a team to investigate as soon as we heard."

Crooked Arm took it in. He felt small and left out and lost somewhere far behind. His father seemed to relish it, all Crooked Arm's brash rudeness at barging in returned. "What I meant," the lord said, "is what would you suggest we do, if the sink really is shifting?"

Crooked Arm lay across the bed, a light sheen of sweat coating him. His bad arm was out beside him, eerily still in the dented mattress. From the elbow down, the arm was withered and turned, as if attached backward. Tendons under the stretched skin were stretched just as tight. What muscles saw fit to grow were clustered and bulbish, like tree tumors around the joints.

Deep Crystal was on the floor beside the bed with her feet propped up straight against the wall. It was the latest trick she'd heard from one of the lord's old maids, a way to get the seed to swim down deeper, to the deepest fertile territory. Try, wait, try again. It was their pattern now, like breathing, eating, periodic Sharpenings in the courtyard fight pit, like the axis of the Slant—twenty-three off absolute, radial one ninety-eight—reliable, constant, something you can plan on.

"It's been fifteen rests," Crooked Arm said, "since that team was sent to Frozen Rock."

"They will return," she replied. "They got off track, caught in an updraft."

"An updraft? They've been gone long enough to get there and back and there again." His eyes traced a miniature version of the trek in the darkness. He'd done it twice himself. Straight shot at forty-five, radial sixteen, couldn't be simpler. "Perhaps my father is correct," he said, "'. . . a shifting in the void . . .'"

"I didn't think you the type to be worried about an old poem," she said.

"I'm not worried about a poem, or some prophetic sign. A shifting is enough. If rocks cannot be relied upon to be where they were before, travel will become impossible. You'd be rising off into your death if you ever tried to go anywhere."

"Would that be so bad?" she countered. "Not traveling the sink? How many of our people have ever left the Slant, or even their home rocks? I never have."

"What about when we're short on water collection and Frozen Rock has shifted and can't be found? Who would we trade our crafted weapons to if we can't get to other rocks and other rocks can't get to us? Rocks that rely on trade will die off. Perhaps rocks we don't want so close to us will suddenly be our neighbors. Those on rocks that run out will come looking for a place that still has."

"But how will they find us if the sink is shifting?"

Crooked Arm pressed his head back deeper into the pillow. "Conflict," he said. "Disorder, strife. That would be the result. In some forms we cannot expect nor avoid."

"And if this shifting is really something more? If a challenger does arrive?"

"All these hundreds of thousands of rests, and no one has ever come for it. Not in any of the histories I've read, and I've read every history in the Slant. All the tournaments, the born names and renamings, the training schools and fighting academies and master weapons, and the only ones we've ever killed are ourselves."

"You really are worried. I can tell by the mean way you talk. You let it bottle up and then unleash on some favorite target."

Crooked Arm sighed. Having this pointed out to him did not, unfortunately, alleviate its effect. Deep Crystal gripped her legs now, making a ball of her body. She rolled back and forth like a cradle. "It's fine to talk that way if you're some bratty youth," she said. "Or a shoemaker in the village. But you're in your middle rests now. Your father won't live forever."

"And then it will be my responsibility to keep parents up and down the Slant entering their children into naming tournaments to the death."

"First Swords come and go. No blade stays sharp forever. Just because no one has ever come for it doesn't mean no one ever will."

Crooked Arm looked over at her. She'd released herself and was laid out flat, naked on the floor. "So you do believe that some rest a challenger will come?" he asked. "That they will arrive via the optical axis? That the rocks of the Slant were arranged by an immortal swordsman, using the Nest? That he's out there, all these rests later, still alive, somewhere in the sink?"

She took a long in-breath, then breathed it out. "Do *you*?"

"I suppose I had better, if I am to be the lord some rest."

Deep Crystal got to her feet. Feeling her way with her hands, she worked into bed on Crooked Arm's good-arm side. He gripped her shoulders, and her head shifted into the bowl of his armpit as they settled into stillness. Crooked Arm could feel her side expanding against him with her breath. Their bodies somehow fit perfectly together, like puzzle pieces. What an odd coincidence, he thought, with all the shapes a body can be.

"I know you don't believe, not fully," she said. "But I know you believe in the importance of believing."

Crooked Arm found himself nodding along. He felt Deep Crystal's fingers moving through his chest hairs, her nails clicking off the follicles. He could barely make out the gray of the ceiling in the dark. It was vague and vanishing, and all above him seemed the deep void, and he could feel the pull of sleep. "Perhaps we've deluded ourselves," he said suddenly, "that this challenger is going to be some warrior with a weapon. We imagine something like what we are. But the sink is wild, strange, and endless. What's more likely to come is something we don't understand at all."

He thought maybe she'd drifted off, but then her voice did come, soft in the softening darkness. "I have a good feeling," she said, "that we have just earned ourselves a son."

AN EYE INTO THE SINK

From the high steps, Crooked Arm took in the clustered buildings of the village below. Farther off, the palace poked from the woods, thin cobble paths weaving together the interlocking courtyards, dojos, sanctuaries, rock gardens, and the personal suites of the lord and his family. Past the palace, the rest of Vertex was the same, high cliffs and jutting ridges, with small villages pocked between. It was the largest rock in the Slant, the size of ten Rosebloods. Each village alone had more people than all of Fairviel.

    A few more steps took Crooked Arm to the high rocks at the base of the Scorched Dome. From the palace, the fire looked fresh, like the flakes of ash would brush away with a gentle wipe or a stiff upcurling eddy from the sink. Closer, the permanence was clear, the scorched peeling thick and dense and firm and as set as a sculpture. It was as if the moment the fire was put out, the dome was frozen, set forever in place.

Crooked Arm circled to the collapsed side, sharing a grin with one of the guards on duty, an old training partner who grabbed his side and smiled, reminding Crooked Arm of when he'd broken the man's rib with his wood sparring sword. Stepping past them and over a charred beam, Crooked Arm came into the hulking interior. Scorched arching buttresses loomed over the remnants of an iron staircase, melted into a strange lacing of droopy curves. The giant gears that once rotated the lens had melted too, the big interlocking teeth fused into an iron, tumorlike mass.

Set upright in the center of the room was a stone plaque as big as a person. On it was etched the kingdom's foundational poem, seven small stanzas arranging themselves downward, like the Slant itself. Two identical symbols framed the poem, one above and one below: three down-pointing triangles, offset and overlapping. Crooked Arm scanned the first few lines: *He came from so distant in the void / it may as well have been another void, / a battle so far away / its words meant nothing. . . .* Then he looked lower, near the bottom. *Some rest, a shifting / in the void will bring a challenger. / Look first in the glass eye of the dome, / to take the anomaly and undo the alignment, / from the topmost rock / to the very / bottom.*

He took a last look at the poem, then crossed to a thinner back hall, where two more guards stood by. At his approach, they opened the far door. Violet and amber light spilled across their feet. Stepping through, Crooked Arm came into the low, theater-like room. The light fell fully over him, cast by an anomaly set out on a central pedestal. It was easy to see where it had gotten the name. It looked like a nest, a loose ball of string, the size of two fists held together, electric ropes of violet gathered around a central pulsating amber core. Both colors radiated but somehow never mixed, falling in dapples and counter swirls over the walls and floor and ceiling.

Each rest, for two thousand breaths, Crooked Arm would come and meditate into its alternating colors. All the naming tournaments, the periodic Sharpenings, the forging of master weapons, all to produce through rigor and ceremony a warrior capable of protecting the Nest from any challenger who would come. This was why they trained and smithed and killed each other in violent tournaments unfolding constantly somewhere on the Slant.

At a young age, Crooked Arm had begun to question the legends. Or perhaps it is better to say he stopped believing them out of hand. An anomaly from the far depths of the sink, with mysterious powers no one knows how to unlock, wielded by a swordsman who would never die. Crooked Arm had decided the code likely came first, the legends written later to explain it, and the Nest simply an anomaly around which it was all hung. But whatever it did or did not do, from wherever it came, its presence and the code to protect it knitted the Slant together.

But Crooked Arm knew something that few others did. This was not the real Nest, nor even what the real Nest looked like. The object on the pedestal was one of several well-crafted decoys. The purpose of their society was to protect the Nest. They employed weapons, training, tournaments, but also deception and trickery. The real Nest was hidden where only the lord and the First Sword knew.

Real or not, decoy or not, appearances needed to be kept up. The people needed a connection to the Nest, something direct, a place they could go and see it, be in its presence, infer what mysteries and meaning they needed from the never-overlapping light. Of course, not just anyone could go in, even though it was only a decoy. That would make it seem unimportant, or that they weren't trying very hard to protect it. People didn't really need to see the Nest so much as they needed to see Crooked Arm passing through town, to his regular meditation. Though a fine fighter, he was no named warrior like his father. He would need to be a different kind of lord, dedicated without question to the Nest's protection, in synch with its unknowable powers. And so Crooked Arm came and sat two thousand breaths each rest, looking into the decoy as if it were the real thing, presenting the wise, in-tune lord in waiting.

After his meditation, Crooked Arm left the central chamber and climbed up to the remnants of the observation platform, where the lord had put on rotating guards to eye the lens and watch the void above. If the legend was true, and a shifting in the void was underway, if indeed it was the sign of a coming challenger, that challenger would appear first in the eye of the dome.

The guard on watch stepped aside so Crooked Arm could have a look. "Nothing but empty sink," the man said. Somehow the glass eye had been undamaged in the fire that melted its gears, but it was locked forever in place now and so always focused on the same spot of overvoid. If a challenger did come, what were the chances they would approach via the optical axis, in all the vast arc of the overvoid, endless as far as anyone could go, a million million rests?

Crooked Arm bent and put his eye to the viewer, which was warm from the guard's diligent looking. His vision adjusted and he blinked, but all there was was a circle of darkness, indistinguishable from any other spot in the overvoid.

▼

Crooked Arm climbed down the angling stairs and walked through the village to the fields that edged the rock. The sink roared louder there, the friction whipping hard as it scraped in from the void. Crooked Arm remembered coming to this same spot when he was a child, holding his wooden sword out into the void and opening his fingers. He would watch the sword float and flutter and turn in place, and when it began to rise, Crooked Arm would reach his good arm out and snatch it back.

He'd so wanted to be like his father then, not some lord in waiting, but a named warrior, and the First Sword no less. Though Crooked Arm was wellborn in station, he was not so in body. To make up for the bad arm, he trained harder than any of the young fighters on Vertex, not because he believed in the legends, but because he believed in himself. His brother Mighty—though that was not yet his name—was less dedicated, but he was huge and powerful, with two good arms thicker than most men's thighs. Mighty didn't need to train; he only had to grow up and fill out. Now Mighty was gone, Crooked Arm thought, and would probably never return to the Slant.

The short walk brought Crooked Arm to the scavenging nets. They were built out from a jutting corner of the rock, five iron spokes welded horizontal from a center hub. A webbing of net hung between each pole. Altogether it looked like an enormous hand reaching out into the sink. Net watchers stood around chatting, but when they saw Crooked Arm, they grunted and went back to their posts. Watchers worked the nets in shifts, through both rest and wake, should any valuable scavenge be caught. This was rare, and so mostly the scavenge piled up and was cleaned out at the start of each shift. Crooked Arm could see it had been longer than that. A dark glinting caught his eye. Something large was gleaming unnaturally in the clumps of scavenge. He instructed one of the watchers to fetch it out.

Slowly, hand over foot, the watcher made his way down and across the netting, a plump spider wobbling on the strings. Reaching the spot, he had to yank and tug the thing free. When he brought it over, Crooked Arm could see it was a large hook, as big as a man's arm, forged from black bonded iron. Its point was a viscous cluster of spiked teeth as fine as needles. It was a hasty smelting, had rough dents and emptied air bubbles left over from its mold, but was strong and lighter than it should be. Crooked Arm was familiar with the weapons and ironcraft on each of the rocks of the Slant; this was of a style he did not recognize. He wondered from how far it had come. Some rock with some other culture and some other purpose, indecipherable to anyone so far above.

Someone was running toward him now across the hillside. Crooked Arm recognized the girl as one of the palace messengers. He turned and waited for the young woman to arrive, gliding in as if slipping on a breeze. "The team has returned from Frozen Rock," she said.

Crooked Arm could see there was more. "What is it?"

"Only one of them came back."

A SHIFTING IN THE VOID

Crooked Arm was gathered with his father and Fast Daggers and the only one who had returned, whose name was Lean. Lean had risen back to Vertex pretty roughed up and dehydrated but had since been fed and cleaned and given plenty to drink. When they brought him in, he was in a palace tunic they used for the staff and one of the lord's own robes over it. He took the seat offered to him and looked at the lord and Crooked Arm and Fast Daggers. Then a man was coming through the room, dropping off a glass filled with something thick and brown. Lean picked it up, sniffed it with a nervous smile, and had a sip.

"Tell me what happened to the others," the lord said, settling into a chair opposite.

"They were killed. At least that's how it seemed."

"How did it *seem* they were killed?" Fast Daggers wanted to know.

The lord held up a hand to her. Fast Daggers stepped off and circled and stood beside Crooked Arm.

"Tell me what happened," the lord said.

Lean nodded. "We followed the line out, everything routine. When we got to Frozen Rock, there was a rock there all right, but it wasn't Frozen Rock."

"What do you mean, it wasn't Frozen Rock?"

"I've run the line before and it was done right, but it wasn't Frozen Rock we arrived at."

The lord exhaled and stood and stepped to be face-to-face with Crooked Arm. Their eyes locked, but neither spoke. With a nod to his son, the lord stepped away, leaving Crooked Arm to settle in front of Lean.

"Tell me about the rock," Crooked Arm said. "The rock that was where Frozen Rock was supposed to be."

Lean nodded again, as if convincing himself before he spoke. "It was bigger than Frozen Rock and had something jutting from it, running almost the whole length, like a scaffolding, something built out into the sink. It wasn't that bluish-white Frozen Rock has either, but more rock- and rust-colored. There was something obscuring it too, like a haze in the sink around it. We didn't get close enough to see any more. As we were nearing, they came out to greet us. At least we thought they were going to greet us, but they attacked."

"They attacked you?" Fast Daggers asked. "No warning? No flare?"

Lean nodded through it all.

"What kind of code is that?" she spat.

"Not the code on Frozen Rock," Crooked Arm said. He took a few steps, unlimbering and then retucking his arm.

The lord had returned his attention to Lean. "How did you escape?" he asked.

Lean looked at him, his face twitching. It was a tiny tic in his eye and the left corner of his lips. "I fled. They had weapons on chains that punched at us through the void. Flinging metals cutting things up. I don't know how to fight. I was there to plot the course. My name is Lean, after all." He took a long drink of what they had brought him. "I know some modified Griswald. So I used it. Sunk as fast as I could, and they couldn't keep up. When I knew they'd given up, I went outwide, then rose back up to here. I was hoping maybe some of the others had made it back too, but they told me I was the only one."

"And your path back. It was as expected?"

"I expected only void space from the lines I'd made out. And that's all there was."

"The distances, the rise and outwide, they were as you estimated?"

Lean nodded, then nodded again. "I've run that line to Frozen Rock before. It was right."

"Yes," Crooked Arm said, "but there was no Frozen Rock. There was something else."

▼

Crooked Arm thought the knocking was creeping in from a dream. Then several voices were hissing back and forth, then shouting farther away. The knocking got louder. Something metal hit the floor in the hall and clanged, and more voices spiked.

"What's happening?" he heard Deep Crystal ask.

Crooked Arm sat up. "I don't know." They remained still, listening to distant voices, doors opening and closing. A bell somewhere started ringing. More knocking now, at the door to their suite.

"What is it?" Crooked Arm shouted.

The door opened, a guard stepping in. "A sinker has entered the overvoid."

Crooked Arm stared hard at the man. "I'm giving you the chance to make this more important than some visitor arriving at the Slant."

"We saw her first in the eye," the guard said. "She descends at twenty-three off absolute, radial one ninety-eight, exactly down the optical axis."

Crooked Arm was up, dressed, and moving down the hall in what seemed like a breath. Soon he was in flank with Fast Daggers and a half dozen of her guards. When they came out on the wide landing platform, Crooked Arm could see the tiny shape of the Sinker high above.

"We got a good look through the lens," one of the guards told them. "She has a sword, and knives in her boots; no helmet; a pack, a small one. So she's only been out a short while or . . ."

"Or she's real good," Crooked Arm finished.

"A sword?" Fast Daggers sighed. "I was hoping for something more exotic."

Crooked Arm watched the Sinker's trajectory angle more their way. Then she was dropping at incredible speed and then somehow slipped even faster into the uprushing friction, coming right at them. "She's going to kill herself," Crooked Arm said.

But her body tilted and cut a swooping angle, and she landed softly in a crouch and stood as if she'd already been there waiting. She indeed had no helmet, and her tie-downs had come mostly undone, dark loose hairs wavering around her head in the friction's lapping eddies. "I must speak with the Lord of the Scorched Dome," she said.

Like the guards, Crooked Arm had drawn his sword. All of them but Fast Daggers, who stood out in front, hands loose as if floating on the friction. "Turn over your weapons," she told the Sinker.

"What is the code here for an audience with the lord?"

"Turn in your weapons, submit to a search and questioning. Then the lord will be filled in and determine himself."

"There's not breath for that," the Sinker said. "Something terrible is coming this way. I must speak with the Lord of the Scorched Dome *now*!"

"Hand over your weapons," Fast Daggers said calmly. "Submit to a search and questioning. Then the lord will determine if you will be seen."

"I won't be made a prisoner. I'm here to warn you. Something terrible is coming. It will destroy this place, and anyone who gets in the way will die. You must tell the lord this. You must make him listen."

"If you will not disarm," Fast Daggers said, "you force us to disarm you. And by us, I mean me."

The Sinker's focus homed in, her weight shifting into her legs, but Fast Daggers was already moving. Like a sudden rush of wind, she let loose an uncoiling of her arm. The Sinker slipped left, a blade missing her face by a hair. Somehow her sword was already drawn. It gleamed silvery in the air.

The Sinker crouched to dodge a second blade, which skimmed her shoulder, but as her palm went down for balance, a dagger dove into the center of her hand, pinning her to the wood decking. The Sinker's scream was cut off by Fast Daggers's boot, a swift kick, square in the jaw. Stunned, the Sinker dropped her sword and her other hand went to the ground. In one smooth motion, Fast Daggers stepped into a lunge and drove a knife into that hand as well. Both hands tacked down firmly, the Sinker fell to her knees, then looked up, somehow still defiant through her bristling pain. "Tell the lord to make everyone leave," she said. "If not, you will all die!"

Crooked Arm was impressed. Not many warriors in the Slant would be conscious after a kick like that, not to mention with a knife stuck in each hand. He watched Fast Daggers draw a new blade, her small fingers wrapped tightly around it, its fine point glinting. He could see the spot she'd aim for, the soft flesh below the curve of the Sinker's jaw. A quick stab, a quick retract, and all would be over. Crooked Arm put a hand on Fast Daggers's shoulder. She turned slightly to look at him. Crooked Arm shook his head, small, slow, but definitive.

Fast Daggers sighed, deflating. Her teeth gritted, and her arm was moving again, blade flipping in her palm to bring the blunt side down hard on the Sinker's head.

A CHALLENGER

The first thing the Sinker saw was a wall of bars, then a guard sitting on the other side, then an iron door, and beyond that only darkness through its single high window. The guard noticed her rousing and stood, looking in through the bars.

"How long have I been out?" she demanded.

But the guard didn't answer. Satisfied she was awake, he turned and left without a word. The Sinker closed her eyes hard, then opened them wider. When she sat up, pain swept into her. She winced and groaned and lifted her hands to see them both bandaged. She could move the fingers on one, but when she tried the other, the pain doubled and radiated down her forearm. She cursed and laid the hands gently on her thighs and waited until the pulsing faded. Peeling back the bandages, she could see under each a few tight stiches. She made a fist with the right hand—the stronger one—and held it, then shook out her fingers. She could hold a sword, she thought, at least with one hand. The other would need five or six rests before it would be of much use.

Getting gingerly to her feet, she went to the cell's one small window and looked out. There it was on the high hill, the Scorched Dome, dark and matte against the shimmering blackness of the void. She'd seen domes like this before, one in person and others in books. They were built to look deep into the sink, in search of other rocks, before the void was much traveled. The Sinker thought back to the glossy pages, the whoosh as she turned them. The images all seemed so impossible to her back then, but now she'd seen so much more, and stranger too, than anything in those old books.

The door reopened. Entering was not the guard but Crooked Arm. The Sinker eyed him as he circled and stood in front of the bars.

"Your hands, how do they feel?"

She glared at him a breath more before answering. "Serviceable, I suppose."

"No broken bones, I was told. You're lucky Fast Daggers uses such thin blades."

"I'll have to thank her."

He smiled, then let the smile fade. "My name is Crooked Arm. I was there when you landed."

The Sinker nodded, remembering his tall, off-kilter stance, the slumping shoulder. "How long have I been out?"

"Not long. Half a rest."

The Sinker traced the path with her inner eye, seeing the map and the rests like a grid in her mind. "There's still breath," she said.

"Breath for what?"

"To get as many people out as you can. You need to tell the lord to tell them. Or whomever they'll listen to."

"The lord is my father," he told her. "He's been informed and has sent me to discuss all this with you."

The Sinker looked at him. "You're lying."

He laughed. "Well, actually, yes, I am. My father *is* the lord, but he doesn't know I'm here."

"Then why are you?"

"Because maybe he will listen to me, but he won't to you. He thinks you are here to take something from us. But I don't think that is the reason you have come."

The Sinker breathed once, long. It seeped from her evenly. Her eyes moved over his face, then down his side where the arm hung too still. She watched him pull over a chair and sit. "I've heard of the warriors who train here," she said. "Weapons from the Slant trade highly in the sink. But it will all be useless. Several Far Machines are set to converge here, any rest now, and the Construct won't be far behind."

"Far Machines?"

"Far Machines range out ahead, plotting a course, hoarding resources. They attack rocks, break them down, prepare whatever can be used or burned for fuel. Working together, they lay out a path for the Construct to follow. When it arrives, the Construct takes it all in, replenishing food supplies, materials, feeding the rest into their engines to keep on the rise."

"And this Construct, the Far Machines, they're chasing you?"

"No. I've been on an outwide plummet, then a rise, to get here before them."

"How do you know they're coming here?"

"I tracked down one of their pilots. I . . . convinced him to share their destination. There's something here they want." Her eyes thinned on him. "You know what I'm talking about, don't you?"

Crooked Arm only looked back, not answering.

"You have something here, something they can use for their engines, a power source, an anomaly of some kind?"

Crooked Arm's reaction gave it away.

"An anomaly," the Sinker repeated.

Crooked Arm leaned back, his mind grinding slowly, a thorough crunching. His head tilted, and a self-aware grin cracked his face. "I'm sure you've come across plenty of local folklore in your travels."

"Yes, lots."

"Here we have a legend about how the Slant was formed, using an anomaly, as you have guessed."

"What does this anomaly do?"

Crooked Arm shrugged. "There's only one person who knew how to use it, and he left here long ago. According to the legend, it holds the alignment of the Slant in place." Crooked Arm opened his hands. "Most of my life, I have considered these legends to be just that. Legends, poetry, art, metaphor, morality tale." He pointed a finger at her. "But now you arrive."

"I have changed your opinion?"

"Not yet, but you've certainly convinced some others. One part of the legend says a challenger will come, seeking to take the anomaly, that they will arrive via the optical axis of the lens in the Scorched Dome. This is the exact angle at which you approached."

"This optical axis. Is it twenty-three off absolute?"

His brow furrowed. "You know more about the Slant than you're telling me."

The Sinker smiled. She shook her head. "No. Twenty-three off absolute is the best angle of approach."

"It is?"

"According to the Blackhurst Method."

"A method of sinking?"

"Of landing."

Crooked Arm looked at the window on the other side of her cell, the small square of empty sink he could see through it. "Rumors have been arriving," he told her, "of something happening in the nearby sink. A small trading rock outwide of here seems to have shifted."

"Shifted?"

"Its position. This is also part of the legend. A shifting in the void is the signal that soon the sink will bring a challenger."

"This rock that shifted—what's its name?"

"Frozen Rock. A trader headed there somehow ended up at the Slant. We sent a team to investigate, but instead of Frozen Rock they found something else."

The Sinker was shaking her head. "Frozen Rock hasn't shifted to some other place. I was there when it was attacked. A Far Machine broke it down, staged it for the Construct, for water, and whatever else they can get out of it. What your team saw wasn't another rock. It was a Far Machine, or maybe the Construct itself. You must convince everyone here to leave."

"Leave?"

"Take what you can and flee."

Crooked Arm hummed low, considering it, an exhale just short of a chuckle. "Even if all of what you say is true, if there is something coming, whether for the anomaly or for some other reason, I can assure you we are more than ready."

She sighed, looking tired. "How far have you traveled?"

"About fifteen rests," he said, "in a few different directions."

"I have been sinking or rising or going outwide since my four thousandth rest. Believe me when I tell you this. The Far Machines will come here. They will take this anomaly from you. They will kill everyone who gets in the way. They will stage this rock, stripping it of every usable thing, killing anyone left. Then the Construct will come and absorb it all, load it into storage, recycle it, reuse it. Then they'll break up the rock itself, melting it down for mineral and ore and fuel. And then the Construct will move on, and there will be nothing left of this place."

A silence hung, but only for half a breath. A strange noise had crept into the room, a high, far-off whine. It was not dissimilar to the distant hissing of the friction, but sharper, piercing, and getting louder. "What is that?" Crooked Arm said.

There was a sudden, hard jolt. The Sinker found herself looking at the ceiling. She'd been thrown against the wall, then to the floor. Through the bars, she could see Crooked Arm getting back to his feet. The chair he'd been sitting in was across the room, one of its legs folded in. There was a shivering in the floor, then another, softer jolt. Then shouting in the hall and more shouting, distantly, in the palace above.

"Now it's too late," the Sinker said.

LAST LORD OF THE SCORCHED DOME

Crooked Arm reached the halls that led to his personal suites only to find the ceiling and the wall collapsed. He climbed in, moving debris aside. He was aware of others helping but never truly saw them. The fingers of his good hand were bloodied and raw, and his bad arm hung, scratched and bleeding, but Crooked Arm could feel none of it. He was on the other side of the collapsed hall now, but no one had followed him through. The doors to his suites were right in front of him and, unlike the rest of the hall, they were undamaged, only dulled under a uniform coating of dust. He turned the knob, and the door clicked and swung smoothly open.

Crooked Arm could not recognize the former layout. There were only toppled walls under toppled ceiling joists under cracked roof tiles and somehow a dead goat torn in half atop the rubble.

A deeper thunk rumbled Crooked Arm's stomach. He felt a pulse of shifting air, then a strange reverse, as if air sucked away. He looked up through the collapsed wall, at the sharp opposite hill and the Scorched Dome high atop it. A gargantuan iron clamp appeared then from the darkness. Wire tail lashing, its jagged mouth widened, hurtling faster, closer, faster . . . until it smashed down on the Scorched Dome. With a deafening snap, the clamp closed tight and the big lens shattered and pieces of glass and charred wood spurted into the void.

Crooked Arm turned back to the room. He stumbled and fell and got up. He climbed into the mess, moving beams and pushing over panels until he found Deep Crystal exactly where he'd left her, lying in their big platform bed. A central joist had broken and fallen down and swallowed her head. There was nothing left above the neck but a raw pulp hinting under the wreckage. Crooked Arm tried to move the beam, but it wouldn't budge. Maybe he could slide the bed, but he yanked at it and could see it was no use. He sat down and looked at Deep Crystal again. Her head was completely gone, but otherwise her body was undamaged and seemed alive and present and capable still of being harmed. "I don't know what to do," he said.

▼

At the front of the palace, the big doors were broken off and lay at odd angles on the ground. A steady stream of guards and servants was stepping over them, eyes watering and wide, skin purple and splotchy where dust clung to their bloodied faces. Crooked Arm stumbled through the crowd until he could see the lower hills. Another clamp had crashed into the village below. Several boxy metal transports worked down the wire umbilicals, drop doors ready to flop open, big gears lowering them into the haze of lingering smoke. Crooked Arm had his long sword, but he could not recall digging it from the wreckage. Nor his trip back through the palace to the front.

There was a sucking pop above, and yet another clamp formed from the void. Crooked Arm watched the sharpness of its giant teeth, its lashing tail whipping off behind. He thought it would hit the palace directly, but the clamp wobbled and careened and smashed into the woods nearby. Vertex thundered with the impact. Already Crooked Arm could see a metal transport working down on a big turning gear. High above, at the farthest end of the wire, he caught a glimpse of the Far Machine's uneven outline, iron fins in jagged angling layers, a shifting viscera of coiled cables, transports swaying back and forth like clinging ticks.

One of the guards was screaming at him, "They dropped down the wires!"

Someone else had him by the shoulder. Crooked Arm turned to look into the face of his father. "The village is overrun," the lord said, eerily calm. "The Dome has been destroyed."

"She's dead," Crooked Arm blurted. "Deep Crystal is dead."

The lord's hardness melted. For one breath he was that funny man with the wooden sword in the yards below the palace. "My son," he said. The rock thundered again with some unseen landing. A cloud of dust and timber debris plumed into the air beyond the trees. Tendrils of dirty smoke curled along the trunk line. Then, from the haze, the forming shape of the droppers, a few dozen advancing in an uneven line. They were sloppy-looking, like rough risers in from a long outwide, in dirty canvas one-zipper jumpsuits, and scuffed-up helmets with clouded safety goggles. Some carried hand cannons, some with big chain spools attached to their backs. Others had liquid vat packs lined with tubing. They moved in from the tree line with semi-coordinated steps, a staggering nonuniform line.

The lord clapped Crooked Arm on his bad shoulder, leaving his hand there, gripping that solid bulb of scar tissue. His face formed the closest thing to a smile he could muster. "You were right," he said. "We were fools, blinded by our own history." A breath of silence passed in the din, and all things, for that moment, seemed pushed back and frozen and waiting for their signal to recommence. "Let us face them together."

Crooked Arm nodded. His father moved to the front and a groundsman appeared, handing him a wood axe. It was no bloody hatchet but would have to do. The lord held it up for all to see. There were fifty arrayed behind him, guards and house servants and farmers, a few named warriors even. Lifting the wood ax high, the lord screamed and ran at the droppers. In one hard wave, the named warriors and guards and cooks and maids and farmers and Crooked Arm all rushed in after him.

The line of the advancing droppers paused and stepped back. From their ranks, odd, tilting contraptions rattled forward, half the height of a man, dangling metal and chain, engines burping black smoke. As Crooked Arm and the lord and their onrushing mass neared, the machines spun up into clouds of lashing hooks and razor wire. The first of the vanguard vanished into a confusion of blood-filled air. Others tried to slow their mad charge but were caught by hooks and pulled into the grinding storm or ripped apart as the hooks retracted to lash and retract again. The droppers were moving forward now, hand cannons firing. Spiked mace balls punched holes in the crowd, wires lashing wildly as they retracted. Other droppers fired charged plugs that stuck into flesh and unleashed torrents of static electricity, reducing whoever was hit to a writhing mass, stomped underfoot in the chaotic melee.

The ground rumbled with another transport landing somewhere. Crooked Arm saw one was headed back up the wire, debris trickling from its seams. He heard the distant high whine of other razor machines somewhere he could not see. The smoke from the village had thickened, spilling from the trees, obscuring everything in a hazy darkness. In the confusion, Crooked Arm came upon his father, lying no place in particular among the dead and injured. A length of broken chain was lodged in his forehead. He was somehow still alive and conscious, though his eyes pointed off and his mouth was full of frothy red foam. Crooked Arm went down to him, and his father's disordered gaze came together and their eyes held. The lord reached up to grab his son, but he had no strength left. Crooked Arm could hardly feel the touch at all.

"The Nest," his father said. "Take it. Take it and escape."

"But the alignment of the Slant..."

There was a final flash of vigor as he gripped Crooked Arm's collar. "Look around you: the Slant is gone!" Crooked Arm did look, but all he could see were vague shapes crossing in the smoke. "The poem...," his father continued weakly, "it is not about the Slant.... It is about all of the sink."

Crooked Arm focused on him, not understanding. The froth had spread down from his father's lips, oozing and bright pink. "Find him," the lord wheezed. "The Immortal First Sword. Bring... the Nest to him...." Then his focus went distant and empty. He patted Crooked Arm's cheek, a light and fluffy touch. His hand stayed there, palm to his son's face, as his lips fluttered, then went still and cold, and his eyes settled and moved no more.

THE NEST

Crooked Arm circled the palace, climbing down to the raw cliffs that jutted inversely from the lip of the courtyard. There he found the black stone door that was all but invisible amidst the similarly colored rock face. Looking back, he could see smoke rising from the village beyond the tree line. Someone was screaming from the high palace road. In the overvoid, the shape of a Far Machine wavered through the layers of smoke, tethers spreading out weblike from its dark belly. Transports halted and jerked, working up and down the wires. Turning back and leaning into the hidden door, Crooked Arm got the huge slab moving slowly aside on its wheeled feet, then he was into the dark passage beyond.

"Who's there?" a voice shouted.

"Crooked Arm," he answered, pushing the big slab back into place.

He moved through the dark hallway and came out in a small subterranean chamber. There was Fast Daggers with a half dozen guards, arrayed along the entrance to the vault door. The hallway was wide enough for only a few people abreast, which made it a good choke point from which to hold off a larger force, or a certain death trap, depending on how it was viewed.

"I suspected you knew of this place." Fast Daggers smiled in spite of the situation. "Mighty spilled the beans before he left?"

Crooked Arm shook his head. "I've known since I was a child." He stepped past her. "I'm taking the Nest," he said.

"Taking it?"

"And escaping." He moved to the vault door.

"Don't," he heard.

Stopping, he turned to face her. Fast Daggers looked relaxed, but Crooked Arm knew better, that soft way her palms floated above the blade hilts. A tiny flick of her wrist and one of those blades would be inside him. The other guards stood by, watching, unsure which side to come down on. "Only the lord and the First Sword are—"

"My father is dead!" Crooked Arm said. "So I am the Lord of the Scorched Dome now."

"Dead?"

"Everyone up there is dead. Or will be soon. It's a slaughter. Vertex, all of the Slant. All of it is doomed. We must take the Nest and flee or they will kill us too, and then they will have it."

Fast Daggers stared back at him. The men too. They could hear the distant tumult from the surface, the dampened thuds, the buzzing fabric of trebly engine warble. There was a closer noise, then more, voices, clanging metal. Then a breath of stillness. Then they watched as the big stone slab was pushed aside. Into the far doorway came the shape of a dropper, with more behind him.

Fast Daggers whipped her arm, and one of the shapes fell back. A voice barked, and a haze of iron ball-and-chain netting leapt from the doorway. Fast Daggers's guards crumbled, bashed to pulp or yanked into the violent retract and torn apart. Crooked Arm grabbed his thigh. There was blood between his fingers, but he had no idea what had cut him. Smoke was bubbling from somewhere and filling the room. Nearby, Fast Daggers bounced up from a roll. Her arms whipped with half-spinning steps, silver glinting knives cutting the air. Blood flit conspicuously from her fingers with each throw, flowing freely from a gash on her upper arm. From the collapsing droppers, a chain ball appeared and skimmed her leg, and, with a hard lash, the whipping tentacle of razor wire bit into her side. The retracting ball followed the embedded wire back down the groove, a sharp crack as Fast Daggers's torso tore open wide.

Crooked Arm came up with the long sword arcing. A hole opened in the swarm of droppers, but it was filled with hazy smoke, and then the floor had him and he felt the daze of his face cracking hard off stone a breath ago. A heavy metal net crashed over him with thick iron pins grinding into the floor. Crooked Arm pushed against it, but the pins only bit deeper in. He screamed and fought, tearing his own flesh in the effort, but it was no use.

When finally he went still, Crooked Arm could see several droppers moving about the hall. The smoke was clearing. More droppers were coming in. One stepped over Crooked Arm, peering oddly through the metal netting. "His arm is fucked-up."

Another yelled, "All clear."

Two men came in wearing the same worn canvas suits, one a young officer, the other a technician. They were monitoring the glowing screen of a small metal box the technician carried. Standing over Crooked Arm, still pinned helpless to the floor, the young officer demanded, "Tell us where it is."

Crooked Arm said nothing.

The officer sighed, impatient. He nodded to the technician. "Well?"

The technician looked deeper into his glowing box. "It's past this door."

One of the droppers stepped forward and shot his chain gun into the vault door. With a hard crack, the door collapsed inward in two split pieces. From inside spilled two colors of light, that same eerie unmixing but now deep gold and green. The technician stepped to the doorway, the different lights falling across his face. "I think we've found it." But then he was still, frozen in place. Crooked Arm noticed something dark protruding from the back of the technician's neck: the handle of a boot knife. One of the droppers suddenly wheeled away. Another screamed and his cannon hit the floor and fired on its own, crushing him between the gun and retracting ball.

"There!" one shouted.

A mace ball launched and impacted something in the haze and stuck. The retract coughed and ripped the gun from the dropper's hand. The haze formed closer, and a blade split his face. A shape was there in the space he left, then gone again. A sword wheeled high, then wide, men falling away and lurching back and lunging forward with the occasional pop and rattle of a wildly fired chain gun. After six breaths, the only one left was the officer, pinned to the wall with a sword at his throat. He looked over the blade, into the Sinker's eyes, and she into his. He was the same pasty-faced officer who'd fired the chain gun at her on Frozen Rock. "You!" he blurted. But that was all. A perfect red line appeared across his throat. He gurgled and sputtered with a look of enraged indignation. Then he fell to the floor, and everything in the hallway was still.

The Sinker measured the sudden calm. She sheathed her sword and winced as she tightened her seeping bandages. She went to Crooked Arm, unsnapping the pinning hooks from the floor. Together they got him out from under the heavy chain netting. Crooked Arm went to the fallen body of Fast Daggers, but there were no last words. She was dead, at the very passageway to the object she had sworn to protect.

"As soon as they realize this crew is gone," the Sinker told him, "they'll send another." She nodded to the glowing box. It was still in the young technician's hands, but the young technician was dead. "The Construct uses a sound-based scan to get a layout of the overvoid, to plot a course to sources of resupply and refuel. They must have figured out some similar means of reading for your anomaly. There's no use hiding it here."

Dodging the stillness of Fast Daggers's eyes, Crooked Arm dug into her bloody tunic and yanked out a key on a chain loop. He led the Sinker past the shattered door and into the vault room. She paused behind him in the doorway as the light fell over her, deep gold and green, both stark and somehow unmixed. Past roping tangles of green tissue-like strings, a dark yellow sphere spun at impossible speed, then slowed, then spun up again another way.

"That's it, the anomaly?" the Sinker asked.

"No. This is a decoy, one of several." Crooked Arm took the tiny key on the chain loop and fit it into an invisible slot. A door at the base of the pedestal popped open. Crooked Arm reached inside and lifted something out. Sitting in his palm now was a roughly spherical gathering of clouded air. Near the periphery, it was perfectly translucent, growing darker toward an inward core that turned hazy, then gray, then into a single point of blackness. The outer clouded layers shifted and shimmered, as if compelled inward by the heavy interior darkness. A vibration modulated thinly from this counter valence. The longer Crooked Arm looked, the more all-encompassing the sound became, until all he could hear was its quiet hollowness.

Crooked Arm had held the Nest once before, in his youth, when it was removed from its hiding spot so the pedestal lock could be repaired. He knew staring at it brought this forcing out of other sound because it had happened then too. The lord—his grandfather—had insisted Crooked Arm see and hold the Nest, hoping it would inspire a dedication to the codes that he would eventually have to uphold. Crooked Arm had found the experience underwhelming, an unsettling of sound but not much more.

The Sinker stepped up beside him, a gentle hand on Crooked Arm's shoulder. Finally he looked away from the inward darkening layers of the Nest. All at once the held-back sounds crashed in. He could hear the muted thump of another clamp impacting the surface, but the rest of the chaos above was only a damp hushing.

"We've got to get out of here," she told him.

With no further hesitation, Crooked Arm stuffed the Nest into the inner folds of his tunic. They slipped out of the vault, down the thin passage below the palace, then circled to the front. From there, they could see the battlefield where his father's body lay somewhere discarded.

The razor wire machines had been turned off. They tilted quietly, clumped meat dripping in their burrs. A few of the droppers smoked roots, their helmets off, laughing, guns leaning against a low wall. Farther off, one of the transports was gearing up the wire. Crooked Arm could hear animal screams and hard metallic clanging from inside. On the opposite hill, the Scorched Dome was completely gone. A transport had landed there, little forms moving about in the charred wreckage.

Moments later, Crooked Arm and the Sinker were descending the palace's long central air duct. The walls were wet with condensation. They slipped and struggled and finally came out a bottom vent onto the underside of the rock. The friction beat hard against them as they struggled to keep hold. In the undervoid, Crooked Arm could see the winking glint of Widescape, already wrapped in the dark wire embrace of another Far Machine. Off below, Haven, only a tiny dot, was yet unattacked. He thought to sink down and warn them, warn the other rocks of the Slant, but as soon as he thought it, he knew it would make no difference and still cost him the Nest. The Sinker was shouting something Crooked Arm could not hear through the roar. She turned away and pushed off and angled her shoulders and hips, then straightened and sliced downward into the undervoid.

Crooked Arm watched her getting smaller as he tucked his bad arm in tight. He coiled his legs and pushed off and angled his head and held his other arm to his side and felt the friction pushing up against him, then felt it split and break and roll down his body. The percussive thumps above came as light coughings now in the roaring void. At a deeper, harder crack, Crooked Arm looked up to see Vertex break in half and separate and waver with the clamp wires limp. The two sections drifted apart until the wires went taut and forced them crashing back together. An explosion of dust and rock engulfed it all. Below, the Sinker had angled and coursed outwide. Crooked Arm rolled and dove, struggling to keep up as she slipped faster into a lateral acceleration. He couldn't figure out where her speed was coming from. He took an angle that would eventually fall in behind her, then had one last look back at Vertex. Through the debris cloud, he could see the two shattered chunks tangled in the Far Machine's wire embrace. Then it was only a gray vagueness and then the absolute darkness of the void, as if the very idea of the Slant had been swallowed up into nothing.

On I sank into the endless darkness, stretching out in every direction, and every direction between those directions, each infinite angle at every infinite radial leading to more points to measure the endlessness from, deeper darknesses cracking apart to reveal more depths filled with endless nothing, more void rolling away so even more could rush up and take its place, until all of it cracked and rolled through, and finally a dim blue speck formed and swelled and expanded out, a vast unfurling of water as endless as the endless sink, and from the water a small rock appeared and got bigger and the ripping friction eased and the bone-chilling cold of the void faded and I landed as softly as stepping onto a pillow, and around my feet I could feel the easy give of the surface, as if it would all slide away, but it only shifted and moved and settled to hold me more sure, and the water was creeping toward me now, over the rock's low surface, rising higher, as if poured from some endless source, and my feet and the surface of the rock blurred as more water churned and roiled in, and my feet were not my feet now but part of the rock, and the water rose higher and rose and rose until I was completely submerged, and above me I could see faint holes of light, then nothing but a blue haze of darkness and a feeling of weight on my chest and sparkling piercings of light and bright sudden flashes and fading bleeds of color blotching and reforming, until there was nothing but the coldness of the water and a darkness even darker than the darkest depths of the void, and a feeling of sinking without sinking, until the coldness and the sinking were gone, and there was nothing, no friction, no overvoid or undervoid or void at all. . . .

PART 4

THE CONSTRUCT

HIRAM GOEGAL

Hiram Goegal was sitting at the table in his breakfast nook, the spreadsheet laid out beside his coffee. As he chewed, his eyes scanned left to right, pausing at the end of each line, staring into each final number. One of the numbers began to move; really it was an ant, making its way across the sheet. He pressed a thumb to it and it popped and curled into a tiny ball. He flicked it away. Where it hit the floor, another ant was passing. It stopped to examine the corpse with its funiculus, then continued along.

Hiram Goegal went back to reading. He was most of the way done with the report when Dugan emerged in a hurry from the bedroom. "I'm always late when I sleep here," he said, pouring himself a cup of coffee. "What are you reading?"

"Estimates from the Slant."

"Already? How did you get them so fast?"

A smile crept into Hiram Goegal's lips. "They were delivered," he said. "I've been called in for a meeting with the barons, at the Garent's direct request."

Dugan grinned back at him and shook his head, holding eye contact all the while. He stepped to the table, put down his coffee, and picked up Hiram Goegal's right hand, the back of which was mottled from a childhood burn. The scar had aged into an uneven smearing of skin up his fingers, a few thick, ropy rivulets worming the knuckles. The palm was worse, dug shallow, dotted with pits and pips, rough, like the surface of an overmined ore rock. Dugan traced his fingers down the grooves of the scar, triggering displaced nerves, sending a shiver down Hiram Goegal's back and into his loins. "I'm already dressed," he said. Dugan laughed and took his hand away and leaned over and kissed him.

Standing, Dugan snatched the spreadsheet and gave it a scan as he sipped his coffee. He turned and leaned back on the counter. "These are good raws if they're right. We're going to be pretty busy down there."

"Would be better if those dolts hadn't broken the top rock in half."

Dugan's eyes went back to the sheet, scanning to the end. "It's a good haul; raws are good." He put it down. "But not good enough. We went far outwide to get to this place. Engines almost horizontal. Forty rests of it. How are we going to stay ahead of the Great Flat that way? Surely the Garent can see the trip wasn't worth it."

Hiram Goegal nodded. He stood and took his coffee to the window. He had a pretty good view of the central router, where the main split and webbed out. Hiram Goegal had grown up right there in Piping. It was the first expansion off Core Rock, and in the beginning only a small build-out, more for housing than pipe making. It was hard to imagine that the Construct had once been only a rock with a single engine welded to the side. It certainly wasn't that anymore. As it expanded, more alloy was needed, and the Piping district grew. The Recycle was added later, a gargantuan interlocking of sorting and reuse facilities, then Waste, to help process all that was left over and unusable. That was generations ago, long before Hiram Goegal. Stacks were added too, a hulking grid of flats like his. More went up whenever materials made it possible. They jutted off, all over Core Rock and the Recycle and Piping too, poking at odd angles, staggering back on themselves, some welded right onto the underside. Hiram Goegal wondered how loud it must be, living down there so close to the Maw. Looking higher, he could see past the tangle of the far Recycle, where Engine One slept, huge on the closest edge. It was rotated perpendicular for repair, its wide belly visible, capped by a soot-black rim.

Dugan was suddenly close behind him. He sighed, the breath hot on Hiram Goegal's ear. "You'd tell me, right?" Dugan said. "If there was some other reason the Garent brought us all this way?"

THE GARENT

A high, leaping, tumbling inferno filled the full-wall fireplace. Heat radiated through the long, low room and circled back in on itself and would have been unbearable to most people of the sink, no matter if they were from Frozen Rock or Boiling Sludge. His guards had started the fire, but the Garent stoked it himself, piling on the combustion sticks until the flames crackled and roared and climbed. It was warm enough now that he'd taken off his heavy coat. He stood in front of the flames in one of the thick cabled sweaters he always wore, his canvas pants lined inside with flannel. All of it was tailored perfectly to his tall, erect frame. His silver hair was looking fluffy and unkempt and thin enough to hint the top of his head.

Perhaps we have simply gotten too big, the Garent thought. Too many people, too much wasted, too few rocks to absorb, and those that can be don't provide enough. The propulsion efficiencies, the reuse schedules, the deep Recycle. All he had sacrificed, of his own and that of others. Maybe all of it was pointless because the real answer was that one simple thing: the Construct had become too big, too big to escape the Great Flat forever. They could rise and prolong their fate, but eventually, inevitably, it would catch them.

The Garent shook off the thought. With a few long strides, he was at the side wall where he kept his collection. It was set up in a grid of stained-wood cubby shelving, each compartment containing a curious artifact arranged expertly in a tight pool of light. All of them were scavenge, oddities found during absorption: small machines, bizarre utensils, confusing half pieces of larger things. The shapes and combinations of materials were odd, unsettling, the objects' functions impossible to determine. Any one of them was only what it was, a relic of some indeterminate use, a reference to a culture so far away in the sink, it could never be reached nor understood. Laid out together, though, the artifacts wove a feeling of familiarity, a ghosted knowledge of a place where such things were routine and recognizable and interconnected on some primal level of creation.

In a central display, there were a few small anomalies arranged on a velvet sheet. Most had been collected during the Construct's rise, but one he'd had much longer. He lifted the front glass and took it out, a small, flat stone with peeking flecks of blue crystal. Anomaly in hand, the Garent went to sit in the cupping heat of the fire. He settled back in one of the high-backed chairs and lifted it toward his face, close to his lips. He inhaled evenly and long, and then, with his lips puckered, whistled and hummed simultaneously, three descending notes. The blue crystal specks began to shine, the flattened rock anomaly radiating a soft, warm glow.

The Garent placed it into the center of his palm and rested his hand on his knee. His eyes went slim, a soft quiver to his lip. A vein on his temple pulsed lightly, bluish through his skin. The air above the anomaly shifted. Something was forming, color swirling in. From a scattering of tiny specks, it fizzed and solidified, becoming the curve of a chin, a dangling lock of hair, a curt line that was a mouth. Floating before him now was the flickering image of a face, the face of a young girl.

There was a knock at the study door, quick, sudden, one of the guards. "My Garent," he heard. "We've arrived at the Slant."

With a last exhale, the Garent clasped his other hand over the anomaly. The girl's face evaporated. The Garent watched the empty air a breath, then crossed the room and put the anomaly back into the glass case. The glow had faded. It seemed only a smooth rock again. He put on his heavy robes and coat and topped himself with a fur hat. Bundled up, he went to greet the waiting guard.

"My Garent," the man said, quieter. "We have the elevator ready."

The guard stepped aside so the Garent could lead the way. The elevator took them down through the center of the tower, past zero level to the sub-Construct, where the big absorption bays bustled with activity. The men stopped when the Garent came in, but he smiled and waved and they all went back to work.

Through the wide bay door, he could see the thoroughness of the staging. The top rock of the Slant had been broken in half and stripped of everything, all of it sorted and packed and bundled into several dozen cubes lashed to each other with thick wire. Farther off, the rock was still smoldering, the surface alternately shattered and flattened. Specks of smaller debris and shape-changing globules of liquid appeared and vanished as the probing beam moved over it all. Vague in the darkness of the overvoid, the Far Machines lurked, tired beasts called to heel.

Around the bay, recycling crews stood by, ready to begin the first sorting, livestock coordinators and assessors from Perishables, with their ice carts and big yellow gloves. Thin clouds of tiny black flies swirled and settled into near invisibility. The high corners were dotted brown and black gray from generations of spider feasts. Thicker, darker beetles scuttled and settled and scuttled, unafraid of the bustle around them.

The first climbers were reaching the cubes, latching on tethers that snaked back to their respective bays. The smaller containers were already wobbling in. Past it all, the Garent could see the climber crews crawling the rock, attaching the cables that would tow it into the Maw. The people and the bugs seemed the same, moving in swirls, settling, then lifting off again, cycling back in a pattern that was no pattern.

"Quartz, magnesium, feldspar." It was the supervisor, who'd come to stand at the Garent's side. "We won't know for sure until we break it down."

"Tell me about this *Scorched Dome*," the Garent said.

The supervisor pointed at one of the stripped rocks, turning idly in the void. "The dome was there, they tell me, on that high rise."

The Garent looked down at the dusty black marring, tiny from this distance, like the leftovers of a firepit.

"They tracked the anomaly to a vault under a cluster of buildings that was somewhere around there." The supervisor pointed again, as if any part of the destroyed rock could be told from another. "The team they sent never came back. They sent a second team, and they found the first team all dead, the anomaly gone. Whoever killed those droppers must have escaped with it."

The Garent nodded, information he'd already acquired. His eyes moved over what was left of Vertex, the two broken pieces, struggling to see how the topographies could fit together. "Are there any images," he asked, "of what the dome looked like before our arrival?"

"I don't know, my Garent. I'll have to check with the Recycle."

The Garent was nodding impatiently. "Please do," he said.

The supervisor removed his hat and scratched his straw-like hair, then put the hat back on. A few gnats buzzed around his ear.

Looking back out the bay mouth, the Garent watched the big mooring cables go taut. With a groan, the wires began winching Vertex in. They were closer to the staging now, the debris becoming more specific. The Garent focused on a headless, armless, legless torso, sinking loose among it all. The first of the larger containers was coming in through the bay mouth. Livestock and reuse supervisors were there and ready. The big door was unlatched and dozens of goat carcasses and burlap sacks dumped out, a few live goats leaping around the mess. Some of the sacks burst open, and potatoes went rolling all over the bay floor. "Oh fuck," the supervisor said, hurrying off to help.

A zinging hum took the floor as somewhere deep below the gears of the Maw spun up. The Garent strode to the edge of the bay mouth to look down. He could see the rock only as far as it entered the rim. First one and then a series of deep crunching bursts gave way to a long sustained rumble, Vertex being ground apart in a thousand whirling iron teeth. Even the rock itself will be used, the Garent thought, melted down for ore or fuel. All the animals, the live and dead, pots, pans, clothing, anything that can be used will be. All this brutality, the unrelenting repetition of absorption, rock after rock, and still it will not be enough.

THE WAY UP IS DOWN

With his leather folder case tucked under his arm, Hiram Goegal was let into the big central boardroom, sweltering with crisp, dry heat. The Garent and the Engine Barons were already gathered around the room's fireplace, their shapes dark and blurry against the roaring blaze. The Garent saw him and smiled and waved him over.

As Hiram Goegal approached, the heat swept over him, an itch in his shirt cuffs, dampness along the back of his neck. The folder case went hot between his arm and side as he shook each baron's hand and then the hand of the Garent. The old man was still upright and lean and hardy in places, but thinning oddly in others. Hiram Goegal could see it in his wrists, in the ropy tendons of his neck. But still he was the Garent, vigorous and loud and simmering with cool energy.

When Hiram Goegal was a child, his father talked about the Garent the same way, an older man with the energy of a younger. They spoke of the Garent then as if he were truly ageless, as if he would lead the Construct for all the rests to come, in whatever stretch of the sink they hurtled upward into. But that was many thousands of rests ago. Hiram Goegal was no longer a child, and the Garent was certainly not ageless. Closer to the man, Hiram Goegal could see the redness of a recently scratched scab, crusty in the Garent's thinning hair.

These gruesome peeks of age made Hiram Goegal curious about the transition, when someone new would have to take the Garent's place. There was no heir nor chief subaltern to pass it to. He'd had a family once—before Hiram Goegal was born—but the Garent's wife and daughter were killed: poisoned by spoiled food absorbed from some backward rock. After the tragedy, the Garent spiraled off, a lonely shadow haunting his tower. For a thousand rests he stayed away. That's what Hiram Goegal was told, anyway. When he was old enough to remember, the Garent had already reemerged and remarried, though he never had any more children. It was mysterious where the next Garent would come from, no one having been around when this one was installed. But they trusted him with it the way they did everything else, knowing it must be the right thing for them all.

Perhaps it would be one of the barons, Hiram Goegal thought. Not Linton. She ran Engine Three and was almost as old as the Garent. Till was younger, but still seasoned and graying with the cool reserved air of a long-serving patriarch. Penn was the youngest, about middle rests, but proud and relaxed in a way that made him seem much older. Linton was the only one Hiram Goegal really knew at all, having worked under her to fit the anomaly-run booster onto Engine Three. His interactions had been mostly with her subalterns. Linton herself treated the whole installation as an inconvenience she was allowing on the Garent's behalf. Once the booster was up and running and Linton saw the effect on engine efficiency and fuel usage, a cold respect bloomed, but never anything more. In the end, Hiram Goegal was still Propulsion staff, and so merely a functionary to the barons.

More important than the booster itself, the project had made real one of Hiram Goegal's central theories, a proof of concept that could be seen and measured. Though Linton did not know of this real purpose, the Garent did. When he saw the results, he and Hiram Goegal began working on a project that could change the Construct forever.

The greetings were over now. The Garent stood to his full height and moved them on to business. "We were discussing the raw numbers from the Slant," he informed Hiram Goegal.

"I've seen them," he replied, nodding.

"Two hundred rests of engine operation," the Garent continued. "Vitals boosted fifty rests, food supply another fifty independent, if the estimates are correct."

"The estimates are always correct," Baron Penn put in, "more or less."

Baron Till cleared his throat, a sound of displeasure. "Adding engine run is a relief with the shortages we've had, but we'll lose out on this trip." The fire crackled in the silence. A building hiss released in a hard pop. "Ten rests of engine run, to be exact." He sipped his drink, eyeing the others over the rim. "If we cannot keep ahead of neutral rise, the Great Flat will catch us too. And everything we have done will be erased."

Hiram Goegal felt the leather folder sweat-soggy under his arm. He shifted to hold it clasped behind his back instead. With the fingers of one hand, he gently stroked the rough scar covering the other. It was a nervous habit he'd decided not to train away. It soothed him, this contact, and evened his breath and so paced the events around him in better tune with his perception.

"You're right," the Garent finally said, smiling at Barron Till. "So very right. Which brings us to our real problem." He opened his hand to a small mapping table. Following him, they slipped from the more intense pool of heat and gathered around it. Adjusting a few knobs, then depressing a pressure switch, the Garent brought his master map to life, a haze of off-red motes clouding the room. "The sink is thinning as we rise," he said. "We've had to angle out further, take costlier detours, even move laterally." The Garent tapped the table edge, and the layout re-formed and racked focus. "Our problem only increases as we rise further. There won't be enough resupply ahead to maintain neutral. We'll have to run the engines on interval, send the Far Machines out staging further. Whether we're passing through a prolonged sector of less dense sink or if we've reached a more uniform thinness, we do not know. We cannot know, not for certain. The echo scan only reaches so far ahead."

The Garent drew his eyes slowly across them, lingering on Baron Till before moving wider again, into the softness of the projected map. "We can keep angling upward," the Garent said. "Stretching things further. Cutbacks may help but will not be popular. Even then, we would still be rising against the rest of the sink, but not against neutral. The Great Flat would eventually catch us. Unless we find some other way to fuel our rise." The Garent took a big breath and held it. "Thankfully, Goegal here has a solution."

Hiram Goegal absorbed the crossing gazes of the barons. He waited a breath, then a breath more. "As you all know, I am from Propulsion," he said. "Most of my work has been studying sink anomalies. Odd objects, inexplicable formations, mutations, if you will, in the very nature of the sink."

The barons peered cagily back, lids thinned to not let one thing slip in unnoticed. Baron Till stroked his beard, his thick, strong fingers mushed together into a pad, like a small pillow he was resting his chin on. "So we were not told the real reason for the lateral movement. We came all this way for one of Goegal's little trinkets."

"I'll remind you," Hiram Goegal said, "that the booster on Three has been running for a thousand rests, at one-third the refit, requiring zero combustion material. All on one of those *little trinkets*."

"So now we can add another booster?" It was Baron Penn, seeming, as always, amused. He nodded at the Garent, some private thing communicated.

"Not yet," the Garent admitted, turning back to Baron Till. "At my directive, Goegal has been searching the overvoid echo for anomalies that could provide a more abundant source of power."

Baron Penn kept his eyes on the Garent, that same smile lingering like an overstayed guest. "And how does searching the void for an anomaly work?" he inquired.

The Garent nodded to Hiram Goegal, who spoke again. "The echo doesn't find rocks in the overvoid. It finds their density, in the displacement of the friction. We've learned anomalies cause a similar displacement. Their energy, in effect, holds back the normal fabric of the sink. In the echo scan, it appears as a density distortion, as if there is . . . more of the sink than there should be. Over the last few thousand rests, I have tracked a half dozen anomalies, two of which were worth altering our course slightly to take possession of."

"My Garent," Baron Linton inquired politely. "Why is it we are only being told this now?"

The Garent nodded. "I do apologize for holding information back. And I must insist you share none of this. Not with your staff, your families, your most trusted confidants."

"But why, my Garent?"

The Garent only nodded more, stepping closer to the fire. It blazed a gleaming halo around him, a red corona coating his edge. "They keep themselves blind to it," the Garent said, "blind to what we must do to stay on the rise. The people living here. But they know. They all know. That burden is one they must bear, that all of us must bear." The Garent went quiet, to let the fire be the only sound, the low rumble of its roar, the hissing and popping sparks, the faint, high-pitch scream of burning air. "To give them a taste of a new idea . . . I worry, then, if the chance were to slip away, become a mirage, the old gestalt brought back in, their will to continue would be . . . compromised. Not all of them, but enough. So . . . until we know for sure, we must not let on what our true purpose is." He lifted a finger to indicate Hiram Goegal. "The math works; as we've neared the anomaly, the closer readings have further confirmed it. Once we have it, we can spread the good news."

Linton was smiling, but the expression was forced. She seemed tired from the effort. "What math is that, my Garent?"

The Garent nodded to Hiram Goegal, who went into his leather folder case, drawing out several packets of paper. "The displacement caused by this anomaly is several orders of magnitude greater than the one running the booster on Three. With it, we can power the entire Construct, all three engines, with no other fuel source needed."

The barons only stared back as Hiram Goegal handed out the packets. They flipped them open, looking at numbers and flow charts.

"What you see are schematics," the Garent told them, "for incorporating the anomaly into our propulsion systems. I suggest you all familiarize yourself so you fully understand the potential. The Forever Rise, without absorption. If we can achieve this, then everything we've done will have been worth it."

Baron Penn's smile was pressed now and impatient. The packet was closed and rolled into a tube in his hand. "'Not yet,' you said, my Garent. So we don't have it?"

"No," the Garent answered. "Two people fled the Slant at the Far Machines' arrival. We think the son of the local lord and one of his subalterns perhaps. They have the anomaly and a little head start." He nodded to Hiram Goegal. "Using the echo scan, we can track the movement of the anomaly. The Far Machines are in pursuit now."

"The Far Machines are sinking?"

"Into the undervoid, my Garent?"

"Yes, they are going to catch them and bring it back to us."

Baron Till's chin dropped with his lower lip pressed out. He glanced to the other barons. "My Garent," he said. "I am to understand we are not going to turn the engines back on? That we're going to sink here until the Far Machines return?"

"Yes," the Garent said, studying them with his warm, friendly eyes. "The Flat isn't so close behind us, Baron. We've made good progress getting pretty far ahead of it. Once we have the anomaly and Goegal has incorporated it into our systems, we can make up for the lost rests quite easily." He measured each baron in turn, a probing search of their eyes and what lay beyond their eyes. "I don't want to do this if we are not in agreement," the Garent said. "I am your Garent, but the Construct is ours, everyone's."

"It will be costly," announced Baron Linton, "but I am with you." Then she added hastily, "Of course, my Garent."

The Garent looked to Baron Penn, who was smiling back. "I am with you too."

The Garent grinned and patted Baron Penn's shoulder. "Baron Till?"

Baron Till was gazing into the fire, his eyes reflecting red watery flames. His head was up, stock straight, posture perfect. A breath passed, then another, then his eyes wavered and floated and landed on the Garent.

"Very well," the Garent announced, smiling. He clapped Baron Till on the shoulder. "It is decided, then."

▼

Outside the Garent's tower, Hiram Goegal paused to look up at the void sucking away. Normally, the engines would be fired back up as soon as absorption was complete, but not now. For now they were off, and the Construct, like everything else, was sinking at the whim of the void. Hiram Goegal considered the change in pitch, the hollow emptiness of the roar, the eerie silence of the engines, nothing but dark hulks on the far edge.

Spread out before him was the wide main way of Core Rock. Everything had started right there, before Piping and the Recycle and Waste and all the stacking expansions. Hiram Goegal turned to look up at the Garent's tower, the Construct's tallest level, ten above zero. If the Flat ever did arrive, he supposed, the Garent could go to the top and be the last one smashed to bits.

Walking briskly, Hiram Goegal made his way down the welded joint into Piping, where the high stacks stacked upward, some as high as five level. Here, you had to look directly up to see even glimpses of the void. If Hiram Goegal kept his eyes only forward, he could imagine there was no sink at all, no Great Flat, that indeed the full arc of human existence was finite and contained, all right there on the Construct.

Turning, he came down the wide stairs that opened into Piping's central way. Around him now was a near-constant hissing of steam.

Puddles of condensation gathered and were stepped in and splashed to slowly regather and be splashed again. The bugs were different than on Core Rock, which had mostly ants and roaches. In Piping, they were moist, maggoty things you could see in every crack and crevice of the ways. Fat flies moved through the air in tumbling swells. But nothing like in Waste, which was basically a uniform haze of buzzing insects.

Hiram Goegal was getting close to home, the same stack where he'd been born, some eleven thousand rests before. Familiar faces flashed. Food windows he'd known since he'd known anything. At a corner, where the steam leaked thicker, kids played tag through the dissipating mists, just as Hiram Goegal had done, the cycles of his life cycling ever onward to bring him stepping once again through the re-condensing puddles.

Entering his flat, he set down his case and keys. He left the lights off as he moved around the low furniture, preferring the cool visibility of his limbic memory. In darkness, the clean lines were stark and severe, a life clear of anything extra. Finally he reached the far side and touched the lighting panel up. Even the dimmest setting revealed the long-lived-in, if exacting, warmth. Shelves, deceptively curved, bowed the wide living room, filled with bound books, manuals, framed awards, and commendations. A side table displayed a row of vacuum tubes, neatly arranged from thin and tall with the filaments gleaming to short and spherical with no hint past the silvered glass. The first relay tube he'd built with his own revised alloy compounds. A bookend was a plaster impression of his scar hand, made when he was a young man. Hiram Goegal liked to place his present hand beside it and see the stark changes of his rests.

Inside a bell-shaped cage in the room's corner was his pet moth. She was gray and white and speckled with dark black dots. Fully grown, from antennae tip to the end of her thorax, she was as long as his hand. Hiram Goegal tapped the thin webbing of bars, and the moth fluttered, a sound like shuffling cards. "How are you, my Florina?" He opened the cage door and put a pinch of food into her bowl. He watched the moth flutter and fractal through the cage and settle again into papery stillness, feeding with her cute little proboscis.

Hiram Goegal poured himself a drink, then went to the far curio. Featured centrally was the anomaly that had first sparked his interest. It was a not quite square of greenish crystal the size of two fists put together. It sat on display atop a three-pronged pedestal. He lit a match and held it beneath, and the anomaly began to glow, bathing the room in a soothing green light. After he whipped out the match, the glow remained, coolly radiating. That was the extent of this anomaly's use: prolonged light output with only a small infusion of heat. He'd tested the displacement but found the power generated canceled out by the power needed to get the cycle going. The anomalies from the Garent's private collection had also been tested. They each generated a little power, but not in usable quantities. The tests had proved the theory, though; the anomalies all shared the same quality of displacement energy; some just had more than others, and some much, much more.

With another card-shuffling flutter, Florina was dancing across the room in several directions at once. She rose, then took a last confusing dive and angled up to land on Hiram Goegal's shoulder. The moth was still for a breath, then fluttered again to perch beside the glowing anomaly.

"Come out for a little exercise?" he said. The moth fluttered but stayed put, then fluttered again and settled, only its small antennae wavering.

In the uniform lowness of the green light, Hiram Goegal caught a reflection in the glass front of the curio, a slight movement behind him in the darkness. "Dugan?" He turned to find two shapes in the deep shadows of his bathroom. It was dark, but he could see both were young adults, their faces sweaty and gleaming. "What are you doing in here?" Hiram Goegal demanded.

The woman pointed a chain gun at him and, with no further hesitation, pulled the trigger. Instead of firing, the latch caught and the gun jammed. Her male accomplice watched her working the switch, his face filled with panic. "It's fucking jammed!" she screeched. The man was moving suddenly, closing the distance to Hiram Goegal in two hurried steps.

"What is this?" Hiram Goegal heard, realizing it was his own voice. He stepped back, seeing a knife flash green in the light. It missed his face and then his chest by the width of a finger. He felt a bite and looked down at the knife, now stuck in his thigh. The young man was terrified by what he'd done, staring wide-eyed at the blood filling the front of Hiram Goegal's pants.

Hiram Goegal breathed hard. His fingers wrapped around the knife handle. With a swift yank, he pulled the blade free, then drove it into the man's chest and yanked it out just as fast. The man was in complete disbelief that this could happen. A sublime ease took his face. He fell to his knees and choked and toppled over and gripped futilely at the gushing blood.

Hiram Goegal noticed something on the man's forearm, a small tattoo, a simple line drawing of three arrows laid over each other, intersecting in the center, each with a tiny triangle tip and a few lines of fletching. Hiram Goegal suddenly remembered the woman. She had stopped trying to unjam her chain gun. Her eyes were gaping and wet, staring at the dying man through a of mop of stringy hair. She raised the gun and tried it again, but still nothing happened. Overcome with panic, she threw the gun at him and ran for the door.

Limping, but moving more smoothly through the familiar space, Hiram Goegal followed her into the hall. Florina went fluttering across the room behind him as he deftly slipped his hand into a drawer. He had his small spring gun now. He angled around the door and found the woman's fleeing shape in the crosshairs. He tightened his grip, and the scar stretched and constricted cephalopodically. With a light squeeze, the barbed spike leapt and lashed and wrapped and spun the woman around, her bones crackling on the retract.

Hiram Goegal let the gun rewind. It was wet the last dozen links and the barbed end coated with gore. He approached to find the woman all but gone. "Fuck you," she managed, then settled into the unmistakable stillness of death. Florina landed weightlessly on Hiram Goegal's shoulder. He didn't seem to notice. He knelt down and moved back the cuff of the dead woman's shirt. There it was, below her elbow, the same tattoo, three intersecting arrows.

THE VOID BETWEEN

The Sinker felt more at ease out in the roaring endlessness, plummeting downward through the uprushing friction, her mind massaged by the counterpoint of her pulse, with only the occasional shouted signal to Crooked Arm as they traded rests to keep watch for risers, for Far Machines, for droppers with tether thrusters in pursuit, but they never saw anything, and they slept and woke again and again and all was cycles in the darkness, the pill, the drop, awake, asleep, again and again, until finally a tiny speck formed in the void below, and the speck became a rock and the rock widened and unfurled its surface, small, brittle and porous, with leafless trees scattered like thinning hair, and a sound too, a whistling, high and nervy and tingling in the roots of the Sinker's teeth.

She aimed at a small clearing and Crooked Arm tilted in behind her, and the surface picked up detail and became a strange cheese of pocks and tunnels and gnarled tree branches pleading voidward. It all wavered and leapt up, and the Sinker swung into her front leg and felt the sureness of the rock press up into the ball of her foot and, with a gentle wavering of her knees, stepped coolly into a single stride, then turned to watch Crooked Arm descending. He was coming in too fast, she could see. He got his feet down, but his weight was ahead of him and he pitched forward with his tucked arm flapping loose as he tumbled and spilled out flat on his face.

Cursing, Crooked Arm worked to free his pinned arm. He rolled over onto his back and breathed heavily, looking up at the last stretch through which they'd come. The Sinker lay down too, made her body flat and let the rock hold her. They breathed together like that, deeply on the friction as it curled up into the overvoid.

"How long was that?" Crooked Arm asked.

"Twenty rests."

"Twenty? I had no idea."

"Yes," she said. "It blends after a while."

"This is the furthest I've ever been."

The whistle they'd heard persisted, quiet but high and piercing and strangely shifting its tone. "We've got to keep moving," the Sinker said, pushing herself to her feet. "They've got some way to scan for that thing. They won't be far behind us." Crooked Arm got up too, wobbling on rubbery legs. He rolled his shoulders around, then pinned his dead arm back into his belt.

The Sinker was already moving, and he hurried to keep up. They leapt over holes that tunneled downward, peeking networks of wind caverns webbing beneath. The friction coursed through, whipping around pockets and curves, resonating right up into their feet. A short hike brought them over some shale rock and down into a small bowl valley, a gravel field dotted with strange gleaming bubbles rising from the ground. The Sinker could see a few scattered huts arranged in the elbow of a distant ridge, and a few more across the flats below. "They're living everywhere," she said.

"Who?" Crooked Arm asked.

"People."

He dug his finger into his ear. "How do they stand the sound?"

The Sinker led them through the field of bubbles, which were some kind of liquid swell, like an inverted drip. The small ones were as big as a hand and the larger ones as high as her waist, all of them perfectly reflective, like liquid mirrors.

"I've come across jewelry and decorations made from these types of swells," the Sinker told him. "They dip things in to coat them with reflected glass. Somehow it's kept liquid by an anomaly in the center of the rock, so they say. You smell it?"

Crooked Arm nodded. "Like something already burnt getting burned again . . ."

"If we get a thick enough shell on your anomaly, it should mask some of the vibration. Maybe enough that the Construct can't keep a read on it."

"But it won't be permanent?"

"It's glass—sturdy, but breakable."

They arrived at one of the camps, a few tents and a small, blackened fire ring. The dirt around it gleamed with tiny slivers of glass and glass dust. A man came out to greet them, the skin on his face loose. Red moons of juicy tissue peeked under his sagging eyes. His mouth hung open. Inside, his remaining teeth were silvery with rot.

"We want to add an enamel," the Sinker told the man, pointing at the closest reflective bubble. The man nodded, then again toward Crooked Arm. "He wants your sword as a payment," the Sinker said. "It's your choice. I don't know what it means to you."

Crooked Arm drew out the long sword. "This had better work," he told her. The man took the sword, looking into the blade, his smile like a slash in a rotten gourd. He went back into the tent flaps and took out a long iron scoop with a gripping handle like a fireplace tong. His hands were as rotted as his teeth, skin dotted with lesions and black calluses.

Crooked Arm took the Nest out of his inner tunic, a dark cloud floating loosely in his hand. The man held out the tongs, and Crooked Arm placed the Nest in the bowl of their grip. Moving to one of the larger reflective drips, the man used the tongs to push the Nest against the bubble. The surface tension dented and bent and wavered, then broke, the thin arms of the tongs vanishing to double back in the reflection.

Gritting his teeth, the man worked with incredible focus, one hand on the tongs while the other moved the handle in curt jerks. His split lips quivered, counting in silence. They were gooey with some kind of ointment. When he finally drew the tongs out, a reflective layer coated the Nest, completely hiding the clouded core. The man smiled at them, nodding with his mouth open. He worked the handle again, and the coated Nest turned in the bowl of the tongs, forming a cooling shell from the liquid mirror. Nodding again, then looking into the surface of the glass bubble, the rotted man pressed the Nest back in. Then a third plunge and then into a vat of oil. When he took it out, the oil gleamed over a perfect mirrored sphere. He wiped it with a cloth and handed it over. Crooked Arm held it up, looking into his bent reflection in the surface of the new shell.

"Where are you planning to go?" the Sinker asked him.

Crooked Arm thought. "To find a man I'm not sure even exists." He tucked the Nest back into his tunic and looked directly at her. "I don't know."

"Well . . . we need to resupply before we go much further." She plumed her map and thumbed and scrolled, and the sink swam and spun around her. She homed in on a tiny dot. "Stayover," she said. "One twenty off absolute, radial ninety-nine, a slight rise outwide." She thumbed, and the map vanished. "It'll take two rests to get there. You have until then to decide."

STAYOVER

"It's tiny," Crooked Arm said.

The Sinker nodded. He was right. It was really only a linking point, and there wasn't much there, six clustered buildings and a store. Farther out was a messy shelving of edge rock where a few campfires burned, each in the privacy of their own stone juttings.

At the store they were greeted by a set of twins and their mother. "Where you headed?" one of the doubled faces asked.

"Outwide, for now," the Sinker told them. She put two zinc bolts on the counter and slid over a list.

The identical sisters scanned it, then snapped to. The mother settled into the vacated stretch of counter. "Don't got quite all of that," she said, eyeing the list. "We make a decent pill. Got plenty of drops. We got all your hards and tacks from a butcher my brother runs right over there. What else we only get when others bring it by for trade or a big trip into Swallow Edge, which my husband makes every hundred or so. But it's been longer than that now."

"We'll take what of it you have," the Sinker said. She lifted a hip bag one of the twins had brought out and tossed it to Crooked Arm. He clasped the straps around his waist and leg. From inside his tunic, he took out the Nest. It looked like a big ball bearing now. He fit it into the hip bag and snapped it shut.

"We're glad you found us," the mother said. "Last people had some trouble."

"It was a bit off from what I have in my map," the Sinker admitted.

"Well, worked out all right, I suppose." She nodded at the high ridges. "You want to set up in the rock shelving for a rest, it's free for those who traded, but after that we charge. That's Ho's land. My uncle Ho. My family runs this whole rock. Always has."

Crooked Arm and the Sinker found an incove and made camp. They could see only one other fire in the rock shelving and a couple of other places where dark shapes moved about. On the ridge above, the thin cluster of houses glowed warmly. Distant talking and laughter trebled weakly against the roar of the edge.

The Sinker broke a combustion stick. She added a single dark rock, and it bloomed and burned low blue. She took two small cups, dropped a pill into each, and set them by the fire. She had taken off her pack and unrolled it. Inside were tiny combustion sticks, pills, hydrodrops, several gels and creams, batteries, all in close-fit pouches and containers and rolls and folds cinched up tight. Carefully she unwound the bandage from one of her hands. A tight scab had formed. She fingered some ointment out of a jar and rubbed it in until the scab gleamed. The cups suddenly fizzled, and a brackish foam bubbled to the rim. The Sinker removed them from the heat. She watched the tiny bubbles on the surface pop and settle as they cooled.

Crooked Arm finally broke the silence. "What was your plan?" he asked. "When you came to the Slant."

The Sinker was winding off the other bandage, creaming the other scab. "I was going to wait out of range, until the Construct arrived."

"And then?"

"Find a way in, improvise. Seek an opportunity."

"An opportunity for what?"

She was looking at the glow of the fire, or past it maybe, where the sink was as empty as ever. "Sabotage an engine. Kill someone important. Both. I would have done what I could. As much as I could."

Crooked Arm tilted his head, looking at her from this slightly new angle. "But you didn't wait out of range," he said. "Your mistake was coming down to warn us." He nodded to her hands. "Now you need to heal. You know they're after the Nest. You don't think they're going to give up. In fact, you know they won't. So . . . you stick with me, you'll get another chance."

The Sinker only watched him, the blue fire glowing in her eyes.

"Do you have any idea why?" he asked. "Why they would be after it?"

"They believe in the Great Flat," she said. "All the propulsion engineering, all it consumes, all to outrun the Flat by rising faster than the friction. For them to stop and sink instead, it must be for a good reason. Or at least they must think so. Does the Nest have some power, some pull of gravity, some combustive property?"

Crooked Arm was shaking his head. "Supposedly the rocks of the Slant were arranged using its power, each one equidistant from the next, a perfect line bisecting them all. It was done this way to prove the veracity of the legend to all future generations, but the method has always been conveniently mysterious. Of course, part of the legend is that only the Immortal First Sword knew how to unlock its power. All we know for sure is that it vibrates, a low noise. If you stare at it, the noise forces out all other sound until it's all you can hear. Some lords in the past studied the Nest. Others in far-off rests ago tried a little harder, but no one ever found any power beyond this slight noise distortion." He cinched his crooked arm into his belt so he could sit up more straight. "Honestly, until all this, I thought it was just some trinket, useful to hang a society on, a good basis for some legends and stories. I figured the Slant was the way it was, and the Nest had nothing to do with it. But why would they come for it if that's all there is?" He shrugged. "Maybe the legends are true, or some part of them. Maybe it does have some power, maybe something we can use against them, or for some greater purpose beyond the Construct, or us, or even the void itself, or . . ." He trailed off, the hope in his voice feeling forced and hollow.

What was in the cups had settled into a black, frothy liquid. The Sinker gave one to Crooked Arm. "Drink this. All at once is better."

He put it to his lips and tilted it back. His grimace turned his face into a whole other face. "It's terrible."

The Sinker had finished hers as well. She was smiling, nodding.

Crooked Arm put a hand on his stomach and burped.

The Sinker burped too, functionally, through her nose. "It's going to expand out again and again for the next dozen rests. Should keep us off pill so we only need a drop."

Crooked Arm nodded. He burped again.

The Sinker took the cups and wiped them, and they vanished into the compartments of her spread-open pack. "Have you decided where you're going?" she asked.

"Yes," he said. "To see my brother."

"He was not on the Slant?"

"No, he left many rests ago." Crooked Arm looked at her, then back into the fire. "My grandfather, when he was the lord, took a long journey away from the Slant. He had been doing research into the legend of the Immortal First Sword. Perhaps he was looking for proof, or maybe it was the thrill of the mystery."

"What did he find out?"

Crooked Arm smiled at her. "Nothing . . . he said. But I always believed there was more. His denials were too pat. Something happened that changed him. He'd found something he didn't want to share."

"And you think your brother might know?"

Crooked Arm shrugged. "The two were very close. If he told anyone, it would have been him."

The Sinker watched the blue flames lap and change shape as they fell and re-formed. "What happened to him?" she asked. "The Immortal First Sword? In the legend."

"The story is an old enemy was loose in the sink and he felt responsible. He trained a successor to be the First Sword and set out the codes for a society dedicated to protecting the Nest. Then he sunk off and was never seen nor heard from again."

A hard bark of laughter pierced from the houses above. The low hiss of the near sink modulated and thickened, then thinned again.

"Every place has a story." The Sinker capped the cream, put it into her pack, and took out a tight roll. She let it loose, and it flipped into a flat pad. She packed the pack back up, tighter and smaller as she clicked the buckles down, then put it at the end of the pad for a pillow. She lay down, thinking. She held her hand up and turned it, fanning out her fingers to see their shape against the void. "Why does it have the name the Nest?" she asked. "That's what it's called in the legends?"

"No. The Nest is just what it came to be called, based on what it looks like, well, what the decoys look like. You saw one of them, like a small nest with an egg in the center."

The Sinker smiled. "The name is based on the decoy?"

Crooked Arm smiled back, grim and self-aware. He put his good arm out behind him and leaned on it. The friction scraped in the silence. The rock shelving must have redirected some of the flow outward; it was relatively quiet given how close to the edge they'd made camp. Even the flame seemed untouched by it, low and steady.

"What about you?" Crooked Arm asked. "Why are you chasing it? For revenge? It destroyed your home too? Your friends, your family?"

"I am from there," she said suddenly.

Crooked Arm was still a few breaths. He turned and got down flat on his own roll, a cheap felt layering they'd gotten at the store. "What happened?" he asked.

She breathed, all out, then a long inhale. "The Construct was huge even then. Ten, twenty of Vertex. They'd been successful. They'd built it bigger, new sections and expansions. But it required more to maintain. Absorption became even more brutal. Too brutal for some."

The sink howled, then shifted, resonating lower, pitching things down.

"My mother wanted to leave. She hated what they had to do to keep rising. It made her sick." The campsite went silent and still, as if that was all there was to it. But there was more. "My father was one of their soldiers and so had some power. When she tried to go, he did the only thing he could to keep her from leaving. He killed her."

▼

Later, when the fire had reduced to a meager glow through a thin coating of ash, Crooked Arm found himself still awake. He could feel that strange liquid expanding in his stomach. He burped again and sat up, and his body shifted and a long fart escaped. He stood and stretched his one good arm, reaching high, high, high. A series of pops popped down his spine. Crooked Arm looked at the Sinker, asleep on her roll with her pack as a pillow. He watched a full cycling of her breath, the long inhale, the long, sweeping exhale.

Leaving camp, he edged the shale cliffs to where they jutted out farthest, then sat with his feet dangling into the sink. The roar was crushing there, scraping up the angled side of the rock and outward into the overvoid. The houses on the ridge were dark, solid shapes against the blacker darknesses of the sink. Crooked Arm wondered for how many rests in any direction he was the only awake person.

Looking up, he held out his good hand to measure the radial and angle versus absolute. It was a way he'd learned with the first two fingers and thumb. Calculating their origin line, he looked back at the sink through which they'd come: the unimaginable ever unfolding of the void, its uniform darkness, the invisible upcurrents of its friction, the roar that was not sound but the sound of falling through silence. The only place and people Crooked Arm had ever known were not anywhere in all that never-ending endlessness.

He closed his eyes and saw again the Far Machines' uncoiling wires, the vicious clamping of the Scorched Dome, the cracking of Vertex, the plume of debris when the separated halves crashed back together. He thought about his father, Fast Daggers, the destruction of the Slant, the crumbling and melting down of the rocks themselves, the bodies that must still be out there, floating limp and forgotten in the sink. Or did the Construct have a way of recycling those as well? And he thought about Deep Crystal, about the child they were trying to have, the mystery of that person who would never be, about his own life too, how sure his future had been, how it was gone now and could never be risen back to, and he felt suddenly empty and strangely free, as if he'd lost nothing at all.

Digging into the new hip bag, Crooked Arm took out the Nest. Even through the shell he could feel the vibration, but all he could see in the new mirrored surface was himself looking back, stretched and bent wide. Extending his arm, he held the Nest out over the edge. The friction curled between his fingers, scooping gently in his palm. He breathed long, then opened his hand and watched the Nest waver in the updraft, then lift, rising slowly into the overvoid. Just before it would be out of reach, Crooked Arm calmly stretched his good arm out, wrapped his fingers around it, and pulled it back in.

INFESTATION

Hiram Goegal's thigh was throbbing after all the exertion. He'd had more pain from the stitches—stretched and rubbed raw—than from the knife wound, which in the end wasn't very deep. Beside him, Dugan lay, gently stroking his hand. Hiram Goegal liked the odd counterbalance of low dull pain in his leg and tantalizing soft contact on his scar flesh. He closed his eyes to better feel Dugan's fingertips moving along the rough skin, gently plucking the tight, stringy windings and squishy pips.

"I brought you something," Dugan finally said.

Hiram Goegal felt the mattress tilting, then tilting back. He roused, catching a glimpse of a flexing butt cheek as Dugan went down on haunches to dig in his bag.

"Here," Dugan said, handing it over as he slipped back into the warmth of the bed. "Somehow got past the sorters and made it all the way down to us." It was heavy and filled Hiram Goegal's whole hand with his fingers spread wide. He turned it over, five evenly angled sides around a golden bowl, its edges lined with squared-off indentations, an odd dental regularity. In the shallow center, Hiram Goegal could see his own reflection looking dimly back. Dugan always found something thoughtful to bring back after an absorption. This was, in fact, how Hiram Goegal first came into possession of the green crystal anomaly. Dugan's crew had found it jammed in the gear. They'd tried to break it with a hammer, but it wouldn't break, or even scratch. Eventually they'd had to get a crane lift to yank it out. Together, Hiram Goegal and Dugan had discovered its power of low illumination; they realized it wasn't a piece of the rock, but a sink anomaly.

Inspired, intrigued, Hiram Goegal had begun testing it. He found the green anomaly emitted a low but inexhaustible displacement energy. With a little rigging, he had a hot plate running off it with no other power input. Not long after, he brought his ideas to the Garent, an alternative way to fuel the engines, a way to end the absorption. He'd been so focused on the idea ever since, it was hard for Hiram Goegal to remember that it hadn't always been so, that it all started this way, with a simple gift found in the low Recycle, one of a dozen or so Dugan had brought him over the rests.

Hiram Goegal tilted the pentagonal object, then drew it closer, then farther, watching his reflection flip and distort. He smiled at Dugan again and set it on the side table with an audible thunk. "Thank you," he said.

"I'm so glad it's over," Dugan said. "The absorption. I get to where I just can't stand watching all that stuff get ground up in there. All these pieces of other people's lives, most of them dead now."

Hiram Goegal had gone down to the low Recycle with Dugan once to see the big gear. He let it turn in his mind, and in the memory both things and people were being crushed by the huge interlocking teeth. "I don't end up seeing too much of it in Propulsion, thankfully," he said. A silence settled over them and extended. Hiram Goegal had a sensory flash then, of himself and Dugan as two tiny forms in a much larger bed with gaping spaces all around and a vast distance between them. He was unsure if he'd slept; his perception was a soupy wave, its troughs and crests gently revealing and submerging.

"Are you still listening?" Dugan asked, and the room rushed back, and Hiram Goegal felt his head nodding. "Absorption is complete," Dugan continued. "Has been for three rests, but the engines are still off. We're just sitting here as the Flat rushes up. Just like the rest of it, the rest of the sink." Dugan shifted in the bed, and Hiram Goegal blinked, coming more fully awake. He saw Dugan had rolled over so he could look him in the eye. Their gazes held. "All the killing, the destruction, the levels of grinding it down, all to stay here at neutral?"

"The Garent must have his reasons," Hiram Goegal intoned.

"The Garent has gone mad," Dugan sighed. The judgment hung in an awkward quiet. "That's what they're saying," he continued, "down in the Recycle. That he's given up on the Forever Rise and is chasing someone. That he's after revenge, or redemption, and will sacrifice us all to get it."

That was the last thing either of them said, though Hiram Goegal lay there quite a bit longer, considering it. When his alarm went off, he sat up, feeling still awake even though he was sure he'd slept at least a little. He was making the coffee when a courier arrived with a note from one of the Garent's top guards. Hiram Goegal read it as the brewer percolated, filling the room with the scent of crisp burn.

Dugan came out of the bedroom a few breaths later, rubbing his eyes, and poured a cup. Hiram Goegal held up the message. "They've found another of them. The same tattoo. Way down in Waste. It was reported seen by a sub-chemist on a floor visit. He remembers seeing the tattoo and which crew it was, but not which man."

Dugan looked frightened. He'd been spooked pretty bad by the whole thing. To Hiram Goegal, it was more of an itch, a mystery, the three intersecting arrows. "What are you going to do?" Dugan asked.

"Catch him. Find out why."

THE ORCHID GARDEN

The Garent began with a cup of coffee, extra dark and bitter with nothing added. He drank it alone at the kitchen block, sip by scorching sip until only a thin film of black remained at the bottom of the mug. After coffee, he lay in the steam bath longer than usual, until his follicles and even his insides were sweated out and cleansed, then into the wood room for a long sit in the dry heat. Finally, he took a walk along the high balconies to overview the Construct before breakfast.

His wife, Delora, joined him as usual at the long table. The Garent hated too much bustling about so employed only one cook and two pages and a few guards, always unseen until needed. For breakfast he had nutrient loaf again, the same distributed to the lower stacks during a food ration. When not hosting some functional dinner, the Garent ate the most bland foods and drank only water. Portion by portion, he cut sections and pressed them to the roof of his mouth and let the mushy loaf slide right down. Delora, as always, had eggs, two, cooked tenderly and set on her plate like gaping eyes. Beside them were her normal toast and short coffee. She was cutting sections of the egg white and slipping them into her mouth. She chewed almost without chewing, like all she was doing was licking the back of her teeth.

"You were talking in your sleep again," she finally said.

The Garent sipped his coffee. "I hope I didn't keep you awake."

Delora smiled and put her hand on his hand. He could feel where her fingers were warm from holding the handleless mug of her short coffee. "What was it? That you were dreaming?" she asked.

"I was dreaming of the rock we just absorbed, Vertex it was called. Gone now, of course, but . . ." The Garent looked to find her peering back intently, frozen but for the occasional eye blink. "It may be hard for you to believe, Delora, but I think I have been to this place before, the Slant. Vertex."

"But how? The Construct has been rising since—"

"Oh, before the Construct. In another life, so to speak. The Slant . . . Vertex . . . It was all much different then."

"I can imagine," she said. "Things change, places change, people too."

"Of course," he agreed. "But let's say *more* different, more different than it would be possible to imagine."

She smiled and blushed and looked at her eggs. She sliced into a big yellow iris, and the cooled yoke ran slowly.

After breakfast, the Garent went to his study alone. Below the right shelving unit there was a swing door with a few books tucked behind it, large books, square and flat. He took one out and brought it to the reading table and spread it open. Strange rectangles of sparkling darkness decorated the pages, charts and diagrams of rock formations all marked out in small pointy dots. There were images of domes like the Scorched Dome too, but unscorched, off-gray, bright and new-looking in way too much light. The Garent paused over a page, looking into the arc of one of the spherical buildings, the strange front opening, like a portion had been forgotten, a wide glass eye gleaming inside. It was then the Garent sensed something and looked up to find Delora standing over the table. "Hello, Delora," he said.

"I'm sorry," she said, tangling her fingers and pressing them into her abdomen. "I know you wanted to be alone, but I was worried about you."

"Nothing to worry about." He smiled at her.

She loosened instantly, like a tiny switch had been thrown. She stepped to stand more beside him, looking over his shoulder at the spread-open book. "I've not seen these before." Her chin flicked to the others in the open swing door. "Where were they discovered?"

"Oh, during an early absorption. Many, many rests ago." He offered her the big book.

Delora took it in her arms like a baby, flipping through the pages with her other hand. "The art!" she said. "Such detail. Such amazing visions." As she flipped to a new page, she found a slip of loose paper. An image filled one side, edge to edge. "It's you," she said. "You as a young man." The Garent picked it up. It showed a dome like the others but with two men standing in front of it, one's arm around the other. Delora was leaning close to him so she could better see the image. "The brushstrokes are so fine they are invisible."

"There is no brush," the Garent told her. "It's a re-creation . . . of a breath."

"How is that possible?"

"A way of capturing light on a page, a forgotten method of doing it. You see it here and there in old books."

Delora touched the image, then pulled her hand back. "Who is that man?" she asked. "An old friend? You both look very happy."

The Garent gazed into the two faces, his own and the other man's, both beaming widely. "This is someone from long ago. He is . . . only a memory now. . . ." His eyes went distant and detached. "All of these ways to look back, but only to look."

Delora still had the big book cupped in her arm. She closed it and put it down and laid her hand on his shoulder. "The void folds out paths impossible if not for the misfortunes that precede. New rocks form from above, and new lifelines branch and diverge and converge again."

A childlike adoration filled the Garent's eyes as he leaned back, looking up at her.

"I do believe," she continued, "despite the fact that you have grown older while we've been together, that you will be here long after me, still in the sink somewhere. I do think you will do it, expand the Construct, eliminate absorption, escape the Flat. But I do not think that is *all* you will do." She leaned down to kiss him, her eyes looking into his. "Perhaps, in many rests to come, you will be doing some other great and important thing completely unrelated to any of this."

The Garent gazed longer at her. He laughed and slipped the piece of paper back into the book. Delora was going to her garden, and he decided to tag along and lend a hand. They took the main hall to the staircase that wound down the center of the tower. The Garent stayed a few steps behind, watching her thin frame sway back and forth as she navigated the steps. When they came into the garden room, the Garent felt the almost coolness of the moistened air settle over his exposed skin. Along the far wall, the orchids were spaced evenly under an overlap of hanging lamps. Low yellow light poured down in several strata of thickness. Air roots spilled out like thick tangled hairs, almost to the floor. The garden was rather costly to maintain, the constant moisture and the lights, but it was the only luxury Delora had ever requested.

"You can help me feed my babies," she told him, handing the Garent the cup grinder.

They went to the supply table, dozens of small wood bins each covered with a separate glass lid. Delora scooped a few species of dried bug carcass into the bowl of the cup grinder. "Two turns over each," she told him.

The Garent stepped to the table. Holding the grinder above the plants, he turned the handle as he moved along. Most of the orchids were still in bud, but two had recently bloomed with their big white flowers like lungs spread open. Wide petals flat and fat, the blossoms looked like strange winged insects caught mid-flight.

Delora appeared beside him with the tweezers. In their grip, she held a wingless bee. The Garent stepped back so he could watch the delicate work. With the tweezers, Delora navigated the bee past the ripe vulva of the orchid, rubbing its writhing thorax on the pulpa way down within. Stepping slightly, she settled over the next orchid and worked the bee in. Then the next, moving down the line with the cool precision of a machine.

"I have another theory about the Great Flat," the Garent told her as she worked.

"Another theory?"

He nodded. "That the Flat is always there, waiting in the undervoid, just beyond the low darkness. That it could arrive any breath, any breath at all. But it will do so only when it is exactly right, only at the very end."

He noticed she had stopped her work, standing frozen now with the bee squirming in the tweezers. She was breathing hard. The fear dancing in her eyes was not unlike the wriggling bug. The Garent found himself close to her, her head tilted back to look up at him, the bee held out at the end of her arm. "You look younger again," she said, and she kissed him and he kissed her back. After some steam had dissipated, their lips parted but remained close, not the width of the bee between them. "I know I can never replace them, your wife and daughter. But I hope I have been something vital to you."

The Garent gripped her shoulders and looked into her eyes, and his face broke into a grin like the one they'd found in the book. It was a glimpse of an even younger Garent, younger than she had ever seen him. "You enrich my life beyond measure, Delora."

When the flowers were all fed and they were putting away the tools, a guard slipped into the garden and whispered to the Garent. He kissed Delora goodbye and returned to his study to meet two men waiting there. One was the bay supervisor and the other—if the Garent's memory served—a manager from the Recycle. They had on the table a long stretch of fabric folded into a few overlapping layers. "What have you brought me?" the Garent asked.

"Something from the Slant, my Garent. It was found in the sorting bins," the Recycle manager informed him. "A hanging of some sort, made of thread and dyed cloth."

The Garent settled above it. The Recycle manager began to gently unfold the flaps. Spread out now before them was a tapestry showing a high hillside with a blackened dome structure on top. "The Scorched Dome," the Garent said, more to himself. "Thank you, gentlemen," he added.

With nothing more, the two men left. Alone again, the Garent went to the compartment behind the swing door and took out the same book he had shown Delora. Flipping the pages, he came upon the loose image of himself and the other man and the dome high on the hill behind them. Setting it down beside the tapestry, it was clear: the contour of the hillside, the irregular octagonal base, the big glass eye, one artful in cloth and string, the other a breath of captured light. "The sink continues to astound," the Garent said to himself.

LOW WASTE

Hiram Goegal sipped his black coffee as he watched the workers coming away from their machines. He was in the floor supervisor's office, its big window looking down on the roiling vats and the tumbling swells of steam. The supervisor was talking about some fuckup a few supervisors ago. A huge rock had been absorbed, and there was so much left over from the Recycle that the vats backed up and reduction sludge spilled over and got to where it was knee-deep in the circuit room. Hiram Goegal tuned in and wondered how long the man had been going on. The coffee was good, at least. No, it was excellent. Whenever he came down to low Waste, he was sure to get a cup of this man's expert brew.

Below, the workers were lining up along the far wall. As their workspace cleared, Hiram Goegal could see the floor was a carpet of tiny, teeming insects, some of them white and mushy and soft as steamed beans, others ticking and sharp, with pointy carapaces and humming wings. Later, when the reducers fired, the bugs would be melted down with the rest of the useless slop. But they'd be back. It was as if the bugs were invulnerable to death, simply vanishing to reappear in full force later. Hiram Goegal knew this wasn't true; when the reducers were on, you could see the bugs wilting and popping. But somehow the eggs survived, or perhaps they used the heat, the next generation boiled to life inside the stomachs of the last.

It was down in Waste where the first infestation had begun: some scavenger beetles picked up during an absorption long before Hiram Goegal. They laid eggs in the reducer vats and were impossible to get rid of, or keep from spreading. More insects were picked up along the way, always managing to survive the grinders and reducers, to find some tiny corner of the Construct to thrive in, adapting, evolving, discovering new ways to live off the people living off the absorption.

There was a knock, and the story of that long-ago fuckup spun off into the din of the floor. The supervisor hurried to the door, opening it to find his foreman there. "They're ready for him," the foreman said.

The supervisor turned to Hiram Goegal. "They're ready for you."

"And none of the men have been told what this is about?"

The foreman shook his head.

Hiram Goegal thanked them, had a last sip of coffee, and followed the foreman down the iron stairs to the reduction floor. Around the vats, piles of mushy tissue had coagulated, or were maybe crusted and permanent. Bugs were everywhere, not just in the vats and on the floor. They scuttled constantly over the mucked rims, stood relaxing on chair seats, wandered in threes and fours up a wall for who knows what purpose. Hiram Goegal tried to imagine working in a place like this, bugs crawling up your legs, dead flakes of them in your hair. It was a whole other Construct within the Construct. An insect Construct, all of them with functions and responsibilities, all part of the larger system.

The foreman had the workers lined up in front of the funnels where all could have a clear view as Hiram Goegal descended the steps. Two of the Garent's guards stood to the side, coolly watching. Hiram Goegal measured the workers' reactions, waiting, holding. A thin segmented worm had appeared on his shoulder. He flicked it away and straightened his coat. "The Garent has sent me," he told them, "to have a look at your process and see if we can trim any fat. He knows you work harder here than anywhere on the Construct, and he wants you to know he appreciates your toil."

Hiram Goegal moved down the line, peering intently at each worker. Many had scars and infected blotches on their necks, their hands, their faces. Working a reduction vat was the filthiest job on the Construct, the lowest of the low Waste. Usually openings were filled by people who'd somehow survived an absorption or were brought on by a population edict. A generation or two and their families would move up into higher Waste, or the Recycle proper, or, if they showed promise, perhaps a low position in Propulsion, or a more steady climb in some alloy shop in Piping.

Hiram Goegal reached the end of the line. He was close to the foreman now. This was the signal to the guards to be ready. He noticed their hands moving to the electric bolt guns on their belts.

"All right," the foreman said. "We need you all to roll up your sleeves." The workers looked back at him, confused. There were a few nervous laughs. Some complied automatically, their faces slack and soupy. "It's not a metaphor," the foreman declared, which got some more chuckles. More had begun rolling up their sleeves, amused but complying. Others wore short sleeves and only looked around, sharing dumb smiles. All except for one, who stood still, nervously dancing his eyes from Hiram Goegal to the guards. Then the man was moving, ducking behind the lined-up workers and making for the door.

"There!" Hiram Goegal shouted.

One of the guards leveled his bolt gun and fired off a shot that hit the wrong man. The workers yelped and scattered as the worker flopped to the floor, his skin coursing with crackles of static charge. Hiram Goegal saw the fleeing man slip through a door. He ran after, the two guards on his heels. In the connecting hall, he caught a glimpse of the far door slamming shut. "He's making for the edge!"

They ran through the door and came out onto the scaffolding of a new stack being built. They were out to the left and above the Maw. If the fleeing man made it across the scaffolding, then a thin crust of edge, he'd be out into the sink and then who knows. . . .

"Come on," Hiram Goegal said to the guards, leading them up the scaffolding. One didn't listen, charging off across the irregular beams instead. Hiram Goegal reached the next level and helped the other guard up. From there, they could see the fleeing man leap from the last beam and land on the far-edge rock. The guard chasing him had fallen. From his stomach, he let loose a bolt that sailed wide, vanishing harmlessly into the sink. The fleeing man was running again, barreling for the void.

"You have a shot?" Hiram Goegal asked.

The guard was breathing flat and even. He'd already gone still and leveled his gun. He tracked the man a breath longer, then calmly squeezed the trigger. The bolt leapt with a hushing pock. Hiram Goegal lost sight of it in the haze of construction. But he saw the fleeing man, only a few steps from the edge, suddenly yank his shoulders back, his arms flipping forward as he pitched face down, electric current snaking over his body.

When they made it down and across the scaffolding to the edge, the other guard had the man in ties, hands behind his back, ankles locked together. Hiram Goegal moved closer. Whether from the cramping or the electricity, the man had gotten sick before passing out. Vomit was splattered all over his face and the ground, but he was breathing and would recover fine. Thankfully, Hiram Goegal didn't have to touch the man to see it, that same tattoo on his arm, three arrows intersecting at the center. He considered it and turned to the guard. "Go and tell them to prepare the wasps."

THE EXILE

Motes formed in the endless darkness below, turning lazily in the updraft, dozens, then hundreds. The Sinker pinched one between her fingers and saw it was a tiny curling feather. All around them now the puffs tumbled and spun and sucked away. Below, a small rock came slowly from the darkness. Details solidified: a few wide fields penned in by a complex of low buildings and barns. Several single-level houses and a high barbwire fence completed the loop. Past the perimeter, a thin, rocky outcrop, and then the edge.

Banking, the Sinker guided them toward the center of the widest field, then angled hard up at the end and swooped and landed as if she'd already been standing there waiting for herself to arrive. Crooked Arm failed to account for the shift in the scooping friction. He landed heel-heavy and still moving too fast, but he wheeled that one good arm and, after a few stumbling steps, managed to stay on his feet. He smiled at the Sinker over his shoulder. "Nice," she said flatly. She looked around at the tiny rock. More feathers floated about, rising into a loose tendril in the overvoid.

"See," Crooked Arm said. "Right where I said it would be."

"You didn't say it would be anywhere. You picked it out of the map and didn't seem so sure."

Crooked Arm nodded absently. "It's good," he said, "not to have to shout every word." He focused on the houses set into the line of fencing.

The Sinker took a few steps, unlimbering. "What's that stink?" But then she could see the ground was coated in a foul mud, a mixture of dirt and bird shit and more tiny feathers. "Gross." She took out her map, plumed it to life, and traced the line from Stayover.

"Something wrong?" Crooked Arm asked.

She eyed the layout a breath more, then thumbed it away. "Not exactly where it's supposed to be, but not so far off either. Maybe some old charting."

A horn pealed and a long barn door fronting the fields opened and a wave of gobbling turkeys dumped out, a thick crowd spreading unevenly around the yard. There didn't seem to be any end to the birds, wave after wave, chests out, snoods high and dangling, wide eyes mad with confused intent. Through the high raucous cacophony of turkey gobble, the Sinker heard someone shouting. A man was wading through the birds. He was wide and heavily bearded and wore muck boots up to his knees. His big square thighs knocked turkeys out of the way as he walked, a pre-wake of flapping wings. "Crooked Arm!" he was shouting.

"That is my brother, Mighty," Crooked Arm told the Sinker.

As the big man neared, Crooked Arm extended his good hand, but Mighty swept by it and snatched him in an all-consuming hug. The embrace lengthened until Crooked Arm was gasping for air. They separated, a beefy hand gripping Crooked Arm's shoulder. Mighty's beard was as black as the void and held his gleaming teeth like distant rocks half a rest away. "How are Father and the rest of them?" Mighty asked. "How is the Slant?"

▼

"Did Crooked Arm tell you about the tournament?" Mighty's eyes hung, wet and misaligned. His cheeks were soupy peekings in the beard holes. His wide, crinkled forehead glistened with sweat.

"He hasn't told me much of anything," the Sinker said.

Mighty cocked a grin at his brother and had a big sip. It was something made from seed extract and bone collagen. They were in the big dining room where the slaughterhouse workers ate, but the workers were all back in the dorms, sleeping. Crooked Arm and Mighty and the Sinker sat around the end of a long table, each with a cup of the seed moonshine, picked-over plates of food pushed off to the side.

"When our grandfather died," Mighty began, "our old man was First Sword, known then as Bloody Hatchet. At the start of each Sharpening, he would scrape the hatchet along his chest, bringing out a thin line of blood and a manic terror in his opponents. He didn't ever wash the blood off either. Layers of it were crusted on there from all his previous fights." Mighty slapped the table, laughing. "Bloody Hatchet was never defeated, and so, when Grandfather died, and Bloody Hatchet became the lord, a tournament was arranged to select the new First Sword." Mighty poked a big finger at Crooked Arm. "We were two of the top young warriors on Vertex. What, about six thousand rests apiece?"

"I was just over seven thousand." Crooked Arm indicated his brother's big frame, almost as wide as the end of the table. "Mighty was not yet the full monstrosity he would become, but still was larger than most grown men on the Slant."

Mighty was nodding along, pouring more into their cups. The Sinker sipped hers and leaned back and put her feet on the table. She slung her arm up on top of her head, leaning even farther back.

"I wasn't Mighty then, not yet." He nodded to the Sinker. "On the Slant, your name is what you are." He gestured to his brother. "Born with a dead arm, twisted crooked at the joint, so . . . Crooked Arm." He slapped his wide chest. "Child Beef!" He burst out laughing. "My name was Child Beef. To choose your own name, you must win a tournament. Then you can be called whatever you like."

"Ah yes, the tournament," the Sinker said.

Mighty nodded some more, remembering. He pointed. "Crooked Arm was older and the better fighter, in a pure sense. That fucking long arm and that long sword."

Crooked Arm held out an empty hand. "Mighty fought with no weapon."

"I'd grab these pipsqueaks and twist them. I got my licks, but once I had a hold of them . . ." He laughed again and guzzled some seed extract. There was no flesh color left to Mighty's face; it was either the darks of his beard or a full red blush from the drink.

Crooked Arm was picking at something congealed on one of the plates. He peeled it free and popped it into his mouth, talking as he chewed. "My father was furious when I told him I wanted to enter the tournament. But he acquiesced because of his belief that all people—even a lord-to-be—needed to steer their own fate."

"And what if both of us were killed? Who would be next in line to be the lord?" Mighty seemed like he really wanted to know. He paused to think. "Child Beef," he said again, and laughed.

Crooked Arm and the Sinker laughed too.

"Most people considered my entry a death wish," Crooked Arm added. "How was a one-armed boy going to survive?"

"In the first round, Crooked Arm beat a much older warrior from Greventon, the fourth rock down. This guy was bigger and salted by loop travel way outwide of the Slant, steel-gray-eyed and unflappable. They parried and advanced, fell back and lunged and feinted, a great display! Slowly, Crooked Arm got beaten back, back against the wall. He was done for. But then he lunged with that long arm and his long sword." Mighty drew a finger across his throat.

"You two met in the final?" the Sinker asked.

Mighty nodded. "Crooked Arm used his long arm and long sword to hold me at a distance. He was better, fast, agile. He was trying to wear me out."

"But?"

Mighty looked to Crooked Arm, who sipped his drink and swallowed. "I was already worn-out when we started," Crooked Arm said. "I'd had several drawn-out duels, while Mighty's were a series of breezy crushings. A thrust got sloppy. Mighty grabbed hold of my back wrist and twisted. The bone inside snapped like dried-out scavenge."

The Sinker winced.

Mighty's beard looked like two big worms had wiggled to the top, working together to make a smile. "But it was the bad arm! It didn't mean a damned thing to him. I knew the mistake I'd made. I could see that long sword held up above me. He had me."

"What happened?" the Sinker asked.

"He ducked," Crooked Arm said. "And the broad side of the sword clanked off the top of his head. It would have cracked the skull of any other warrior on the Slant."

"Or in the sink."

"Mighty had my hand again, but the good one. He yanked down on it and kicked me in the chest. I was suddenly on my back, sucking breath. My vision cleared and there he was, lowering one of those huge meaty fists. I woke up a rest later, and Child Beef was Mighty, First Sword of the Slant."

The Sinker considered it. "You never ended up winning a tournament of your own?"

"It was the only one I ever entered," Crooked Arm answered. "I was in line to be the lord." He shrugged, shook his head. "If I had won that tournament, I'd be dead now. How many Sharpenings before some named warrior figured out a way to beat a one-armed swordsman? So Crooked Arm it is." With his good arm he held up his bad so they could all see the scar where Mighty had snapped it in that tournament so long ago.

Mighty jumped in to play along, pulling down his shirt to show a rude curling of healed flesh. "My seventh Sharpening, what was his name?"

"Lance."

Mighty barked laughter. "How could I forget? As soon as the hand dropped, he threw the thing right into my shoulder. But then he didn't have a weapon and . . ." Mighty shrugged, releasing the scar to the underdarkness of his shirt. "All the events of my life were set in motion by my grandfather's death. He was the one who suggested I fight with no weapon. Came up with the name even, Mighty, though he never got to see me earn it. When he died, I was suddenly First Sword and thought I would be forever. But High Hammer beat me. Knocked me out cold. The bastard only let me live because I was the son of the lord." Mighty shook his head. Clearly some part of him wished he'd died in that sunken fight pit in the palace courtyard on Vertex. "I couldn't stay after that, so here I am, way out on this farm." Mighty guzzled some more seed extract. His mouth was a bottomless hole in the beard where he poured the stuff. His gaze landed on the Sinker as if by accident. "What about you?" he asked. "I bet you've got your scars."

The Sinker had a long sip. She stood and showed them a spot of tangled skin on the side of her stomach, then, turning, showed a similar scar on her lower back. She remained on her feet, leaning back on the table. "I was on Brackenrock," she said. "I'd only stopped for supplies. I was headed for an ore market, still a dozen rests away. Out in the Zs. You know the Zs?"

Neither of them did.

"I'd had a little to drink. I didn't even see him coming." She pointed to that place on her stomach. "Went in the front and out the back."

"Then what?"

"I slashed open his throat and that was it for him." The Sinker shook her head. "I had to keep that fucking sword in me a whole rest, waiting for the doctor to sober up."

They broke into laughter again. They refilled their cups from the big pitcher. Mighty put his feet out on the chair opposite and rested his cup on the mound of his belly. "What became of High Hammer?" he asked.

"He didn't last that long," Crooked Arm answered. "His third Sharpening, he lost to Stone Mace. Stone Mace only lasted one. Then it was Fast Daggers. She held it until the very end."

"Fast Daggers?"

"From Widescape, fierce and small and as fast as shifting air. She was Wild Breeze before she won her name." Crooked Arm laughed, but the laugh turned cold. Each took a long sip, a few contemplative breaths.

"Hard to believe it's gone," Mighty said. He looked at them, glassy-eyed and drunk. When Crooked Arm had first told him the news, the brothers had gripped each other and cried it out. Then they'd started drinking, more and more until they'd almost forgotten and the old stories came out. Now the darkness was circling back around.

"It was a hard thing to see," Crooked Arm said.

Mighty nodded. "I wish I had been there, but . . . it doesn't sound like it would have made a difference."

Crooked Arm nodded, pouring the rest of his drink back in one long gulp. He looked into the empty cup and put it down. "With his last breath, Father told me to find the Immortal First Sword, to bring the Nest to him."

Mighty looked directly at him, seeming suddenly sober and sad. "Father died still believing in superstition, Crooked Arm. That doesn't mean you have to."

"The Nest may not be what those poems and legends suggest, but it's more than nothing. Why would they come for it otherwise?"

"Why does anyone do anything?"

"Grandfather believed. When he returned from that journey, his research into the legends, the Immortal First Sword, he was never the same but never said why. He found something, didn't he? Something he did not tell the rest of us."

Mighty made a noise, part sigh, part burp. "You will be disappointed."

"What did he say?"

Mighty looked at the Sinker.

"You can tell her," Crooked Arm said. "What does it matter anymore?"

"It doesn't matter. It never did."

"What was it, then?"

"He didn't tell me then, when he got back from that trip, but you're right. There was something different. Like he still believed but didn't want to. It was only much later, when he was sick and dying . . ." Mighty leveled his gaze on Crooked Arm. "He told me he'd discovered where the Immortal First Sword was from."

Crooked Arm sat up more straight, like his head had been pulled by a string. "Where?"

Mighty eyed him a breath before continuing, "It was not some distant place in the sink but a little farming rock, a hundred rests away." Mighty shrugged. "That's what changed Grandfather. He found out our founder wasn't some immortal warrior but just a person, like you or me or anyone else. The Nest is not some cryptic weapon from a far distant battle. The Slant was not arranged by some power it has. It's just an anomaly, one of who knows how many, a simple trick of sound and nothing more."

"Did he say what the name of the place was?"

Mighty smiled, looking more drunk again. "Hidden Rock," he said, and laughed.

Crooked Arm looked to the Sinker.

"Never heard of it," she said.

"Had Grandfather been there, to this place . . . Hidden Rock?"

"He said he had, but who knows. He was sick then."

"Did he say which direction it was?"

Mighty let a long breath out. His cup was empty. He set it down without refilling. The beard made a motion like someone pulling up loose pants. "He said Hidden Rock couldn't be found. That it was invisible."

"Invisible?"

"An invisible rock. Hidden. A rock that was there but not there. There but could not be seen. Could not be found." Mighty laughed. He shook his head. "It was babble, Crooked Arm, just like the rest of it. A metaphor, a story. Or the ravings of an old man, scared of death."

THE MILKER AND THE VENOMIST

The room was dim but for a few milky pools of light. Illuminated in the center was a man strapped to a metal gurney. Three others moved about, Hiram Goegal and two men in lab coats: the Milker and the Venomist. There was a faint chemical reek to the place and a low intermittent buzzing from several flies caught inside the lamp casings. Coming to the gurney, Hiram Goegal settled and gazed down at the man they'd captured. He was lolling under the straps, biting on his own lip, a pearling of blood at his denting teeth. His eyes were squeezed tight; tears pooled and spilled from the contracting skin. His tattoo, the three intersecting arrows, was obscured in the sweat coating his arm like a sloppy gloss finish. His whole body was wet with it, in beads and streaks and pools.

"You were not born on the Construct," Hiram Goegal told him. "How did you arrive here?"

Shivering, the man swallowed. His lips parted, tearing a film of frothy drool. His voice was even and far off. "You arrived at us," he said.

"Well, then, when did we arrive at you?"

The man turned his head in the gurney, his eyes strangely focused now on Hiram Goegal. "You killed them, didn't you?"

"Who?"

"Looris... and Fred."

"You mean the ones with the tattoo like yours?"

"They were just dumb kids."

"Those dumb kids tried to assassinate me." Hiram Goegal pointed at the tattoo. "Tell me what this marking means."

The man's eyes leapt and tumbled. "It... it... it is a family emblem... my whole family. John Arrowcross is my name. A family emblem." He started laughing. He couldn't hold it in. Tears were streaming from his eyes, laughing and crying at once.

Hiram Goegal nodded to the Venomist. The tiny man turned back into his case. He took out a new bag and hung it from the metal caster hook. With half scissors he spliced the line and ran the new bag in. They watched the man swim into the effect, the bull's-eyes of his pupils making big loops. His muscles tightened and loosened in waves.

"That is the latest venom going into your blood," Hiram Goegal told him. "This one comes from the Giant Grudle Wasp." He nodded to the Milker, who was taller than the Venomist, but also rail thin. Behind him, his workspace was lit up so it could be seen clearly from the gurney; it was good to have a visual, it had been found. Above the workspace, the wasps were pinned up, their pulsing thoraxes tapped, mandibles quivering. Over generations, the Milkers and Venomists had bred the wasps larger and larger until they were as big as a shoe, with proportionally enlarged venom sacs.

"You can probably feel it cold in your veins," Hiram Goegal told the man. "There's a dial for it, one way less, one way more."

At the mention of more, the Venomist, for a demonstration, turned the lever even farther. Fluid gushed into the tubing. The man's eyes rolled. Legs stretched long, then twitched with cramping. He made soft "hoo hoo hoo" sounds, then went slack but for his head, which hovered an inch above the gurney.

"Where are you now?" Hiram Goegal asked.

The man's voice was far-off and raspy. "In the fields . . . back at Flux."

"Flux was absorbed more than a hundred rests ago. You and the others, you planned this for that long?"

". . . For longer."

Hiram Goegal considered the answer. He looked to the Venomist, but the man only shrugged. "How many of you were there on Flux, with the tattoo?" Hiram Goegal asked.

". . . Five."

"And how many survived the staging and absorption?"

". . . Three. Only three of us."

"And you planned this, all three of you, for a hundred rests? For revenge for Flux?"

The man shook his head, languidly, back and forth. "We didn't give a shit about Flux. Just making sure . . . sure you would keep on going. Rising, until you'd gone too far. Then we were going to slip off, sink back, get reassigned." The man was talking fast now, as if when he got it all out, it would be over. "We'd never heard of it," he said, "of the Construct. We thought you'd rise on past. But then you slowed, started going outwide. We couldn't kill the Garent, couldn't get to him. But we thought if you were dead, the Garent would give up on it and start to rise again."

Hiram Goegal's hands had entwined behind his back. He moved his thumb over the gouges and creases and crags of his scar. He caught eyes with the Venomist's obscured face through the hanging bags. Stepping alongside the gurney, Hiram Goegal came to the man's feet. "You were *assigned*?" he asked. "To be at Flux? Doing what?"

Another slow nodding. "Flux was the only rock for fifteen rests in any direction. A linking point between three sectors. We were there in case any information turned up about it. We'd erase it or trash it or alter it. We'd discourage anyone from heading that way. We were clerks. We were just . . . watching mostly. . . ."

"Where are you trying to keep people from going?"

The man was breathing deeper. His lips parted so he could lick them, leaving a film on his tongue. He tried to swallow, but his mouth was too dry. He choked, then coughed, then coughed some more. "I won't tell you," he finally said.

Hiram Goegal nodded to the Venomist. With obvious relish, he turned the dial more. The man's eyes fell open wide. His skin went flush, then pale. A long smile wormed across his sweat-slicked face. Hiram Goegal spoke slowly, so as to reach him in whatever fog he was in. "Where are you trying to keep people from going?"

"... To ... Hidden Rock," he finally said.

Hiram Goegal smirked at it. "Hidden Rock? That's its name?"

The man laughed, ghosted and thin. "There, but not there."

"'There, but not there,'" Hiram Goegal repeated, more to himself. "What are you so worried about people finding? What's on Hidden Rock?"

Now the man smiled, as if he'd given up and decided to enjoy the venom. "It is a hole ... a hole in the void."

Hiram Goegal looked at the Venomist. "He has to be telling the truth," the Venomist said. "He has to be!"

Hiram Goegal realized he was leaning in over the gurney. He stood more straight. With a touch of effort, he set a curt grin on his face. "Where is it?" he asked. "Hidden Rock, this hole in the void?"

The man swallowed. He shook his head. He melted away, then flooded back, his eyes wide and searching. "Three ... ," he mumbled, "at twenty-three ... one ... ." But the words sank away, and he lolled and smiled and bubbles of saliva popped along the crease of his mouth.

"You can hear me still?" Hiram Goegal asked.

The man nodded. His face settled into a resting contentment. Urine spread across his pants and pooled along the sides of the gurney. His smile widened even wider, and a line of dark fluid ran from his ear.

"Too much!" the Milker hissed, stepping out of the shadows to loom above the gurney. The Venomist was turning levers back, but it was too late. The man's eyes went soft, then liquefied, filling his sockets to the brim. His breath slowed, calming, extending longer and longer, and then he was still. The Venomist looked bashfully at his mistake, not able to meet the Milker's eyes.

TWO AGAINST THE VOID

There wasn't anyplace for them to bunk down except in a loft above one of the turkey barns. The ground was no good for an open camp anywhere because it was all shit and feather goo. So they climbed up the barn side and into the long, low loft, cluttered with crates and empty seed bags stuffed full of other empty bags. They rolled out their bedrolls and lay down. The Sinker felt the loft floor turning under her, like she was on a spinning plate in the dark void, when really it was her eyes closed and drunk.

"Tell me what you think," she heard Crooked Arm say.

"Think about what?"

"Were you listening?"

"You were talking?"

"While we were drinking."

"But not just now?"

Crooked Arm laughed. "Hidden Rock."

The Sinker laughed too. "All places have a name," she said. She swallowed and burped. "I don't need to eat for ten rests."

"So you think it's not really hidden? That it's only a name?"

"Or it's not there at all," she said. A louder squawking erupted below them, then settled. "Maybe they named something they can't find Hidden Rock. No one knows where it is or has been there, because it's not. Not there." The Sinker rolled over. She could see his profile now as he looked up into the barn roof. She yawned and closed her eyes. She could feel the pulling of it, the sink she would slip into past the waking edge.

"How would you hide a rock?" he asked. "Maybe it's only hidden in the sense its location is kept secret. So it would be there if we only knew where."

"Maybe." The Sinker came back into a little pool of clarity. She realized her eyes were open. She rolled over a quarter turn, looking up at the pitched ceiling. The spinning had slowed to a tiny ticking rotation. "There's a mapping archive," she said. "Most thorough in the sink. But it's not close."

"How far?"

"Fifty rests, give or take."

Crooked Arm whistled, a far trailing note. Some turkeys below cackled and wings fluttered, and Crooked Arm and the Sinker both laughed. "You mean far far," he said.

"Yes, far. Very far."

"Fifty rests," he repeated.

Silence filled the loft. "Did you consider taking it from me?" he asked suddenly. "The Nest. Giving it to them so they would stop?"

"Yes."

Crooked Arm remained still, the Sinker too. "Why didn't you?"

"Maybe I will."

He laughed.

"The Construct won't stop because they get something they need or want. They'll only find some other way to justify needing more, wanting more, some other way to justify taking it." She burped. It was the first in a series. When they'd passed she said, "For so long, I'd let it all go. Long blocks of rests without it crossing my mind, the Construct, what had happened there, what it could become if it kept expanding."

In her mind's eye she traced the line they had made together, her and Crooked Arm, from the Slant to that bubbling ore rock, outwide and down to Stayover, then almost straight sink to the turkey farm. Then farther back, to her line before that: Fairviel, Roseblood, that long haul through the Degloss, Frozen Rock, Big Iron . . . For a breath, the blanket of cornstalks wavered and moved through her mind, shifting in unison with the flow of the friction, in tune with the curling upwinds of the sink. She saw again the corn farmer's limp body, pulled into Big Iron by the magnetic cuff. She couldn't remember his name anymore, or the names of so many. And still . . . all of everything she'd traveled through was only a tiny squiggle in the greater scope of the sink, a point, if the map was zoomed out far enough. With all that endless void for her and the Construct to be separate and far away, somehow their fates had tangled again. Perhaps because they were not actually two fates, but one. One line through the void.

"I'll take you to the archive," she said.

"You will?"

"We can trade data from my map for information. If anyone knows about Hidden Rock, it will be them."

"So we are in this together now."

The Sinker didn't respond.

"You have a plan?" he asked. "For when they do catch up to us? It's going to take more than charging at them through the void, no matter how strong your hands are."

"I guess I'm going to have to know it when I see it." A few breaths cycled through. The turkeys were as silent as a barn full of turkeys could be. Past the walls, the Sinker could hear the friction rushing by.

"You've never told me your name," he said.

But she had settled into stillness, and no answer came.

THE THINGS FROM BEFORE

A page led Hiram Goegal through the sloping portico of the Garent's tower, the wide front entrance like a book flopped open face down. He was in his finest suit, dark shoes and a dark undershirt to match. Tucked into his side, he carried that heavy pentagonal object Dugan had brought home from the Recycle. As Hiram Goegal followed the page along a curling corridor, what Dugan said about the Garent rattled through his mind. Others were no doubt reaching similar versions of the same opinion; how could they not be? After the long lateral movement to arrive at the Slant, the engines were turned off and still remained dark. The absorption was completed more than a dozen rests ago. No one, from the barons down, could remember the Construct stopping its rise for so long. How much closer to the Flat were they getting just waiting there? How much of the hard-earned distance between it and them had already been given back?

Perhaps it will all be over soon, Hiram Goegal thought with grim relief, though not with the outcome he'd wanted. The Garent had called him in, and not to some public function room, but to his private study. He wanted an update on the search for the anomaly, the Nest, as the people of the Slant called it. Unfortunately, Hiram Goegal didn't have any progress to report. No matter how politically he put the matter, they still did not have the Nest; the signal they'd been tracking had gone dim and was hard to pinpoint with accuracy. They still knew the general direction it was headed, and some speculation about where they could be going, but that was it.

The page was trudging up the central stairs now, Hiram Goegal clomping behind him. They went up who knows how many steps, then down a short hall to the double wood doors of the study. Hiram Goegal expected to be shown in and told to wait, but when the page swung the tall doors open, the Garent and his wife were already by the fire. Hiram Goegal had been in the boardroom the Garent used for meetings with the barons, and a few other public spaces in the lower levels, but never in one of the Garent's private rooms. All of it was lined with wood panels that shone dark and reddish from the firelight. To the side, Hiram Goegal could see the Garent's famous collection, laid out expertly in a full wall of ornate shelving.

Hiram Goegal's sweat had already broken from the ascent. Now he was wet all over inside his clothes. He felt his breath slow, his lungs working hard to suck in the hotter air. As gracefully as he could, he moved toward them, clasping the Garent's offered hand.

"Hiram," the Garent said. "You have not met my wife, Delora?"

"Madam," Hiram Goegal said, taking her hand in a more gentle shake. She looked oddly at him as their fingers came apart, a reaction to the rough flesh that Hiram Goegal had become accustomed to.

"My husband has told me much about your work," she said.

"All good," the Garent reassured.

A door opened, and another page approached. He handed Hiram Goegal a tincture, a single sip in a tall glass vial. Hiram Goegal put it to his lips and drank it back—a harsh cinnamon in his nose, then on his tongue. His eyes watered, but he blinked and they cleared. "Very good," he said, smiling at the Garent and Delora, then giving the vial back to the page.

"That hand," Delora said, "did you injure it in the lab?"

Hiram Goegal held it up between them, as if refreshing his memory. "I was a boy. I had misbehaved, and as a punishment, my father threw a favorite toy into our stove. Without much thought, I'm afraid, I reached in to retrieve it." Hiram Goegal turned the hand so they could see the melted flesh on both sides. "The shape of the toy was gone as soon as I touched it. I was holding not the toy but molten plastic."

"Quite a philosophical story," Delora said. "Tell me something else you remember about it, burning your hand."

Hiram Goegal could feel the intensity of her gaze now. It had built and built as her eyes held on him, combining with the fire, increasing his sweat. "I remember my father's bald spot," he said. "He'd put me in a chair and knelt down, removing the plastic from the burn. This kind of tenderness was . . . unfamiliar. He was such a hard and quiet and unforgiving man in all things. A true product of Piping."

The Garent looked at Delora, and they both smiled. "And you live there still," she said. "You've not requested something on Core Rock?"

"Piping is my home. I suppose it always will be."

"That's very noble of you," Delora said. "And how is your leg?"

Hiram Goegal leaned on it, testing it out for them to see. "A touch sore is all."

"Who were they?" She was genuinely curious: foreigners in the Construct attempting assassination. Hiram Goegal could see the thrill of fear it gave her.

"They came on at Flux," he said. "Slipped the absorption and took up in the lower stacks. They'd been in one of the deep reducers and blending in fine. It seems the plot was an effort to protect a rock in this sector. Luckily for me, they were not very competent assassins."

Delora laughed nervously, looking relieved.

"What was it?" the Garent asked.

"What was what, my Garent?"

"The toy. That you tried to retrieve from the fire."

Hiram Goegal looked at his hand, turning it over to see the rude misshapings of his palm. He tucked it into his pocket. "I don't remember," he said. "When I think of it, all I can see is liquid."

Delora shifted her weight more into her heels. Without looking his way, she put a hand on the Garent's shoulder, then removed it and entwined it with her other. The Garent nodded to the pentagonal object. "You have brought something."

"For you," Hiram Goegal said, offering it over. "It was found in the Recycle."

The Garent took it into his hands. "It's heavier than it should be."

Delora looked on. Her smile had gone vacant. "It's lovely," she intoned.

The Garent turned the object over. He ran a finger along the fine detailing, looking into his dim bronze reflection in the shallow bowl. He watched his upside-down face blur and flip as he brought the object closer. He touched a fingertip lightly to one of the dark splotches on his forehead.

"It was discovered on the third rock down," Hiram Goegal told him. "Neither its style nor ore content matches anything else we found on the Slant. The craftsmanship is too precise to be handmade, and the type of machining capable of producing it would require a rock much larger than the echo has found anywhere in this sector."

"What do you think it was used for?"

"Perhaps it was one of many like it," Hiram Goegal surmised. "A part that formed a larger object or mosaic. Something curving or maybe a large sphere."

The Garent turned it over again, feeling the angled pentagonal sides and how it could all fit together. He tilted it so Delora could see her face, distorted in the reflection. "Oh," she laughed, touching her cheek, then her chin.

The Garent smiled at Hiram Goegal and clapped him on the shoulder. "Thank you, Hiram. Good. Good," he said. He hefted the pentagonal object again to feel its dense weight. His eyes turned inward, down some labyrinthine contemplation; then, as if stepping from a fog, he moved to the grid of wood shelving along the wall. The Garent scanned the layout and found a place and set the heavy object down without the faintest sound. He stepped back and went still, his eyes moving slowly over the array.

"I don't think it's quite right," Delora said.

The Garent was nodding as he went back to the shelf. He moved the object to a different spot and stepped back. Now he was pleased, and Delora seemed so too. The fire crackled, and the light shifted and shifted again, overlapping shadows leaning and swaying across the collection. It was Delora who broke the spell, turning and extending a hand to Hiram Goegal. It struck him then how upright she stood. She looked nearly as old as the Garent but was perfectly postured and alive with a simmering thinness. Her grip was firm too. "Good to meet you, finally, Hiram Goegal."

"And you as well."

She nodded and smiled and said, "I will leave you two to business." The Garent took Delora's arm to walk her to the door. Hiram Goegal watched them go, then turned to look over the collection. He could imagine uses for several of the objects; others were less obvious and some too strange to possibly understand. His eyes focused on one, a twist of chrome tubing around a thick iron beam, the chrome so stark and bright it seemed to glow with reflected light. Beside it was a plastic man in a green uniform, no bigger than a coffee cup. Then a device made from a dozen interconnected cranks with a protruding handle on top.

The Garent was suddenly at his side. "How far some of this must have come over the countless rests," he said. "I wonder, from where did each begin. Where was it first assembled or molded or who knows how half this stuff was made?" The Garent chuckled. He shook his head. He smiled at Hiram Goegal. "It reminds me, the collection does, about how much sink is out there, how far it goes. We have our own great distances to travel, Hiram, if we are to stay ahead of the Flat."

"Yes, it is true, my Garent."

The Garent nodded again. He glanced at the door where his wife had exited, then held a hand out to the roaring fire. They left the collection and waded back into the thicker pool of heat. There were two chairs there, with high backs and a low table between. Looking into the flames, Hiram Goegal could see a few long boxbugs tittering in the back of the fireplace. A hissing from the combustion sticks hissed higher, reminding him of the underhum of Engine Three. A high pop startled him, and the hissing noise was gone.

"We got rid of most of them in here," the Garent said, gesturing at the boxbugs with a fire poker. "But there's no holding them back, not completely. Those creatures thrive in heat that would roast most living things alive."

"They always find a way," Hiram Goegal replied dutifully.

"Resistant to the poisons too, those tricky bastards." The Garent pointed the poker at one of the high-backed chairs. Hiram Goegal sat, watching the Garent load even more combustion sticks into the fire. A page came in with two plates of finger foods and new drinks and set it all on the table. The Garent was arming the bellows now. With each puff, the flames grew and the heat poured over them. Hiram Goegal could feel the air singeing his nose hairs. The boxbugs were indistinguishable now from the ashy black flecks of wood tossed by the rising inferno.

Satisfied with the blaze, the Garent lowered himself into the other chair. His eyes glowed with the lappings of the fire. "A strange thing," he said, "these people from Flux. You had a chance to question the one they found."

Hiram Goegal nodded. "They had done some sniffing and come to the conclusion that if I were gone, the Construct would go back to the rise. Their rock would be safe."

The Garent laughed, short and loud. "They were probably right, Hiram. How could I have undertaken all of this without you?" The Garent thought longer. "What was the name of this rock they were trying to protect?"

Hiram Goegal's mouth tilted into a curl. "The man I questioned called it Hidden Rock."

The Garent laughed again.

Hiram Goegal lifted his new drink and sipped it. This one was bitter, like old medicine with a whiff of strange rot. He pushed back a deliberate swallow and set the drink down. "They've been at it awhile," he said, "from what I could gather, trying to keep this place a secret. He said they had people stationed at access points and intersections all around the sector."

The Garent hummed with curiosity. "Were you able to get him to divulge what they are hiding on this place called Hidden Rock?"

Hiram Goegal had a breath half out. He finished it, then took a slow, even inhale. "The man described it as . . . 'a hole in the void.' Some kind of destructive anomaly, if my guess is correct. It's impossible for them to lie on the venom, but the truth they tell is often clouded and a little cryptic from the side effects."

"Side effects, yes," the Garent repeated distantly. "And you were able to locate it, Hidden Rock, using the echo scan?"

Hiram Goegal smiled, pleased that the Garent considered him so thorough. "Yes, I had a look. I did find a small displacement that could be something, in the general area of Flux. A place where, indeed, there is no rock in any of our maps. But the displacement is minor, and pretty far low outwide of our current position. Their Hidden Rock is safe after all."

The Garent nodded some more, nods that got smaller and smaller until his head was still again. "Hidden Rock," he said. "A hole in the void," he laughed, forced and breathy, tired. "All places have a story, no?" The Garent lifted his drink and pointed to some papers stacked on the table. "Like this Kingdom of the Scorched Dome," he said. "You have familiarized yourself with the local lore of the Slant?"

Hiram Goegal nodded. "I've read the summaries Culture put out."

"The anomaly—the Nest as they call it—a great weapon? Powerful enough to move rocks around in the sink, to arrange the perfect alignment of the Slant. And these decoys they'd constructed. Two decoys. A fake decoy and a real decoy, so to say. Quite brilliant, don't you think?"

"People make up stories, add customs, traditions, to give things some explanation, to put some structure around their lives, to make it all make sense, to make it grand."

"Yes, grand indeed," the Garent said. "To move rocks around in the sink, isn't that what we hope to do with it?"

Hiram Goegal nodded. "Yes, in a way."

"In our own way," the Garent said. "You have your math, your science. But for most of the people of the Construct that is no different than a strange legend from some absorbed rock. They must simply believe. I'm not sure if we told them that they would. But I know they believe in me . . . for now."

The Garent pressed down on the arms of his chair to resettle his body. His chin had come down a bit, so he could look at the fire through the haze of his brow. "Things have a way of converging in the sink," he said. "Symmetries revealed, strange connections, legends proving to be cryptically true. How it has unfolded this way, I do not know . . ." The Garent trailed off. He absently scratched at one of the sores high on his pate. He looked at his fingers, annoyed to see a thin arc of crusted blood under the nails.

"I don't think I understand, my Garent."

The Garent wiped his hand on his pants and laughed and smiled. "I sure do love those reports," he said. "It'd be such a monotonous slog without Culture." The Garent sipped his drink, gazing into the fire. "We set out on this together, Hiram. To find a way to end the absorption. Are you uneasy, worried that we may fail?"

"Things have become more complicated," Hiram Goegal said. "The signal the Nest gives off has somehow been dampened. It's more of a pulse now and hard to follow. We know the general direction.

Communicating this to the Far Machines with the relay, however, has been a challenge."

"What would you suggest we do?" the Garent asked.

"The last strong signal had them almost straight down, fifteen-ish off absolute. This son of the lord has a brother. He left the Slant long ago for a farming rock in the path of their descent. It seems pretty certain that's where they're headed. A Far Machine has been sent there to intercept them."

The Garent leaned his head against the chair back and stroked his own neck. "And if they slip away again? And we have to relay again, or recall and relay?" He sucked on his teeth and took a big breath and seemed suddenly robust. The firelight on his face was red and dark and hid his age lines. "I'm not sure how much longer we can wait here, Hiram."

Hiram Goegal nodded. Heat swept through him, an inner heat. He could feel the dampness of his clothes between his skin and the chair. The Nest had been in their grasp; the Far Machines were right there. It should already be over but in a different way. When he looked up, he found the Garent staring back at him. Hiram Goegal knew no matter how long he waited to speak, the Garent would wait longer. "We got a lot of information from our closer scan of the Nest," he finally said. "We can recalibrate the echo of the overvoid and try to find another anomaly with potential. Perhaps it will be an issue of collecting several, like the one on the booster."

The Garent nodded and nodded some more. "I have an idea," he said, "that could significantly shorten our pursuit."

"You do?"

"Recall the Far Machines. Rotate the engines full inverse."

"Turn the engines on inverse? You mean take the Construct down? Sink after them?"

The Garent nodded. His head had lifted high atop his wide shoulders. "Put everything we have into it, our full resources. Alter the bays here on the Construct so we can absorb rocks with as little slowdown as possible, without stopping if it can be done. We chase them ourselves until they stop, run out of food, or hit a long stretch of sink with nowhere to go."

Hiram Goegal could not speak. Dugan's words ran fresh circles in his head. The Garent was indeed after something different, or the same thing, but for a different reason.

"We are close, Hiram. We are closer than we've ever been."

BILL'S TURKEY FARM

Crooked Arm went to the dining room first to get some coffee. A bunch of workers were eating, eyes all set forward, half-dead with sleep as they packed in flat cakes and eggs and pitchers of hot, fresh brew. When he asked where he could find Mighty, a few looked at him, then went back to eating as if nothing had been said. On the slaughterhouse floor, Crooked Arm found a supervisor. He was watching a row of workers pulling feathers off dead birds, the naked carcasses loose-fleshed and floppy and spanked-looking.

"Where is Mighty?"

"You mean Bill?"

"Who's Bill?"

"He's in the office." The supervisor whistled and waved, and a kid came running over. "Take him to Bill's office," the supervisor said.

The kid led Crooked Arm deeper, past the big vat reducers, the bone presses, the wrap rollers wrapping turkey carcasses into gleaming bundles. They went up an iron staircase, to a wood door. The kid knocked and a voice boomed from inside. They stepped into a sweltering room, where Mighty sat behind a wide desk. The walls were lined with black-painted piping that steamed with hotness and clanked and tittered. Mighty was scribbling something in a book. Other books lay open on the desk all around him. He finished what he was writing and set the pen down and leaned back and smiled. He nodded to the kid, and the kid left and closed the door.

"Hungover," Mighty said.

Crooked Arm nodded, only slightly. "I've felt better."

Mighty regarded the pipes. "Turkey guts. We pump it through so fast it liquefies, stays malleable in the sink as the couriers pick up speed. Less friction, faster delivery, faster return, more turnaround, higher profit. It sells good, for pills, for cooking." Mighty shrugged. "Makes the room a bit too hot, but I kind of like it, most of the rest of the sink being as cold and dry as it is."

"Who's Bill?" Crooked Arm asked.

Mighty looked at him. He laughed. "Bill is what they call me here."

"Why Bill?"

Mighty shrugged. His cheeks moved as if he was chewing something. "What are you going to do next?"

"The Sinker knows of a mapping archive. A place called the Axium. They've been charting the sink for a hundred thousand rests."

"And what if this Axium isn't real, or isn't where she thinks it is, or they don't have any Hidden Rock in their map, because that isn't real either?"

"You can't be sure of anything in the sink until you get there."

"Did she tell you that?"

"What other choice do I have?"

"The choice to let it go. To forget about it. Toss the Nest into the void and do what you will with the rest of your life. The codes, the tournaments, the master weapons. We killed each other to see who was most fit to protect that thing. *Killed* each other! To protect what? Why?"

"I hope to find out," Crooked Arm said. "Did Grandfather tell you anything else about Hidden Rock, anything that could help me find it?"

Mighty sighed and shrugged. "All he said was it was about a hundred rests away." He puffed out some air and pointed at Crooked Arm. "You were right, you know. You were the cynic and skeptic. I was the true believer. I wish I listened to you back then. You were droll and boring about it, but you were right. And now you believe it all? That there's some immortal swordsman out there, still alive after who knows how long? And what, you think he'll be able use the Nest to remake the Slant? Is that why you're doing all this? To get it all back? To get everyone back?"

Crooked Arm glared at his brother. "I'm no fool," he said. "The Slant is gone. There's no magic that can bring it back." Crooked Arm paused. Saying it out loud had affected him more than he'd expected. He could see it settling on Mighty too, and when their eyes met, both sets were damp. "I know what I don't believe," Crooked Arm said. "I don't believe the Nest is nothing. Not anymore. There must be some greater use or purpose, even if the legend is only a metaphor. Grandfather found something on Hidden Rock. And I'm going to find it too."

"And what if the something he found was a dead end? What if you do manage to get there and find the same thing. Then what? Keep looking? Where? How long? Forever?"

Crooked Arm didn't answer.

Mighty looked at him and chuckled and retreated into thought. "She's been to it, the Axium?"

"No. But she has a map, more detailed than anything you or I have seen. It's in the map, so it should be there."

"Why does she give a shit?"

"She has a vendetta."

Mighty nodded. He was quiet with himself a breath. "And had you hoped I would go with you?"

"Yes, I thought maybe you would."

Mighty slumped in his chair. He rested the heels of his hands on his big belly and tented his fingers. "Like you said, the Slant is gone. Take your life and live it for yourself."

"The Nest is the only piece of my life that's left."

"Lord of the Scorched Dome even though there is no Scorched Dome. It makes you the lord of nothing." A smile spread slyly through the beard. Pressing his big frame up out of his seat, Mighty moved to a closet in the corner. He took something out and gave it to Crooked Arm.

Crooked Arm grasped the wood handle and held it up. "The bloody hatchet. I thought Father had it in a case somewhere." Crooked Arm turned it over. "It seems so small."

"He gave it to me before I left. Said it had served him well as First Sword but needed a new purpose."

Crooked Arm felt the weight in his hand. He tossed the hatchet, and it flipped once and the handle landed perfectly in his palm.

"I know you could have killed me," Mighty said suddenly. "In that tournament, after I snapped your arm. I saw the point of your sword rotate. If you'd gone for the kill, you'd have won. But you tried to knock me out. Where was your belief then? The best warrior is to be First Sword."

"High Hammer let you live too," Crooked Arm said. "He could have crushed your skull with that thing."

"He was about to become First Sword. Didn't want to serve under a lord whose son he'd killed in the fight pit. Another benefit of our birth, I suppose. Another thing I inherited from Father."

"What do you mean?"

"Bloody Hatchet. I know he was a great warrior, but . . ." Mighty trailed off.

"Are you trying to tell me all those named warriors he fought, they just let themselves be killed because Father was the son of the lord?"

"No. But the rocks below, they weren't sending their best up to Vertex." Mighty shrugged. "Politics, Crooked Arm. Father retires undefeated and becomes the lord, and the whole Slant is happy." Mighty sighed and nodded to the slaughterhouse out beyond his office. "When I got here, they were all wild, the turkeys. I used that hatchet to kill the first dozen and rose them up to Revellville to trade, then came back here with the profits, and the cycle began. Now look at it."

Crooked Arm gazed around, but all that was visible was the inside of the office and its one big desk and cabinets and the steaming pipes coursing with liquid guts.

"I could give you a job," Mighty said. "Training the guards. Have to have a damn guard with every shipment we send out." He nodded to indicate the sink, out past the edge of the rock. "We've been having some trouble. A couple lost shipments. They've gotten off track and had to come all the way back and set out again. We could hire her too, your friend there, the Sinker. Help us tighten up our routes. Would save us more than it would cost to pay you both. Been a real mess out there lately."

"I don't think she'd go for it."

Mighty stepped to face him and put out his big hand. Crooked Arm took it and they pulled each other into a hug. "So you won't come with me?" Crooked Arm asked. "Even if you don't believe any of it, it would be good to be up to something together again."

"It would. But . . . too many people rely on me here. My life is not what it was."

They separated and stood there, each with a hand on the other's shoulder. Mighty's smile wobbled and tilted high on one side. "I hope you find him."

▼

"I'm sorry about your brother."

"That wasn't my brother. That was Bill."

The Sinker yanked a strap, and her pack tightened to her back. Crooked Arm had two hip bags now, mismatched, with a strap around each thigh. When he told his brother he'd traded away his long sword, Mighty made him take the hatchet. It hung now, hooked in Crooked Arm's belt. Mighty also gave them two old helmets, half spheres pocked with dents and chips, but they had visors and earmuffs to deaden at least some of the roar.

"It's going to be a long one," the Sinker said.

Crooked Arm put on his helmet, the Sinker helping him tighten the straps. Exchanging a nod, they slid down the visors and stepped to the edge. Feathers floated pleasantly about them. Above, they formed a haze that thinned into the overvoid.

The Sinker pointed the other way. She shouted to him through the roar and the layers of padding, "Seventeen from absolute!" And she leaned and slipped forward, off into the roaring friction.

Crooked Arm watched her tilt, then straighten, picking up speed as she rocketed away. He turned to look back at the house, set in the center of the long fence. He could see Mighty, out on the porch, looking over with his big hand up. Crooked Arm waved back, then turned and tucked his crooked arm into the back of his belt. He leaned his bad shoulder forward and down, rolling off after the Sinker, into the dark uprushings of the void.

THE FOREVER RISE

Hiram Goegal stood with the barons on the top veranda of the Garent's tower. It was the only place on the entire Construct from which all three engines could be seen, far out past the stacks and the hulking expansions. Distantly the sink howled as the friction scooped inward from the far-out edge, skimming by in a curling tangent. It had an even, gentle lift way up there above it all. Drinks had been brought to them, which they sipped uncomfortably, waiting for the Garent's arrival.

Baron Till was already done with his, but he kept rattling the ice, then drinking off whatever melt had gathered since his last sip. "It's hard to believe," he said, "full inverse." He made a circle with the glass and watched the ice cubes continue their momentum. "The Garent has taken quite a liking to your work, Goegal. What do you think about him flipping the engines and sending us downward?"

Hiram Goegal took a breath to form the answer carefully. "The

Garent seems to believe it will be worth it," he said, "so I will too . . . for now."

Baron Penn laughed. "I can see why he's grooming you."

Hiram Goegal turned to see whom he was talking to, but he was talking to him. "Grooming me for what?"

"He is getting old, very old," Baron Penn said. "Someone will have to be the next Garent."

The idea struck Hiram Goegal like a cold flush of venom into his veins. He had no desire to be in charge of anything. All he wanted was to change the absorption, a cleaner way to rise. That and prove his theories true, he supposed. But suddenly he could see it from their perspective: a young engineer brought into the inner circle as the Garent neared his end. What else could it look like to them?

Linton laughed now, but it was forced and sad, with a touch of cold malice. "Think what you want. Believe it, or don't." She peered at the other two barons. "I had this same conversation when I was your age, Till. The others and I, we all thought the same as you. The Garent seemed so old that it was only a matter of breath. But here we are. I'm an old woman now, and he's the same as he's always been."

Baron Till was shaking his head. "He's aged since I've known him." But Hiram Goegal could see the touch of uncertainty clouding his eyes.

"He *has* gotten older, more so recently," Baron Penn put in. "I've known him long enough to see it."

"It may seem like it some breaths," Baron Linton said, "but then . . . then you see him, and he's slightly more hale, or the light hits him right, and . . ." She smiled inwardly, shaking her head. The others had gone quiet, Barons Penn and Till sharing a look Hiram Goegal could not read, some secret baron language. "It's all right," Baron Linton concluded. "Your faith is harder. You have to simply believe. But I've been around long enough to remember it. I've seen how little he's changed, how little he's aged."

They all looked down at a long centipede wiggling out, as if onto a stage made by their gathered feet. Even the top floor of the Garent's tower was not immune. They watched the tiny legs flashing, the thick spine forming an S curve one way, then the other. Baron Linton lifted her foot and gently set it on the centipede. She shifted her weight and turned her boot until there was a sharp triple crunch, then left her foot there so they wouldn't have to see the mess.

Linton looked at each of them, Hiram Goegal included. "The Garent may live forever, but that doesn't mean he should be in charge forever." She shook her head. "Full inverse." Hiram Goegal could see how angry she was, furious but holding it in, playing politics and maneuvering along.

Baron Till pointed his mostly empty glass at Hiram Goegal. "What would you do?" he asked. "If you were in charge, Goegal. Would you keep sinking after this thing, no matter what, no matter how long it takes? Because that's what it appears the Garent is willing to do."

Hiram Goegal did not realize it, but he'd gone perfectly still. He'd never considered it anyone's choice but the Garent's and so no choice at all. The Nest could power their engines; Hiram Goegal knew that. He knew he could make it work, but was the Nest really the only way? Couldn't there be other anomalies out there as powerful? Certainly there must be, if the sink really is endless. Or maybe the Garent was right, maybe this was a singular chance, a singular anomaly they were after.

The barons, all three, were looking at him, waiting for him. They wanted to hear his answer, but they wanted to hear more than the answer as well. Before Hiram Goegal could form any response, a door on the far side of the veranda cracked open, and the Garent emerged. He had on a huge jacket and what appeared to be two hats, one small and tight with a furry puff of a hat stuffed down on top of it. Hiram Goegal could not help but think of what Baron Linton had said. The Garent did look old and feeble, old enough to be the father of the Garent Hiram Goegal had drinks with the rest before, yet it was the same man smiling at them as he shuffled over, his hand like some blind creature probing out ahead. Each baron shook it in turn, then Hiram Goegal last.

"It is the beginning of the end," the Garent told them.

Hiram Goegal watched Baron Till share a grim look with the others. It was not the best word choice, he had to admit. The Garent went still then, looking around until a page came scurrying across the veranda and handed him a drink like the others had been given. The Garent smiled at it with caged relief, and his big piled coats moved and shimmered as he swiveled to face them again. His drink wavered in the air, and they all reached their glasses out to toast.

"The Forever Rise is a short sink away," he told them. "All of us will be able to look back on this breath and say we were there when it all changed, when the Construct found a better way to keep ahead of the Great Flat."

They toasted again, and all of them sipped, even Baron Till, whose drink was down to clear water with a single, faint oblong of ice. There was a deep clunk that drew all their attention to the faraway edge. There, slowly, Engine Three was moving, its blackened underside rotating up. Hiram Goegal stole looks in the other directions, the other two engines moving in synch, until all three sat upsidedownly on the edge. He'd seen them rotated this way for repair, but never had they been fired up in inverse. Not until right then...

There was a hushing, as if sound sucked away, then a series of low, deep coughs. Soot plumed from the upturned mouth and vanished immediately into the darkness of the overvoid. Then a low glow, golden on the rim, then a rumbling that was more of a feeling, a tickle in the guts. Smoothly the rising growl of ignition gave way to a sustained fabric of layered bass, all three engines resonating in low harmony. It held like that for the space of a breath, then the thruster fire burst. The engine's fat belly jerked back and up. Its seams glowed, turning deep red with specs of vanishing blue. The other two engines joined in, all three firing at full.

Hiram Goegal could feel the motion distinctly at first, as if his outer body had begun to sink while his inner body protested. It lasted only a few breaths of acute acceleration, then it was gone and it felt suddenly no different than rising, or sinking at neutral. Hiram Goegal looked up. Above, the overvoid was no longer empty darkness but a spiraling vortex of milky exhaust.

THE ENDLESS SINK

It was the first thing they'd seen since leaving the turkey farm, and no more than a faint glimmer in the darkness of the undervoid and not getting any larger as it neared, which made Crooked Arm think maybe it was sinking away from them, but as he watched, it shifted and was suddenly coming closer, and he could see now it was a skeleton, some riser or sinker lost long ago, the uprushing whipping through the loose bones to resonate in the hollow cavity of the skull, like a distant, off-tune singing, and he remembered reading that a skeleton adrift in the void was a sign, but could not remember what of, or where he'd read it, so many signs and portents and legends, old tales, old ways, adjustments to the old ways and the old tales, no two rocks the same understanding, versions as endless as the void they were plummeting through, sleek and bulletized, rocketing downward, those old helmets strapped on tight, the Axium still forty rests away, and they swallowed their pills, and dropped their drops, and the hunger passed, then swelled back and passed again, until it too gave up and was gone, and the roar became a hollowness, not a sound, but an inverse of sound, the removal of sound, and it seemed impossible that any rock or any thing at all could ever form again from the darkness, that they'd search and search until they were dead and picked clean, skeletons given to the whim of the sink, and there was the occasional shouted question or signal, but most was in silence, and they swallowed their pills, and dropped their drops, and traded rests to keep watch for risers, and while the Sinker slept, Crooked Arm would hold up the Nest and look at his own reflection in the warped darkness, and he would feel the friction coursing over the tight bulbs of his bad arm, through the ropy knots of muscle, and he would watch the Sinker in the submissions of her sleep, aware that when he was sleeping she was likewise watching him, and the pills and the drops and the rests, and then the Sinker was pulling them up and the map expanded out like a lung, and she poked and re-formed and reshaped it, and pointed out the line to the Axium, but it was so far Crooked Arm couldn't conceptualize the distance, and then she was pointing into the outwide, and they sidetracked that way a full rest to arrive at Resupply, and she told him it was the third rock she'd been to with that same name, and they stocked up on pills and drops, and the Sinker bought a few creams and a powder, and Crooked Arm was surprised to see they had a small anomaly for sale, and the owner told them it wasn't really for sale because no one would ever come with as much as he was asking, and he took down the anomaly, which was a cylinder and small enough to be closed in the palm of a hand, and he tapped it with a metal hobby hammer, and a dull ringing came from it and the owner smiled and put it on a table, and then the table was ringing too, then the wood floor and walls and ceiling and everything in the room, all in different tones, and when the owner lifted the cylinder up again, the ringing stopped, and he smiled and got onto a stool to put it up on the high shelf under its staggering asking price, and it was as if no breath had passed between the shop owner's gap-toothed smile and the endless void unfolding forever as they sunk helmet first into its depths, and more rests passed and curled and cycled into cycles of drops and pills and waking and sleeping, and then the Sinker was shaking him awake and Crooked Arm could see they'd come upon a moisture cloud but, unlike others he'd encountered, not spread and loose but condensed into a molting near sphere as big as a tiny rock, and past its shifting, translucent surface was a thin system of green roots webbing cardiovascularly, and tiny leaf pads had formed along the thickest tendrils, which shifted and winked like sequins, and when Crooked Arm pushed his finger into the water, breaking the surface tension, oblong pools and drops and droplets were released out loose to waver in the void and then rejoin the shifting ball, and the sphere molted and warbled but stayed together as they sunk on, through more rests and pills and drops, and Crooked Arm could not remember if the moisture cloud was real or something he'd dreamed, and when a speck formed far below and off outwide, Crooked Arm thought it was some meaningless object that would pass just as distantly, but it came loose from its point in the sink and seemed to be adjusting to keep them in its path, and the Sinker was suddenly screaming at him through the roaring friction, "Far Machine!" and Crooked Arm could see a long central hull, not half as big as the ones that had come to the Slant, with two enfilading wings stretched out from either side, and the Sinker shouted, "It's a small one, not using its thrusters," and Crooked Arm was astounded it was coming up so fast on the drag alone, the wings like iron fingers webbed with wire and gleaming mesh that sparkled and crackled with static charge, and a bright light erupted on the front, a thick spearing beam into the sink, setting Crooked Arm and the Sinker aglow, and he heard her shout, "Rods!" and he could just make them out, tiny glints forming from the blinding light, and the Sinker flashed her sword and a loud clang rattled and a tear opened in the back of her leather suit, and Crooked Arm slashed with the hatchet and felt a hard metallic thwack and then was turning randomly through the sink, and a rod sliced his arm and another passed clean through his calf and he let out a curt yell to refocus and could hear the Sinker shouting something but saw only the blinding light of the Far Machine, and both heard and felt a deep thunk, and then the Sinker was there, pushing him out of the way as the huge clamp screamed by, and the light atop the Far Machine went out and all was gone but for the rippling friction and the odd colors and blobs of inner-eye spasms and the cold smell of the chain flying by, and with a crack it went taut, and somewhere above the big clamp snapped shut with a deafening clap, and Crooked Arm rolled through the roiling friction to dodge the lashing chain as it retracted, then turned his hips to barely miss the clamp smearing by, and the Sinker released something from her belt that latched onto the clamp and she braced and was yanked violently away, and as the giant spooling gear was about to swallow her, she leapt clear and turned over gracefully to land feetfirst on the Far Machine's wide front carapace, and then she was crawling along to a side hatch, and she reached into a fold in her suit and slapped something onto the hatch, then pushed off before a curt white flash sent the hatch top spinning into the darkness, and a spiked ball chain shot out from the open hatch, missing the Sinker by a hair as she looped back and landed on the hull and rolled and threw something into the hatch that smoked and sparked, and a dropper came flailing out and was cut in two by a crisp flash of the Sinker's blade, and more droppers were dumping from the other side, and the Sinker saw them and dove into the smoking hatch, and now Crooked Arm was bearing down on them, and two of the droppers noticed and turned and fired their chain guns, but Crooked Arm tumbled hard, rolling through the tugs of the updraft to bring the flat side of the hatchet down, and he saw the odd tilting of the dropper's face as his skull shifted two ways under his skin, and the hatchet and his long arm were like a grand wheel, its farthest arc opening the throat of the other dropper, and the Sinker emerged from the Far Machine covered in blood and with a flick of her arm threw something, and another dropper went still as if he'd lost interest and fallen asleep, and there was a pop inside the Far Machine and one of the draft wings groaned and bent, then snapped, flailing along the hull, and with the other wing still extended the Far Machine tilted and rolled over, and the Sinker slid clear as the rotating wing bashed a dropper into wet pulp, and then the Far Machine was rolling faster, then faster, spinning wildly and rising away, and the three remaining droppers looked from Crooked Arm to the Sinker to their disabled Far Machine, and Crooked Arm drove the hatchet into one's face and the Sinker cut the other two into four and all the pieces floated up and away with their wildly tumbling Far Machine until they were long-ago specks, lost in the nothingness above, and the void was dark and empty again, and the Sinker inspected Crooked Arm's wounds and took a little tub from her pack and placed a few flakes of chalk in the hole in his calf, then licked her finger and touched the moistened tip to the chalk flakes and the wound foamed and Crooked Arm shouted, but the pain was gone just as quick, and the Sinker tied a strip of ghostly white fabric tight around it, and she handed him a cube wrapped in wax paper and a second one for herself, and the map expanded, and she ate while she poked and zoomed and recalculated the angle versus absolute and found true outwide zero and set a new guideline, and Crooked Arm ate the cube, which was moist, brown, and almost translucent, and then the map was gone, and they were sinking again exactly as before, as if nothing had happened between, back into the endless darkness of the void and the roaring friction and the pills and the drops and sleeping and waking into darkness, and it seemed as if whole rests were gone in a breath but each breath a full rest, for rests on ends of other ends of rests, and Crooked Arm was having trouble placing the events of this sink, when they fought the Far Machine or visited Mighty or which was first, and how long since that desolate rock with the pools of liquid mirror and the destruction of the Slant and the Far Machines pulling Vertex apart, and the darkness, and the void and all the space and breath between, and they stopped at a rock that was really three rocks winched together with a system of ropes and pulleys, and some small structures and homes had even been built out in the central webbing, and like Mighty's farm and the Slant before, the people there were anxious about recent shiftings in the sink, rocks not exactly where they were supposed to be, confusing trips out into the void, lost shipments and people, and the Sinker had a look at their maps, which were spare but did have the Axium in the same location as hers, and after a quick resupply they sank and slept and woke and sank, and the rests stretched and contracted until a ghost rock formed below them, sharp clustered hills laced with staircases and walkways connecting small homes, and inside one of the houses they found piles of ultra-fine dust where even the skeletons of the people who'd lived there had decomposed, and Crooked Arm wondered if others would ever come and remake something there, another life, another family, another culture amidst the fine particles of the last, and they tilted off and downward into the void, and the rests smeared into sleep and awake and pills and drops, and for a brutal stretch of twenty rests there was only one rock, which was not a rock at all but an enormous ball of mostly clothing and pieces of clothing and scraps of cloth, and the Sinker told Crooked Arm the pieces were drawn together and that's why the ball crackled and glowed with static charge, and Crooked Arm could not fathom how long those scraps must have floated in the sink to be drawn together that way, and he watched it turn and radiate and crackle with sparkles more and more faint, until new endless darknesses had taken its place, and the map plumed and the Sinker adjusted their angle and radial so they could stop to resupply, and the people at the little trading rock were astounded to see anyone coming from that direction of the sink, and over a big group fire they drank a lot and heard more stories of recent travelers getting lost and that the sink had become unreliable and even the Axium was at a loss as to what was happening, and Crooked Arm and the Sinker slept in beds and then were sinking again, and the beds and the fire and the stories of the shifting sink were as if a blink in an endless stretch of staring into the darkness of the void, and the Sinker told him they were getting close, and the map plumed and expanded and spun around them, and they had to backtrack a half rest, then a slow swoop outwide, until finally a speck did form from the darkness, and they bent their angle to sink more exactly toward it, and the speck spread evenly and became a rock, unnaturally circular with a greenish surface that shimmered and undulated as if liquid shifting and sloshing about, and the Sinker moved in close to shout to him over the roaring friction, "The Axium!"

LOST IN THE OVERVOID

Above the bend in his elbow, along the outside of Hiram Goegal's upper arm, Florina had perched, her compound eyes swiveling over his work. Her antennas crossed and uncrossed and shimmered. "Checking my numbers," he cooed, just above a whisper. The moth fluttered and resettled as he drew over a new, fresh page. He was hunched over his small corner desk in the living room, with the rest of the apartment unlit and formless around the lamp's concise pool. Sheets of scratch math fanned out in sloppy piles with numbered rows tilting oddly. He had the last of the bottle they'd opened in a small jar, sipping just enough to keep some bitterness on his tongue.

"You're back at it?" Dugan asked.

Hiram Goegal turned to look at the open bedroom door. All beyond it was a soupy pool of black. "Sorry," he said. "I thought you were asleep." Florina fluttered off and fractalled and dropped and rose and settled near the lamp, shuffling her hind wings and folding them in.

Hiram Goegal heard the rustle and creek of the bed. The darkness gave the sense of motion.

"I was lying there awake when you got up," he heard Dugan say. "I'd been building up the nerve to tell you."

"To tell me what?"

Only silence. The moment extended and still no answer. Hiram Goegal looked a breath longer, then went back to work. Numbers edged out from the tip of the pencil he was constantly sharpening. He finished one row and moved on to another. Then a hand was on his shoulder. He could feel the tight bulge of Dugan's crotch against his arm. He looked back and saw him there, smiling dimly in the pool of light.

Florina fluttered up and alighted on Dugan's shoulder, hanging there with her tiny feet hooks. "Hi, sweetie," Dugan said, swallowing the words. His eyes looked wet. The moth fell off and fluttered away.

"Are you all right?"

Dugan nodded. He turned and faded back into the darkness. "I'm leaving."

"You don't want to sleep in?"

"The Construct," Dugan said. "I'm leaving it."

Hiram Goegal stood. "I don't understand."

"We're sinking. And not just sinking but racing down at it. First we go outwide, then sit there, engines off, and now . . . And all the while the Great Flat comes up at us. What does that mean, for all we've done, for all the death and destruction we participate in? It makes it all mean nothing, less than nothing."

"But it won't be for much longer." He took a step closer. "We found it, Dugan. A way to end the absorption. An anomaly powerful enough to fuel our engines without consuming other rocks. Once we have it, we'll rise further, faster than ever before, faster even than the Flat coming up. We can stay ahead of it forever. We're so close."

"I'm sorry," Dugan said. "I've already decided. I was just trying to figure out how to tell you."

Hiram Goegal felt a constriction of his inner volume. He kept himself frozen there between breaths until he could hold it back no longer and then he breathed and breathed again and the forward flow resumed. "I thought you were happy here," he said.

"I am, with you. But here?" Dugan gestured in a way that meant the wider life around them. "What am I doing but watching a big grinder crush the last bits of some rock, trying to keep those idiots from getting their hands caught in it, actually and metaphorically."

Hiram Goegal laughed, but it was too light for the mood.

"All that killing, all that destruction, the blood they're always mopping up, the fucking bugs, only to sink even faster than the rocks we've absorbed? We're not saving anyone from the Flat; we're only killing to kill more and faster."

"But we'll turn back around as soon as—"

"Don't."

Hiram Goegal stopped.

Florina fluttered and tumbled through the air to lift up into her cage and go still.

"Where will you go?"

"We . . . we can go wherever. Come with me," Dugan said.

"I can't."

"Why not?"

Hiram Goegal searched the space between his outer edge and the inner point of his consciousness but in the end said nothing. When Dugan left the apartment, he did go with him. They went down the crisscrossing stairs, through the wide underbelly, and out an access hatch to a landing above the rim of the Maw. There were four others there waiting for Dugan, all Recycle management. They'd acquired a set of small tote engines that could take them to a tiny rock they'd picked out from the scan. As they readied, Hiram Goegal looked over the lip, into the Maw, the frozen violence of the overlapping gears, the inner-winding iron teeth, sparkling with fine-pointed gleam. Its layers parallaxed away, teeth upon teeth upon teeth. A thin, nearly invisible haze blurred it, thousands of tiny flies living off whatever got stuck in the gears.

One of the totes lit and then another, and then they were haring off into the outwide one by one. Dugan waited until last, until it was him and Hiram Goegal alone.

"Once we have it," Hiram Goegal said, "the Garent will turn us upward again. We'll pass through this same stretch of sink, and you can get back on." But he knew he would never see Dugan again.

"Can't you feel it, the sinking?" Dugan said. "That lift in your stomach? Doesn't it make you nervous? That sound, that counter-whistle."

Hiram Goegal tried to turn his awareness inward. He had felt the flutter for dozens of rests now, long before they'd turned the engines on inverse and started to sink. It had nothing to do with the physical way they were moving through the void; it was nervousness about a reality he'd helped to shape. It was the Garent who'd ordered them to sink, but it was because of Hiram Goegal that they were doing so.

"Do you really believe it?" Dugan asked. "That you can do it, keep the Construct rising forever, get rid of absorption?"

"Yes," Hiram Goegal said. "But you don't believe in me."

Already the other totes were tiny flickering lights shrinking in the distance above. "It's good to see you the way you've been lately," Dugan said.

"What way have I been lately?"

"After something." Dugan smiled. A last kiss and he was gone.

THE AXIUM

As they sunk closer, Crooked Arm could see the strange liquid-green quality of the surface was an illusion created by lush gardens lacing the buildings and walkways. The foliage wavered with the friction's lapping eddies, creating green waves of motion surging back and forth. The rock itself was a near-perfect oval, made so by stretches of iron rimming added where the natural edging didn't jut far enough. Within this patchwork metal-and-rock rim, the surface was developed to the very edge, with squat buildings in concentric rows staggering inward to a small, hive-like complex at the center. From there, thinner walkways spread out radially with a wide main way bisecting it all.

 The Sinker drifted in closer, shouting at Crooked Arm and yanking his sleeve. Crooked Arm looked where she was pointing, at a cleared area with flat red stones inset to form a huge X. They tilted and sank that way, and the rock oblonged out below them. They saw a dozen tiny dots coming out onto the landing place. The dots became a security force. The rest of the rock was swallowed by perspective and the surface rushed up at them. Crooked Arm swung his legs forward and lunged and came down as smoothly as stepping off a stair.

He cocked a smile at the slick landing, but the Sinker didn't see it. She was focused on the security captain, sauntering over with his cadre of men. He was big, with a barrel chest and an ill-fitting vest. His soft-featured face was like soup with stubble floating on it. His men were younger, hard-eyed and silent; they looked like rough risers brought to heel. Half carried crossbows and the others long batons. Their uniforms were clean, crisp, with starched, sharp angles. In contrast, the captain's was a mess, sweat-stained and dirty, like he hadn't washed it in a hundred rests. "You're Rorrey's crew?" he said. "There were supposed to be six."

"Who's Rorrey?" Crooked Arm asked.

"From Teelgarren, he was supposed to send me six new recruits."

"No," the Sinker said. "Rorrey did not send us."

The captain sighed, tired and frustrated. "Well, they're five rests late as of right now. Either of you looking for work?"

"We've come to use the Archive," the Sinker said, "for mapping data."

"Oh ... well ... all data transactions are frozen until they can figure out what's wrong with it."

"Something's wrong with Archive?"

The captain hooked a thumb behind him. "We've been getting complaints the data is off—well, more than complaints. People coming back angry, those who can find their way. They're demanding their trades returned, or more, compensation for lost blah blah blah. The archivists aren't giving out any data until they can get it sorted out, so the Agency has stopped even trying. Things are kind of a shit show right now," he confessed with a final shrug.

"And how long is that going to take?" Crooked Arm asked. "For them to sort it out?"

The captain only shrugged again, his mouth moving like he was chewing something. He looked them over, a longer look, their packs, their weapons, their eyes. "You two have come pretty far," he said.

"About seventy-five rests, all told," Crooked Arm said.

The captain whistled. "Where did you start?"

"We came from the Slant. The Kingdom of the Scorched Dome."

The captain was nodding, but it was clear he had no idea. "I started on Inglethorp," he said. "You ever heard of it?"

"Yes," the Sinker said, "out past the Zs."

The captain smiled at her. There was something soft and kind about his eyes, buried as they were in the sweaty vulgarities of his face.

"I have a pretty extensive map of my own," the Sinker told him. "Most of it the upper sink. The Agency, the archivists . . . they're going to want to know about it, whoever's in charge of collecting mapping data, frozen or not."

The captain glanced up into the overvoid. "The upper sink," he said. "What's the highest you ever got?"

"Jerrellong," the Sinker said with no hesitation.

The captain laughed. "Never heard of it. But I believe you. I suppose you can file the request and see what they say." The captain nodded to his guards. "You two stay here, and come get me if Rorrey's recruits show up. The rest of you, back on patrol." As the guards peeled off, the captain was smiling again. "Well . . . we have to check your weapons first."

▼

The room they entered was empty and nondescript but for a counter and several doors. All the walls were painted flat white. It was gaslit, and Crooked Arm had trouble seeing clearly after so long in the darkness of the void. The Sinker drew her sword and put it on the counter, Crooked Arm the hatchet. They unclipped their helmets next and slipped them off. Both their hairdos were matted and folded strangely. They caught sight of each other and grinned. Setting her helmet down, the Sinker ran fingers into her hair, massaging her scalp. Her eyes rolled with primal pleasure.

A clerk was sitting back there, chewing something. Dozens of weapons and helmets hung on hooks behind him. He got up and took their gear and punched up two cards and set them on the counter with a soft double click.

"The boot knife too. Both of them." The captain was smiling at the Sinker, holding out his hand. She drew the first boot knife and turned it and held it handle out and then the second. The captain took them and gave them to the clerk. The clerk sighed and punched up another card.

Sufficiently disarmed, the Sinker and Crooked Arm were led down the wide central way with the captain a step ahead. They went past a leatherworks and ironsmith and specialty shops with everything you could need or want in the sink. At several places along the way, people had bunched into groups or were waiting in lines, those in back cursing the ones up front. They passed a drink house that had been completely smashed, the big front wall pulled down, broken tables and chairs barfed out from the gaping hole. Snippets of arguments were overheard, people shouting, bickering. Motley groups of traders were wandering angrily about, disgruntled transporters smoking roots, impatiently waiting for customers who weren't coming. Guards were conspicuous throughout, armed like the captain's men, all of them nervous and tired.

"Seventy-five rests." The captain whistled again, that same fleeting note. "You've been a long way," he said. "Anything of interest between here and this Slant of the Sacred Dome?"

"Mostly empty void," the Sinker said.

"Ain't that the story?"

They were passing a depot. A big crowd had gathered at the front windows, all of them waving receipts and punch cards. Something was happening way at the front that neither Crooked Arm nor the Sinker could see. "It's not usually like this," the captain told them, not slowing down.

"What's it usually like?" Crooked Arm asked.

"Boring, peaceful. People pay for a route, they get it, we don't hear from them again, but now . . ." He nodded to a cluster of matching buildings ahead, the central complex they'd seen on their descent. "That's the Agency," he said, "where your request gets filed and processed."

The place looked deserted. "Is there anyone even here?" Crooked Arm asked.

The captain laughed. "You should have seen it a few rests ago. Usually there's a line down to the gate. But with approvals frozen . . ." He shrugged.

"What happened?"

The captain rolled his hand in the air as he led them on. "Big conglom wanted their trade back for a route system the archivists drew up. Said they lost most of everything cuz the lines were off. When the Agency said no, the conglom sent a bunch of goons here, busted up half the main square before we could chase them off." He looked at them over his shoulder. "We're always hiring more guards. It's a sweet gig. No one really gives you any trouble usually, but I guess every once in a while you have to get some exercise." He smiled at the Sinker and even winked. "But you didn't come all this way for a job."

He'd stopped them outside one of the buildings. Closer, they could see each was constructed of metal sheets, riveted together along neatly folded seams. "You're lucky," the captain said, cracking a grin, "about the line. People have to wait all rest usually." From his side belt he took a punch card and a tool. With a half dozen clicks, he punched up the card. "Make sure to give them this. It will get you started." He cracked a grin and held the card out to the Sinker. When she tried to take it, he held it tighter, smiled at her, then let it go. He winked again and strolled off.

The building they went into was almost identical to the weapons check, painted all white, gaslit, with a small counter, but the counter was empty. They looked around and tried the other doors, but everything was locked. The Sinker held up her hand, and they both went still to hear a distant clicking and a mechanical groan. A door behind the counter opened, and a clerk came out. "What are you two doing here?" she asked.

"We're here to use the Archive."

"But all transactions are frozen. Didn't they tell you?"

Crooked Arm handed over the card the captain had given them. The clerk was surprised to see it. "They already started you? But it's frozen?" She took the card, scanning the punched holes. "Data for data? They don't approve data for data. It's data for trade, trade for data. Well, now they're not approving anything, but even when they are..."

"But approvals come from the Archive," Crooked Arm said. "The Agency is still operating and so has to at least run our card."

She looked at him like he was an idiot. "Of course I do, but it doesn't matter if the Archive is saying no to everything. I can file and refile it all rest long." She ran the card through a roller and punched in a few more holes, then handed it back.

"What does this mean?" Crooked Arm asked.

"It means good luck."

They were led down a hall, into a small, plain room. Like the others, it had welded seams and was painted flat white. It was bare but for a few chairs and a table. They were told they'd have to wait and, when they asked how long, got only a shrug. Alone again, Crooked Arm asked the Sinker, "What do you think is going on with the maps? Yours has been off too, hasn't it?"

The Sinker nodded, troubled by it. "There's usually a bit of natural drift, but everything has been off, and not just by a drift, off pretty far and inconsistently too."

"A shifting in the void," Crooked Arm offered. "Maybe there is an Immortal First Sword after all."

There was a knock, and the door swung open. A man entered in a white canvas jumpsuit, custom cut and starched. "I'm sorry," he said. "I'm here to close you out. I hope you haven't been waiting long. They never should have started you."

"Who are you?" Crooked Arm demanded.

"Oh." The man's face opened into a smile. "Sorry. I'm from the Agency. I'm the agent . . . the one in charge of the transaction, but didn't they tell you the Archive is frozen?"

Crooked Arm held up the card. "But you haven't run the card yet."

"There's no point, you know," the agent told him. But he took the card and ran it through a crank roller on his belt, then looked into the numbers. "Mapping data for mapping data?" he scoffed. He held up the card, punching new holes with his own puncher. Finished, he ran the card through his crank again and put it into his pocket. "I'll need to see the mapping data you propose in trade. A formality, as approvals are frozen, but I still need to see it."

The Sinker took out her map. She turned the dial, and the green light blossomed and the room filled with a haze of dots and specks. The agent's puncher hung loose and forgotten in his hand, the light of the Sinker's map reflecting in his dancing eyes. "What scale is this?" he asked.

"One thousand rests into the upper sink."

The commotion at the depot had gotten worse while they were inside. A few of the high windows were broken now. Below, several guards were failing to control the surging crowd. Crooked Arm and the Sinker could see the captain in there, pointing and barking orders. He spotted them and smiled and shrugged, then went back to yanking someone around by the collar.

Some of the agitators were seated, strap-cuffed together, watched over by a few more guards. Closer, some other guards were beating the shit out of two people they'd pulled from the crowd. The guards' eyes glowed with ecstasy as they brought down their batons. With a new surge of shouting and shoving, the crowd swayed. A separate fight had broken out farther off, and the guards went wading back in.

Leaving the chaos of the depot, Crooked Arm and the Sinker rented two rooms at a flop inn, then, asking around, found the Dive, a local stopover bar for sinkers. "That's what you are now," she told him. "You've sunk a lot further than most of the people in here."

Crooked Arm was rolling his bad shoulder, massaging the dead arm with his good one. "There was a pain," he said, "dull and had been getting worse. But ever since we started sinking, it's gone." He shrugged. "What does that sound like to you?"

"Sounds like not banging around on a rock all rest. The sink may be cold and loud and boring, but it's good for the joints."

They got some concoctions with vapor leaking off the top and took them to a booth in the corner. The room was low and cellar-like and speckled with others seated alone. "That's the longest I've been out in a single stretch," the Sinker said.

"I'm honored." Crooked Arm drank his drink, swished it around, swallowed, burped. A cloud of vapor leaked from his lips. They laughed.

"You know," she said, grinning at him, "you would have made a pretty good leader."

"Lord of the Scorched Dome," he said, a little bittersweet.

The vapor lapped up from their mugs in the silence. No one else seemed to be talking. The lights were darker, and now Crooked Arm's eyes were tilting back the other way. Inky splotches moved across his vision when he blinked, mixing with the vapor to disintegrate above the table. "What do we do if they don't let us use their maps?"

The Sinker pressed her lips together. "Find the head archivist, put a sword to their throat, make them."

Crooked Arm laughed. He had another sip. He was getting used to the light. He felt the push and pull, a tiredness in his eyes from adjusting. "My wife was blind," he said suddenly. "She had enlarged irises. So not enough light could get in. She could really only see with a light so bright it would blind anyone else."

There was a commotion at the bar. Three guards had settled there, the same ones beating on people in the depot crowd. The bartender gave them some drinks, and they retreated to a corner, laughing and telling stories the rest of the place could overhear.

"It's the first you've talked of her," the Sinker said. "Your wife, your family."

Crooked Arm nodded. "She was killed in the attack. After I let you out of that cell, I went to find her. When I did, she was already dead."

The Sinker tilted her head and looked longer at him. "Don't you ever want revenge? Don't you want to hurt them?"

Crooked Arm inhaled fully. "I want to know why," he said. He resettled in his chair. "The sink needs its vengeance and justice. And it needs its understanding and curiosity too. But it doesn't need them all from the same person. I guess we make a good team."

The Sinker sipped her drink, swallowed. Vapor leaked from her nose. Finally she cracked a grin.

"Everywhere you look there's some injustice," he said. "Some murder, some theft, some cruelty, some unfairness. What do you let pass and what do you stop and take issue with? If you hadn't warned us at the Slant, you'd already have your revenge, or be dead from trying."

The low fabric of the room punched up higher with the laughter of the guards. Crooked Arm and the Sinker looked over to see they'd knocked the busboy's tray on the floor, laughing as he picked up a few broken glasses. "You're right," the Sinker said. "The sink is endless. It's impossible to right every wrong." She nodded to the table full of guards. "But we're here now. And so are those assholes. Let's go fuck them up."

Crooked Arm laughed again, but the Sinker was already up and headed that way. She walked over to their table and leaned on it with both hands. Crooked Arm had gotten up now to stand behind her. It took the men a breath to notice, half-drunk smiles turning slowly their way. "The next head you bust with one of those batons," the Sinker said, "I want you to think of this."

The one in the middle seemed to be their leader. His cocky smile floated out above the table. "Think of what?" he said.

The Sinker grabbed his head and slammed it into the table. Crooked Arm planted his fist into the center of another one's face. The guy took it all right, but he was struggling to get up from the table. Crooked Arm hit him again, and he dropped as if he'd been picking up speed for a dozen rests. The Sinker was on top of the third one, punching until his arms went limp and he sagged down, vanishing into the darkness under the table.

Suddenly there was a fourth one they hadn't seen, the big one. He surprised Crooked Arm with a solid punch in the jaw. Crooked Arm took a wobbly step and sat in an empty chair that shattered below him. He fell back, and the Nest popped out of his hip bag and rolled across the floor. The big guard went still when he saw it, the fight around him forgotten. He picked it up, looking into his own bent reflection.

The Sinker landed suddenly in front of him. Her foot flashed, catching the big man on the side of the head. He dropped the Nest but shook off the kick, eyeing her with an off-kilter smile. The Sinker's other foot cut the air, and the big guard's expression went blank, his body stiff. He fell over like a board, flipping the table up with drinks leaping and smashing on the floor.

The first one the Sinker hit was the only guard left conscious. He looked up at them from his chair with his face a mess of blood. There was something new in his eyes: fear, or maybe like he recognized them somehow. The Sinker stepped toward him and the guy flinched, and she punched him anyway and he slumped back in the chair and would have looked peacefully asleep if not for the bright blood dripping from his face.

Crooked Arm got to his feet. His first step was a little unsure, but then he was fine. He bent down and picked up the Nest and slipped it back into his hip bag. The busboy had run over, looking at the mess with a dim smile. "You two better get out of here."

Leaving the bar, Crooked Arm and the Sinker went out to the far edge of the rock to sit with their feet dangling, looking down and up and outwide into the sink.

"You have any damages?" Crooked Arm asked her.

The Sinker looked at her hands, turning them over, then back. "One of them hit me somewhere," she said. "But now I'm not sure where. My knuckles are sore."

"I think that's a sign things went well." Crooked Arm rubbed his jaw. "That big guy got me pretty good," he said. "Didn't it seem to you like he recognized the Nest or knew something of it?"

"He was probably thinking how much he could get for selling it. Hired muscle will nick anything to pad their pay." She thought a breath. "Where the fuck did he come from anyway?"

"Maybe he was taking a shit."

They burst into laughter, long and hard. "The ribs," the Sinker said. "That's where he hit me." They laughed some more and, when things went quiet, started laughing again, then went quiet for real.

The friction howled, lifting the Sinker's hair, then letting it settle, then lifting it again.

"I've been thinking about it a lot," Crooked Arm said, "during that whole sink from Mighty's. About something my father said right at the end. That the poem, the legend, was not only about the Slant but all of the void. Maybe the Nest wasn't just holding the Slant in place but everything."

"So if you stopped moving, the shifting would stop too?"

"I don't know what to believe, but if I stop, they'll catch up to us and take it. The Construct isn't about to go stationary with it either."

The Sinker contemplated it. "Every place has legends," she said. "When I was a child, people said the leader of the Construct didn't age, that he would never die, that he would be with them always. But he was just a man, getting older like the rest of them. Of course, some believed it. Maybe even most. They believed in him, which I think was the real point of it all. They would do anything for him."

"Why?"

"He promised them their own immortality, in a sense. A way to escape the fate of the Great Flat so their lives would mean something beyond their lives. So the places they knew, the families they built, could never be snuffed out, forgotten, erased by the Flat."

"But you don't think the Great Flat is real?"

She shook her head. "Another lie. A way for the Construct to justify what they do."

Crooked Arm nodded. "Or maybe—like all legends and poems—the Great Flat is more of a metaphorical ending, a way to make the undoing of the sink understandable, defined, something we can see or at least imagine. Maybe the Great Flat began when the Construct came to the Slant, when the Nest was removed. Maybe all this shifting is a wider undoing, not of the Slant but of everything, and now we're headed right for it, all of us, no matter what we do."

The Sinker found herself peering at his face. She shifted her gaze, back to the darkness of the void. She breathed deeper, and the friction rushed into her, thrilled to be invited. She forced it out slower, pushing against the counterpressure of the uprushing. It extended, two breaths for one, a lengthening of the sink, a slowing of it.

"Avon," she finally said.

"Avon? What's that?"

"My name. The one I was given. But no one has called me it since I left that place. I've told a few people over the rests. But I . . . the sound of it. It doesn't sound like me, feel like me."

"All right."

"My father said it was a type of water they had where he grew up."

"What type of water?"

"He said it was how it moved. As if from an endless source, always running on, finding new ways, gentle but unstoppable. It was called an avon. He said even as a baby I moved like water."

Crooked Arm hummed. "I've seen it," he said. "That quality of flow. He was right."

"He was full of shit. He was born on the Construct, just like me."

"You think he's still alive?"

The Sinker leaned against him, resting her head on his shoulder. Together, they looked out into the far outwide. "I don't know," she said, "but if the sink really does have some inner symmetry... then... yes."

MIGHTY

The Garent and Hiram Goegal came into the dining room together. The heat was near unbearable, radiating aggressively from a huge fireplace along the widest wall. Inside it, the stacked combustion sticks were a single molten mass with giant orange hands dancing above. In spite of it, the Garent had on one of his thick fur jackets, long, with what looked like fur pants underneath. His hat was small but dense, more like a felt helmet, with flaps covering his ears. The table was set for a formal meal, plates with lumps of side dishes, a few small pitchers of various liquids, and at the far end, chained to a big steel chair, the prisoner.

His face was swollen as shut as a fist, mangled and gleaming with bright red blood and dangling tendrils of drool. His mashed lips were huge and purple in the thickness of his black beard, his face so swollen and misshapen and his hair so matted with blood that it made his head seem the head of a giant. One of his hands was pinned to the table by a big buckle that held his wrist flat, palm up. His fingers were bolted down too, each with a thin U of iron. The other arm hung, chained to another bolt on the floor. His legs were also chained, tight to the chair, and his waist strapped down and latched. He couldn't so much as shift his weight forward. There were three droppers there too, with chain guns, just in case.

The Garent paused as he came around, looking long into the ghastly rearrangement of the prisoner's face. Hiram Goegal could see more clearly now how huge the man was in proportion to the Garent and the droppers. Even seated he was nearly as tall and twice as wide. "He's a mess," the Garent said. "Was all of this necessary?"

"He put up quite a fight, my Garent," one of the droppers said.

The Garent nodded and moved closer, finding the slit of a single eye peering at him from the wreckage. "Well, we needed you alive, didn't we?"

"I don't know what you need," the prisoner said, his voice startlingly clear through the disassembled face.

The Garent and Hiram Goegal stepped around the table and sat. The big form at the end didn't move, besides the swaying of his drool. There was the occasional soft pock of blood drops hitting the floor. The fire crackled and hissed and popped, its uneven light shifting darkly over him, making the bruising seem like caverns dug into his face. Hiram Goegal noticed a fat roach had settled on the prisoner's arm, only its antennae moving. A few dark gnats could be seen shifting in his matted, bloody beard, despite the sour reek of a recent spraying.

The Garent waved a hand at one of the droppers, who moved to the door and signaled someone in the hall. A breath later, the door reopened, and a turkey was brought in on a big steel sheet. Hiram Goegal had eaten fowl before, but they'd all been hand-sized or smaller and had to be picked apart and explored to find a meal. This one had heaping slabs that could be sliced right off. They put the cooked bird on the table, steam trickling above it. One of the aides stopped beside the prisoner, flicked the big roach away, and stomped it.

The Garent waited for the aides to clear the room. He nodded to the droppers, then smiled at Hiram Goegal. Slowly the Garent turned back to the prisoner, looking long at him. "So, you are Bill," the Garent said. "But on the Slant they called you something different. I am correct?" No answer or movement came, and so the Garent pondered it out loud: "Mighty."

Hiram Goegal nodded at the big, cooked bird. "Can we trust you enough to take the chains off one of your hands so you can eat, Mighty?"

The eye not swollen shut glinted from the clumped bruising, skin like rotten fruit piled in the gaps between beard and hair. "I can't eat that shit anymore, not if it was the last food in the sink."

The Garent smiled, amused. Reaching forward, he plucked a succulent morsel of white meat. He dropped it gently into his mouth and chewed. He smiled, the crushed turkey steaming and gray in his teeth. "It's delicious," he said.

"That's good," Hiram Goegal put in. "We have a few thousand of them now."

The Garent finished chewing, then had a sip of something already poured into a glass. The taste wasn't what he was expecting. He coughed, then laughed at himself. He had a second, steadier sip. Then he settled back into his chair, staring at Mighty. Neither looked away nor spoke for several breaths. The light high crackle of the fire was the only noise. "You are one of his descendants," the Garent finally said.

"Whose descendent?" Mighty asked.

"The Immortal First Sword, as you would call him. I'm guessing when he left the Slant, he put one of his sons in charge, the first Lord of the Scorched Dome." The Garent grinned, his eyes twinkling.

Mighty glared at him. "How do you know about all that?"

"We have read the poems from the Slant, your legends and tales and superstitions."

Mighty's big head swiveled, taking them all in, the sinewy Garent, the droppers and their dangling chains, Hiram Goegal with his mottled hand resting on the table. "You're the animals that destroyed the Slant," Mighty said.

"Not destroyed," Hiram Goegal corrected. "Recycled, absorbed, put to better use."

"What use?"

"Fed into our engines so we can rise faster than the Flat comes up." Hiram Goegal held out a hand with his palm level. "Everything in the sink is sinking. Even when rising, you're only sinking slower than everything else. All of it will reach the Flat some rest, all except for us."

"You're sinking now," Mighty said. "I can feel it, even in here. You're sinking faster than a normal rock."

"Yes," the Garent admitted. "That is what we are here to discuss."

"We happen to have a few open spots right now," Hiram Goegal said. "A new stack is being completed with several flats still free."

"Unfortunately," the Garent broke in, "we cannot offer you a place on the Construct. You strike me as the type who would plot and plan ten thousand rests for some dramatic act of revenge."

Mighty affirmed with his shimmering stillness. Blood had gathered in the lower half of his open eye. The flies shifted in the edges of his hairline, seeming to multiply by the breath.

"But we can offer it to your people," Hiram Goegal said. "The ones from the farm. They will be given a place in the stacks to live, a job in the Recycle, or Waste, or lower Piping, depending on their skills. Of course, they are welcome to leave and find their own way. When given the choice, most choose to stay and become productive. Soon they see how much better we have it here. That we are not just another rock sinking meaninglessly at the whims of the void. The Construct makes its own fate."

"How many?" Mighty demanded. "How many survived?"

"Ten. And we have places for them all."

"Ten? There were twenty-three on that rock!" Mighty stared at them with his one slivered eye. "And how many survived from the Slant?!"

The Garent and Hiram Goegal shared a look, but neither answered.

Mighty stared at them. He looked at his bolted-down hand. His forearm flexed, but all that moved were the very tips of his fingers. "You fucking murderers," he seethed.

"And how many died in your Sharpenings?" the Garent challenged. "How many did you kill with your bare hands, Mighty?"

"Eleven," Mighty answered, without hesitation.

"I know this may seem barbaric to you," Hiram Goegal put in. "I can assure you it is anything but. It may be the most advanced idea in all the sink. We will create a place where people can live free. A beacon for humanity, liberated from the fear of the Great Flat."

The Garent pressed his ashen face into a long smile. "To become forever, we must rise."

Mighty snorted, wet and bloody. "What the fuck does this crazy shit have to do with me?"

Hiram Goegal answered for the Garent. "That anomaly from your home rock, *the Nest*, is how we're going to do it."

Mighty scrutinized him, then the Garent. "You're insane," he said. "That thing is nothing! You destroy and kill, all for nothing!"

"We already have one small engine running on an anomaly," Hiram Goegal said. "They all share a very special characteristic, the anomalies. Each generates a certain amount of displacement energy, similar to that created by a friction turbine, or one of our engine furnaces. But more efficient, self-fueling, needing no other power source at all. With the engines running off the Nest, we can then put all of our resources into expansion, more stacks to save more people. As we rise, the Construct will continue to get bigger. More and more will be saved from the coming of the Great Flat."

The Garent smiled, his head tilted back. Now he shifted to look at Mighty. "Would you like to save people too? You can save all those who remain from your farm."

Mighty only stared back, his lumped face slack, leaking blood and drool. A tiny fly crept from the beard and crossed his lip. "Yes," he finally said.

"Then perhaps you can help us with a few things we would like to know."

"And they will all live?"

"Yes."

Mighty thought and nodded.

The Garent was pleased. "Your legends say this anomaly, the Nest, that it arrived with the Immortal First Sword, who then used its power to arrange the rocks that made the Slant. Do you know how he did it, how he used the power of the Nest?"

"Legends, stories, that's all they were. Made up, to teach us lessons as kids."

The Garent thought. "What was the lesson?"

Mighty's single open eye went hard and piercing. "You came all this way to ask me about an old poem?"

"No." The Garent answered. "Your brother recently visited you. He had the Nest with him. That is correct?"

"I don't know where they're going. And even if I did, I would never tell you. Kill all the people you want, destroy all the rocks you want, there's no way I would ever betray my brother."

"How noble," the Garent said. "But I already know where your brother is going."

Hiram Goegal was as surprised as Mighty.

"Hidden Rock," the Garent said.

"Hidden Rock?" Hiram Goegal repeated. "How do you know that?"

"Because things have a way of coming together in the sink." With his head high, his lean face smoothed by its broad, welcoming look, the Garent seemed a man barely past middle rests, perhaps younger than Hiram Goegal had ever seen him.

Mighty was shaking his head. "If you know where he's going, then why come here?"

"Hidden Rock is almost straight down. Once we're up to speed, we'll catch them quite easily. But it's an expenditure of engine power I'm not willing to commit to until I am sure."

"Sure of what?"

"That the Nest really is what I think it is."

"And what exactly do you think it is?" Mighty spat.

The Garent smiled at him, upright and firm and filled with a simmering vigor. "You know," the Garent told him, "the Slant is not the only place in the sink that believes anomalies hold secret powers. One maybe can move rocks, for example, or roll back breath or heal or kill or make something that never was have been."

Standing, the Garent reached into his robes and took out his rock anomaly with the flattened side and the flecks of blue crystal. "This anomaly, like others, has a cute quirk about it." The Garent placed it flat side down into Mighty's palm. "Feel that vibration? Strange, no?" The Garent picked the rock back up, holding it out where all of them could see. "But its other power, its secret use . . . for that, one must know the method of activating it. The difficult thing is each anomaly is different, and it could be anything, any random pattern of actions. Submerging it in water, moving it through a certain sequence of precise rotations, exposing it to an open flame." And here the Garent's eyes shot to Hiram Goegal, and a thinner, knowing smile spread.

Disengaging, the Garent held up the flattened rock anomaly again. "This one's secret power? It lets you relive a memory, brings it to life to hover in the air so you can see it and feel it again."

Mighty laughed. "Turkey shit," he declared.

"Luckily for us, I happen to know how to activate this one. So I can show you firsthand." The Garent lifted the flat rock anomaly to his lips and, puckering slightly, whistled and hummed simultaneously, three descending notes.

To Mighty's amazement, the anomaly began to glow. Hiram Goegal was stunned as well; it was very similar to the glow from the anomaly back in his flat. After letting the two of them take it in, the Garent placed the glowing anomaly into Mighty's bolted-down hand, right into the open palm. Mighty and Hiram Goegal only looked on, confused, as the Garent stood back to his full height.

"Think," the Garent offered Mighty. "Think back to when you've seen the Nest."

Mighty's confusion deepened, but the glow from the rock anomaly drew his attention back. It was changing color, radiating brighter, then dimmer. The air above it was swirling now, a crackling image forming, fractured and broken. The perspective was low, a few people passing back and forth. When the people cleared, there was the Nest, sitting in the center of a table.

Hiram Goegal watched the Garent staring. He looked older again, his eyes fixed on the flickering image, his skin ashen, but then rushing with color. He smiled a different kind of smile, an amalgam of awe and appreciation. "See?" the Garent said. "Do you believe in the secret powers of anomalies now? Think back to when you may have seen the Nest activated. Perhaps you know without knowing."

Mighty shook his head. His brow found new ways to fold the bruising in. There was a raggedness in his breath, a low gurgle in each inhale. "I only ever saw it this once," he said. "I was a child." The image thinned as someone crossed, and the whole thing turned and swirled and broke apart.

"You really don't know," the Garent said. He reached down and plucked the anomaly from Mighty's hand. The last remnants of the floating image slipped away, and all there was was the empty air above the table. The Garent held up his flattened rock, its glow gone. "Whistle the right tune, put your hand to it, let the memory flood into your mind." He smiled at Hiram Goegal, then turned back to Mighty. "The anomaly you were once sworn to protect is capable of much more. More even than aligning some rocks. It is capable of destroying us all. But only if one knows the method of activation."

Hiram Goegal's eyes thinned. The Garent was looking at him, opening a hand in his direction. "But thanks to this man here," the Garent continued, "we have found a better use for it. A way to save instead of destroy." The Garent's look deepened, eyes damp as he stared at Hiram Goegal. "And all the people we have lost, all we have sacrificed, all will be worth it if we succeed. If we succeed, we remake the sink."

Hiram Goegal blinked away his own misting. The look between them held another breath. Then the Garent turned and disengaged.

Hiram Goegal watched him step around the table to settle in front of the fire, looking into the flames, silhouetted by the blaze.

"It doesn't matter if you know where they're headed," Mighty said. "Or how fast you can get this monstrosity going. You won't catch them. My brother travels with a sinker who knows all about this place, knows how to evade you. They won't be caught unless they want to be, and that won't be good for you either."

A combustion stick hissed and popped. Another began hissing lower. "Tell me about this sinker," the Garent said, "the one who travels with your bother."

"She arrived at the Slant just before your machines. That's how they escaped. And they'll do it again. The sink is as wide as it is deep. Lots of places to hide."

The Garent stared into the dark compaction of the sticks, the near-blue flames at the heart. With a sudden turn and step, he was at Mighty's side again, the flat rock up to his lips. The Garent whistle-hummed the same descending notes and set the rock into Mighty's palm. "Remember her," the Garent said. "The Sinker."

A long breath popped a mucus bubble on Mighty's lips. The air flickered, and another ghosting image took shape, a woman's face, lean, dark hair, darker eyes. The Garent stared into it, his mouth hanging open. "It's her," he finally said. All eyes in the room had focused on him, all except for Mighty's. Mighty was watching the droppers, none of them looking his way.

With a sudden explosion of tensing muscle, Mighty yanked his arm. The chain broke and a bent link went skittering across the floor. His other hand was still bolted to the table, but he stretched his free one wide and grabbed the Garent by the throat. Mighty's arm was like a tree limb and the Garent's head a baby bird caught in the crook of the farthest branch. But the chain hooks were already leaping. They lashed and wrapped Mighty's big body and dug in, and all three retracts twisted him different ways at once.

Freed, the Garent stumbled off, gasping for breath. Hiram Goegal and the head dropper went to him, but he waved them off and, in a long, sweeping exhale, regained his extra-human composure. Reaching down, the Garent plucked the flattened rock anomaly from where it had tumbled to the floor in the tumult. He held it tight in his palm, put the hand into his pocket, then looked to Hiram Goegal. A strange half smile pressed onto the Garent's lips, a touch mad or frightened. "Offer his people a place in the stacks," the Garent finally said.

The head dropper nodded, and they all turned to look at the mess the chains had made. Mighty's lips were still trembling, a hissing, almost inaudible breath. His hand twitched as if trying for one last crushing clench. The wide black centers of his eyes stared up blankly past them, long past the tiny confines of that interior room, into the ever reaches of the void above, and all he had fallen through.

▼

After returning to his flat in Piping, Hiram Goegal hung his jacket and went to see his little Florina. First things were always first, and she had not been fed since he left for the absorption the rest before. The cage fluttered and settled and fluttered again as he approached. When he reached it, her feet were hooked over the thin metal bars. He unclasped the small door, and she flew out and settled on his arm.

"Thank you, my dear," he said, his eyes welling. He blinked the tears away and pinched some food into her dish, then stood there in a stillness tugging like the passing void. The rests were stacked up right then, as if they'd occurred all at once and he'd just read an expert brief that covered every breath. He looked at the space around him and wondered how far the Construct had moved through the sink since he'd walked Dugan down to that lip above the Maw, since he'd watched those exhaust trails dissipate into nothing in the overvoid. What was Dugan doing right now, out there in the endless sink?

As Hiram Goegal made for the far curio, Florina lifted off and fractalled back into her cage to settle at the bowl. Like a paper cutout, she wavered, only her proboscis moving, little sucking kisses into her dish.

Across the room, Hiram Goegal was standing before the gift Dugan had given him so long ago. The green crystal anomaly was the defining marker, a pivot from which to tell before and everything that came after. It was clear that there was more to the Garent's quest than he was letting on. And more to the anomalies as well. More than Hiram Goegal's science had unveiled. Baron Till's question still haunted his mind. . . . What *would* he do if he were in charge, if it was his decision to make: Keep hurtling after the Nest, even if it destroyed them all?

Shaking off the thought, Hiram Goegal took down the green crystal anomaly. He brushed his fingertips along the shale-like contours of its flattest side, feeling the rough tug against his calluses. In the sterile neatness of the kitchen, he flicked on the burner and turned it to its lowest setting and watched the thin blue radiation of the flame. Gently he set the green crystal anomaly on top. The same glow began to emanate, as he'd seen it do before, as the Garent's anomaly had done when he whistled those three hollow notes. "What else can you do?" Hiram Goegal pondered, half to the anomaly and the rest the out-loud wandering of his mind.

Hiram Goegal put the palm of his hand on the flat top of the anomaly. The scar flexed as he widened his fingers and pressed down so there was no space between skin and its shaley side. A breath passed, then another. Hiram Goegal felt himself slump. He really had expected it to work, to do something, but what? Then he began to feel it, a light electrical current tingling his palm, then a warmth spreading into his fingers. The scar pulsed with heat. Beads of sweat formed and the skin became loose and liquid. He left his hand there longer, watching the skin pool, then settle, then regain its consistency. Amazed, Hiram Goegal lifted his hand off the anomaly and held it close to his face. The scar was gone.

ALL THE KNOWN SINK

The Sinker woke to a knocking at her flop inn cubby. She opened the view door to find an unfamiliar man in a white jumpsuit. "Who are you?"

"I'm from the Agency," he told her. "I'm the agent assigned to your transaction."

The Sinker opened the full door, looking around. "What about the other guy?"

The agent's face broke into a wide, toothy grin. "Oh . . . he's not in approvals."

The Sinker came out, and they went to get Crooked Arm. The streets had thinned and emptied. Most of the people they saw were guards, stationed at intersections, wandering the walkways in groups. The agent led them through a big gate into an exterior waiting area, set out in one of the gardens. Vines climbed the walls and thin metal trellises, all but encasing them in greenery. Several small flower blooms were so vibrant, they seemed to glow with their own source of light.

It made Crooked Arm think back on all the distance they'd come and how grim and gray a place the sink had been. From the garden, they could see a team of traders coming back in from some long outwide, a half dozen swooping toward the rock in formation. Guards were gathering on the other side of the gate, then peeling off, a shift change, it looked like. "This place is on edge," the Sinker said.

Crooked Arm nodded, agreeing. "I hope we didn't come all this way for nothing." They shared a grim look.

The agent returned and, with his big smile leading the way, took them down a hallway into a descending staircase. "We're going to the central Archive," he told them. "It'll probably be one of the bigs, not some adjunct. They're being pretty careful since the trouble, which I understand, but even with it open wide, the archivists can be real bastards about data for data, but we'll see. We have the approval, so what can they do?" The agent pressed a nervous smile, reminding them of the extreme whiteness of his teeth. They reached a door with two guards dressed like the captain's men. The agent handed over a punched-up punch card, which they rolled through a gear and handed back. One of the guards unlocked the door, and they passed through into a low-ceilinged, subterranean room.

"We're on the underside of the rock," the agent told them. He stomped his foot. "The sink is right on the other side of this floor." He smiled.

Crooked Arm could feel it with each step through the interlocking rooms, a subtle springing back, the friction trying to push the floor up past them. They went down a few hallways with small mapping rooms branching off. Through tiny windows, Crooked Arm could see archivists and their assistants bent over exposed hardware, some of the rooms glowing with sections of projected map. Finally they arrived at a room with a high, domed ceiling cut upward into the under rock, roughly semispherical with deep lines gouged down the inside. At the center of the room was a hulking map apparatus, a huge tube and projector with a protruding ring of panels. Two people were huddled over it, talking quietly as they adjusted settings and dials.

The agent spread his smile out wide, all his teeth lined up. His skin had drained pale and gleamed with the first crackings of a sweat. He took a few steps toward the big apparatus but then stopped, as if scared of getting too close. He had one of his cards out, up in the air like an invitation. "I have the approval here, for a data-for-data."

From the main control, the tidy bald head of the archivist arose. It was unnaturally round, an exact sphere, it seemed, the bottom half thinly bearded. "So this is them." He broke into a smile and slipped on some glasses. His noticing them was the cue for his assistant to do the same. She looked over, a densely freckled young woman peering from a board of wired crystals. Her gaze lingered long enough to make Crooked Arm uneasy.

The archivist came across the room and took the offered card. Only after scanning it did he finally look at the agent directly. "This seems to check out, thank you. You can go."

The agent blanched. He managed a scornful look at the archivist and got only a dull, impatient smile in return. With a last glance at the Sinker and Crooked Arm, the agent crossed and slipped out. The archivist watched until the door was closed and the room had fallen silent but for the humming of the sink through the floor. "That's better," he said, his attention returning. "We don't meet people who have traveled as far as you," the archivist said. "I've heard about your map. A thousand-rest radius and most of it the upper sink!"

"I didn't chart all of it," the Sinker confessed. "I traded for a few uploads. And there was plenty on there when I got it too."

The archivist was shaking the objections off. "You know how many rocks I've been to? We've got several hundred mapped out in the Archive. Me, I've been to five. Five rocks." He laughed like his life was some big joke he'd just let them in on. He held out his hand. "Your map?" he said. "I'd like to begin the transfer."

The Sinker took out her map but did not hand it over, not yet. "You upload my data to your map; then you upload your data to mine. All of it."

"You want the whole main master?" the archivist said.

"Everything you have for everything I have."

He smiled at her. "Well . . . we're not approved for that exactly, but . . . I don't see any problem with it. You have a deal."

The Sinker nodded and handed him the map. The archivist turned it over. He ran a finger along the input jacks, feeling the rough welding. His hands shook with age but looked soft and supple and incapable of breaking anything.

The assistant had come over to watch; her eyes and hair were the same reddish brown as her freckles.

"A five nine three should do," the archivist told her.

The assistant took the Sinker's map to the apparatus and started patching it in. A green light came onto the panel. "Transfer initiated," she called out.

"Very good," the archivist said, more to himself. He peered at them, his eyes rolling around inside the round frames of his glasses. "Let us get down to the real business at hand, then." He focused on the card the agent had given him, examining the tiny square holes. "What you *are* approved for is route line and location of a rock." He smiled. "I'm honored that ones as traveled as you have come to us looking for a place you cannot find. Let us see if we can be of any help. What is the name of this rock you seek?"

"We're looking for a place called Hidden Rock," Crooked Arm said.

"Hidden Rock?" The archivist frowned, moving to a control panel. He keyed in several combinations of buttons and looked into a thin scrolling screen, scanning a list. "Hidden Rock," he said again. "We don't have anything in the Archive with that name. Perhaps it has another?"

"Not that I know of. But I know its approximate location."

The archivist smiled. "Well, perhaps that will be enough. Bring up the main master," he said to the assistant. But she had gone still behind her controls, her eyes staring out hard from her speckled face. "Main master," the archivist said again, gently. The assistant came to, focusing back on her panel. "Get us zoomed out on this sector," the archivist said, "a three-hundred-rest radius."

The assistant turned a few cranks, and a low red light bloomed from a central lens. A shimmering projection of crimson dots and specks filled the room. "As you can see," the archivist said, "most of our charting is of the lower sink."

The Sinker studied the bottom-heavy spectrum of dots and motes. "How deep have you charted?" she asked.

The archivist smiled. "All of it? Only a sliver? It's impossible to know. But we've charted pretty deep, to what we think is the bottom of it, the Spear, it's called, the bottommost rock in the sink. Of course, there could always be more, but in all the charts we've compiled, that's the deepest it goes." He turned to Crooked Arm. "Tell me what you know about the location of Hidden Rock, and we'll see what we can do."

"Our orientation point is the Slant," Crooked Arm told him. "The Kingdom of the Scorched Dome."

"The Slant? I'm not familiar with that either." The archivist looked to his assistant. She was already keying it in, eyeing a low readout. She looked up and shook her head. "We don't have it," the archivist said, frowning. "We're better with the lower sink, candidly."

"Can you lay my map in over?" the Sinker asked.

The archivist thought and nodded, then looked to the assistant and nodded to her too. The dots fizzled, and a new mist of green appeared overlaid. The archivist moved around under the integrated projections. Crimson dots and green dots and purple where the data overlapped. "Amazing."

The Sinker pointed out a perfectly aligned formation. "Here," she said. "The Slant."

Crooked Arm stepped close to it, looking into the ghost of his former home, a place gone from the sink, except in old maps. "We think Hidden Rock is about a hundred-rest sink from here," he said. "Though we're not sure of the angle."

The archivist was still swept up in the Sinker's data. But the smile crackled away and his glasses settled and a cold formality entered his voice. "Set a hundred-rest radius downward from this formation. Angle twenty-five from absolute along all radials." The assistant went to it, turning and taping. The map fizzled and re-formed, and a ghosted white arc appeared below the Slant. The map moved again, scrolling along the arc.

"Nothing very close," the assistant's voice came. "Glaxon, Turbis within fifteen."

The archivist was shaking his head. "Try wider," he said. "Set a full radius in all directions."

The assistant adjusted the dials, and the arc became a sphere around the Slant. They all studied the perimeter. Only a few dots were close. The assistant read off the names. "Burgerburg, Hallotrap, Freedford."

The Sinker was walking through the projection, the dots and specks gliding over her. She indicated a distortion, a tiny inconsistency in the projected shell, as if that one spot were being seen through water. "Zoom in here," she said.

Nothing happened. The Sinker turned and, through the tangles of machinery, caught sight of the assistant's gleaming eyes, staring hard at her. The archivist went to the controls. At his shooing, the assistant stepped away. The archivist's fingers danced nimbly. The map zoomed and re-formed, and the distortion became a distinct wavering cube. "It's not empty," the archivist said. "It's been erased."

"What do you mean, erased?"

The archivist started turning and dialing and reading off a thin scroll. "Someone has wiped it," he said, "from the Archive, this section of the main master. This has never happened before. Maybe I can call up an old cache path or—"

"No!" the Sinker shouted, startling Crooked Arm.

The archivist had gone suddenly still, his face soft with a thought. His body slumped and fell forward across the controls, then down to the floor on his back. The assistant stood above him, her eyes wide, a knife, covered in blood, clutched in her hand. "I'm sorry," she whispered. She stepped forward and pushed the knife into the archivist's chest and pulled it out.

Her eyes shot up then, as if remembering suddenly where she was.

Her face tightened into a scowl as she slammed her hand on the control panel. The map and the rest of the room went dark. Crooked Arm looked to where the Sinker was, but she was gone. Past the big mapping apparatus, he saw a door open and the assistant slip out. He ran to it, yanking the nob, but it was locked. The Sinker had reappeared at the panel where her map was still patched in. She waited a breath more as the transfer finished. When a small light on its side pulsed green, she unplugged the map, and it vanished into her coat.

Crooked Arm was there. "She locked the door behind her. We'll have to go out the way we came in."

They noticed the archivist was still alive. Weakly, he reached for the Sinker with pleading hands. She moved nearer to him, close enough to hear him ask, "Is it endless . . . the sink?"

The Sinker thought a breath. "Yes," she said. The archivist smiled, but his face looked rubbery and dull. The last gleam in is eye dried, and his body softened. "He's dead," the Sinker said.

Crooked Arm was looking at the dark control panel. "You know how to use any of this stuff?"

"No idea."

"Do we have enough information to find it?"

"Maybe. But right now I'm more worried about getting our stuff and getting off this rock. I don't think they're going to believe us that his assistant did this."

"No," Crooked Arm agreed. "I doubt it."

Pushing back through the door they'd come in, Crooked Arm and the Sinker found a guard waiting there. He seemed like he was about to ask something, but the Sinker drove her foot into his face. His head cracked off the wall, and he slouched to the floor. Quickly they moved back through the same interconnecting rooms, the sink pulsing up through the floor. Both expected more resistance, but the rooms and halls were empty. "I'd have thought she'd blamed it on us by now and have the whole force mobilized."

"Yeah," the Sinker agreed. "I don't like it either."

Only by the exit did they encounter more guards, four of them, busy putting on riot gear. Crooked Arm and the Sinker readied for a fight, but the guards gave them only a quick glance. "I'd get out of here if I were you," one said. "Shit's about to get messy out there."

Outside the complex, there was a heavy guard presence, all of them dressed in padded vests, with riot shields and batons. None of them seemed to care or even notice as Crooked Arm and the Sinker crossed the garden and went out the gate. Soon they found out why. A new, even bigger crowd had formed at the depot. Rocks and trash were flying through the air, glass smashing, shouts and shrieks of pain. More and more guards were arriving to line the front, banging on their shields and showing off the bristling charges of their batons. "They're going to break in," someone told them.

Leaving the depot, the Sinker and Crooked Arm passed stores being looted, some of the owners futilely trying to save their goods. Guards were flitting about, but there were far too few to keep any order. The sinker bar they'd been at was smashed open. Some people had dragged all the booze out to drink right there on the main way. "A shame," Crooked Arm quipped grimly. "I kind of liked that place."

They made it to the weapons-check building, but the door was locked. They could see the clerk in there, peering wide-eyed through the window at the chaos outside. "Open the fucking door!" the Sinker demanded.

When nothing happened, Crooked Arm threw his shoulder into it; it didn't budge. Without hesitation, he stepped back and kicked it, and the lock burst and the door flew back and banged shut again. The Sinker pushed through, Crooked Arm right behind her. They could see the clerk plopping out a side window and running off.

"That's far enough," a voice said behind them.

Crooked Arm and the Sinker turned to find a few guards stepping in through the broken door, then a few more. Two they recognized from the bar fight, mostly because of their black eyes and fat lips. There were seven of them in all, some with long batons, others with crossbows, already loaded and pointed. The archivist's assistant came into the room behind them.

"It was you," Crooked Arm said, "who erased that portion of the map."

"Give me the anomaly," she said. "Then you're free to go."

Crooked Arm eyed the two crossbows pointed at him, one at the Sinker. There was the mistake, he knew. "You'll just kill us after we give it to you," Crooked Arm said.

The assistant nodded to the guards around her. "These men want to kill you and then take it. I just want to take it. We can do it my way or their way."

Crooked Arm glanced at the Sinker. A single breath passed between them. Slowly he reached into his hip bag and took out the Nest. "This is what you want?" he asked.

The assistant's eyes went wide, then slimmed. "So it is true," she said, more to herself. Then, louder: "Give it to me and I promise they'll let you both leave."

Resigned, Crooked Arm nodded. The assistant held out her hand, and he stepped slowly toward her, the bowmen following him. Just as she was about to take it, Crooked Arm leapt. He felt an arrow skim his back as he tackled one of the bowmen to the floor. The other guards were on him at once, swinging their batons. Crooked Arm felt the hits landing hard all over, but it didn't matter. He knew the move: keep them occupied long enough for the Sinker to get into the room full of weapons.

When one of the guards landed on him, Crooked Arm thought, that was fast, even for her. Another guard fell back, and the baton strikes stopped. The others were looking up, and one more fell as Crooked Arm scurried back and got to his feet. He watched the Sinker spin down as her blade hand swept up, a perfect red line drawn across two separate guards. Crooked Arm picked up a fallen baton. With a wide swing of his long arm, he slammed the end into a guard's face. Turning, he saw another not looking his way and brought the baton in square.

There was only one guard left, somehow so quickly, baton in hand, squared off against them. The assistant was crawling on the floor. She had an arrow sticking out of her side. Another guard got to his feet but was still mostly knocked out and fell over again.

"Get the fuck out of here," the Sinker said.

The last guard held a breath more, then dropped his baton and ran out the door. The Nest had fallen to the floor in the fight. Crooked Arm picked it up and put it back into his hip bag. Together, they went to the assistant. She was lying on her side now, breathing low, looking up at them. On her arm, they could see a strange tattoo, three intersecting arrows. She coughed, and blood splattered down her chin, a spread of droplets across the floor around her.

"Take it there . . . ," she said, "to Hidden Rock." She pointed weakly at his hip bag. "From Purseon . . . a three-rest sink . . . twenty-three . . . one ninety-eight . . . take it there . . . take it to Hidden Rock."

They waited a breath, but there was no more.

"This one has it too," the Sinker said. It was the big guard from the bar fight, seated against the wall with a boot knife in his forehead. There on his forearm was the same tattoo, three intersecting arrows. Crooked Arm considered it. "Twenty-three off absolute . . . radial one ninety-eight . . ." But he trailed off.

"What?" the Sinker asked.

"That was the same angle and radial as the Slant."

The sink was familiar now, the angle, the radial, the void spreading out endlessly below with only more endlessness expanding out above, and the friction roared and more darkness unfurled and the descent slowed and the void thickened into a soupy gray mass as far as I could see, and a speck formed below me and became a haze of blue and then an endless water as wide as half the sink, and a rock formed itself from the water, and I landed and felt its sandy surface give beneath me, and my feet settled into it and it held me softly and the friction was a warm stillness now, and even the sound of the roaring void was gone and a voice came again from some unseen place, and I turned and found myself facing a wall of water rising somehow in a vertical plane before me, and through the shifting water I could see a vague hint of some other place, as if the water was a soft doorway or portal, and on my side the warm stillness of the friction and the sandy grip around my feet, and on the other, a shifting chaos of motion and a muffled voice dully piercing the tumult, calling me back, or warning me not to return, and I looked down and saw my feet sinking not in sand but into a soft carpet of moss, and beside me was a gnarled tree no taller than a man, and a smell of salt and charged air reached me and my hand was heavy and I looked into it and saw myself looking back. . . .

PART 5

HIDDEN ROCK

REFLECTIONS OF THE VOID

From Purseon, they sank three rests straight at twenty-three, radial one ninety-eight, exactly as the archivist's assistant told them. The Sinker had run the line in her map, and it did go into the area erased from the Axium Archive. But when they reached the location, it was dark and empty and indistinguishable from any other place in the void. The Sinker pulled up and took out her map, and the projection plumed and she turned and zoomed it and zoomed it further, scrutinizing the mist of dots as it rotated and swelled.

"This is the spot," she shouted. "She could have been lying...."

"Or it could have shifted," Crooked Arm shouted back. "The Axium maps, your map. It's not the maps that are off." Crooked Arm scanned the void, the overvoid, the undervoid, outwide along the whole radial.

"We'll have to start lateral sweeps," the Sinker shouted. "It will take a while, but if it's here, we'll find it."

"Look!" Crooked Arm pointed, far off in the undervoid, at a distant glimmer of light. When the Sinker collapsed the map, the distant light vanished and all was dark again. They tilted and sank that way. As they neared, two shapes wavered and formed from the darkness: risers, coming up at them. The Sinker's hand went to her hilt. Crooked Arm readied himself as well, tucking his bad arm even tighter in, then grasping the handle of the hatchet. But they could see now the risers were not risers at all but themselves, reflected in a gigantic mirror. Only when they got close enough to touch their own fingers could they see exactly where void ended and reflection began.

The Sinker looked off in each direction but could not tell how far the mirror extended. They picked a direction and pawed along, hands on the hard, cold glass, their own silent forms moving in parallel until they reached the edge. But it was not the end, only a seam before another mirror began at a slightly different angle. The Sinker could see now the mirrors angling off ahead and behind them and to either side. "It's a shell," she shouted. "Built out around the whole rock."

Crooked Arm nodded. He could see it too. He looked into the seam between the two mirrors. "We can fit." With a nod from the Sinker, Crooked Arm went in first. She watched as he slipped through, looking like he'd melted into a fold of the dark void.

"What's in there?" she shouted, but the only answer was the howling of the friction, hissing and warbling off the mirrors and whatever structure was holding them up. The Sinker moved in, following Crooked Arm. She saw herself working between herself, reflected twice back, then again, then so many they overlapped into a gray void, and she felt the hard lashing of the friction, but from inside her body, and the gray splintered darker and became a deeper blackness than even the far-off empty sink, and she could feel it rushing down her body, faster than ever before, so fast she lost direction and went tumbling wildly, and she gave herself over to it and felt it take command of her flailing limbs, and then she was turning slower, to be smoothly gripped by a soft flatness, and she blinked and blinked again, and roused finally, finding herself lying on a cot.

Crooked Arm was seated on another nearby. "You're awake," he said.

The Sinker's head pounded. She held it with two hands and cursed under her breath. "It gets better," he told her. She breathed, and her head pulsed lower. She sat up and groaned and rubbed her temples and looked around. They were in a holding cell. On the other side of the bars were a small table and a few chairs and a single door.

"We were electrocuted," Crooked Arm said. "I think a static field when we went in through the mirror shell. A trap. And we got caught."

The Sinker groaned and worked to her feet. She stretched her arms high, and her spine gave a few thankful pops. Lifting her leg, she swung her knee wide, her hip popping too, but deeper, like something heavy falling.

"The Nest is gone," Crooked Arm told her. She turned to look at him. "So is your map. Both gone when I woke up. Weapons too, but the rest is there." He nodded to where their things were arranged neatly against the wall inside the cell.

The Sinker went to her pack, poking through, finding the map was indeed gone. She cursed under her breath. "How long have you been awake?" she asked.

"Not long. There was a kid." And Crooked Arm nodded to the other side of the bars. "He got up and ran off when he saw I was awake."

As he said it there was a sound from beyond the room. Voices. Someone laughing. They listened, but all had gone quiet again. Then the door on the other side of the bars opened and a man came in, about middle rests, with soft, friendly features. His hair was soft too, silky and slightly curled, with a beard that was thick but short and more like a coating of fur. "I am Foster," he told them.

"You're the leader here?" Crooked Arm asked.

Foster only smiled, mildly amused. "No, we have no leader. I have been elected by the others to come and talk to you." His eyes thinned on them. "Have you dreamed of it?" he asked.

"Of what?" Crooked Arm asked.

"Of the other way it can be."

The Sinker and Crooked Arm traded a glance but offered no answer. Foster watched them, withdrawing into his own thoughts. "Then how did you find this place?" he asked.

"A woman at the Axium." Crooked Arm nodded to Foster's forearm. "A woman with that same tattoo."

"Clarabelle," Foster said. "She was stationed at the Axium to *keep* people from finding this place. Why would she have just told you where it is?"

Crooked Arm stared back through the bars. "I think we both know. Because of that anomaly. She tried to take it from us. There was a fight and she was killed. As she was dying, she told us how to get here."

Foster took it in. "Clara is dead?"

"Where is it?" Crooked Arm demanded. "Where is the anomaly?"

Foster pressed a smile, looking suddenly more comfortable. "Safe."

"And my map?" the Sinker put in.

"Also safe. I hope you understand our caution," Foster said. "Many people have dedicated their lives to keeping this place hidden, for as far back as anyone knows. Some, like Clara, have died in their efforts. Once everyone here is satisfied you are not a threat to this place, you'll be free to go." He shifted and resettled and focused on Crooked Arm. "I do not think you are a threat, but there are some who are unsure." He smiled. "Tell me about this anomaly."

"I come from a place called the Slant," Crooked Arm said. "The Kingdom of the Scorched Dome."

Foster nodded. "We heard the Slant was destroyed."

"Do you know how?" the Sinker asked.

"Yes. Something called the Construct. We had people stationed at Flux when it was attacked."

"But you don't know what it is, the Construct?"

"Just from the reports," Foster answered.

The Sinker shook her head and sighed and leaned back.

"The Construct came to the Slant for the anomaly," Crooked Arm told him, "the Nest, as it was called there."

"Why do they want it?"

Crooked Arm looked to the Sinker. "Energy," she said. "To run their engines, somehow. That's our best guess."

"Yes." Foster nodded. "Some expansive propulsion technology, we've heard. Large enough to move their rock around in the sink. Why did you want to bring it here, this anomaly?"

"On the Slant, there was not much known about it beyond our local folklore. Many rests ago my grandfather went on a quest to learn more. He somehow found this place and determined it to be connected to our legends."

"Connected? How so?"

"He thought the Nest was brought to the Slant from here, long ago."

Foster seemed troubled by it. "You say your grandfather found this place. Do you know how?"

"No, only that he found something here that changed his mind about our legends, about what the Nest could be and the man who brought it to the Slant."

Foster nodded. "And now you are continuing your grandfather's quest?"

"My home was destroyed, everyone I know there killed. I want to know why. I want to know what the Nest really is. Does any of that story mean anything to you? Do you have some foundational texts or legends that relate in any way?"

Foster shook his head. "Our methods of deception change," he said. "Old protocols are floating around out there still. If your grandfather did find this place, they could have told him anything to keep the real truth hidden. There's no way for us to know what he may have learned, but whatever it was was likely made up as a layer of protection, a misdirect, something to make him give up."

Crooked Arm scrutinized Foster through the bars. "That mirrored shell around the rock, the static field. The people with that tattoo. What is it you're working so hard to hide?"

Foster answered without hesitation, "The Overlap."

"The Overlap? What's that?"

"Let's leave it there for now. I'd be betraying everyone here if I shared any more. We would like to help you, but first I must consult with the others. Once we have discussed it with everyone, we can work together to figure all this out."

"How long?" the Sinker demanded. "How long are we to remain in this cell?"

"The others are gathering right now. It won't be long. I'll return shortly, and you'll be let out and your things returned." With that, Foster slipped out the door. They could hear some low talking, then all went quiet again.

"There's more they're not telling us," Crooked Arm said. "More than what they're hiding, the Overlap, whatever that is." He looked around at the cell and the room beyond the cell. "How hard would it be to break out of this place? You've been measuring it up since you woke."

The Sinker smiled low at him, then turned her attention to the walls and bars. "Hard but not impossible. We'd have to smash our way out. It would be loud and take some work, but we could do it."

"Then what?" he asked.

"I don't think they pose much of a threat. If they had any substantial force here, they would have made it known to us."

Crooked Arm nodded, considering it. Food was brought to them by two kids, and while they ate, Crooked Arm and the Sinker decided they would lure the next adult who came in close enough to the bars for one of them to grab. They didn't have to wait long. Soon they heard more noise on the other side of the door. A faint knocking, then two voices talking, then talking louder. Crooked Arm and the Sinker both remained seated on their cots, watching as the doorknob rattled. With a click, the door creaked open and someone stepped into the room.

The Sinker stood from her cot, staring through the bars. "It's you," she said.

She was right. It was me. That was it, the breath when I reentered the Sinker's story.

THE SINKER OF FAIRVIEL

After leaving the destruction of Fairviel, I thought only of sinking, of getting as far away as fast as I could. I scrapped my plan to go to Roseblood and plumed the map and set the radial and picked a rock almost straight down at absolute, and I tilted and sank that way and made with my body the smallest resistance I could, and the sink wavered and hummed and increased its roaring and the speed accumulated and the friction pressed back, and through the pressing back I picked up even more downward speed, and what was left of Fairviel was swallowed into the overvoid with the fading image of Del and Tim mushed into that uprooted house, and I slept and dreamed of *the endless water and the rock floating in it with the downward pull calling me in,* and I woke and checked my place in the map and had my drop and pill and slept again, and the edge of my body felt vague and mixed into the near void and then condensed, the real me a smaller me hidden deep inside concentric shells, and the friction pulsed and roiled and the map plumed and collapsed and the drops swelled out and absorbed into my tongue and the strange hollow expansion of the pills as they worked through my guts, and more rests passed than my charting calculated, then more, and I worked to stay calm and maintain the routine, the pills, the drops, until I came upon a rock by accident, not the one I'd planned for at all.

It was a trade stopover where something in the rock had rotted out the teeth of the people living there. One of them had to talk the others out of robbing me of everything. She helped me find where I was in the map too, but demanded all my silver disks and drops in return. I considered the bolt gun but was too scared to use it. I could load it and threaten them, but if they called my bluff, would I be able to pull that trigger? And if I did, then what? One shot, then they'd surely kill me before I could reload. With the others leering on, I had no choice but to give over the disks and drops.

Then I was out in the void again, with nothing more than what it would take to get to the next rock, with no room for mistakes, and if not for the map, the dark, endless featurelessness of the void would have been impossible to distinguish, but I stuck to the angle and the radial for three rests straight, and when the next rock finally did form from the undervoid, it felt like a miracle, and the map was suddenly more familiar, and the resupply smoother, and I was sinking again.

When I reached the next rock, a place called Mollannoo, I took a ten-rest contract weaving rope to pay for a resupply, then renewed it once to get a little ahead. Sitting there weaving rope, the strings over and underlapping in the rhythm of my fingers, I ran through my last moments with Del and wove it and ran it through again and again until it was my own private endlessness in the sink of my mind. When the others went out to the drink houses, I would bunk down early and study the map in the hammock they'd given me and dream a version of the dream where *I was in that same hammock, in the same bunk room, but a surge of warm downward friction was pushing on me, trying to force me through the hammock and the floor and the rock and back into the endless sink.*

After a few rests, I had worked out a path downward, three rocks to another resupply where I could reassess. When the second contract was paid, I gave my thanks and set the angle and radial and plummeted off into the void and was rock to rock this way with the next two always picked out and the angles and radials laid in and the drops and pills all sectioned off in a chart I could see in my head, and the sink unfolded with each new edge, and new unfurlings revealed more and more of the endless void rushing up, and the cupping hands of the friction would hold me, the sink exactly the same *except the water there below me, and I would gaze into the dark blue, as deep and wide and endless as half the sink, with even more void above, just as empty but changing color in phases of long breath until it was the blackest void again but pocked with holes of light, and the rock had formed itself from the water, and its sandy surface held my feet with the same warmness as the friction, and the sparkling lights above doubled and tripled and quadrupled, and a softer, easing light was forming, and a strange horizontal line separated two types of darkness, and all of it was fading to a void of emptiness so pure I knew* I was back in the actual sink I was sinking through, and the rocks got more frequent but were not always where the map said they'd be and often took a little outwide back-and-forth to locate, and I learned I was in a new sector and traded some scavenge I'd collected to upgrade my map with more of the undervoid, and the rocks thinned again and my supplies thinned too and the path downward was both a puzzle and a maze and the rocks riddles for me to dissect over fires as I ate alone, and so much darkness unfurled and unfolded and was gone above me with only more rushing upward to fill the space with more endless void, and in the long sink between Gill and Teelhoof, I saw some specks headed up and tried to angle off, but it was risers, and as they got close, I saw the nearest one had a big knife in his hand, and I got out the bolt sling and clicked in a bolt and when he was close enough, I pulled the trigger and felt a click and a thrust and saw his face yank in and go pale with waxy youthfulness, a kid not much older than Del, and the others were closing in now too, and on the same inhale of the same breath, I turned and pointed headfirst into the uprushing and vanished all resistance and could feel them right there on my heels but knew looking back would be the thing that killed me so I held tight and picked up speed, and the friction melted around me and more unfolding void broke apart in huge gaping chasms, as if the very fabric of the sink was torn open and I was dropped into the breach, and everything felt far behind in some other place I had traveled beyond, and when I finally looked back, I saw only empty void above me and the ghosted imprint of that riser's eyes, and it tumbled and wove like rope fiber with Del and Tim and the shattered debris that had been Fairviel, and I plumed the map and found true outwide at zero and picked a rock and set the angle and radial and sank that way and restocked my pills and drops and got a few new bolts for the bolt sling and was sinking again just as before with two destinations always picked out ahead, and the sink spreading out wide with rocks plucking themselves from the darkness, and then more darkness rolling out in sheets with more void rolling in or swelling up, until I ran low on pills and drops and had to stop to work a stint at a sheep operation on Lylette, where friction turbines slowly turned the whole rock. By this rotation, the farmers paced out their planting and mating and slaughter. I got a contract shearing sheep and a second grinding gourd dust they manufactured into pills. After work, I'd sit out on the edge as the sink rotated above, and I'd laugh at the table with the others and study the map in my bunk. It was as simple as my life on Fairviel, back when I was a girl who thought she would never leave.

Unsatisfied with the stationary nature of my work, the dream began to churn and intensify the longer I stayed on Lylette. *There was the endless water and the speckled darkness above and the pull downward, toward and through anything in the way, and the sandy rock with my feet sinking in and the shimmering, vertical plane of water and past it even more of the sink or some other sink I could cross into and a voice, far-off and strangely familiar yet unplaceable, and I looked up and outwide and all around the sandy rock but could see no one, so I called out, hoping whoever it was could hear me through the watery plane or through the endlessness of the overvoid or through the distances and layers of dream until* I was shaken awake by a worker in the bunk below me. I'd been talking in my sleep, he said.

The next rest, while we were shearing, that same worker asked me what it was I saw when I dreamed. I told him ever since I left my home rock, no matter where I went to sleep, the dream was the same, or of the same place, a rock surrounded by water as endless as half the sink.

He nodded. "And the dream has changed," he said. "Since you left, there's more of a"—and he looked around to see if any of the other shearers were listening—"downward pull, a force propelling you, calling you." I was nodding my head, staring into his eyes, the centers wide and dark as he continued. "And the longer you stop, the longer you stay in one place, the harder the pull. And there is something else, a plane of some kind, a doorway or passage it seems you could step right through."

"How do you know all that?"

He went eerily quiet for a few breaths, then took a stick and drew in the dirt three intersecting lines. He added pointed heads and fletching so the lines became arrows. He told me I should go seven rests to Grygor's Rock and talk to a man there named Grygor. I should tell him about the dream and draw this symbol out for him. I asked him why, but he refused to say more. The next rest he was gone, skipped out on the remainder of his contract without even taking his wages.

When mine was done, I made sure to get my pay and set out for Grygor's Rock, which took some stagger sinking to get to and was more like ten rests. It had a gently sloping surface, leveled into tiers to serve as holds for traders. Each tier had its own bar, and in the third I found a man named Grygor. He took me to see his father of the same name, who had tattooed on his forearm the same symbol I'd seen scratched in the dirt of the sheep pen: three intersecting arrows. I told Grygor Sr. of the dream, the rock in the water as endless as half the sink, the vertical plane, and the voice beyond it. He told me there was a place where others like me had gathered. I asked how they were like me, and he said all of them had seen different arrangements of the sink, in visions or in dreams. He told me the location of this rock was a secret guarded by people like him to protect something there. I asked him what, but he told me I would have to learn for myself. Once I was there, the dream would make more sense to me. If I wanted to go, he would arrange for my approval and assign a guide to help me get there.

The guide took me four rests straight down, to a small stopover, then outwide three more, then down again at an angle he must have had in his head, because he never looked at a map or checked to see which way was true outwide zero. The guide chatted the entire trip, small-talking constantly even though most of it was lost in the roar. He didn't shut up until we landed on Purseon, where he was to hand me off to another guide, but for three rests we couldn't find him. The place was in a bit of an uproar over a lost supply run that it seems everyone on the rock had been invested in.

"Things are off," the clerk at the trade store told us. "Seems like the whole dang sink is turning around on itself."

Tensions were high, and I went out with only the bolt sling hidden in my belt and a few extra bolts in the deep of my pocket. When the second guide finally did arrive, he said he'd gotten lost on his transit back from some far outwide place I'd never heard of. This guide was the opposite of the first, never talking unless he absolutely had to. After a brief conversation with the one who'd brought me, he snapped down his visor, and we dove off together with hand signals for me to keep close and follow his lead. We sank three rests on pills and drops and finally pulled up into some indeterminate stretch of emptiness. With his visor clicked firmly down, the guide plumed his own map and pointed and made a zigzag with his hand. We set off outwide, then doubled back lower, and after several such back-and-forths, the guide pointed off at something I couldn't see until we sank closer and found our own reflections hovering there like two strangers we'd come across in the void.

The guide made a deliberate motion of pressing his hands over the sides of his helmet. Understanding, I covered my ears. He brought out a small tuning fork that he tapped on a metal wrist guard. Even with my ears covered, the piercing highness of the note cut through, tickling in under my teeth. He tapped the fork again, then waited. There was a hiss, and the mirror shell of Hidden Rock came into view as it crackled with a quick dance of static discharge. Only then did the guide's visor come up so he could yell through the roaring friction, "All clear!"

He showed me a seam in the mirror shell. Following behind him, I came into the inner side of a huge iron framework encasing the rock. The uneven metal frame held up a shell made of hundreds of sheets of mirrored glass, the inward-facing sides all shades of silver and gray. From a high view station welded to the framework, a kid waved at us as we went past. Below, it was like any other small farming rock, a few ranches and fields dotted with cows and goats. Several dozen houses were arranged in clusters along the edge. Closer, a small factory burped smoke from a brick stack.

We sank the short distance from the mirrored shell, landing on a surface that was moss covered and spongy and gave with every step. The barns were climbing with it too, up their corners and in soft splotches of orange-green on the roofs. Only around the houses and in some of the pens was the moss cleared. To do so, they'd sliced it into long sheets and rolled it back, and somehow it all stayed alive in big green and brown spirals. I gazed up at the inner shell, the dark iron framework crossing and recrossing in nothing close to symmetry, the mirror backs an abstract mosaic blocking out all of the overvoid.

THE OVERLAP

I was taken past the rolled-up mosses to a small farmhouse and told to wait at a table in the kitchen. A kid brought tea, then left me alone. I looked out the window at the cows lumbering through the moss, the goats chewing and staring back crookedly, until finally the door opened and a man came in. He introduced himself as Foster and told me he'd been elected by the others to come and talk to me. Like Grygor Sr. and the man at the sheep farm, Foster asked me to describe my dream. I told him about the rock and the endless water and the emptiness of the sink still there above it but with colors that changed and rotated through and became a blackness like the sink but pierced by tiny holes of light, and I told him about the vertical plane of water and the indistinct voices and about my feet sinking into the rock.

Foster seemed pleased or was maybe just overly friendly. "We can help you figure out the meaning of this dream," he said. "We can also tell you what compelled you to travel all the way here. Others, just like you, have been coming for countless generations, drawn by its pull."

"By what's pull?"

"The Overlap." He smiled. "I would be betraying everyone on this rock if I told you more without a vote. It won't take long, a rest or two at most. While you're waiting, you can stay here."

I looked around. The house was clean, well furnished. "No one lives here?"

"No," he answered. "Not anymore."

▼

I had the house all to myself but was told I'd not be able to leave it until the vote. I could see a man out on the porch with that same tattoo, sleeping in a chair. Another was standing at the back gate. He waved and smiled when he saw me. The house was cozy, well-thought-out, and clearly lived-in. All the closets and drawers were empty, but otherwise it seemed like someone could come home any breath. Only with the bolt sling under my pillow was I able to get any rest. Lying in bed, I could hear the distant wailing of a cow. The moo extended and repeated and the details of the room blurred in the dark and I felt as though I was *back on Fairviel, leaning over the edge, except the sink below me was not a bottomless void but the mossy surface of Hidden Rock, somehow only a step away, and I leaned out farther and leapt and felt its spongy give beneath my feet and watched it roll out around me to a closer edge, where it dropped off and became not void but water, the surface of the rock only a small moss-covered oval in all the vastness of it, the single feature a gnarled tree with long-dead branches, and the water all around the moss surface was churning now and lapping and slapping up over the edge, and, turning around, I saw there was a perfect square missing in the moss and above it was the vertical plane of water, through which I could see a different rock, craggy with high rises and valleys full of trees, all of them on fire, and there was a pressure in my fingers and I realized I was holding something, and I looked into my hand and saw myself looking back, and the* softness of the bed pressed up as another long wailing of the cow mixed in with the strange sound of the friction there. I sat up in the bed. I could feel a closeness to the things I'd seen. A lingering pull had come over from the dream, pressing on me as I slipped down the stairs to the front door.

Peering out the window, I saw the guards had left. The rest of the rock was quiet and still. I couldn't see anyone or any signs of life at all. But then I did notice something strange. In the front yard across was the same gnarled tree from my dream. Beside it, instead of a hole in the moss and a plane of water, there was just a house. A small field extended behind it with fat cows chewing on moss and wading in muddy pools where the moss had been rolled back.

I went out the door and across to the tree. Maybe it was not exactly as it had been in my dream. Maybe I'd just seen it on my way in and it got lodged in my subconscious. Still, I could feel a distinct pull. It seemed to be emanating from the house. It was like a voice calling, but with no voice, no sound.

Entering through the front door, I came not into a real house but only a timber frame shell. It had no interior walls or ceiling or even a floor. A dark line was painted all the way across the ground. Past it was an empty dirt square marked off by stone pillars. On the ground between the closest pillars was a flat slab with several strange symbols engraved into it. Otherwise, the timber frame was completely empty. But there *was* something there, pulling me toward it. It was the same feeling as back on Fairviel, all those rests ago, an urge to let go and dive in, to plummet forever into its depths. I looked down and saw my foot hovering over the line, about to step across and me with it.

"Stop!" Someone grabbed me suddenly from behind. I turned to see Foster, his soft beard like a tiny blanket to warm his face. He smiled grimly. "You would not be the first," he said. "The first to try to go in. The dreams, they pull us toward it, those who can see. It is how we all came to be here. For some the pull becomes too much."

Foster pointed to the four stone pillars. Each had a symbol etched into the front, three overlapping arrows. It was not like the tattoo, though, more like three block triangles laid asymmetrically, one on top of the other. "Those mark its edges and height. You must not under any circumstances go past those markers."

"Why?"

Foster had a scrap of wood in his hand. "Watch closely," he said. Slowly, he extended the board out, toward the emptiness. When it crossed over the line, it went rigid as if taken. Foster let it go, and, with a hushing contraction, the board was pulled in. It hung up in the air a breath more, then broke apart into a fine mist that thinned and faded. Then it was just the empty timber frame again, as if nothing at all had occurred, and there never was that scrap of wood.

"That's what happened to them? The one who lived in that house before me? The pull became too much? They tried to go in and . . ."

Foster nodded. "This is the Overlap," he said.

I stared into the emptiness, trying not to see through it to the timber frame behind, but *into* it, to see it itself.

"We believe this space here overlaps with someplace else," he continued. "Our best guess is it's a hole or a tunnel or puncture, if you will, in the very fabric of the void."

"What do you mean, someplace else? Where?"

"We do not know. We think the dreams are a glimpse of what is on the other side. You have passed the test. Getting here to Hidden Rock, finding the Overlap on your own. If you decide to stay, you can help us. Your dream could even be the key."

"The key to what?"

"To getting across."

A PUNCTURE IN THE SINK

The sink thinned and grayed and the friction slowed and warmed and the rock was beneath my feet again, and it was not flat or sandy or spongy moss but hard and brittle and craggy, with high jutting rises as far as I could see, a rock without edge, without end, and a hard crushing roar beat suddenly on my ears, and I turned and saw in the distance a faint glimmer of blue and a roiling whiteness and then water was pouring in and crashing over the farther rises and then the closer ones, and all around me the rock was vanishing under the blueness and the white frothy tumult, and there was a heaviness in my fingers and in my hand a curled-up version of my face looking back, and the water crashed and spread out below, and past its farthest edge the coming of a darkness as dark as the endless void, and all I could think to do was call out, hoping if someone or something heard, they would reveal themselves to me before all was consumed in water and darkness, and I could feel the shouting coming out of my mouth, the loudness of it, but it didn't sound like words, just muffled pulsing waves, and the water crashed harder and rolled back and crashed again and the rock

began to shake, the trees whipping like edge grass, leaves torn free to swirl and be lost in the roiling water, the water raging even harder, throwing itself in gargantuan heaves, brutalizing the edge, and huge chunks of rock broke loose, ejecting thunderous plumes of spray as they vanished in a storm of white froth, and the shaking had spread into the void itself and I could feel the fabric of it shivering, the pulsing rhythm the same as my muffled scream, and the rock and the water and the void above all began to meld and mesh and cone away into a swirl of messy colors and textures and I was suddenly awake in my bed on Hidden Rock.

I sat up, the shifting uncertainties of the non-dream becoming real and solid, first underneath and then around me. The rhythmic crashing of the water was something else now: voices, several, rising and falling into overlapping waves of sound. I got up and went to the window. Where the front walk met several other branching walkways, a small crowd had gathered. Farther off, the glassworks was quiet. It was just there to make replacements for the mirror sheets, but they seldom broke. Mostly the glassworkers worked only enough to keep their skills up.

I'd been on Hidden Rock a dozen rests then, living in that same house. No one ever mentioned the person who'd lived there before, the person who'd thrown themselves into the Overlap. Seamlessly I worked into the routines and patterns of the place. There was some guard duty and lots of farming, all of it done by everyone, rotating through shifts assigned via a long-ago agreed-upon formula. There were cows, just as on Fairviel. There was more space, though, on Hidden Rock, and fewer people, so no need to keep them out on a tether, the cows. On Hidden Rock, they rested and slept right there in the moss fields where they spent the rest of their lives between milkings. On Hidden Rock, instead of standing on the edge and watching the cows floating out, rippled by the friction, I would lean on the field fencing and watch them sleeping on their sides, captured in an eerie stillness but for the big mounds of their bellies and barrel chests, rising and slowly falling with their breath.

I was never sure of the exact amount, but it seemed forty or so people lived on Hidden Rock, most of them lured by some image in some dream or vision, though there was wide variation in the detail. Some people were the children of those who'd been lured, or their relatives, and there were a few I'd have to call fanatics, who seemed to just believe it all for no reason. I wasn't sure how they'd ended up there, or what exception had been made or why.

My attention was drawn again to the crowd on the front walk. There were more people gathering, the talk more animated. When I went out to join them, they told me there had been some kind of attack.

"Who was attacked?"

"Not who," someone said. "Purseon. Purseon was attacked."

"They said it was a metal rock, with wire arms."

"How could a whole rock be attacked?" another asked.

I left them still talking and tracked down Foster. He was working manically to organize another supply run to a different depot, down and outwide.

"The resupply isn't what you should be worried about," I told him. "If this is what I think it is, we need to be ready to leave."

"Ready to leave?"

"Plan out a line, start packing and gathering supplies. Send out a scout to learn more."

There were three of them working on charts spread out on the table, but now they stopped and all looked at me. "We know what it is," Foster told me.

"You do?"

"Something called the Construct. But it can't find us here."

The Construct. The Sinker had never told me its name, but how could it be anything other than what had destroyed Fairviel? The images of my home rock, broken up, the scattered field of debris, the dead faces of Del and Tim and all the others surged back into me. Suddenly there was a noise from outside, a high pealing horn. Foster and the others rushed to the door. Outside, the noise was louder, an alarm ringing from several places. Foster yelled to a kid running by in a glassworker's apron. "What's happened?"

The kid stopped running. He stood there panting, unable to speak. His eyes were big and frantic with his lids crushed to tight multifolds of skin. "A meeting's been called," he finally said. "Two intruders were caught." And he took off running again.

▼

I joined the others, heading to the meeting hall. From outside, it also looked like a regular house. The inside, however, was an open floor plan with a mishmash of benches and stools and overstuffed bag chairs. Twenty or so people were already there with a few more trickling in. Foster was absent, having been elected to question the intruders. All around the hall, people were talking about what had happened: two intruders caught trying to sneak through the mirrored shell. They'd been neutralized by an electrical protection system rigged inside the iron framework. It was unclear to anyone why these intruders had come or how they'd found Hidden Rock, but they had with them an extensive map and an anomaly.

Foster entered then, the big room quieting as he went to the front. He had a box, which he set down on the central table. There was more shuffling, people shifting in their chairs, looking around. Someone stood and said, "Motion to begin the meeting."

"Second," someone else said.

"A vote to start the meeting has been called," said a third. "All for?"

Almost every hand went up, but still the person who called the vote did a count, their lips moving silently as they ticked off the hands.

Now someone else was standing and talking. "First order of business is the intruders."

"The code is the code," someone said.

"We still have to vote, though!"

"Were they guided here by the dream?"

People all looked to Foster for the answer. "No," he said. "They don't know anything about this place."

"How did they get here?"

"It seems Clarabelle told them."

There was another wave and waveform back, a low hushed panic. "Why?" someone shouted. "Why did she tell them?" A few others were shouting the same question.

Foster took a breath to let the room settle into silence again. "Because of the anomaly they have with them," he said, "perhaps the one we have been waiting for." More speculative conversation broke out, bubbling, then fading into a tense quiet. "I think Clara was right in sending it here," Foster continued. "The anomaly is what's important, and the intruders seem completely unaware of what it can do. If they weren't guided here by the dream," he concluded, "I don't see how we can make an exception." There was a lot of head nodding and affirming.

Someone called for a vote. Hands were going up, slowly, then more and more. Someone else yelled out, "Against." Hands went down, and only a few came up. I hadn't voted either way.

A totally new person stood up to declare, "Passed, that no exception to the code can be made."

I leaned toward the person sitting next to me. "What will happen to them, the intruders?"

"Killed, and the map they used to get here destroyed."

"Killed?"

"The code is what's kept this place hidden for countless generations. Anyone who finds Hidden Rock who was not guided by the dream . . ."

Killed? It didn't seem right. But the meeting had moved on, coolly and efficiently. Foster was speaking again. "Next is our most crucial order of business. The anomaly." The energy in the room shifted. This was what people had really come to the meeting for. Anticipation, excitement, fear, all simmered around me.

"Let us see it," someone said. People near the front were already standing, stepping toward the table.

The first person to reach it folded back the box flaps and looked inside. "That's it!" they shouted. "It's what I saw in my dream!" Now everyone was standing, or standing on their chairs, trying to get a clear view.

"It's true!" someone else shouted.

"It's what I've seen too!" said another.

"You're only saying that because someone else said the same thing!"

More people were crowding around the table, arguing back and forth as each got a look and came out with their own opinion. Foster raised both hands, palms out. Slowly, the commotion settled and faded and everyone was looking at him again. "What about you, Emery?" he asked. I was surprised to hear my name. All eyes turned to me as Foster continued. "In your short rests here, I'm sure you've gleaned that the visions that brought us all to Hidden Rock have begun to change. For many, a new image is emerging. There is some disagreement about what this could mean, about what exactly it is people are seeing. As you've recently arrived, your opinion won't be tainted by the opinions and descriptions of others."

I stared back at him over the small crowd. It was hard to know how much of this was calculated. Was it really a democracy, or predetermined mechanics Foster was working us through?

"In your dream," he said, "you saw the Overlap. And you saw someone come across, and they had with them an anomaly. Is that correct?"

"That is one interpretation, I suppose."

"Take a look at it," Foster said. A space had cleared at the front table, people spreading apart to give me a path. I walked to the table and looked into the box and saw a mirrored sphere, and inside it was a curled version of myself looking back. "Is this the same anomaly you saw in your dream?" Foster asked.

"Yes," I had to admit.

The room unraveled into a commotion that drowned out any one voice until Foster spoke up again. "The new images that have appeared in our visions," he said. "The shifting of the rocks. The attack on Purseon. Maps have become unreliable. Operatives have gone silent, and not just on Flux. Perhaps all of it is the sink coming apart around us. And so the dream has brought us the way out. Perhaps we should follow the signs and make an attempt. If it opens the way back, then all of us can go, before whatever happens next."

A voice broke suddenly from the back of the room. "Second!"

Then another: "All those in favor of attempting to cross."

Hands went up. It was not unanimous, but a clear majority had voted for. "Are there any volunteers?" Foster asked the room? "Anyone who would like to be first?"

The murmur went down to a dull whisper until: "I nominate Foster."

"Second."

"All those in favor of electing Foster to make the attempt."

Foster tried to interrupt, but hands were already raised, with more joining them. With a glance, he could see it was well over half. Foster wobbled a little and turned as white as a ghost of himself. Swallowing deliberately, his voice cracking, he managed to say he was honored.

I was still at the front table. Inside the box was something else that caught my eye. It was the map they'd taken off the intruders, but it wasn't just any map. It was a map I recognized. Suddenly it felt like I was back on Fairviel, leaning out into the friction. The pull from the dream had been pulling me here all along, even way back then. But this was a deeper pull, a pull into some more grand facet of the sink, not down, or up, or outwide, but through.

▼

As the whole rock gathered at the Overlap, I snuck back to the house I'd been given. In the bedroom closet was my pack and gear, most of it untouched since my arrival. I took out the bolt sling and the extra bolts and then hurried off for the house where the holding cell was. Like most of the buildings, it looked from the outside like any other home. Sliding the bolt into the groove, I pulled back until I heard the hollow click, then knocked on the front door. The man watching the place opened it, his smile fading when he saw what I was holding.

"What's that?"

"A bolt sling," I told him. "Loaded with enough force to shoot the bolt right through you."

"Why, though?"

"Step inside," I told him, pointing with the pipe barrel. He did as told, backing slowly into the holding cell's outer room. It was her sword—I was sure of it—leaning in the locker with a few other weapons. "Sit there," I told him, pointing to a chair on the other side of the room, "and give me the keys." He took a small ring of keys from his pocket, handed them over, then sat where I'd indicated.

I peered into the cell room through the tiny one-way window, and there she was, the Sinker, the same one who'd come to Fairviel. I unlocked the door and slipped into the cell room with only the bars now separating us. It had been more than a hundred rests since I'd watched her plummet off the edge of Roseblood, and there we both were, in that small room on Hidden Rock. How, in all the sink, had we ended up at the same place, arriving just a dozen rests apart? My eyes locked with hers. The ghost of a smile flickered between us, and for the space of that breath, it felt as if we were old comrades, thrust into a strange situation where we knew no one but each other.

"It's you," she said.

I nodded as I rushed to the bars and worked in the key. The Sinker looked past me, where the guard had come to stand in the doorway. When he saw us see him, he turned and fled. I found the right key, and the cell door clicked open. The Sinker came right up to me, her faint smile spreading into appreciation. I held out her map. "Your weapons are in the next room," I told her. "A hatchet, some knives, your sword."

Smiling coyly at me, she took the map and vanished it into the folds of her suit. "I knew you would leave that rock, but not that you would make it so far."

"That thing you went chasing after . . ." But I stopped, the words caught in my throat. For some reason I'd thought it'd be easier say out loud. Then I realized I hadn't yet at all. I hadn't spoken a single word about it to anyone. "The rock that consumes other rocks," I finally managed. "The Construct . . . It . . . came to Fairviel. . . ."

The Sinker was set again in one of her eerie stillnesses. The centers of her eyes had retreated, looking inward.

"I'd already made up my mind to leave," I continued. "I'd already said goodbye. Then . . . it was just there. We didn't even see it coming. I was knocked out and somehow thrown clear in the first part of the attack. I woke up, maybe a rest or two later, and . . . they were dead. All of them." I thought about Del's strangely circular head, the smaller curl his face made inside it.

"I'm sorry," the Sinker said. "If I'd had any idea . . ."

I was shaking my head. "There's no way you could have known it would come that way." I thought again of that darkness I'd woken into, of the confusion. "If I'd left the rest before, I suppose I wouldn't even know it happened."

"You did the right thing," she said, "deciding to leave. It's impossible to stay alive in a place if you know it's a lie. You leave to stay alive, or you stay and are mostly dead."

I swallowed and then swallowed again and felt the swelling knot, first huge, then dissipating in my guts, like a pill working its way through. "It's on its way here, isn't it?"

The Sinker breathed once, then nodded.

The other intruder had come to the cell door. I wasn't aware of it right then, but I would come to know him as well as any other person in my life: my mother, my husband, my son. He would tell me countless stories about his family, his life on the Slant, its histories and legends and poems and rumors and the fuzzy line that separated them, but that was still to come. Right then, he was just another unfamiliar face. "The anomaly," Crooked Arm said. "Where is it?"

CONVERGENCE

I took the Sinker and Crooked Arm to the timber frame house. From the outside, it looked as plain and normal as always. There wasn't even anyone watching the door. When we pushed in, we saw most of the residents of Hidden Rock gathered up against the far wall. Foster was standing out in front of them, holding the Nest. His face was pale and sweaty, clashing oddly with his dark, felty beard. He was only a step away from the line, looking into the emptiness past the stone pillars.

"What is this?" Crooked Arm demanded. The Sinker had drawn her sword at some undetermined point. It quivered the air as she scanned the crowd for any threat. A bit of terror evaporated from Foster's eyes when he saw us, or perhaps was pulled deeper in. He flashed a last look to the gathered people, the people who said they believed as much as he said he did. Then his back straightened, and he turned and stepped into the emptiness of the Overlap. For a single breath it seemed like it would work. He was there, past the stone slab and the tall pillars, *inside* the Overlap. Foster flushed with relief. The fuzziness of his lower face spread into a huge, wide grin. But it was as fleeting as a random curling eddy from the sink. A blink of intense pain took Foster's face. He jolted minutely, and his body burst into a fine red mist.

The Nest hit the ground with a dense thunk and rolled out of the Overlap, unharmed, to settle on the ground just past the line. No one saw Crooked Arm bend and pick it up. They were all looking at the bloody cloud, still the shape of Foster, hanging ghostlike, then fading to a shimmer, and then a wavering dust, and then gone.

"What do we do now?" someone said. There was no answer or even a noise.

The Sinker had sheathed her sword as invisibly as she'd drawn it. With a few even strides, she stepped to the line. For a breath I was worried she'd be pulled across, but it was the Sinker; she moved only in the direction and how much she desired. Stopping at the line, she reached into her pack and took out a rope. After gazing into the emptiness a breath more, she swung one end of the rope out over the line. It went taut, suspended in air, as if grabbed by something on the other side. All was still a breath, the rope held out straight from the Sinker's grip. Then a sudden hard tug, as if something in the emptiness was pulling it in. Where it crossed above the line, the rope began to dissolve, coming apart into tiny fibers that shrunk and faded away. The Sinker held the rope a breath longer, then let it go, and it whipped and lashed and was sucked in like a noddle.

The Sinker's eyes thinned, the ghost of a rope burn buzzing in her palm. "Some kind of destructive anomaly," she said to Crooked Arm.

"I know this symbol," he said. He was pointing at the etching on one of the pillars. "It was carved into a plaque in the Scorched Dome. But these symbols"—he pointed at the markings in the big stone slab—"these I do not recognize." Crooked Arm turned back to the people of Hidden Rock. "Does anyone know what these symbols mean?"

After a breath of silence a single voice broke out. "No. All of it, the stone markings, the slab, all was set up long ago."

Crooked Arm looked back into the emptiness of the Overlap. "What did he think was going to happen?"

When no one answered, I spoke up. "He thought he could pass through to a place on the other side. Everyone who has come here has dreamed of it, though the details vary widely."

"So they believe this is some kind of passageway?" Crooked Arm said. "That this place you dream of is on the other side? What made him think the Nest was the way across?"

"In the dream, someone crosses through the Overlap, from one place to another, and they're holding something that looks a lot like your anomaly."

"But this mirror surface is only a shell. It's not what it really looks like."

"It's what it looks like to us, to everyone here now."

Crooked Arm nodded and looked longer into the emptiness, struggling to see more than nothing. "Tell me about this place," he said, "that you imagine is on the other side."

"It's different," I told him, "to different people. No dream of it is exactly the same."

"What does it look like to you?"

"Glimpses," I told him, "of a place being destroyed, falling into nothing, water smashing it away. To me it doesn't seem like a beginning but an end."

"What about the rest of you?" Crooked Arm asked, turning to the others. "That's what you see, destruction?"

A few were nodding, others shaking their heads. "Yes"—one of them spoke up—"but many believe it is *this* place that will be destroyed, and on the other side is what comes next."

Crooked Arm disengaged and stepped up close to the Sinker. "We'd always understood our legends to be about the Slant, the fixing of the angle and radial. But maybe, as my father said, it is the story of something bigger." He pointed at the symbols carved into the slab. "'. . . *so distant in the void it may as well have been another void, a battle so far away its words meant nothing.* . . .'"

"They do look like letters," the Sinker said, "but not ones I've ever seen."

Crooked Arm pondered it. "Perhaps the First Sword did not come *from* here but *to* here, through the Overlap, just as these people have dreamed. From here, he goes to the Slant, but then where . . . ?"

"The arrows," the Sinker said, nodding to the stone pillars. "They all point down."

Crooked Arm looked back at the symbols, the three overlapping arrows. "Your map," he said. "The data from the Axium has been added in?" The Sinker got out the map and turned the dial. The projection plumed, motes and dots filling the empty timber frame. "Bring up the Slant." She thumbed the control. The projection swirled and zoomed and racked, until seven perfectly aligned dots hung before them. "Now, can you run a beacon from the line formed by the Slant?" he asked. "And then zoom out. As far as possible?"

The Sinker complied. A thin tracking line speared out from the perfect alignment of the Slant. She thumbed again, the sink condensing, the scale getting smaller and smaller. Finally the zoom stopped. The Slant was up high, the beacon line extending downward, through the map's haze of motes and dots, all the way to the very bottom, to perfectly bisect the lowest rock in the sink.

"'*Look first in the glass eye of the dome*,'" Crooked Arm recited, "'*to take the anomaly and undo the alignment, from the topmost rock to the very bottom.*' But not the bottom of the Slant. The bottom of it all." He pointed at that lowest rock. "How far away is that?"

"Two thousand rests," the Sinker answered. "Of course a guess, and depending on how it's done."

"Two thousand rests," Crooked Arm repeated to himself.

The Sinker held up a hand, tilting her head a little and almost closing her eyes. "Do you hear that?"

Crooked Arm shook his head. I was listening too, but there was nothing. Then suddenly there *was* a sound, but not one difficult to hear. It came sharp and high, reverberating off the wooden timbers of the empty house. It was the repeating peal of the alarm.

▼

The Sinker was the first one through the door, the rest of us spilling out behind her. We looked up at the interior of the mirror shell, the alternating silver and shades of gray blocking out all of the overvoid; Hidden Rock was hidden from the sink, but the sink was also hidden from Hidden Rock. Just as suddenly as it had started, the alarm went quiet, leaving only the harsh crosscurrents and hissing misdirects of the friction off the iron framework. For a breath, everything was calm and still, but I could feel it, a lessening of the pressure, as if the very air of the sink had thinned. From somewhere unplaceable, a sound unlike any I'd ever heard, a deep, hollow thunk.

Above, the largest of the silvered panels influxed and warped and splintered away and became instead a gigantic iron clamp. It crackled with dissipating static charge as it dove, wire tail lashing, to impact in a nearby cow field. Everything shook once, hard. Through the hole created by the shattered panel, we could see a dark complex of gears and dangling chain. Already a transport was descending the wire. A few people took off running, perhaps for their homes, perhaps for the edge. Most stayed where they were, looking up, awed and confused.

"You need to leave!" I shouted at them, surprised by my own voice. "This thing will kill you all! It will destroy everything!" Eyes turned to me, wide with uncertainty and simmering panic.

"Leave?" a voice said. "How can you ask us to leave?"

"We can't leave," someone said.

"We've got to stay and fight them!"

"Fighting them isn't an option," Crooked Arm said.

"She's right," the Sinker told them. "If you want to survive, you've got to go now while you still have a chance."

Before anyone could move, there was another deep thunk from above as another grapple fired. This one hit the iron framework, and the whole shell buckled and all the mirrors shattered at once. There was no sink above us now; it was only the Construct, filling all of the overvoid with its jagged, rocky belly, its thick metal understackings, rough, mechanical edges, angles of iron angling upward from the staggered absorption bays. In the center gaped the terrible sleeping gears of the Maw. A crushing bass rumbled, the propulsion engines spinning down. Loose mirror shards turned and winked as they sucked up into the friction. Two more grapples fired, impacting farther off with a terrible double shudder that shook up through our feet, knocking a few people to the ground. The first transport descended past the barns. Debris could be seen pluming into the air where it hit. The overvoid was a webbing of cables now with boxy transports working down.

"You can't fight it." It was the Sinker. The coldness of her voice cut through the chaos. "But there is something you can do." She stepped out in front. "Is there any paint on this rock?"

Like me, they were all surprised by the question, but one did speak up. "Yes, in the glassworks."

The Sinker pointed at the empty timber frame behind her. "Get as much as you can and pour it on the roof of this house, only this one, the one with the Overlap. As soon as you're done, you clear out, into the sink, and try to escape."

She got some confused looks, but then a few disengaged and went running for the glassworks. "Ladders!" one of them shouted, and more left in another direction. Like a bubble, the rest of the crowd burst and hurried off, some fleeing, others deciding to help with the ladders and paint.

Crooked Arm had stepped up close to the Sinker. "I don't know what you have planned, but I hope it works."

"Me too. You need to go," she told him. "They'll sweep the rock looking for it. And they'll have more in the void to intercept any escape." She turned to me. "Is there some way off this rock, that someone would not expect?"

"Service tunnels," I said, "that lead down to the moisture coils."

The Sinker and Crooked Arm shared an affirming look. As he readied his pack and tightened his straps, the Sinker came closer to me. "You could go with him," she said. "Until some other line pulls you off. He's good; you can trust him. It means a lot out there, having someone you can rely on. It can mean everything."

"I could go with *you*," I said.

"You don't want to go where I'm going." And her eyes ticked upward, toward the Construct looming above.

I nodded, realizing right then that I already knew. "If you'd never come to my rock," I blurted, "I'd be dead. And I'd have died believing all those lies they told me."

"If I had never come to your rock . . . ," she countered, "I'd still be off on an endless sink. My past life was done, all but forgotten, not connected in any way to my current breath. Then, there it was again, that unbalanced code. Suddenly all that breath wasn't just some other life but exactly what I needed when the two converged."

The surface shook with the landing of another transport, then another. A few more were almost down the wire. The Sinker put her hand on my arm, and I looked at her and our gazes held. I felt my breath, the wholeness of it, felt it scrape in off the edge, broken into pieces by the mirrored shell, pulled in through my nose, then rebuilt inside me and exhaled as one, and with a last push I found even more, something borrowed from the uprushing, a piece of the friction held too long, and with a final exhale the breath was gone.

Turning back to Crooked Arm, the Sinker went into her pack. She took out her map and put it into his hand. "Take it," she said.

When he looked up, his eyes were rimmed with brimming tears. "I thought I'd spend my life on Vertex," he said, "that I'd have to, and I really didn't care, one way or the other. Now I'm headed to the bottommost rock in the sink, to the very end, if there is one."

The Sinker cocked a grin at him. "Not if the Great Flat gets you first."

He held out his hand and the Sinker gripped it, and he pulled her into a one-armed hug. Her arms went around him too. "You will buy me some breath?" he asked.

"It may have that effect."

They held the hug a breath more, then parted and looked into each other's eyes. Then she was running off across the mossy field until we could no longer see her, and the chaos above seemed to fade to translucence, and a breath of false quiet settled, then too was gone.

A RIVER THROUGH THE VOID

Only a ripple in the natural curling of the friction marked the Sinker's path across the surface of Hidden Rock, plummeting into the darkness between the cisterns and the barn, vanishing and reappearing at the side path, at the cluster of back sheds, at the corner fence post near where the transport had touched down. A dozen droppers, early salvage, out for perishables. She advanced on them in the same cold and efficient way she cut through empty void, not silent, but lower than the background fabric of the roar and so unperceived. A series of sinks: barn corner to toolshed to the big, curled moss that edged the muddy watering place. Two of the cows lay there dead from something thrown up when the grapple impacted, one's head so thoroughly bashed it seemed a different animal. Nearby, the droppers were encouraging the live cows into a big group. Others were using a steam lift to load the dead ones onto the transport. One of the droppers was pointing her way. She ducked down farther behind the moss roll.

"There're a few over there," she heard him say. "Get them on so we can start to load the live ones."

The Sinker cut an eye around the corner of the rolled moss. A dropper was pushing the steam lift over, puffing and hissing along. Above, the big wire snaked upward from the transport, lost in the hazy, complicating layers of the Construct. All of the overvoid was swallowed by it. The big teeth of the Maw seemed to swell and ebb with breath, an effect of the changing distance as the engines worked to hold the delicate balance. In subtle shifts of tension, the wires slackened and tightened and groaned and warbled almost musically. The Sinker could see the sharp enfilading edges of the Far Machines, invisible but for their movement against the Construct's expansive underbelly.

She crept around the big mossy roll and got down beside the cow with the smashed head. The dropper was to the other dead one. The steam-lift tines slid under it, and there was a sudden high hiss. The Sinker peeked over the closer carcass, watching the other dead cow being whisked away, deposited in a pile in the back of the transport. The lift was turning and heading back her way. The Sinker hid behind the smashed cow's huge body and steadied her blade and readied herself for it. When the dropper reached the cow and got the tines under its carcass and with a tremendous hiss lifted it away, the Sinker was nowhere to be seen.

▼

The transport wobbled and turned against the dark backdrop of the sink, swaying from the grapple wire as it winched into the wide mouth of the absorption bay. A team of sorters was finishing with the first one. The container was empty now with the small herd of goats led off. Other sorters worked in twos, one at each end, to lift the dead goats one by one onto a slow-rolling conveyor belt, beginning their long journey to Vitals. A dozen droppers entered. Laughing at the sorters, they helped, huffing and grunting and laughing louder as they tossed the rest of the goat carcasses onto the belt. Then the droppers climbed into the emptied transport and strapped themselves down. The door was cranked shut and, with a lurch, the transport lifted away. Swaying back and forth, it descended toward the rock below.

The foreman took it all in with his hands in fists at his hips, trying to look like the biggest person in the room now that the droppers were gone. The second transport was settling into place, and the sorters approached and threw over the boot levers and cranked open the door. A few cows wandered out of the darkness, heads lolling, mooing confusedly. Behind them, a few more with broken legs were unable to stand, throwing their heads back, bellowing forlornly. There was one with no head at all, only a red mush where its head had been, and still the rib cage was expanding, contracting. Something was under the soft belly flesh, a small lump moving slowly. The protrusion went still and then swelled, the cow's flesh rising in a point, then splitting. The tip of a sword emerged, then more, until the whole blade shone wet and greasy with blood. Then an arm, and then a shoulder, and then she was climbing out, red and black with gore but for her gleaming eyes.

One of the sorters approached and something flashed, and the sorter turned back to the others with a brand-new red line across his throat. He fell face down on the bay floor, still but for a spreading pool of blood. The others could see her now, lean and blood-slicked in the open transport door. A slim edging of her sword winked through a streak of fresher, redder blood. Only her eyes moved, counting them and their distance in breaths.

Another transport was wobbling and winching its way in. A panicked bleating could be heard from inside. The bay door opened, and the next batch of droppers was there, horsing around as they readied to board. Their laughter faded when they saw the Sinker.

A single breath of stillness took the bay. On the exhale, her sword blurred into a wheel of motion, sweeping back and rolling out smooth. Chain guns launched, haphazard, panicked, tangling with the chains of other chain guns on the retract. The Sinker's blade flicked fresh blood in artful arcs. She was gone from where she was and somewhere else instead. Like a lashing wind from the sink, she swept the bay. In thirty-seven breaths she stood still again, scanning for what could be next, but all the droppers and sorters were dead. The only motion was the smoky swarms of flies and a single lumbering cow. It blinked at her, not comprehending in the least. "Mooooo."

The Sinker crept to the edge, gripped the rim of the bay mouth, and swung underneath. She could see the central chassis where the axle joint connected Core Rock to everything built after. She remembered her father explaining it to her, how the Construct all fit together, how it could be separated only in the axle room and only with the Garent's ring.

Closer, swarms of bolts hung in perfect rows, charging on the up-rushing friction, and she realized then how near she was to the end and the beginning, to both the long arc of her transit through the void and the smaller one of her life. The circling cycles of the sink had brought her back, not only to the Construct, but to that same space she'd hidden in as a girl, unexpectedly right in front of her. Not the same exact beetles—but ones like she remembered still clung to the bolts, somehow evolved to feed off the static charge.

The Sinker climbed lower, coming to the weld in the joint where the metal joists had been forever melded with rock. The space there in the elbow of it was even smaller than she remembered. She pulled herself to it and stuck her head in. Closer to a helmet than a hiding spot, but she'd fit in there at some point. I must have been so small, she thought. She pulled herself out and went still, listening to the friction scrape past it, the empty howl it made, that low note that had rung in her head ever since, and always would.

▼

The people she passed were technicians and sorters. They slowed and their eyes went wide, but none made any move to stop her. She was, of course, still covered in blood and cow gore and carrying a sword likewise decorated. The halls seemed shorter to her, thinner. Everything smaller after so long in the wideness and depth of the sink. And she'd forgotten about the bugs. Every few steps she'd feel a sharp crunch and look down at some shattered exoskeleton. Overall, things hadn't changed, and she found the grapple pit with ease. She slipped in and closed the door and made it to the bottom of the cast-iron stairs without a sound. There were only three of them, a target master and his two techs.

"Turn around," she told them, and when she saw the target master's face, she knew he was the kind of righteous prick who would not back down. His teeth clenched and he leapt at her, and his two technicians, emboldened by his courage, charged in after. The Sinker took a short forward step, an overlapping second, then a lunge, the sword dancing in perfect counterbalance. Then she was still again, and the target master and his techs lay on the floor, their slimmed eyes pointing off at nothing.

The Sinker approached the big crank and the three smaller dials arranged underneath. A fat, furry caterpillar was making its way across the wheel. She let it climb onto her finger, then set it on a counter nearby. Looking into the periscope, she could see the surface of Hidden Rock below, enlarged in the lens. The fields and goat pens moved by in amazing detail as she rolled the crank, a central spot of focus around a distorted muddiness. She watched it wobble and move, and then she had it moving the right way, the viewer gliding over the rowed houses. And there it was, after a few turnings of the crank, the roof covered with spilled paint.

"Good job," she said under her breath. She squeezed the release and felt the percussive thrust of the grapple launching out. She watched it in the periscope, the wire spooling loose. The grapple hit with an explosion of dust well wide of her target. "Shit."

The Sinker wasted no breath. She looked into the periscope and adjusted the crank to compensate. There was only one release left. One more grapple. One more shot. "Stop!" A dropper stood in the doorway with a chain gun. The Sinker turned and whipped her sword arm and the sword vanished, and the dropper looked at where it was now, embedded in his chest.

The Sinker went back to the periscope. A last quarter turn of the center dial brought the target to a new position, a little off from the painted roof. She took the only remaining release, held her breath, and pulled. She felt the hard intake of the launch letting all springs loose. In the periscope, she watched the mooring wire lash and lash back, the huge grapple getting smaller as it rocketed away.

All things hung then as if suddenly asleep out in the wide-open void, given over to the cupping hand of the uprushing friction, whatever it would do. In the periscope's central spot of focus, she saw the grapple impact the painted roof, exploding the timber frame shell beneath it. Instantly the thick mooring wire went taut. The Sinker slammed the retract, and the big shoulder spool began to wind in. With a lurch, she was thrown to the floor. All around her, iron groaned and resettled. She could feel distinctly now the even and measured descent. She struggled to the periscope. Her eyes fell down the lens's blurred outer rim, toward the clarity at the center. The timber frame was smashed and scattered, the thick mooring wire being pulled into the Overlap, and the Construct with it. She could feel the answer of the engines as all three revved up to full power. But it only added noise.

LAST DESCENT

The knock came as he was finishing lunch. At the sound, Hiram Goegal did not go to the door. Instead, he took his plate to the counter and stood still in the quiet, listening for the second knock, wanting again some sound inside his life that was not of his or Florina's making. He pressed his hand flat to the counter and looked at the smooth, soft flesh, marred only by freckles and moles and the squishy, tubey lumps of crisscrossing veins. Even now, almost a dozen rests later, he still had trouble accepting that this was indeed his own hand. He moved his fingers and watched the fingers of the healed hand move the same way.

    The first thing he'd done, immediately after his scar vanished, was to check his thigh. The cut from the knife was also gone. The stitches were still there, now just useless loops through his flesh. He'd snipped them and pulled them out one by one, then tried the anomaly again. The tiny pinpricks left from the stitching sealed up and smoothed out too, until there were no marks left from the wound at all.

Hiram Goegal had waited patiently a few rests for a message from the Garent. When none came, he sent in a request of his own, which was never returned. Since the Construct set out for Hidden Rock, the Garent had not come out of his tower, nor, to Hiram Goegal's knowledge, had anyone gone in, not even the barons. Hiram Goegal conducted several follow-up experiments to gauge the green crystal anomaly's method of activation and effect, then a few rests in the lab, rerunning old tests and implementing new. He had a way to heal—it seemed almost any injury—but still no usable energy could be produced from it.

Hiram Goegal kept the findings to himself. The green crystal anomaly would certainly be useful, but exactly how he did not yet know. His only option became to wait and see what the Garent would do next. A few rests became five, then ten, then eleven. By Hiram Goegal's calculations the Construct had reached the void around Hidden Rock earlier that rest, and, indeed, he had felt their descent begin to slow.

When finally the sound of the second knock came, Florina fluttered inside her cage. "I hear it," Hiram Goegal assured her. On the other side of the door was one of the Garent's guards. Hiram Goegal recognized the man but could not remember his name and felt a fleeting twinge of guilt.

"Mr. Goegal," the man said. "The Garent requests your presence."

"He does?" but Hiram Goegal was not surprised. He'd had faith the Garent would bring him back in when the breath was right. As the guard led him through Piping, then down the main way of Core Rock, Hiram Goegal could feel the distinct lift in his stomach as the Construct slowed further. There had been rumors of more defections, people leaving or grumbling about doing so. Hiram Goegal wasn't sure how true they were. Could there be others like Dugan, slipping silently into the overvoid? How many? On the far edge, he could see Engine Three rotating back upright. Its fat bottom rumbled, and a low blue radiance upfaded, burning along the whole rim. There was another, more subtle lift, and then the friction shifted and their rapid descent was suddenly over.

"Mr. Goegal," the guard said. Hiram Goegal realized he'd stopped walking to watch the engine. His stomach was reorienting itself to the rudder of upward thrust. The guard was feeling it too. He laid a hand over his lower abdomen and pressed a frown. "I sure don't like that feeling," the guard said. Then they were moving again, through the tower's front entrance and up the central stairs to the Garent's study.

He was waiting by the huge fireplace and, even in the blazing heat, was still bundled in several layers of wool and a puffy frock coat with fur trim. It was all topped off with a hat twice as large as the Garent's head. He was standing perfectly upright as always, seeming impossibly tall and wide with the hat and jacket, but the face inside all the layers looked as old as Hiram Goegal had ever seen it, a rotten water fruit set in the furry mounds of his collar.

Turning toward Hiram Goegal, the Garent extended his hand, and the two men shook. As they came apart, a gleam lit the Garent's eyes. "Your hand," he said. "You found it!" He smiled. "The method to unlock that anomaly: any open flame will do it."

"How did you know, my Garent?"

The Garent returned his gaze to the bursting flames, engorged on a heaping stack of combustion sticks. "In a different life," he said, "I was like you, in a way. I too studied anomalies. Or looked for them is more correct. Like you, I had a partner in this endeavor. I searched for them, and he deciphered them, unlocked them. That one you have in your flat, I'd seen it before, long ago. My partner had unlocked it, like he'd done with many others. It was his specialty." Hiram Goegal watched the Garent's distant eyes, reflecting back mirrored fingers of branching flame. "The Nest, as it is called, is also an anomaly with which I am familiar."

Hiram Goegal breathed once, long and even. "What can it do, the Nest, when activated?"

The Garent looked into the floor. "I do not have an exact answer. I do not know all of what was done with it before or how. I believe it did arrange the rocks of the Slant, and quite a lot more."

"How many are there?" Hiram Goegal asked. "Anomalies."

The Garent thought. "Thirty? A hundred? An infinite amount? I do not know. Nor do I know nor understand how they could have survived all that happened, but they have."

"I wanted to come and tell you," Hiram Goegal said. "I wanted to ask you more about it, but you'd shut yourself away, my Garent."

"Yes," the Garent said regretfully. "In addition to the planning of all of this, I have had much to think about." The Garent turned more fully to him and smiled. With one hand, he gestured to the view screen set into a bubble on the table. They stepped to it and looked into its liquid darkness. "What do you see?" the Garent asked.

"Empty void."

"This is the undervoid, right now," the Garent said. "But it is not empty. There is something there. . . ."

Hiram Goegal looked longer into it. "Hidden Rock."

"Yes." The Garent seemed more tired than pleased. "We are about to launch the first grapple. Far Machines are in the underoutwide, the bays prepped with droppers on tether engines to intercept anyone who tries to escape."

As promised, there was the hollow thunk of the first grapple releasing. Hiram Goegal could see it in the bubble viewer, slipping into the darkness, its wire tail unspooling into spiraling oblongs. It hit something and opened a hole in the void and through it a tiny glimpse of a cow field. Another grapple was fired, and the darkness of the void gleamed and glinted and became a thousand tiny pieces of glass. A bluish discharge of static electricity crackled away, and there it was, Hidden Rock, hidden no more. A grapple was already attached, a transport gliding down. A second, then a third fired and impacted, and the wires snapped taut.

"My apologies that I planned all this in secrecy," the Garent said. "But it had to be right. I do hope it is enough, that we will capture the Nest, that you can use it to achieve the Forever Rise, but . . ." And here the Garent trailed off.

"Yes, my Garent?"

He nodded. "I believe my fate has become separate from the fate of this place, though how it is to happen is very confounding and mysterious to me still. Something unexpected, I am sure, if the sink is truly symmetrical, if it has all come together again as I suspect."

They settled in above the viewer, watching more transports gliding down, the first ones returning. All of it was a haze of far-off motion, impossible to follow in any detail. A courier arrived, and Hiram Goegal felt a lift of anticipation. Had they finally captured it? But it was a report about a fight of some sort in one of the bays. The Garent dismissed the man and came back to the viewer.

"Anything we should be concerned about?" Hiram Goegal asked.

The Garent seemed lost in thought. Another thunk suddenly reverberated up through Hiram Goegal's feet, another clamp firing. He saw a flush of confusion wash the Garent's face. Another thunk and another clamp was sailing away. Hiram Goegal watched the second one impact far below. The wire snapped tight, and then he was on the floor, looking up at the table's thick pedestal leg. He felt his stomach compress with a sudden drop. The room around him was shuddering, the whole of the Construct, it felt like. A distant roar kicked up, then another, humming in harmony, the unmistakable sound of the engines firing to full.

Hiram Goegal pulled himself to his feet, looking back into the viewer. The Garent was working his way up as well. The room shuddered hard again, and they swayed and swayed back. "What happened?" the Garent asked.

Hiram Goegal steadied himself on the rim of the bubble viewer. "Something has the clamp wire! Something on the surface. I can't imagine how, but . . . it seems to be . . . pulling us in."

Baffled and wide-eyed, the Garent came to see for himself. The small rock below was getting larger as they were inexplicably pulled toward it. "I should have left this place," the Garent said, suddenly ghost white, "back when I first suspected, when we first reached the Slant." He sighed at himself with a final curse. "Another of my selfish decisions."

The Garent watched it all unfolding a breath more, his eyes scanning over the bubble as they drew ever closer. Finally his gaze lifted, and he stepped away and seemed again a younger version of himself. "I have guaranteed the people here that I will save them from the Flat. Perhaps I cannot follow through for them all, but I can for most." The Garent put a hand on Hiram Goegal's shoulder. "You must help, my friend. Go to Piping. Get as many people out as you can, into other districts, or into the sink if need be."

"What will you do?" Hiram Goegal asked.

"The only thing I can. Release that section of the Construct and hopefully save the rest."

RETURN TO THE SINK

I led Crooked Arm through the access passageway they used to service the moisture coils. It was a narrow descent through the center of the rock, slippery and slow going, everything coated with paper-thin sheets of ice. The coils gleamed with drops that swelled and sucked into the mineral filters. We felt no more thudding or percussive bursts from above. We couldn't hear anything from the surface at all.

Finally, we made it down the last of the thin passage and came out on the underside of the rock. Below, the iron framework was bent and sagging. Sub-webs of it had broken off to drift away. Mirror shards dotted the undervoid, larger ones rotating to show fleeting glimpses of what the destruction looked like from farther off. We could hear more thumping from the rock above now as another clamp impacted the surface, then another.

Scanning the undervoid, Crooked Arm cursed. I could see them now too, a half dozen Far Machines circling the perimeter below. We watched them moving smoothly along, dark jagged bleeds against the more pure blackness of the void. From their fronts, cones of searing light ignited, probing the void in slashing overlaps.

"We're not going to be able to get past them," Crooked Arm said.

But then we saw the Far Machines shift and begin to rise, and suddenly they were gone from view. Below us, past the twinkling debris of the broken shell, the undervoid was empty.

"Where are they going?"

"I don't know," Crooked Arm answered, "but I bet she had something to do with it."

"It destroyed her home too?" I asked. Right then I still didn't know. The Sinker had actually never told me anything about herself, not really.

"You could say that," he answered. "The three of us are the same in that way." He turned to look up at the underrock, as if he could see through it, to the Construct, to whatever fate the Sinker was rushing toward. "If you're coming," he said, "we'd better go." Then he was moving again, climbing down into the coils.

I thought, for only one compacted breath, of the line I'd made from Fairviel and where it would go next. What would it look like when laid out in a map at the very end? Then he was pushing off and I was right behind him, hurtling into the uprushing void. He pointed—four droppers sinking hard on us, tether engines flaring. Past them, Hidden Rock and the Construct and the Far Machines firing their clamps and rods at what I couldn't tell. Crooked Arm was shouting at me to make some space, and it reminded me so much of that first trip to Roseblood with the Sinker.

As the droppers closed on us, Crooked Arm's hatchet warbled through the friction. The lead dropper's face fell in. His engine tether careened and tangled with another tether, and the two engines wound around each other and crunched a dropper caught between. A chain gun fired off wildly, lashing its razor tail. Crooked Arm rolled and threw his hatchet into the draft of the retract, and the blade side lodged in the dropper's chest. The last dropper was on him, chain gun aimed at Crooked Arm's head, but I'd closed the distance. I pointed the bolt sling into his back and pulled the trigger, and his body jerked and went still. I could see the bolt had passed clean through, turning off slowly into the void with droplets of blood in shifting patterns around it. Crooked Arm retrieved his hatchet and pushed the body off, and it tumbled up and away with the others.

By then we'd sunk far past the scattered debris of the mirror shell, now just odd winkings of light above. Farther off, the hulking Construct with Hidden Rock a tiny morsel at the end of its many tethers. More droppers were coming, fiery dots against the chaos. Crooked Arm and I took the tether engines and pointed them down and pressed them full throttle and held on and sunk hard until the engines gave out and the Construct and Hidden Rock and the Sinker were gone, and all above us was the dark emptiness of the void.

THE EMPTY CAGE

Hiram Goegal was running to get back to his flat. People had come out of their homes, crowds gathered around the bases of the stacks, demanding information, arguing, some packed up and heading for the closest edge. When he finally made it to Piping, he was sweating and had fallen and torn his pants. Outside his building, a neighbor he recognized grabbed him by the jacket. "Goegal, what's going on?!"

"Get yourselves and your families into the Alloy District as fast as you can." But it sounded crazed and foolish, and the woman only stared at him like he was mad. Hiram Goegal said nothing more, pushing past her and into the building's front door. The lift was crowded with people screaming and shoving with the doors jammed open. Hiram Goegal circled to the stairs and bound up several with each step, then down the floor hall to slip finally into the relative quiet of his flat.

He went to the cage first and gently opened the door. He watched Florina, hanging from her foot hooks, completely inanimate. "My sweetie," he said. Next he was at the kitchen window. He cranked it open and pulled out the screen. A few flies buzzed in and swirled and flew in deeper. The roar from the distant engines was impossibly loud, even from so far away. One side of the Construct was being pulled harder now, and he could feel a slight tilt.

Florina had finally come out of her cage, dancing crookedly toward him. She landed on his arm—so light he could not feel it at all—then lifted off again and fluttered out the open window. Hiram Goegal watched Florina's fractalling rise until she was a dot, then a speck, and then too far to see at all. Another hard shudder increased the tilt, and Hiram Goegal turned and watched one of his high bookcases fall over forward.

He found himself with a bag slung over his shoulder, standing in front of the remaining shelves, but then realized he would take only one thing. He lifted down the green crystal anomaly and slid it into the bag. The room shuddered hard again, and more crashed to the floor around him. The Garent should have released the axle by now, he thought. He snapped the clasps of the bag down as he went into the hall. From the drawer he took his spring gun, then paused and turned and looked back into the flat where he had spent most of his life: the small kitchen, the bedroom, dark beyond the door, ghosts of Dugan in the dented sofa cushions, the empty wire bell of Florina's vacant cage.

THE SYMMETRY OF THE VOID

The Sinker found the axle room and climbed up to the higher catwalk and became one with the shadows and waited, and when the Garent and his guards arrived, she waited more, until they were in the room and the door was closed, and then she dropped on them and one of the guards was dead before her feet landed in near silence, and her arm lashed and the boot knife appeared in one's throat and he fell too, and when the other guards looked, she was at the base of the stairs that led to the big axle, her sword out before her, and there was a stillness in which the Garent peered over the shoulders of his guards, and the three in front widened their legs and leveled their chain guns, and there were several overlapping clicks as the triggers tumbled free and the spiked balls leapt and the Sinker dove and rolled and felt the vibrating clang off the stairs and the rattling clatter of the retract, and she leapt up and saw another ball already retracted and punching out again, and she sidestepped and stomped the chain at the perfect tautness so the ball swung back wildly and shattered the legs of the one who'd fired it, and she slashed and leapt and dove and rolled up to her feet and was among them at close quarters now, and the counter wheeling of her free arm fell into synch with her steps and her sword became liquid, with the blade cycling smoothly through each counter into the next until a hard clang off a hidden forearm guard broke her flow and her sword rang and almost vibrated out of her hand, but she used the parry to re-collect and spin the other way, and her sword made a whimper through the air, then a soft tug, and she was splashed with an arcing of blood and felt a dull thud in her hip and the floor was suddenly above her and a kick landed hard between her neck and shoulder and she yelled and saw through the pain the Garent and two of the guards making for the stairs to the shoulder axle, and she threw her second boot knife, which stuck in the Garent's arm, and the guards caught him falling back and the Sinker's knee bent sideways and she screamed and rolled, and above her was a contorted face with a chain bar wheeled back but already she'd sliced through the tendons on his leg and he folded backward, and the ceiling opened up and the chain bar clattered away and a click came from somewhere and she put everything she had into a roll as another spiked ball punched through, and she saw the chain go taut and the spiked ball streak by again, now sopped with blood, and she rolled but was kicked in the stomach and looked up and saw them clustered around her with quarter swords slashing and chain bars whipping down and iron club shafts bristling with electric current, and she flailed at their legs and one went down nearly on top of her and all she could see was a mess of angles and fluid and her own gleaming sword blurred in drunken streaks, and something solid hit her face and she gasped and was helpless for a breath, and the whole Construct shook suddenly and she slid and crashed into a heap with at least two others grabbing at her and yelling, and one had her hair and she bit into a wrist until she felt bone crack, and she pushed up and the floor was turned again and she was standing somehow with one eye squinting through the stinging blood, and the ones left were more of a single shape and she slashed at the farthest tendrils and, feeling with her foot, found the bottom step and pushed back against it to thrust forward, and her slashes were parried by one or two or three of them, and she retreated up a step and then another, and when they came, she was above them now with their faces turned up wide and red slashes appearing and more screaming faces filling the bloodied emptiness, and a sharp current bit her side and her leg and left arm went numb and she smelled the sparks and scalded flesh and something had wrapped her wrist, and she tangled it further and yanked and lifted her sword tip into the guard pulled forward by it, and she lowered her shoulder and pushed him back and several of them were falling and her hand was on the lower stair, and through the swirling haze of motion she saw the Garent lying on the floor, holding his arm, but then he was swallowed by the chaos of the closer men, and she slashed holes in their solid shapes and pieces of them fell away, and from the smear of blood and sweat and flesh the flashing of a sword, and she parried, but the force shot the sword from her hand and another slash went all the way down her other leg, replacing the simmering numbness, and she fell and rolled and felt a guard looming over her and reached up and grabbed his collar and pulled him down hard onto the top of her head and felt his jaw crack and saw his wide mouth falling crookedly away, and sparkles were clearing from her eyes as she grabbed her sword and slashed across a stomach and stood and spun and felt the easy give of an opened throat, then an artful parry, and with a last simple wheeling, all went still but for the blood dripping through the grating, plopping sounds somewhere far below.

 The Sinker ended it where she'd started, blocking the stairs to the shoulder axle. Only the Garent was left. He'd been thrown in all shaking and was just getting to his feet. He had fresh bruises on his face and the boot knife was still in his arm, but he seemed unaware of it. The Sinker locked her eyes on him, not bothering to wipe away the blood that dripped from her face. "I was unsure if you would come," she said.

"No. You were certain, or you would not be here. You knew what would happen if one of the grapples made contact with it, the Overlap." He nodded at the room's central joint, the slot for his signet ring. "Here is the only place the shoulder can be released. And I am the only one authorized to alter the central chassis."

"If you do, everyone in that sector of the Construct will be killed. The whole Piping district."

"And if I do not, *all* will die. We're getting as many people out of Piping as we can. Some will make it into the sink, and hopefully we can pick them up after. The Far Machines are trying to break the wire, but they won't be able to."

The room shuddered hard, followed by a high ringing reverberation. The Sinker could feel the increased speed of descent as her stomach pushed back against it.

"That was one of the engines giving out," the Garent said. The knife in his arm was bright red down the handle now. But he wasn't concerned, looking only at her, long at the details of her face, breaking down the smallest features until even the Sinker could not bear it and looked away.

"I wondered if it could really be you," he said. "After all this breath, after how far we both must have moved through the sink. It seemed impossible, but I also knew it must be true." He opened his hands to her. "Here I am. You've gotten me here. You have what you want. Let me release the shoulder axle and then we can talk."

Her blade wavered out before her, soaked and soaked over with blood and dried and resoaked again. Her own blood was seeping in, shiny with fresh wetness. "I did not come here to talk," she said. "This place ends. Everyone here ends. Everything the Construct was or is or could be is over."

Metal groaned and clanged somewhere. Roaches began emerging from seams in the floor. Others made their way up the walls. An engine had burst and the fire spread to Waste; now it was the bugs swarming upward, desperate to escape their fate.

"Each person must decide for themselves what they are willing to believe," the Garent said. "But I saw the Flat with my own eyes, the horrible finality of it, the endless outwide, but finite too, in that there can't be anything past it. After that, I rose, fast as I could, spreading the word. The smart ones listened, then more. We built the engines, added the stacks, saving more and more, getting further and further ahead of it." His face paled, turned waxy and gray. "But the sink thinned. The absorption became forced . . . brutal . . ." The Garent's eyes filled with tears. He looked at the Sinker through the blurry wetness. "She was right about it, the absorption. I have tried, with every breath since, to find some other way of doing it. Strangely, it is that quest which brought me to this place, to you. It was when I lost you, when I lost her, that this ending began."

The Sinker only stared back, as unchanged as the empty void. "You didn't *lose* her. She hated what this place was. She was going to leave and you killed her, you . . ." She stopped. The bottom had fallen out of whatever she was going to say.

The Garent was nodding. "Yes," he said. "I know what I did." His eyes tracked a big roach scuttling over his boot. He followed it to where it joined with a few others, forming a line up one of the support columns. All around they scurried, climbing over the dead guards as if they were part of the floor. The Garent gripped the knife handle suddenly and yanked it out, then tossed it to the floor. He took a step and was still again. "Maybe she did hate this place, or maybe it was just the reason she gave. I offered to go with her, to take you, and the three of us would leave together." He expanded with a breath, then was smaller again. "She said no. That she would go alone. We fought—or *I* fought, I suppose—yelling, screaming at her. And then it was as if . . . as if having awoken into it, from some other place. And I saw her there . . . then you. Your shape vanishing from the door. The smacking of your bare feet down the hall, quieter and quieter."

The Sinker's eyes shimmered, a crack in the coldest, most empty void. "I see it every rest," she said. "The red blood on her neck, that short blade in your hand. Your knuckles were white and bloodless inside and speckled with it on the out. With her blood. I remember too a thin smoke. Maybe it was a candle put out in the scuffle. But I thought it was her soul, leaking up through her torn-open dress, through her skin and the ceiling of that tower room, off into the void above. A breath later it was just as you said, as if waking into it. I was clutching a stolen sword, *this sword*, and leaping from the edge, into the endless sink...."

A tear broke a cleaner path through the blood and gore, a single gleaming streak on the Sinker's face. She saw the arrangement of the room from above, briefly, in a flash through her mind. She was back in this place, sword in hand, with him. What more proof could there be of the silent, invisible converging nature of the sink? It was like Big Iron, lurking above that corn farm so many rests ago, pulling things toward it, not for any reason beyond its natural function. She could feel these same mechanics permeating the local fabric and so likely all of it, some indifferent force, some magnet at the heart of the void. "I was gone forever from this place," she said. "It was the sink that brought me back, that aligned our paths to cross again."

He nodded, agreeing. "It is amazing how it has come together. That somehow, only by looking for something else, was I able to find the way out again, and the way to remake it too. But I no longer want it, no longer want either. I want to save the people here. I wanted to see you again." Tears were wet now on his face. He held out his hand, opening it to reveal the small flat rock anomaly, heavy-looking and dark in the cup of his palm. He lifted it and pursed his lips and hum-whistled those three descending notes. The flat rock began to glow, and above it formed the face of a child, a smiling girl. "I've looked at you every rest since," he said. "It is as fresh as the breath you left."

It was no shard of mirror glass, nor still pool of water, but a reflection through all the breath that had passed since. The Sinker stared into the young face, a glimpse of someone else entirely, but still connected to her in a way that could never be severed, no matter how far she sank or how far outwide, no matter how many layers added, or rocks plummeted past, or codes set to right. It would always be her, a sliver that could never vanish in the void, even an endless one.

The Garent closed his hand, and the floating image flicked away.

He smiled at her more current face. "No matter what happens next," he said, "I am glad I got to look at you one last breath. The real you, as you really are now." Flies had begun to swirl the room, corkscrewing swarms spiraling upward. There was a shiver, and a few pipes cracked and more beetles poured up, spilling across the floor like brackish water. The Garent tried to embrace her with his eyes, a soft pleading. "I am sorry," he said.

The Sinker let an exhale finish, then drew in so even and complete that the room bent into the rhythms of her aliveness. "Lots of things seem endless," she said, "until they end. I forgive you. But the sink does not."

With a long step, she closed the last distance between them and drove the blade into his heart and withdrew it cleanly and without a noise. Blood flowed from the wound in great profusions. The Garent looked confusedly at it, his hand already there to stanch the gushing. He peeked under his palm and saw it splashing out in burps. "It does not hurt," he said, amazed.

"It is my final kindness. You are still my father for a few more breaths."

He peered at her, and it seemed only their eyes were left with the rest of the sink wiped away. "Save them," he said. "You have your revenge, your redemption. The code is set right. Now you can save them, the people who live here." Already he had turned ghost white. When he tried to step, he found he had not the strength so went down to one knee, then fell forward onto his face. After all the endless rests he had lived in the void, he was dead. The Sinker breathed long and slow. A grand dedication had righted an old code. The sink, its long-forming shapes uncertain, had found again a bit of symmetry.

It was then that it appeared, poking out of the Sinker's chest, a long barbed spike, slimed with blood. Behind her stood Hiram Goegal, spring gun in hand. He flicked the retract, and the Sinker lurched as the spike was hastily withdrawn. She saw the actual shape of the hole before it filled with blood, then felt the hard embrace of the cold iron floor. She was aware of him approaching and picking up her sword.

Then he was down over the mostly bloodless corpse of the Garent, then standing again, holding the Garent's severed finger by the signet ring to let the digit drop out.

Roaches crackled under Hiram Goegal's boots as he stepped over several bodies to reach the joint drive. He inserted the ring and pulled down the central axle levers, severing the Piping district from Core Rock. There was the hollow sound of bone popping, and the shimmying and lurching ceased as the Construct snapped free, back into the softer embrace of its two remaining engines.

The Sinker felt the floor settle and calm into smoothness, then slowly melt away as the cone of her vision tightened. There was a bright spot at the center, but all else was dark. From the coldness of her body, there came a stretching and expanding as the most crucial parts floated free, up the darkness of the cone and through the bright center, once more into the uprushing frictions of the sink, the trembling along her edge, the roar dulled in the soupy confines of her helmet, the empty endlessness of the void, her gaze sinking away forever into flatness.

PART 6

THE GREAT FLAT

Water coursed below me, as endless as all the endless sink I'd traveled through, and above as much endlessness as always, and from the distance the same sandy rock formed and was getting larger, drawing nearer, or it was me being drawn toward it, closer and closer, until I was placed gently on the surface, which gave softly and held my feet, and I could feel the whole rock was turning as the overvoid rotated colors until it was all blackness and the tiny holes of light poked and were gone again and there was the sharp, pickled smell of brine, and then I was moving, pushing through the trees into a place where there was only rock and not even the endless water could be seen, and the sink above was obscured by the overlapping branches of the overhanging trees and all was green and shimmering in a strange friction that didn't feel like it was curling up from below, and it was warm, not cold, and there was a clamor in the din, a hushing through the trees, and a hard cross friction whipped and the branches above waved and swayed and a swelling of light spilled in, so bright I looked away and saw where my shadow cut hard on the ground, and there were more

shadows too, overlapping and stacking up, and I turned and saw faces that had crowded close all around me, and I gasped and wheeled backward and a hand clutched my shoulder and my body yanked away and the rough cupping of the friction surged up and the void spilled in, and a form in the near dark wavered and smeared and took the shape of Crooked Arm. Seeing me awake, he let go of my shoulder. "It became a terror on you," he shouted, loud to be heard above the roar. I rubbed my face, roughing out the echoes of the dream.

"You were gasping and trying to wake up." The edges of his body rippled and blurred, and I realized how different this was from the dream where an overall stillness pervaded and things looked settled and whole and untouched by the friction. "It was the same dream?" he shouted.

I nodded. "But there were people," I shouted back.

"Who?"

I thought how to put it. "Everyone," I finally shouted.

We were in that final stretch of it, the void between Penultimate Rock and the Spear. If our charting was right, we'd reach it within the next rest. We still didn't know much about what awaited us there. An ore mine manager on Flatvesh told us a poet lived on the Spear who'd collected every legend in the sink. According to the people on Vestige, it was the first sinker, sunk further than anyone ever has. One rock insisted there was no Spear, that they were the bottommost rock in the sink, and even when Crooked Arm showed them the map, they laughed and refused to believe it and told us we were sure to die if we sank on because there was nothing. One rest later we came to Sturgis, where most of their amusement was making fun of the idiots only a rest's rise away. We never met anyone who'd actually been to the Spear, or anyone who knew anyone who'd been there. It was all rumors and hearsay, and we'd begun to wonder if anyone had ever been there; or if it was real at all; or if the Spear was not the bottommost rock but only a border to another stratum below, a new endlessness unfolding out forever, undetermined, unmapped; or if the endlessness was only an opening to the top again, and we could sink through it all over and over for as long as we lived; or if there was some other ending past it all, a flat, or a thinning, or a meniscus that could be broken through to something else?

When the Spear finally did form below us, it did so like every other rock in the undervoid, at first only a speck in the vast unrolling darkness but then coming on fast, as if rising up as we plummeted down. It was so small, the smallest rock we'd encountered in all our sinking, or seemed to be at first, for all we could see was a flat, jagged surface around a sunken courtyard, all of it bisected by crumbled walls and collapsed doorways. As we swung outwide to approach, I finally learned how this rock got its mysterious name. From the tiny upper surface, a huge spear-shaped understructure extended downward into the sink. It was all metal and glass and angled with thick gridding beams, converging into a point in the far distance below. Hanging from the undersurface, two gigantic statues of men in armor pointed swords downward into the sink.

We swooped in and landed on an edge that was brittle with chunks broken off and thin iron beams poking out like unkempt hair, bubbly and sharp with rust. The giant statues and the distantly converging point of the Spear were invisible from there. Below the edge, the void was dark and empty, just another bottomless depth of the sink.

We found a section where the lower wall was caved in, making a rough but easy enough descent into the courtyard. An obscuring maze surrounded us. It was empty and nondescript but for the crumbling walls that seemed to have once been a grid of rooms with passages cut between. There was no sign of life at all, only broken stone and piles of rock debris, some of it as fine as powdered dust.

"What do you suppose it is . . . or was?" I asked.

Crooked Arm only shrugged. Neither of us had seen anything like it, not on this scale or any other. There didn't seem to be any natural shape, as if the whole rock had been chiseled and formed with nothing left of how it began.

"Sure doesn't seem like anyone lives here," Crooked Arm said. "We'll have to find a way down into the understructure. Or maybe we can sink along the outside and . . ." He went quiet and held up his hand. I could hear it too, piercing the fabric of the roar, a strange, higher resonance, an eerie whistle.

Chamber by chamber, we followed the sound, climbing over the half-standing walls and through strangely square doorways, all with short step-overs. We found, in the center of the courtyard, a rectangular hole with stairs descending into a darkness below. The soft, hollow whistling we'd heard was the friction coming up through the hole even faster than in the wide-open sink. After all the distance we'd traveled, all the people we'd met, all the sink we'd plummeted through, what we'd found was another darkness, a darkness within the darkness, a void inside the void.

▼

Looking up, we could no longer see where we'd begun, and still below the staircase squared and squared around itself and blurred into a fine mesh and seemed to be as endless as the sink. We paused and opened doors into strange rectangular rooms long abandoned, with smashed-up floors and tangles of wires and thin, curling slivers of broken white glass spread all over. We tried to plummet right down the center of the stairwell, but some opening at the bottom was funneling the friction in. It rushed up with amplified force, lifting us faster than we could sink down against it. Crooked Arm decided it was set up for some kind of training, a place to learn sinking forms in the controlled chamber of the stairwell. It made me think of the meetinghouse back on Fairviel, where the boys practiced Kolatchi over the funnel hole.

As the monotonous descent extended, my mind circled back there, to my son's curling face and his hair, clustered and thick as piled barn hay. It seemed so long ago, the accident with the meat knife, Del's infected leg, the arrival of the Sinker, the things those people said at the fire on Roseblood, the truth about my home rock and my father and husband and that kid chopped in half by the centurions, the destruction of Fairviel. The Sinker was such a large part of it, but all total it was four or five rests we were together. The entire journey since Hidden

Rock had been without her, though it did feel like she was there, guiding us through each unfurling of her map, each plunging stretch of void.

I thought of her again, right then, as the staircase kept on angling in, how her honor simmered around her, the wrongs she'd tried to right—through violence, through balance—on a scale as big as the Construct or as small as Del, whom she'd never met yet still felt bound to help. It was Crooked Arm who'd known her better. Avon, the river through the void. He said she was like Hidden Rock and the Nest; somewhere she'd added a mirror shell, a layer that reflected the sink around her, hiding what was really inside. I pictured her running off into those pastures on Hidden Rock more than two thousand rests ago. We'd been sinking ever since.

Finally the stairs stopped and flattened into a tiny landing with a single open doorway like the others, set high up with a low step-over. Past it was a hazy grayness. The hollow roar was louder there, all the force of the funneled friction pushing up through that one spot. So strong was the friction, it created a kind of door where there was no door. Only by gripping the frame and pulling while Crooked Arm pushed was I able to get through the invisible barrier. On the other side, the stairs widened into a last flight down. Once past the confluence of the doorway, the resistance eased, and we took the last flight together, down into a wide square room, the same flat gray as the courtyard high above.

One side of the room was dominated by a gigantic fireplace, dark and still and more like a scorched hole. Otherwise, the chamber was empty and nondescript, bare walls and a flat gray floor interrupted only by a central porthole and a plain stone bench set beside it. There must have been intakes in the low corners because the friction hissed along the sides of the room, rushing and howling up the walls, across the ceiling, through the lone doorway, and into and up the ever-angling staircase.

"Hello?" Crooked Arm said, his voice coming back strangely louder, then again, but softer and softer until all was quiet. "I really thought there would at least be something," he said. "A village, some old tales about a traveler who once came here. Maybe they'd have some legend about the Nest. Maybe it'd be an answer. Maybe enough of one, maybe not." He'd stepped to the central bench. Now he leaned forward to peer through the porthole.

"Anything there?" I asked.

"Only more of it."

I stepped over and looked in, and the sink stretched out its uniform darkness. "Do you think this is really the end?" I asked. "The lowest room in the lowest rock in the sink? Could there really be nothing more, forever, no matter if you sank a million rests?"

Crooked Arm didn't answer. His eyes had focused on someplace deeper in the room. "We are not alone."

He was right. A figure moved along the side of the room, then turned and slowly made its way toward us. It was a young man, dressed in bulky robes so dark he seemed only a head floating on velvet folds and a pair of pink feet peeking way down low. He said nothing as he came closer, and I could see now he was possibly older, his age harder to determine the longer I looked. As I stared, I found I could not understand one specific thing about him. He was there and whole but left the impression of translucence, someone impossible to remember even when looking right at him. He came to the edge of the porthole and breathed deeply on the newness of the air around us. He looked at me, and when his voice came, it was resonate and silky. "It is fitting that it's you," he said.

"Why?"

"Because you are the one who has dreamed what comes next."

I felt that same pulse of more awakeness as that breath long ago, when the Sinker moved through the crowd at the Deciding and somehow her eyes landed on me. "How do you know that?" I asked.

"Or else it wouldn't be you who is here right now. . . . It's confusing, I know, but makes perfect sense as well. It has to. Have you brought it with you, the anomaly?" But then he paused. A look of dim recognition lit his face as he turned to Crooked Arm. "No," the man said, "*you* are the one who has it. You are from the Slant. What is your name?"

"Crooked Arm."

"You never earned another?"

"I had a chance. A tournament for First Sword. But I would have had to kill my brother, and I couldn't bring myself to do it."

"What would your name have been? If you had earned it back then? Back when you could have killed your brother and become First Sword of the Slant?"

Crooked Arm's gaze went distant, looking back at the inner sink of his life, the path through within. "The Long Sword," he said.

"And now?"

"Now . . . after all this . . . the Endless." The howl of the friction modulated lower, a throaty hum.

"I'd like to see it," the man said. "The anomaly, the Nest as you call it now."

"It was you, wasn't it?" Crooked Arm said. "You brought it to the Slant. But how? How are you still alive after so long?"

The man pursed his lips. One eye went slim. "It doesn't always seem so long."

Crooked Arm thought a breath more, then reached into his hip bag and took out the Nest. Our reflections curled away on the surface of the glass shell. "Can you tell me what it is?" Crooked Arm asked. "Our legends said it was used to set and hold the rocks of the Slant in place."

"Not only the Slant," the man replied, "but all of the sink. That is why things have shifted around you. It was the same for me before I found the observatory again. Once the Nest was settled into one spot, the sink around it settled too."

"The observatory . . . ," Crooked Arm said. "The Scorched Dome you mean?"

The man nodded, still looking curiously into the Nest. "You added this casing," he said, "to keep it hidden, to mask the echoes?"

"Yes. Someone came for it. They had some means of scanning the sink to know its location. They destroyed the Slant, Vertex, the Scorched Dome, all of it."

The man sighed and made a clicking sound. "Yes, that was him, my counterpart. He had his own anomaly, one that allowed him to see into the past, back at all we'd lost. This connection made him long for it more and more, trapped here for endless rests with only the memory for company. He thought the Nest was the way back. I told him he was mistaken; our home was gone; the way back led to nothing. I told him the Nest had been destroyed as well. That part was a lie, but a necessary one. I don't know if he believed me. I was the only one who knew the method of activating it; even if he could find it, it would be useless. So he sought a different way to escape. A way to escape *into* instead of *out of*, to escape within. He thought he could build a mechanism, a machine that would negate the sink's power to constrain him."

"The Construct."

The man nodded. "He is dead now, I know, my counterpart." His eyes went distant and his breath long. The only sound was the hissing of the friction as it swept up the sides of the room. He looked back to us, and a dry smile settled on his face. "Living forever does not mean you cannot be killed, by yourself, by someone else, by the effects of your actions."

"This counterpart," Crooked Arm said. "He was the old enemy you left the Slant to hunt?"

"He was not my enemy. We'd worked on it all together, studying the anomalies, searching for one that could save us, that could save everything." His head tilted and his eyes found more space to push open wider, peering distantly at nothing. "We thought we'd located the proper anomaly, but the method of activating it eluded us. Finally, at the last possible moment, I worked it out. So simple once I unlocked it." He laughed, then pressed his face down closed, a strange pile of overlapping skin. "But I was wrong, about how the Nest functioned, about what it could do. I did not understand then that it was how the last arrangement was set as well. I failed to recognize this cycle and so ignored too much of what had already been built. Instead of creating another arrangement, I destroyed ours. And all that was left was shattered and spread out in the endlessness." He held out a hand, palm up, to indicate all of the sink above us, and below too, and outwide, in all directions.

"I thought I was alone here at first but soon found others, though they had no memory of anything but the void. It was as if it had always been, an endlessness before the endlessness. I began searching for a place to rebuild, to begin again, when I stumbled on a familiar remnant, the same observatory where it all began. I took it as a sign and settled there, Vertex, as it came to be known. Soon after, or perhaps it was long after, I began to dream that he had survived as well, my counterpart, that he was *here*, trapped on the bottommost rock. I understood then the true nature of the endlessness." He nodded down at the floor. "One of us must always be here, to mark its furthest extent, a way to have a finite infinity. Before leaving, I stamped the alignment of the Slant as a means of finding me if needed. Twenty-three off absolute, radial one ninety-eight. It's how you knew to come here, correct?"

"Yes. We followed the optical axis of the lens." Crooked Arm thought longer on it. "So, after leaving the Slant, you came here and took his place?"

"In a manner of speaking." He thought a breath, his face lacing with confusion. "How long has it been? How long have I been down here?"

"I have no idea," Crooked Arm said. "Thousands and thousands of rests. Hundreds of thousands."

The man nodded absently and held out his hand. It had the same qualities as his face: it could have been the hand of a child or an elderly man or anything in between, and looking at it longer made it harder to determine. "May I hold it once more?" he asked.

Our reflections tilted and wobbled as Crooked Arm placed the Nest in the man's open palm. "You said your home was destroyed," Crooked Arm said, "that you couldn't go back. Back to where?"

The man thought how to put it. "To what you would call *Before*. It's hard for me to imagine now what it was like, so different from this place. My connection to it has grown thin, or atrophied, or aged like anything else."

"Before? Before when?" Crooked Arm asked. "When did this happen?"

The man seemed confused. "Just now," he said, "or right then. The observatory was on fire. The very start of this whole thing. When I reset the alignment. When I . . ." But he trailed off, sensing something we couldn't. "The small details are not important, not anymore." He looked down, into the porthole. "It is the nature of the infinite," he concluded. "Its greatest strength and greatest flaw: that everything does happen . . . eventually . . . somewhere . . . even the end."

The sink howled, then howled louder. There was a shifting of the friction, a compression. Then, through the porthole, I could see it, at first a hazy point of lightness, then a blossoming gray, soft and out of focus, and then unfurling endlessly in all directions, rushing up at speeds impossible to comprehend, or it was us, I suppose, who had found such speeds hurtling downward toward it, for all the rests of all the endlessness of the sink.

The Great Flat.

"There's not much breath left," the man said. He looked to Crooked Arm. "The only way for you to know is to see what happens next." Now the man held out his other hand. "Your hatchet," he said.

Crooked Arm drew it from his belt and handed it over. The man gripped it like shaking hands with an old friend. He felt its weight and raised it high and brought it down hard. The sharp edge hit the glass casing perfectly, cracking it into several pieces. As the jagged chunks fell away, I watched the Nest emerge, the cloudy haze, the pulsing tendrils, smoky, simmering in counterbalance with the dark center point. No, not dark, but void and endless-seeming in itself. The vibration that could be felt through the casing was stronger now, tickling the depths of my ears, a thin unease in the gut, and I realized then that all sound had been pushed back. The only thing I could hear was the Nest's humming vibration. When I looked away, it all rushed back in, and I was there again in the bottommost room on the lowest rock in the sink with the Great Flat real and rushing up.

"It has been so long since I last saw it," the man said. He looked at me. "You could have figured out how to activate it. It was there in the visions as well. But traveling here, I suppose, crossing the sink, was just as necessary for the wholeness of the dream."

Pressing a thumb and forefinger into the Nest, the man seemed to pinch the inner core. With his other hand, he gently gripped the outer, vaporous surface. His face contorted in concentration to hold it two ways differently. With a turn of his wrist, he rotated the outer core until it clicked, then rotated it back. There was a second, softer click, and the low vibration of the Nest hissed away, leaving an odd emptiness in the lower spectrum of sound. From the dark inner core, a faint glow arose.

"It is activated," the man said, looking right at me. "Make sure your dream is whole, as whole as you can make it."

He held the Nest out over the porthole and let it go to float there perfectly in the updraft. The eerie glow persisted, radiating coolly, coating the rim of the porthole with bone-colored light. He was right about the long descent. How could my dream not be altered by it, by the events and rocks and people we'd crossed along the way, and the long stretches of empty void, and Hidden Rock, and the cows sleeping in the moss or floating out on their tethers, and by Del and by Crooked Arm and by the Sinker most of all.

Below, the Great Flat had solidified into a gray stone expanse, out-wide as far as could be seen and coming up fast. There were only a few breaths left. I reached out and took the Nest and felt my fingers sink into its ghosting smoke, and the core was cold and vibrant, and the most recent version of my oldest dream flooded into my mind, and I thought of this—

ACKNOWLEDGMENTS

This book would not have been possible without the early editorial work of Yishai Seidman and Jennifer Burwell. I also owe a debt to Naomi Henderson, Ben Loory, and Baynard Woods for critical reads and feedback at just the right times, and my agents, Peter Steinberg and Brandi Bowles, whose excitement and enthusiasm inspired me to continually push this manuscript further. James Engle at Navigation Media and Mark S. Temple have provided invaluable support and friendship throughout my career. Gavin Grant, Kelly Link, and the staff of Lady Churchill's Rosebud Wristlet first published the short story "The Endless Sink." Richard Horton included it in *The Year's Best Science Fiction & Fantasy 2015*. Daniel Liang allowed us to see the void with his amazing illustrations. I cannot say enough good things about the team at Saga and Simon & Schuster who brought this book around the final bend and into the real world: Charlotte Trumble, Ella Laytham, Caroline Tew, Brian Luster, and especially Tim O'Connell, who has championed this novel from his first read. Lastly, a big thanks to Zebulon Ober; I hope this novel brings readers a fraction of the wonder you inspire in me.